D1534821

CRY OF
THE OWL

CRY OF THE OWL

A Novel

Francis Mading Deng

LILIAN BARBER PRESS, INC.
New York 1989

Francis Mading Deng was a Distinguished Fellow in the Jennings Randolph Program of the United States Institute of Peace 1987–89.

The publication of this book was supported in part by a Fellowship from the United States Institute of Peace, Washington, D.C. The Institute of Peace is an independent, non-partisan government institution, created and wholly funded by the United States Congress to expand available knowledge about ways to achieve a more peaceful world.

First published in the United States of America in 1989 by

LILIAN BARBER PRESS, INC.
P. O. Box 232
New York, NY 10163

© by Francis Mading Deng

Library of Congress Cataloging-in-Publication Data

Deng, Francis Mading, 1938-
    Cry of the Owl: a novel / Francis Mading Deng.
        p.   cm.
    ISBN 0-936508-25-6   (0-936508-26-4 pbk.)
    I. Title.
    PR9408.S83D44 1989   89-15041
    823 – dc20   CIP

Manufactured in the United States of America

CONTENTS

PRELUDES

A review by a Sudanese

Dear Francis:

It was an extremely enjoyable and instructive experience for me to read the manuscript of your novel, *Cry of the Owl*, last week-end. I found the manuscript so fascinating and provocative that I couldn't put it down or do anything else until I finished reading it.

Your earlier novel, *Seed of Redemption*, had already introduced me to the potential of the fiction form in addressing the complicated and sensitive issues of national unity and social transformation in the Sudan. I must admit that I have found *Cry of the Owl* much more effective as a tool for exposing and discussing the most sensitive and deep-rooted issues in our individual and collective psyche. In fact, I can now see far-reaching and even revolutionary potential for the fiction method.

Coming from the *Ja'aliyn* tribe of the northern central Sudan, known for their strong prejudice and shameful commercial exploitation of southern Sudanese since the days of the "institutionalized" slave trade, *Cry of the Owl*, has succeeded in provoking deep emotions and reflection on my part.

1

As you probably know from my short piece in *The Search for Peace and Unity in the Sudan*, I am of the view that all Sudanese must undergo the painful but extremely beneficial process of exposing deep-rooted prejudice and social discrimination before they can hope to evolve a genuine sense of national identity and achieve lasting peace and justice in the Sudan. Through *Cry of the Owl*, I have had a most revealing personal experience in practicing what I preach.

For example, I have found that the most moving parts of the manuscript were those explaining and exploring Dinka culture. Besides confronting me with my shameful ignorance of this profound cultural tradition so close to home, I found myself deeply resonating with many aspects of that extremely rich and humane tradition. I came to a greater appreciation of what you mean when you say that the so-called "animists" of the Sudan are as religious, if not more so, as the adherents of Islam and Christianity.

In terms of its immediate and profound contribution to resolving our country's chronic state of instability and insecurity, I was particularly struck by the manuscript's skillful and very convincing analysis of the subtle elements of individual and collective self-identity. The manuscript's very clear exposition and analysis of the shifting and intricate ingredients and processes of identity, with their far-reaching practical implications, offer both diagnosis and treatment for some of the deep-rooted causes of conflict and tension in the Sudan.

For this novel to achieve its full potential, it must be translated into Arabic, and widely distributed throughout the Sudan. As you know, the majority of our educated compatriots cannot read English well enough, and cannot afford novels published in the West. A skillful and artistic Arabic translation, preferably prepared under your personal guidance, and published locally in the Sudan, would make this wonderful novel available to the people who need to read it most. Moreover, I wonder whether it is possible for this novel to reach, in some form, the vast majority of our population who

*[Produced by the Wilson Center Press in 1987 from the papers and discussions of a workshop organized by the Center earlier that year on the problems and prospects of peace and unity in the Sudan]

are illiterate. I even dreamed of its production as a movie or television drama for broadcast in rural Sudan.

Wafaqk Allah wa sadada khutak—May God bring you success and guide your steps.

Abdullahi A. An-Na'im, Ph.D.
Associate Professor of Law
University of Khartoum, Sudan.
March 8, 1988.

Extract from a Dinka song

"The Curse of the Owl"

My grandmother, my grandmother,
Aluel, daughter of Chol,
Came with a glory that God denied;
A great woman who bore multitudes of children,
Then consumed her hoes digging their graves,
Leaving my father a lonely bull of the buffalo.
The owl cries all night in our home,
The evil bird of the night has bedeviled us,
The Great Bird cries: "When it dawns, when it dawns
"0h son of Deng, when it dawns,
You will bury another child."
The bird of the night has cast an evil spell on my father;
The bird knows our burial ground;
That is why my father remained a single child,
Struggling alone in the wilderness:
Our land, our land,
Our land at Giem,
My father covered with dead bodies;
No ground was left for a foot to step.
That is why I have become a slave
Forced to labor in foreign lands...
Oh Marial, what I have found I will not say.

DEDICATION

In memory of my beloved sister Awor, who was the very embodiment of human virtues, but who, with all the promises of a good and happy marriage, died in childbirth after an otherwise successful delivery of a handsome baby boy. The baby followed his mother a few days later, and both were followed a few months later by Awor's only surviving child, a girl in her third year, whose beauty, charm, and intelligence had already become evident. In the Dinka frame of things, without an offspring to continue her name and "stand her head upright"—*bi koc nhom*—my sister had perished forever—*aci riar.*

May this Dedication rekindle their memory and remain a symbol, modest as it is, of their place in our hearts and minds.

PART ONE
SETTING

ONE

ELIAS BOL MALEK WOKE earlier than usual, feeling heavy in the head from sleeplessness. News had reached him the night before that his father, Malek, popularly known as Malengdit, the chief of the Mathiang Dinka tribe of North-western Bahr El Ghazal District, was seriously ill, probably dying, and wanted his son by his death bed. Elias had gone to bed early as though that would shorten the night so that he could prepare for immediate departure the following morning. But he could not sleep. Tossing about in bed, turning from side to side, engrossed in the possibility of his father's death, his sleep fused reality and dream, a long nightmare. With the morning, the nightmare gave way to the dreadful reality of his father's illness and probable death. He must move quickly if he was to see his father alive one more time.

Having brushed his teeth and washed his face, Elias took his morning tea—a ritual performed every morning in much the same way one showered and dressed for the day. After his tea, he took a shower and got into a safari suit. But Elias was not going to work that day—he was going to make his travel arrangements.

It was a blazing hot April day in the Three Towns that formed the country's capital—Khartoum. Elias got into his Peugeot 504, which he had only recently borrowed the money to acquire, and driving faster than usual, he took the Medani road from Erkewit, where he lived, toward the center of town, onto Nile Avenue, and then turned left toward Omdurman Bridge. Across the bridge, a massive building of red bricks trimmed with ivory paint, rose like a mountain at the confluence of the White and Blue Niles. Only a few years earlier, this had been where the "People's Assembly" met to rubber-stamp the presidential orders of the reigning field marshal, Jabir El-Munir. Since the popular uprising that had toppled Munir and restored parliamentary democracy, the building had become the meeting place of the newly elected Constituent Assembly that was to formulate a new constitution for the beleaguered country. Elias was a member of that Assembly, representing the district of Northwestern Bahr El Ghazal of which his father was paramount chief. That was one of the few southern areas in which the civil war permitted elections, the rest of the South being in the prohibitive war zone.

The Assembly was in session and the grounds of the building were congested with cars, but the blazing heat of the tropical sun and the enthusiasm for the return of democracy ushered the crowds into the magnificent halls of the building. The decor was breath-taking: skyward cathedral ceilings featured majestic chandeliers with sparkling crystal bars; floors glimmered with polished marble; fountains flashed and flowed wistfully into partially hidden streams; a dramatic lighting system spotlighted the wide steps linking the split levels lined with planters containing trees of mature size. It was a sight to drown the dull, gray desert environment of that part of the country.

Elias passed the Assembly hall toward the Speaker's office. First he went through an office occupied by the Speaker's personal staff, then stopped at the secretary's desk in the office immediately before the Speaker's. The secretary, an attractive young woman in a light fashionable tobe, with a flirtatious smile on her face, immediately ushered him into the huge office where the Speaker, Sayed El-Jaylani, sat far back behind a magnificent mahogany desk. The light brown Jaylani, a man in his late fifties, rose to greet Elias. He was dressed in a beige Arabian abaya with a Sudanese imma neatly wound around his head.

"Welcome, welcome, Brother Elias," he bellowed with considerable cordiality. "Take a seat."

Elias took one of the chairs in front of the Speaker's desk.

"I take it you got my message. I sent a messenger with notes to you and Brother Baraka Mohamed to come and see me."

"I just came to the Assembly and headed straight to your office," explained Elias. "I didn't encounter the messenger."

Somehow, Jaylani detected a sadness in Elias's tone and mannerism. "I hope all is well? You look downcast."

"I have received disturbing news about my father. He is said to be seriously ill, perhaps dying, and would like to see me as soon as possible. I would like to take leave to go immediately."

"I am awfully sorry to hear that," Jaylani responded feelingly. "Of course you may leave as soon as you wish. I called you and Baraka to discuss how we should approach some of the more critical and sensitive issues facing the Assembly. But that can wait until you return."

As he spoke, the door opened and a young man dressed in a jallabiya and imma entered. "*Salaam aleikum!* Peace be upon you!" Baraka Mohamed El-Jak said in greeting.

"*Wa aleikum salaam wa rahmat-u-allah wa barkatu*—and upon you be peace, God's mercy and His blessings," Jaylani and Elias responded in unison.

"Welcome! Welcome!" Jaylani added, as they both got up to receive Baraka.

As Baraka approached Elias, he betrayed both surprise and cold curiosity, as though wondering why on earth the Speaker would bring them together. But it was a subtle response, noticeable only to those who knew the prevailing atmosphere. Jaylani was one of those. He was not in the least surprised by the look on Baraka's face, for he had noticed for some time that there was a coldness in the mutual attitude of the two men.

"*Ahlan wa sahlan*—come with ease, you are among your people," Jaylani continued with his greetings.

Baraka shook hands with Jaylani and turned to Elias, "*Salamat*—greetings," he said with a restraint that made the greeting a formality, barren of any cordiality or sentiment.

"Ahlan, ahlan—relatives, relatives," Elias responded with a shortened greeting. There was warmth in it, though it was deliberate, almost calculated, which only confirmed that disharmony marred the relationship.

Although Baraka looked a little older, he and Elias were both in their early thirties. They were both over six feet tall, slender, finely sculptured, dark brown in color, and handsome. That was all they had in common though, for the two men represented groups that were not only ethnically, culturally and religiously different, but antagonistic.

Baraka Mohamed was the spokesman for the ruling Nation of Islam, which believed in the Arab Muslim identity of the Sudan and advocated the application of sharia, Islamic law. Using the numerical majority of the Muslim communities and the vast financial resources available to them from the oil rich Arab and Muslim countries, they had set for themselves not only the task of upholding the cause of Islam and Arab civilization in the Sudan, but also the sacred mission of spreading the message of Allah and Arab civilization throughout Africa.

Elias Bol Malek was the spokesman of the newly formed Association of the Revolutionary Minorities of the Sudan, whose acronym was ARMS. The Association was a radical political movement that aimed at promoting the interests of the disadvantaged rural communities of the country. Although it was spearheaded by the Christian elite from the South, the movement catered to the non-Arab population throughout the country and was making headway in the West and East among tribal groups which, though Muslim, had retained their indigenous ethnic and linguistic identities. In recent history, their identities had been overshadowed by Islam and Arabism, but now they were beginning to reassert themselves.

As a political faction, ARMS was in the minority and a member of the opposition group of parties, but there was no doubt that the people whose interests the opposition represented were an overwhelming majority, labelled as minorities because of their disunity and peripheral share of power. ARMS knew that this group of disadvantaged communities was a potential force in the future of the country What was required was to make them realize their power. This naturally posed a grave threat to the ruling Arab elite.

The coldness in the relationship between Baraka and Elias could not however be explained merely by their political differences. Such differences were normal among the politicians, but they rarely affected personal relationships. Jaylani was particularly disturbed because he felt that as spokesmen of opposed political factions, the attitude of the two men was capable of influencing the conduct of parliament positively or negatively. One of the reasons for his calling them to his office was to broach this issue and hopefully to clear the air and improve their personal relationship.

"There are several things about the work of the Assembly which I would have liked to discuss with you gentlemen," Jaylani explained. Then turning to Baraka, he went on to say, "But I have just learned from Brother Elias that he has to rush back home to his father who is reported to be seriously ill."

"Oh! I am sorry to hear that," Baraka reacted with a formal gesture.

"I appreciate your sympathy. It's God's will."

"So, I guess there is not much we can do at this point," Jaylani continued. Then discreetly and cleverly hinting at his objective, he added, "But one thing I would like to see more of is closer and more cordial contact between the two of you, with me as mediator if you like. Let's not talk about that now, but think about it and let's pursue it in our next meeting."

The two responded with a solemn silence, indicating that they realized what he was talking about. "And now, Brother Elias, since you are understandably eager to get going, I think we should let you go."

"Thank you, sir," responded Elias. "I shall be back as soon as possible."

That same day, Elias flew by plane to Wau, where he was given a government truck driven by an Arab policeman, and accompanied by another policeman from the Balanda tribe. They drove northward over a rugged dirt road toward his village at Dak-Jur.

Throughout the journey, he thought of his father, how close they had been, and what the world would be without him. He recalled the highlights of their relationship, from the time he was still a child, through his years in school and military college. The more he thought of their ties as father and son and the dependence of the tribe on his father, the more he could not swallow the thought that he might die. He sighed soundly, hoping that his father would recover and live for many more years.

As it was rapidly getting dark the driver put on the headlights. Suddenly, an awesome sight brought them to a halt. Right in the middle of the road lay a huge lion, roaring, his mouth wide open, his canines frightfully exposed, his hind legs, neatly folded under his heavy body, his left foreleg stretched forward holding a firm grip on the ground, while his right foreleg wavered aimlessly in the air, indicating that he was blinded by the headlights. The driver blew the horn, but instead of moving, the lion thundered with the mighty sounds of the king of the beasts that he is known to be. The driver pulled out his rifle from its hanging place under the roof of the front seats.

"Don't!" protested Elias. "Don't you know that lions are among the most peace-loving creatures on earth? They only kill when they must and should only be killed when they must."

The Arab driver was flabbergasted. "But sir, how do we pass? He could be dangerous to a small vehicle like ours! If he should overturn the car, where would we be—in heaven?"

Elias felt challenged. Although he had succeeded in stopping the Arab driver, he worried in fact that the Balanda policeman in the back might shoot. He lowered his glass window, stuck his head out, and told the policeman to refrain from shooting.

Elias had deep-rooted reasons for not wanting the beast to be hurt. He had heard that the lion was a sacred animal in his clan and that the relationship between the Lion World and his family went back to the history of Arab raids for slaves. As he understood it, the Arabs once attempted to raid their villages in the middle of the night, but were intercepted by a pack of lions, which killed several people and dispersing the rest to run away for their lives, averting a catastrophe. The elders of the ruling clan, his family, subsequently got together and carried out a ritual of affinity with the Lion World. They undertook never to attack lions and ritually committed the lions to a reciprocal undertaking. Whichever side would violate the accord would suffer fatal injury in the ensuing conflict. The elders took out a sacred bull, prayed, and then tied it to a tree in the forest as a gift of friendship to the lions. According to the legends of the clan, the pact had been observed by both sides. Even in more recent years, lions were known to have provided protection to the Dinka against Arab raiders. In gratitude, Elias's clan had honored the lion kingdom with dedication and sacrifices of cattle, some kept in the herd as the sacred property of the lions, others slaughtered as sacrifices in their honor, and yet others left in the forest to be found and consumed by lions. It was a close affinity which a member of the clan could not afford to disregard with impunity.

Elias felt that, although he was a Christian convert who was not supposed to believe in the pagan ways, he could not violate the family word of honor which had become part of his ancestral tradition. Deep inside him, he felt apprehensive that if he disregarded the word of his forefathers, evil would befall him or some other members of his family. With his father at the brink of death, this was an especially wrong time to act irresponsibly.

All these thoughts came to him in a fraction of a moment. His mind quickly made up, Elias asked the driver to turn off the headlights. The stars were shining brightly and it was still possible to see the lion, defiantly poised in the middle of the beaten track.

"I will go to the back with a loaded gun," Elias said to the driver. "And then I'd like you to drive very slowly without headlights. At the crucial moment, he will jump aside. You can then put on your headlights and speed up. If he doesn't move, I will shoot at the critical moment."

"But sir, if you should miss at such close range, he might jump onto the back of the truck, and then what?"

Elias had made up his mind not to entertain any fear. "One must sometimes live on faith," he said. "Let's try!"

Elias asked the policeman, together with the assistant driver, to move to the front, leaving him alone at the back. He was adamant that he should not endanger anyone else to honor his family tradition.

"Impossible," protested the Belanda policeman, a short stout man who saw his honor in his profession, which, at that moment was the protection of a Member of Parliament. "After all, we are here to protect you, whether from humans or from beasts."

"I assure you, I will be safer without you in the back with me!"

"How can that be?" queried the policeman, somewhat insulted.

"It's a matter of religion. I cannot explain it to you now, but please take my word for it."

Reluctantly, the policeman moved to the front seat. Nonetheless, he loaded his gun and pulled down his window, ready to shoot, should the situation require.

As the truck moved forward without lights, the lion seemed calmer and more receptive to the object that was approaching. He still roared and waved his right foreleg in the air, but there was something more passive about him, which made Elias even more confident that he was right. Despite the diminishing distance between them, he did not seriously contemplate having to shoot the beast.

Suddenly, the lion jumped off the road. Before the driver could put on the headlights and accelerate, the beast had leaped onto the back of the truck. It had all happened so unexpectedly that Elias had had no time to think of shooting the animal. But that was no longer possible anyway, for the lion had knocked the rifle out of his hand. Too petrified to reach for the gun or make any move, even a frightened sound, Elias gazed into the lion's face, without words or thoughts.

Then, an astonishing thing happened: the lion snarled, stretching his left and right forelegs alternatingly at Elias, as though he were a domesticated cat. Dumbfounded, Elias did not fully comprehend what was happening, far less how to react.

Not realizing that the lion was on the back of the truck, the driver put on the headlights and accelerated. As the truck was picking up speed, the lion gave a loud but benign roar and jumped off to the wayside. The driver heard the roar and assumed that the lion was still running after them, all the more reason to go fast. It was some time before Elias regained his senses and banged on the roof of the front seats to stop the truck, now clearly far away from the scene of the incident.

Elias's account of what had just transpired sounded like a fairy tale to his companions. But they realized that whatever exaggerations his account might have entailed, a miracle had just occurred.

As it was now quite dark, the state of insecurity in the area dictated that they should spend the night at Chwei, a police post only a few miles away. After a night restlessly spent between reality and the dream world that the episode with the lion had dramatized, they woke up early, had tea and took to the road.

As they drove through Dinkaland, their truck announced their approach with the roar of the engine and thick dust rising up to the sky. Dogs and children from villages along the road ran toward them and chased after the passing vehicle, an opportunity that rarely came their way. As it was still the dry season, most of the wild life had migrated and left behind a wasteland, shimmering with mirages that shot the tall slender figures of the Dinka and their herds into the skyline. Exhausted by the heat, people clustered in huts or under trees as if to hibernate for the season and preserve energies for the toil of the rainy season, when they would once more burst forth with activity to cultivate the land.

As they got closer and closer to his village, Elias's heart beat faster and faster. How was his father? Was he really dying? Might he already be dead? Oh, what a thought! What would he do?

As though to distract himself, his mind flew back to the Assembly scene he had left behind, the racial tensions that underlay its political currents, and his brief encounter with Baraka Mohamed. The name of his village helped induce this flashback, for it was called Dak-Jur—"Where the Arabs were tired out" —because oral history had it that it was here that the Dinka had taken a firm stand against the Arab slave raiders and forced them to retreat and eventually withdraw.

Dak-Jur emerged from a distance. Although encircled by trees on three sides with an all-season river on the fourth, it was located on elevated ground with a spectacular command of a vast panorama of open plains, dotted with water spots surrounded by clusters of vegetation. When the sounds of the approaching lorry were heard, dogs came running, only to realize that this was no easy game, and chased at a distance. Children ran excitedly to watch the roaring cyclone roll toward their village, not knowing that it was Elias returning home.

TWO

ELIAS FOUND THE VILLAGE bubbling with activity as people moved up and down between the huts that encircled the compound and the shady trees that defined and accentuated the homestead. Between the huts were two cattle byres, several times the size of ordinary huts. The grounds in the central area of the homestead were covered with pegs, several yards apart, to which the cattle were tethered when not accommodated inside the byres. The herd had been released to graze in the pastures nearby. The small calves, still tethered in the sun and waiting to be moved to the shady trees, bellowed mournfully, yearning for the company of their mothers. Two boys, their naked bodies smeared in ashes, were busy clearing the cow dung from the area, spreading it to dry as fuel for fires to smoke the flies and mosquitoes away from herd and human alike. Their jubilant singing as they worked, contrasted sharply with the cloud of apprehension that hung over the village on account of Malengdit's illness. But that was not the way the villagers saw it. Singing was merely a rhythmic accompaniment to work and while it sustained the momentum for labor, it did not signify insensitivity to the tragedy looming on the family and the tribe.

As children clustered around Elias, he went back to the lorry and grabbed a big bag of sweets and another one of dates for them to feast on, while he pushed his way through the greeting crowd wondering where his father was. He soon learned that the old man was in a hut that the elders entered and exited on their knees through an oblong doorway not more than three feet high. When he reached the hut, Elias got on his hands and knees and crawled inside, which wasn't too difficult, as it was his mother's hut and crawling had been part of his upbringing. Also, the safari suit he wore made stooping relatively easy.

Word had already reached Chief Malengdit that his son had arrived and was coming to see him. No sooner had Elias crawled inside than his father first sat up and then tried to stand to receive him. It wasn't easy. Elias saw his father, a figure about six feet five inches tall, struggling to free himself from a sheet cover, revealing a close cropped head with white sprouting hair. Naked to the waist, Malengdit appeared reduced to skin and bones, looking like a living skeleton, and upon seeing him thus tears nearly came to his son's eyes. Elias knew that nothing would depress his father more than to see tears in the eyes of his favorite son. Certainly, his father's condition could not stand any more gloom. Wiping his eyes to brush away the tears as though some foreign body had intruded, he moved toward his father's bed to save him the agony of standing up.

"Is it really you, my Bol? Have you truly come, my son? Nothing is bad; even if I should die now, I will go with a sweet heart."

Elias wanted to tell his father not to think about death, but in the condition the old man was in, that would be hypocritical, the kind of fake encouragement that could only insult the old man's intelligence and wisdom.

When they had exchanged greetings, Elias reached for a *mangan*, a wooden headrest on three legs, and sat opposite his father, now precariously seated on his bed. "Perhaps you should lie down, Father," Elias suggested, careful not to be too alarmist.

"No, I am fine. And even if it were sitting up that would kill me, what better moment can there be?"

It had been years since Elias had seen the inside of his mother's hut. Like most Dinka dwellings, it was a circular structure about twelve feet in diameter with a low wall of wooden poles arranged in a cluster, plastered with mud. Resting on the wall was a high conical roof of tall rafters, with rings of tightly wound branches around the frame, over which rested a thick thatch of long savannah grass. Although the thatch was smooth on the outside, the ceiling inside revealed the bare frame of the rafters, the rings wrapped around them, and the mud tunnels of the termites that infested the wood.

On the side opposite Chief Malek's bed was a small fireplace used at night to burn the leaves which produced a pleasant fragrance for humans while smoking away the mosquitoes. Toward the back of the hut and resting on four tall wooden pillars was the storage platform on which utensils and other household possessions were kept. At the very back of the hut, two large spears rested on a heavily oiled piece of leather. One spearhead was leaf-like and the other lance-like, each joined to a long slim shaft, heavily decorated with metal rings. These were the Sacred Spears of the Chief, passed on to him through a long line of ancestors, all of whom had been the spiritual leaders of their people.

Chief Malek had been left alone to rest but was wakened by the commotion of his son's arrival. No sooner had Elias entered the hut than he was followed by increasing numbers of people, some to visit his father but many to see him. Within a short time, the hut was congested to the point of suffocation, while even more people gathered around outside. Apart from the narrow doorway, only three small holes, each several inches wide, spread far apart, provided the needed ventilation. Elias wanted to scream from the heat and stench, but he could not insult his people, whom he knew very well to be proud and acutely sensitive.

Suddenly, voices were heard, "Please make way for the diviner; the diviner is coming, let him pass." People were urged to leave the room to give Ayueldit, the diviner, a chance with his patient and the patient's son. Ayueldit crawled through the doorway and then stood up to greet Elias, who was already standing to receive the holy man. In the Dinka priestly manner, Ayueldit held his right hand up and opened it as he solemnly exchanged greetings with Elias without touching hands.

Ayueldit stood over six feet tall; he was a lean man, with an elongated face and sharply sculptured cheekbones. His gentle but firm look shifted alternately from a discreetly penetrating scrutiny to a beaming smile that revealed sparkling white and well-ordered teeth. Even his long braided hair strung with shells and beads seemed more of an aesthetic touch than the usual paraphernalia of spiritual decorum. Although in one of the anomalies of changing times, he was wearing shorts and a T-shirt, a soft leopard skin, which was part of his ritual attire, hung across his shoulders. It could be used as a rug or a cover to provide protection against spiritual impurities. So, whether he sat on a bed, a stool, a piece of wood, or the ground, Ayueldit always spread his leopard skin over whatever he sat on.

Elias offered Ayueldit a stool, but the diviner respectfully declined and chose the mat, making sure that his leopard skin was tucked under him. After a courteous pause, which seemed long and tense, Ayueldit began to speak. " The truth must be said: when confronted with you, the educated, we do our work with fear of intrusion because your ways are different."

In this he was correct. Christian missionaries had encouraged their Dinka converts to discard and disparage those pagan ways which were viewed as the work of the devil. But Elias had matured enough to realize that such an attitude was too simplistic. Besides, the man was only trying to help.

"I don't think you should feel that way," Elias said conciliatorily. "After all, we are all after the same thing and that is the physical and spiritual well-being of man."

Ayueldit was touched by these words. "As they say, people are not all the same. There is always the son who will listen to the words of his elders and be enriched by their wisdom. And there are those who get captured by the adventures of youth and whatever is new. Even though we have accepted the advantages of learning and of modern medicine, there should still be room for the ways which have served our forefathers for many generations."

Chief Malengdit was pleased with this exchange and signaled his approval by gently smiling in his son's direction.

Elias, now relaxed, asked, "I understand that you have already divined the cause of my father's illness?"

"It goes back a long way," began Ayueldit. "As you know, your father was named after the spirit Malengdit. I don't know what you have already been told about your father. The story of his life is connected with the terrible smallpox epidemic that almost wiped out our people of Mathiang. Many, many people died from the disease. It was only after your grandfather made a great feast for the spirit Malengdit in which a bull having white and brown spots—the color *malek*—was sacrificed that the disease was arrested. Your grandfather named your father Malek in honor of Malengdit. In my divination, it has been revealed that Malengdit now wants to claim his son, your father. That is why we have suggested that the bull Malek which is tethered outside under the shrine be offered to the spirit Malengdit to redeem your father. Malengdit is well known for his benevolence; if called upon with the right words, he will respond to the prayers of the people he once saved from disaster."

Elias could not share the diagnosis of the diviner, but he was not about to voice disagreement either. Instead, he listened politely, nodding his head in courtesy from time to time, and when the diviner had finished, Elias was saved the embarrassment of having to comment when his uncle Akol entered the hut and called out, "Master, shouldn't we begin the invocation now? It is getting hot; sacrifices should be conducted in the coolness of the morning, not in the heat of the day."

Akol was Malengdit's half-brother, from their father's second wife. He was a man in his fifties, of medium height and, like the Dinka of their time, very lean. There was an element of the usual half-blood tension and rivalry between the two, but this was well disguised and in fact overcompensated for by a display of family solidarity and brotherly cordiality. The two brothers were considered quite close by normal half-kin standards.

"Your word is correct. Call the elders to the shrine," responded Ayueldit with a lowered voice of spiritual authority. He himself was not required to participate in the ritual, but he had to spray the bull with holy water before the invocation could begin. Word was soon echoed throughout the village. "Let the elders go to the shrine. It is getting late for the sacrifice."

At that moment, a lady stooped through the doorway and announced with conventional respect, "I am coming." Once inside, she stood up to reveal a noble-looking figure, tall, in her mid fifties, with a sheet wound around her waist and another hanging across her shoulders and opened on one side. Aluel and Elias greeted each other with concealed emotion, for among the Dinka, mothers and sons are not supposed to display love and affection for one another.

"Son, the women are also longing for you. They are tired of waiting. While the elders gather for the sacrifice, you should go and greet your mothers and sisters."

Being the chief, Malengdit had the largest number of wives in the tribe. Elias Bol's mother was the first, but there were scores of others, all classified in a very rigid system of seniority in which Aluel was the "chief" of the women, revered by all the other wives. They referred to her not by her name, but as "Mother" or Man-Madit, Madit's mother, after her oldest child.

It was in the presence of both his parents that Elias Bol decided to tell the story of his encounter with the lion. They were engrossed by the account, from time to time expressing their fascination, but without interrupting him. Aluel especially kept repeating, "Just see that," whenever a particularly dramatic point came in the story. When Elias was finished, she said, "I am not surprised. Now you have seen with your own eyes what you used to hear about the ancient pact between the Lion World and your clan!"

Malengdit made a sound of soft laughter. Then gesturing to Aluel went on to say, "Stop there! You speak of ancient events, what about this more recent incident with you and the twins?" Then turning to his son he said, "You know the incident in which your mother and your twin brothers were captured by the Arabs. That was how your brother Madit fell from the Arab horse and broke the hip that left him lame for life, until he disappeared from here. Your mother and the other twin son, Achwil, were taken away by the Arabs, until she was later rescued; Achwil was never heard from again. If it were not for the intervention of the lions, our people would have suffered greater losses. So you see, Bol, my son, your mother's word is correct. It is good that you have now seen with your own eyes what we elders keep telling you educated youth about the powers of our ancestral spirits. Our spirits are God's messengers; their words are strong. But education has turned your ears away from our words. You do not hear what we say. And even when you hear it, you do not take it into your hearts. It goes in one ear and out the other. That lion did not come to you for nothing. Let me now tell you, my son, that lion had a message. And that message will be revealed. I am quite sure about that. We should not worry our heads by trying to guess what the message is. What is important is that the lion came to you and did no harm: that means he was a messenger. However long it might take, his message will eventually reveal itself. What we need to do now is honor his appearance by sacrificing a lamb. But that can be done later, when all this commotion is over."

"Well, let me go back to the more simple words of the family," Aluel resumed. "The hearts of the women are breaking with waiting. Let Bol go to greet them."

Chief Malengdit agreed and Elias stepped out with his mother. As they passed by, he saw the bull tethered to a peg under the shrine on the right side of the largest cattle byre. The main structure of the shrine was a barkless tree trunk, stuck to the ground with branches shooting out like a sculpture. Hanging from the branches were a wide array of objects: gourds, shells, rings, beads and the like, relics of previous sacrificial gifts to the ancestral spirits. Around the trunk and the branches grew creeping plants, among them *kwol-jok*, the "sacred cucumber," used for blessing. Scattered all over the elevated grounds of the shrine were bones and skulls of animals from previous sacrifices.

When the elders had all gathered, they formed a large circle around the bull, ready for the invocation. Malengdit's brother, Akol, called on their oldest uncle, Mijak, "Uncle, please call the word!" That was the Dinka expression for prayers. Mijak, also known as Mijangdit, was over eighty years in age, with a tall stooping figure that seemed to focus his modest weight on the forked stick he carried to support himself. His face was emaciated, his eyes sunk deep into their sockets. Removing tobacco from his mouth with a shaky hand and placing it in his snuff box, he rolled the remaining pieces around with his tongue and sprayed them out several times. Then he cleared his throat and declared, "Hold this word of mine."

The rest of the elders, until then waiting in dead silence, echoed the traditional response in a chorus "Hold the word."

"You God, and you spirits above, together with you our ancestors in the ground, it is to you all that I address this my word."

The chorus repeated Mijangdit's last word.

"And it is not for a bad thing that we are calling upon you; it is life that we are asking of you."

Echoes of the crowd followed with the last phrase, "we are asking of you."

"Throughout the entire history of our people, it is because of the chief that people live in a land."

The chorus continued to repeat the last word or phrase of the prayers as the invocation proceeded.

"When people become used to the leadership and protection of their chief, then comes the spirit of death and takes him away, that is what destroys a people. Our people have suffered a great deal. Times have changed for the worse. But this one child of yours, whom you placed in charge of your people, has been a source of inspiration and strength for our people. His presence has given our people's hearts the ability to endure and keep the land.

"And why was it that you, my brother, gave your son the name Malek? Was it not to honor the spirit that had saved your people from disaster? And did God and you the spirits above not bless him to grow up to be the chief you wanted him to be to his people? Why then take him away when his people now need him more than ever before? You God, and you our ancestral spirits, that is not the way to treat one's children. We know that you know everything; the ultimate wisdom is with you. But we trust that you also want to hear how your children see things and the pain they feel deep in their hearts. You have the last word, but you should not close your eyes and your ears to the cries of your children.

"Our people are finished; there are no elders left to guide our youth. I am an old man and my remaining days are few. Malek will soon be your most senior son in this world. How can you take him away when he still has the strength to lead? No, I have rejected the word of death. Save him to do your will and protect your people in this world. And accept in his place this bull, Malek, which we are about to sacrifice as a special gift to you."

Focusing attention on the bull Mijangdit went on: "As for you, Malek, this is the reason for which you were blessed as a sacred bull when you were still a small calf. You were chosen and given to the spirit of Malengdit so that you might one day be sacrificed to redeem people from evil. Yours is not a bad death; it is a good death. We shall all die some day, but you are dying today for a noble cause, to save the life of the leader of this land. From the Byre of Creation, God gave man the cow to be an ally in the war with the spirits of death. It is your sacred duty to assist man in the pursuit of life and well-being. And it is only the cow whose life is valued by the spirits as a worthy substitute to human life. So, accept the sacrifice in good grace; you are not being disdained, you are being honored. That is my word."

Another elder took the turn to speak. "Hold this word of mine. I will direct my word to the Spirit Malengdit. This bull we are about to sacrifice was consecrated and dedicated to you in honor of your life-saving powers that once redeemed the people of this tribe from the disaster of the smallpox. The man whose life we are praying for today was named after you to honor you for the good thing you had done. How can you take him away from the people you had blessed with his life and leadership? You spirits may see things differently from us humans, but in our view, you should accept this bull with which you were honored from the time it was a calf. Save our chief for us. We need him. I am not a man of many words. That's all I have to say."

At that moment, someone drew attention to a group of people who were approaching, carrying a man on a bed. "That must be Uncle Mithiangdit," said Akol. "We did not expect him to come because he himself has not been well."

As the group approached, the crowd quickly made room for Mithiangdit's bed seat.

"Let Uncle Mithiangdit say his word, now that he is here." said Akol, as all eyes focused on the old man, prominently located in the circle. "We cannot sacrifice the bull before his invocation."

Everyone agreed and also decided to give him time to collect his breath and thoughts. Mithiangdit must have thought a great deal on the way, for he feebly sat up on his bed, his hands shaking, his mouth munching on nothing and drooling with the spittle of old age. Adjusting his worn and soiled jallabiya, he spoke in a trembling voice that seemed to be a bridge with the world of the dead and the spirits.

"I am the oldest person in this group, older even than the son of my father, Mijak. I have seen a great deal in this world. I lie awake most nights reflecting on what has become of our people. What my heart sees is not comforting. During the days of our grandfathers, some of which we witnessed, God and the spirits above were close to man. People lived by the word of God and the ancestral spirits. When an elder called on God and the spirits, they listened to his words. Even if things had gone wrong, God, the spirits and the ancestors would let their wishes be known and man would obey. Once their wishes were met, God and the ancestral spirits would remove the threat of evil and things would go back to normal. People united their words and followed the path of God which our ancestors had bequeathed to us. Now, words have lost their meaning. The ancestors no longer listen to the voices of their sons, pleading for help. And God does not heed the prayers of the ants in this world.

"But I do not blame God, the spirits or the ancestors, for the generations of today have departed from the ways of our ancestors. And that cannot be pleasing to our spiritual Fathers. I do not have long to live and I am already thinking of what to report to my age-mates who have departed before me. What

I will report will not please their hearts. But what can we do? We have to tell the truth, even if it hurts."

Mithiangdit kept rambling on while the chorus repeated his words or phrases with increasingly less enthusiasm as he trod the bridge between the dead and the living.

"And yet, we have to appeal to you, God, the spirits, and the ancestors. Whatever wrongs your children on earth have committed, wash your hearts and bless them with a breeze of cool air to give them health."

A voice was heard directing the drifting thinking of the old man. "Gear your prayer to the issue at hand, the health of Chief Malengdit."

The old man looked offended by the interruption, for it was not the traditional Dinka way to interfere with a speaker's train of thought on such solemn occasions, especially when the speaker was such an elderly man as Mithiangdit. Turning to see who had made the impudent remark, Mithiangdit bit his lips angrily and remarked, "This is just the kind of youthful restlessness that I was talking about. It hurts me perhaps even more than it does our ancestors. But we have to accept that life is passing on and that does not free us from the obligation of protecting our children. You God, and you our forefathers, and you our ancestors, who else is left to speak for you in this world? Save Malek and take the bull. That was the way God decreed at creation, that cattle would be man's means to redemption. Let him sleep well and wake up healthy. As for you Malek, accept the sacrifice and urinate the way sacrificial animals should do when reconciled to their fate. My words are finished."

Dead silence followed. It was as though the group wanted to see the effect of Mithiangdit's words. Then, to everyone's satisfaction, the sacrificial bull bellowed and urinated. "*Nguoth*," chanted the congregation, signifying "on target," an expression used in war when the enemy is hit with a spear. On religious occasions, it was used to signify the victory of righteousness over evil. "The bull has accepted the sacrifice," commented someone.

It was now time to slaughter the animal. Young men moved in and using ropes, subdued the beast and turned its front eastward for the ritual. After touching the animal's neck with the sacred spear and pointing it away from the homestead, one man moved in with a sharp spear and made a small cut on the neck as though careful to minimize the wound he inflicted on the animal. Then digging the tip of the spear deep into the wound, he made sure that he cut the arteries, causing a flood of blood to flow into a gourd which had carefully been put in place for the purpose. The meat of the sacrificial beast was to be cut up and distributed according to specific rules of kinship, age and gender. But in the meantime, a selected number of elders went to Malengdit's hut to perform the rest of the blessings. Mijangdit and Akol were among the people who went to pursue the ritual.

Mijangdit cut the sacred cucumber into halves and threw them up. Everyone watched to see how they landed. The rule was that if both landed upward, that indicated a good prospect for recovery. If one landed upside down and the other upward, the one that had landed upside down would be thrown away and the other used to bless the sick person on the forehead, chest and feet. If both landed downward, that meant that the prayers had not been heeded.

At first, both halves landed upside down. The elders tried again and the same result occurred. People exchanged worried looks. "God, spirits of our clan, and you our ancestors, you are not going to dismiss us lightly." Mijangdit voiced what everybody seemed to feel. "It is Malengdit's health we want from you and we will not leave until you show us that he will recover. Please answer our prayers."

The ritual was performed again and again; it was not until the fourth time that the desired result was achieved—both halves landed upwards. "*Thithiey, thithiey,*" they all reacted in a chorus of gratitude to their Lord. After blessing Malengdit with both halves of the cucumber, the sacrifice was declared a success and the prospects for the chief's recovery were believed to have been considerably enhanced, even though of course no one could speak conclusively for God, the deities and the ancestors.

The festivities of the sacrifice were barely over when the clouds began to gradually form and by late afternoon, the world was suddenly covered by the shadow of a thick mass blocking the sun. It was close to the beginning of the rainy season, but even the optimists who would have expected the sacrifice to be blessed by the heavenly Fathers could not expose their secret hopes that it might rain. With the clouds spreading like heavy smoke in the sky and beginning to roar and thunder with the mighty voices of the Spiritual Kingdom, it soon became obvious that God and the spirits above were responding to the call of the ants, the humans, below. As the cool breeze that announced the imminence of a downpour started to blow, the village went into frantic tempo as people rushed about moving their belongings into huts and cattle byres.

"Don't you see the rain has come? Can someone fetch the sheep and the goats? And who is after the cattle?" Men and women's voices crisscrossed in the air, and people ran all over the place. It was a moment that combined jubilation over the blessing from above with panic over the practical inconveniences of the sudden change in season. And there was also fear that even in responding to the prayers of their children on earth, the Fathers above might also express their anger by striking with the club which accompanies a thunderstorm. The elders were implored to say a few prayers and spray the compound with grain.

"God, our Great Father," Ayueldit spoke looking up to the sky, holding a gourd of *durah*, sorghum seeds, in the left hand, his right hand filled with grain. "We welcome your blessing and the cool breath of life which your rain will bring to our homes. It is the coolness of health and general well being for Malengdit, his people and their herds that we prayed and sacrificed for. Let it pour down; that will sweeten our hearts. But do not allow destruction to spoil your good work. Deflect the club from your children's heads and let your thunder be a drum to which they will dance and not an angry voice to silence them or leave them mourning. Let your lightning be a torch to guide our path in the darkness and not the blow of death."

He spat on the grain in his right hand and threw it up in the air. He spat on the grain in the gourd, took some more and sprayed them in all four directions.

Akol then took over. "I speak only to add my voice to what Master Ayueldit has said. You our Fathers above are giving us hope with the blessing of the rain. Do not let any evil spoil that hope. That is my word."

He too blessed the grain by spitting on it and threw it toward the sky, turning around and repeating the ritual in all directions.

Then came the downpour, so heavy and with thunder and lightning so strong that people pulled together with mixed emotions of relief and awe, with men crammed in the cattle byres and women in the huts, finding some comfort in their closeness. It was a testimony to Dinka dedication to their herds that they were able to bring them all back and tether them inside the cattle byres. The goats were easy, for at the smell of the rain, and certainly with the first drops they all came running for the byres as they dread the feeling of water on their straight hair. The sheep were another matter, for while disturbed by the rain, they were too confused to know what to do, except to stick together as a herd and follow wherever anyone of them happened to forge the way. Nor were the cattle much better. But those were the kind of critical moments for which the Dinka had developed herding skills from childhood. Not a single animal was missed in the confusion of the rain.

Elias and his companions sheltered in the mud-wall-thatched-roof structure which his father used as his courthouse. The downpour stopped only intermittently and otherwise continued virtually throughout the night. The reward of the night's adventure was the almost miraculous transformation of the environment the following morning. Sounds of frogs and crickets filled the air. The plains around Dak-Jur suddenly turned into one big lake, with birds of varied colors, sizes and shapes flapping their wings and singing their distinctive songs of relief and joy. Butterflies and moths added their configuration to the colorful world of flying creatures. On the dry spots, there emerged teams of small velvet red insects called *alueldeng* and dark blue-red ones called *nyankwetkumeth*. The beauty of the sudden appearance of so many living creatures was accentuated by the contrast with the bleak and blazing conditions of the day before, the season of yesterday.

That was how a land of contrasts, where seasons reduced to a dualism of dry and wet, drastically changed the environment like day and night, creating conditions of life and death for all God's creatures on earth. Man did not pray for sunshine, but for rain and the cool breeze of the accompanying winds. But even that blessing could be a source of danger and death, as the seasons of heat, dryness, and want and of rain, lushness, and plenty alternated in a delicate balance. But for now it was all blessings from the Fathers above.

THREE

ELIAS WOKE UP BY daybreak, brushed his teeth, washed his face, and sat on a chair outside his father's courthouse. He was soon joined by his companions. They were having their morning tea, marvelling at the transformation of nature when a boy came to say that Elias's father wanted to see him. Elias hurried to his father's hut and found him with his mother. His father was drinking tea.

Elias could not believe how improved he looked. "How did you sleep, Father?"

"Quite well. I feel much better than I have done for some time now."

Turning to Aluel, Malengdit said, "Pour your son a cup of tea!"

"No, thank you. I have just had my tea."

"Have more."

"Well, let me pour it then," Elias conceded.

"Aluel, perhaps you should leave us alone now. I want to talk to Bol."

"What keeps me outside your talk?" protested Aluel mildly.

"There are some things which only men should know," Malengdit explained. "But on second thought, perhaps you too should know this one. Only I want it to be strictly between us. You women have a way of betraying secrets. Keep this one to yourself."

"What secret have I ever betrayed?" Aluel questioned with a conciliatory laughter that took Malengdit's comment not as a criticism, but rather as a teasing emphasis on the confidentiality of what was about to come.

"Son, as I told you, I slept well last night; I certainly feel much better today," resumed Malengdit. "Several things happened which I thought I should tell you about. What I told you yesterday about the message of the lion seems to be already manifesting itself. I was sleeping when I was woken by the sound of a lion. It was not the sound of a hungry lion; it was a peaceful roar. When I woke up and tried to listen more carefully, I could hear it no longer. I asked the woman, your young stepmother who was sleeping with me, but she said that she had not heard any lion's roar. She dismissed it as a dream. I did not argue with her, although I was sure that I had heard the sounds of a lion. I recalled your experience and felt that even if it were a dream, there was a message in that dream. Anyway, I decided to go back to sleep.

"I had gone back to sleep for only a brief period when I woke up again and this time heard an owl cry. It was on top of this hut. The rain had stopped for a while. Your stepmother also heard it. She wanted to go out and chase the owl away, but I prevented her from doing so. Our people consider the owl an evil bird because it functions at night. But for the same reason, it is a wise bird that sees things in the darkness—things others do not see. I felt that its visit might have some significance, a purpose. So, I called a few words of prayer for our ancestors to reveal to me the purpose of the visits by the lion and the owl. Both brought to mind the tragedy our family faced once when the cry of the owl was followed by the Arab attack and the intervention of the lions against them. Anyway, I prayed for the significance of these revelations.

"Then I went back to sleep and saw an astonishing vision in a dream. Our sacred spears, the symbols of our divine leadership, were blazing with a white flame and lying coiled around them was the snake totem of our clan, the puff adder. He was not at all affected by the heat of the flame. Indeed, there was no heat; it was merely a ring of light. I took it to be the illumination of our spirit, Ring, the Flesh. So, still in the dream, I got up; I prayed for explanation in front of the spears; I anointed the puff adder with butter; and I placed a gourd of melted butter in front of him. Then my father appeared next to the spears and with him was a creature who looked human but which I could not easily identify. That creature was holding the rope tied to the neck of the bull Malek, which was sacrificed yesterday. The bull looked as alive as any animal in the herd.

"It was my father who spoke first. 'Son,' he said, 'listen to our words very carefully, but do not try to touch us. We are not of your world. The man with me is Malengdit, the spirit after whom you were named. You know that I named you after him because he had saved our people from the disaster of smallpox. He is a life-giver, not a killer. And yet, Ayueldit was correct in divining that Malengdit wanted to bring you into our world of the dead. His intention, which he discussed with me, was to save you.

'We have been watching over the affairs of your world and have been deeply distressed by the changes we have observed. Our people have been transformed by foreign powers. First, the English came and introduced our young people to their religion, their language, and their ways of doing things. But at least they left most of our people under their chiefs to live their lives the way their ancestors had always done. Then the Arabs of the North and the Egyptians sent the English away and said that they wanted the Sudan to become free of foreign rule and that they wanted the Arabs of the North and the Black people of the South to be united into one people. This has now turned into a disaster for our people. They have been subjected to the kind of wars that destroyed this country before the English came. And now, our people are being turned into Muslims and away from the religion of their forefathers. Our people have been changed twice in your own lifetime, first to adopt the ways of the English and now to adopt the ways of the Arabs. Your power to control things through the ancient ways of your ancestors is being undermined and diminished.'

"My father went on: 'To hold your position only means to make your people believe that their ancestral powers still prevail when they have lost control. It is now being said that chieftainship should be abolished and chiefs replaced with elected leaders. That will be the end of ancestral leadership through divine chiefs. Malengdit argued, and I agreed with him, that it would be disastrous for our people to have our ancient leadership terminated by foreign rulers. It would be better for you to withdraw naturally and let the young educated generation assume their power through the ways they know best.

"'We, their ancestors, including you, their fathers, will then keep a close watch on them and bless their efforts from here in order for them to keep the names of our people alive and retain effective control over their own affairs. That was indeed why we sent the lion to meet with Bol so that he would know their clan spirits are with them even in distant lands. Malengdit and I have heard the prayers of the elders to save you for the people and have decided to grant their request for now. But, son, we have appeared to you in order to advise you to prepare your sons to take over and provide the people with the leadership required by the new conditions that now prevail. To be effective in meeting the challenge, your sons must come together. Convince Bol to look for his lost twin brothers, Achwil, whom the Arabs captured while an infant, and Madit, who later disappeared. We have spotted them. One is living a dangerous life in an Arab town. The other has met with a smoother success, but has become completely Arab. Bol must look for them and bring them back to the service of their people together with him. Those are our words. You will live long enough to fulfill this prophesy and then we will come to fetch you so that you retire with dignity and preserve the ancestral legacy of our leadership. We must now go. Farewell, my son.'

"Then I fell into a deep sleep from which I woke up this morning feeling much better. So, my son, that was what happened last night and those were the words of my father. I do not have much to add except this."

As he spoke, he pointed to the sacred spears at the back of the hut. The two large spears, one leaf-like and the other lance-like, had been passed down the family line from time immemorial and represented the power of divine rule. They rested on a piece of oiled leather and lying coiled next to them was a huge puff adder with a gourd of melted butter in front of it.

"What is that?" shouted Elias, who until then had been silently absorbed, mesmerized by the story.

"I woke up early to find him there. So I got up and said a few words of prayer and gave him the butter. You see, son, I have survived this illness and will live for some time yet, but the will of the ancestors must be fulfilled. You must find your brothers and work together for the cause of peace and well-being among your people. It will not be necessary any more for you to stay here. You must return and get to the task."

Elias had noticed that his mother's eyelids were heavy with tears. When his father concluded his words, she lost control of herself and broke down, sobbing. Malengdit was angered by her conduct. "Aluel, this was exactly what I was afraid of when I asked you to leave," he said. "How dare you cry over a prophetic word from the ancestors? Have you not heard that I am not dying as yet? Is that news to cry over or did you want me to die? Now, let me see no more tears or else you will make my tongue say bad words."

"How can you talk like that?" Aluel complained as she wiped her tears. "How can you talk in such a cold-blooded way about our twin sons? And how can you recall their memory and expect me to show no emotions? Can't you see that I have struggled to forget, but can't? Now you speak of them as though they are still alive and you expect me to remain calm? You may want them for leadership, but for me, I don't care whether they are to be leaders or not; I only pray to God that you are right and that they are still alive and well." And as she spoke, she began to wail.

"Woman, it is not my words that I say; I am only a tongue for the words of our ancestors. You must not doubt the truth of their words. You speak as though your children were born of a woman without a father. Are they yours alone or ours together? Stop crying: you will offend our ancestors and make them take those children away forever."

Elias felt so removed from their world that he did not even know how to respond. He certainly knew the story of his lost brothers, but he had never fully realized how much their memory still meant to his parents. In fact, he felt shaken by the reference to their role in leadership. Was his father, whose idea all this obviously was, disappointed with Elias's role? Or was it merely that he was pained by the loss of his other sons and wanted to justify the renewal of the search?

Elias quickly dismissed these suspicious ideas and relished the thought that his brothers might still be alive. How wonderful it would be to be reunited with them! Perhaps, since they were older than him, they could help in the burdensome task of leadership. All those thoughts crossed his mind in a flash as he listened to his parents, while continuing to watch the snake.

"Father, this is a deadly snake," Elias spoke out on a topic he felt needed most urgent attention. "We must kill it or dispose of it in some way."

"Son, this is exactly what your ancestors were talking about. Your ways are different. But you must understand your people's ways. You see, a power that is deadly is equally effective in protecting life. Our clan is known for its power to destroy by curse, but we are equally famed for providing spiritual protection for our people. That is what these large sacred spears stand for. And just as our destructive power is only effective in punishing wrongdoing, this ancestor you see lying by the spears is only deadly against those who deserve punishment. Otherwise, he is a protector. Can't you see that he is here by the will of God and the ancestors?"

"Is there really nothing we can do, Father, to protect people from a possible accident with the snake?"

"Malek, Bol is telling the truth," interjected his mother. "This is a village of many people. It is possible that our ancestor, the puff adder, might wish to stretch a little by moving around the village. Cattle could trample over him. Humans might accidently step on him. He might take that as disdain and strike back. We will have opened another front with the spirits. I suggest that he be taken away for his own protection and to prevent harm to anyone."

"Go and look for a lamb of *chuany* color, one whose pattern is as close as possible to that of the puff adder," Malengdit conceded. "And ask Ayueldit to come with my brother Akol. We shall dedicate the lamb to him before we have him removed. We must pray to him and the ancestors to explain that his removal is not rejection, but protection."

"There can be nothing bad in that," confirmed Aluel, pleased that the chief had heeded her advice. "After all, his message has been received and will be honored."

The village of Dak-Jur was now festive with celebrations that honored the miraculous blessing of a downpour and the recovery of Chief Malengdit. The reputation of Ayueldit for diagnostic accuracy and curative powers, already well deserved, was enhanced. Drums were brought out and the distant tribes, invited by their sounds, joined in the singing and dancing display of joy and gratitude. Animals were slaughtered and abundant foods prepared. The festivities continued for days, but the secret of the divine message remained exclusive to Elias and his parents.

Within days of the heavy rains with which the prayers for the chief's well-being had been received by the heavenly powers, more rain fell and the land continued to be transformed. The plains were now covered with a green carpet of virgin grass while the trees began to bud colorfully and the rivers teamed with minnows and tadpoles. A symphony of sounds in the air provided both lullabies for sleep and tunes for waking up in the morning. Children gratified themselves with a cool bath in the rain pools surrounding the village, while the cattle spread out feasting lavishly on the sprouting grass.

Although Elias was now more assured of his father's health, he felt that he should take him to Khartoum for a medical check up and whatever treatment he might need. "I don't see the purpose, my son," responded his father. " Our ancestors have revealed their will to us; we must act accordingly. I have no need for medical advice."

"Father, I trust the wisdom of the ancestral will, but I see no harm in complementing that with the benefit of modern medicine."

"That can only make our ancestors believe that we do not have full faith in them."

"Now Father, in this day and age we cannot continue to believe in a conflict between the ancestral ways and the ways of our advancing world; the conflict must be resolved."

Elias allowed the matter to rest knowing very well that he would have to rally the support of the elders, including Ayueldit, the Man of God. As soon as Elias found the opportunity to talk to Ayueldit in the presence of his father, he raised the question, making sure that the diviner did not read his suggestion as a vote of no confidence in his efforts. "I really think that we are better off using all the defense we have against the disease," he said. "It is better to overkill than be the victim."

The task of persuading Ayueldit proved far less difficult than Elias had thought, for the diviner saw no contradiction in the various approaches to Malengdit's well-being.

"I have always maintained, as you said the other day, that we are all working for the same end, the well-being of man," he reasoned. "We appeal more directly to God and our ancestors to remove any evils that threaten life, to restore health and to safeguard the well-being of man in society; doctors on the other hand rely more heavily on their man-made medicines. But without God's blessing or will, their treatment would not work. So, you see why I say that we are all working for the same thing?"

It was eventually agreed that Elias Bol should take his father to Khartoum. One of the old man's younger wives was designated to go along to nurse him. Aluel insisted that she too should go. "We pray that Malengdit will recover," she said, "but I want to be by his side in his illness and even more so, should he die."

The matter ended on her word, even though her reference to Malengdit's possible death was dismissed as unnecessary fatalism.

Eager to combine caring for his father with his duties as a member of the Assembly, Elias saw to it that they left as soon as the necessary arrangements for his father's departure were made.

When it was time to leave, a spot was prepared for Malengdit to lie on the back of the truck with Aluel and the junior wife sitting next to him. Elias and the security officer sat next to the driver. Malengdit insisted that they take a lamb and leave it where the lion had appeared as a gift or a symbol of gratitude. The lamb was tethered to the frame of the truck in the back.

The journey itself was trying for the rains had penetrated the land transforming the pavement-like soil into a heavy muddy clay. The beaten track suddenly became a long trail of mud in which the truck frequently got stuck. The passengers, except Malengdit and his wives, and of course the driver, would all get down to aid the engine with a push. No one cared anymore about protecting their clothes, or for that matter their bodies from the mud. Indeed, the muddier they looked, the more hard working and conscientious they appeared and the more self righteous they felt. When they came to the spot where they had encountered the lion, the driver, who had been informed of the plan stopped.

"Was this not where we found that lion?" he asked Elias and the other companions, who quickly confirmed his judgment.

Chief Malengdit was too exhausted to perform the full rituals of dedication. But he said a few words of invocation lying down, and reaching for the lamb, rubbed it on the back and said, "Tie him to a tree; his owner will come and find him there."

That done, they roared on, leaving the lamb crying in a voice that sounded pitiful to Elias Bol but which to his father and mother confirmed a fulfillment of the ancestral obligation and a promise for a successful search for of Achwil and Madit, the missing twins, which had just been revealed in Malengdit's dream.

PART TWO
GENESIS

FOUR

VIRTUALLY EVERYONE IN DAK-JUR knew the tragic story of the twins, Achwil and Madit, and Aluel, their mother. Malengdit and Aluel had already lost their firstborn, male twins for whom the conventional names of Ngor and Chan had been predetermined. The "birds," as twins were metaphorically called by the Dinka, had "flown away," died in their infancy. The parents had only just begun to feel compensated by their second set of twin sons, Achwil and Madit, when tragedy struck again.

Much talk about independence from British rule was in the air and with it rumors about the impending return to the days of the slave trade when the Arabs of the North had raided the African tribes to the South for slaves. These rumors continued to spread as the British began to withdraw and were replaced by Sudanese administrators from the North. Only a few months before the declaration of independence, the mounting fears of the South exploded in a rebellion that soon developed into widespread disturbances in which hundreds of Northerners in the South were brutally killed. With the intervention of the withdrawing British governor-general, the rebels were eventually persuaded to put down their arms and order was restored. Northerners and Southerners agreed on a unanimous Declaration of Independence by Parliament. But things soon began to fall apart. Contrary to the promises for a fair trial of the rebels and redress of Southern grievances made by the governor-general, the independent government retaliated with a vengeance against the rebels and the South in general. But not all the rebels had surrendered; some had taken to the bush to pursue anti-government hostilities that progressively escalated into a full-scale North-South civil war.

The sentiments of racial and cultural animosity which these hostilities fanned began to open old wounds and revive intertribal warfare between the Arabs and the Dinka. This was particularly acute in the northwestern regions where the Dinka Mathiang came into violent confrontation with the Baggara Arabs. And in their clashes, the Arab tribes reverted to the age-old practice of raiding for cattle and slaves.

For Malengdit's family, the tragedy went back to the night the owl cried, alerting the village to the impending raid. The Mathiang Dinka had just clashed with the Baggara Arabs and had inflicted heavy casualties on them. It was a dreadful fight that ended with the Arabs withdrawing and leaving their dead unburied, to be eaten by the birds. One night, some time later, the owl cried and though chased away, persisted in returning and crying. Malengdit was in a hut with a junior wife. He got up, went outside holding his sacred spears and sang the secret hymn of leadership, meant to be invoked only when the tribe was facing imminent disaster.

"You of my forefathers," he said in the prayers that accompanied his hymn, "whatever the owl is crying about, divert it from my people. We have only recently fought with the Arabs and knowing them as I do, they will be back for vengeance. Block their way, Oh God of my Fathers. It was not we who invoked the fight; it was the Arabs who hunted us like animals. That was why You the powers above granted my people victory. Do not abandon us! Stand behind us. Let Your blessings be our shield. Let not the Arabs spill even a drop of blood in this tribe."

Chief Malengdit had barely gone back to bed when he heard a lion roaring some distance away. Like all Dinka adults, he knew the hazards of their countryside and the behavior of the wild beasts. Clearly, that lion was struggling with prey. He wasn't running; he was fighting. But with what or whom? Was it an antelope, a cow, or a human being?

Malengdit was listening carefully to the sounds of the lion when suddenly he heard the neighing of horses in the village compound. Almost immediately, he heard the sounds of a woman and children crying, their voices mixing with the sounds of the horses. He rushed out, and so did the other men in the village. But what they found caused utter dismay. The Arabs had disappeared with Malengdit's wife, Aluel, and Achwil, one of her twins. Madit, the other twin, had fallen from the horses and was lying on the ground crying, unable to move. He had broken his hip.

The twins were then about two years old. That night, they had been suffering from diarrhea and in a fit of blind courage or compulsion Aluel had opened the door and taken them outside against the advice of the women in the hut. Perhaps she had been concerned about the feelings of the people in the hut, but in retrospect it all seemed unbelievably reckless, especially in view of the fear from both animals and humans which then prevailed.

War cries were sounded and the young men of the village, soon joined by many others, went out looking for the Arabs. But, no evidence could guide them in any direction. It was a senseless and dangerous hunt. On the advice of the elders, the hunt was called off to be resumed in the morning.

Word soon spread that the Arabs had come in a band of horsemen and that they had been intercepted by a lion, the one whose roaring had been heard in Malengdit's village. The beast had attacked the Arabs, killed one whose remains had been found scattered on the spot the following morning, and judging from the horse marks and the footsteps in the area, must have mauled several others. Apparently, the people nearby had heard the sounds of the Arabs and their horses and had concluded that their enemies were at war with the beast. They had chosen to ignore the plight of the slave raiders knowing that it was the lion or themselves against the Arabs.

Scouts were sent to trail the horses, but there was so much crisscrossing of footprints and hoove prints that it was not easy to detect where they headed. Besides, Arab camps were scattered and it was not easy to spot the one where the culprits might have settled. People had virtually given up all hope of finding Aluel when travelers brought news of a camp where the Arabs were reported to have nursed the victims of an encounter with a lion. Since no other incident with a lion was known to have taken place, the reports suggested that those must indeed be the enemies they were looking for.

A plan was drawn up to ambush the camp at night. Once it was entered, the attackers were to shout out in Dinka instructions as to where Aluel and her baby, if they were together, should head for rescue. The rescue mission went as planned. When the team reached the Dinka settlement closest to the Arab camp, they hid in the village and waited for night-fall. When the camp was sound asleep, they approached and then formed themselves into two rows. The front line, composed of a few people, advanced toward the camp and initiated the attack, their main objective being to create confusion among the Arabs and their herds, while shouting instructions to Aluel in Dinka to run to the next row. The Arabs' cattle, not tied to pegs at night, were loose within the zeriba, and consequently stampeded, running over some people, and breaking down the fence. The men were hardly ready to repel the attack when instructions for Aluel's escape were shouted. Aluel responded in Dinka as she followed the orders. But there was a hitch: Achwil was not with his mother. Aluel kept shouting as she withdrew: "My son, my son; I don't know where the Arabs are keeping him."

But there was no time for doubts. Within minutes, the remaining attackers had swarmed over the camp and withdrawn with Aluel and a herd of Arab cattle. The Arabs retreated further from Dinka territory. Achwil was not heard from again.

Although the tragedy of Achwil's disappearance kept Malengdit and his family mourning, Aluel's return was a significant reward. Yet Aluel suffered from the emotional pain of having lost one of her sons. She could never forgive herself for having taken the twins out that fateful night. She felt guilty for having escaped from the Arabs alone, leaving Achwil in Arab captivity. But perhaps the one who suffered the most was Madit, for despite his having survived the raid, his broken hip left no prospects for full recovery. Among the Dinka, whose quest for physical attraction and wholesomeness was exaggerated, this was a great personal tragedy.

As though to compensate for these events, Aluel became pregnant again. And precisely because she and her husband regarded this pregnancy as compensational, they attached great importance to the development of the baby. Even Malengdit followed her pregnancy with unusual attention for a Dinka husband. Aluel's diet was closely watched and anything she craved was promptly provided. Malengdit forbade her from any physical labor or activity that might in any possible way affect the growth of the child.

Aluel's delivery proved to be very difficult. When it began with the pangs of labor, female elders who were particularly knowledgeable in these matters, were surprised that a woman who had had twins would experience a painful labor. The labor continued, the pain intensified, but the baby did not come. As was always the case under those circumstances, no men were allowed into the delivery hut. When the ordeal went on for longer than was reasonable, senior women clustered around Aluel and began to subject her to a different ordeal.

"Aluel, wife of my brother," said one senior kinswoman from Malengdit's clan, "our people have customs which we turn to under these conditions. Women confess any wrongs they might have committed to avoid any dangers in pregnancy or delivery. You are a woman and any woman can commit a mistake. What is important is that you do not endanger your life or that of your baby by concealing your wrong. All you need to do is tell the truth for we have rituals for removing the curse of wrongdoing."

"Aluel," spoke another elderly woman, "it is for these occasions that our ancestors left us with certain customs to follow. It is true that the thought of your having had another man is appalling to anyone here in this hut and I know it would pain the men in this family severely. But it is for a matter of death or life that we are beseeching you. Confess and let this evil pass. So what if you have slept with another man? You will not be the first or the last to have done it. The heart is a feeble organ which can be swayed easily by a breeze of passing attraction. It is only human and that is no reason to risk death."

It was as though salt was rubbed on her wound. Shrieking in physical pain, she cried, "Oh my back; my back is broken! I am dying; I am dying! Oh I am dead."

"Confess, confess," the assembled women continued to press. Combining physical and emotional pain, Aluel shouted back, "Oh my people, I have nothing to confess. I have committed no wrong. God knows I have committed no wrong. I have sought no man. Even as a girl, I was never known for eyeing men. Oh God, let me die and be over with it all; I cannot endure any longer."

A female diviner, Acholdit, was hurriedly fetched from a nearby village. She entered the hut looking calm and that gave people some ground for hope. She even rebuked the women for showing so much anxiety which she seemed to believe aggravated matters. "What if she should die?" she said sarcastically. "Will she fill the ground so that there would be no place for burying others?" Having asked for people to leave, except for two or three to witness her performance, she felt Aluel in the belly, the back and the thighs, and mumbled a few words to herself. And then she began to gradually transform until she was in a state of trance. She chanted in a language that was not intelligible to the women. Then standing up and going around the hut, she shouted, waving her hands as though chasing something away. So powerful and overwhelming was her performance that even Aluel became mesmerized. She almost forgot that the woman was there because of her condition. The diviner went and sat facing Aluel. She was still breathing heavily and looking physically transformed, almost frightening with her fierce and penetrating eyes. "Now, look into my eyes very closely. I am telling you that they are gone. They are not our spirits; they are foreign spirits and with the help of our ancestors, we have chased them away. Now, stop being frightened and have your baby."

With the other women, they let Aluel lie back and push, as they massaged her belly and back. Suddenly, the baby came out smoothly and cried, signalling a successful and healthy delivery; a beautiful baby son. The women greeted the delivery with a chorus of *Thithiey*, "Praised be the Lord," while withholding any compliments that might turn into a bad omen for the baby.

"Let a brown lamb and a brown chicken be taken at night to a forest far away from here," Acholdit said to Malengdit later. "Let them be left there alive, they will be found by those foreign spirits; we do not want them to come back to Aluel, looking for food."

As the baby was born after twins, he was named Bol according to the Dinka system of naming.

The sad circumstances under which he was conceived, the compensational nature of his conception, and the dangers of his difficult delivery, all combined to make Bol a special child. The fact that he was special to his parents attracted favorable attention from the wider circle of relatives and others who clustered around the chief's household. But Aluel's devotion to her child was exceptional. It was she who composed the verses that soon became the praise song of those who held the baby, jouncing him tenderly and rhythmically to the chanting of the lyric:

Brown baby, brown baby
Your mother was bedeviled by the Arabs,
But she was not forsaken by the Dinka.
Born in tragedy, you are a child of destiny,
Smile, but do not attract the evil eye;
Those who gaze on your brown skin with envy
Wishing to cast a spell on my darling one,
May their sight be dimmed by the powers of our clan
And by the will of God.
My little one, rest in peace
Your land is in safe hands.

Malengdit always liked to hear the verses chanted, somehow fancying his leadership as the safe hands ensuring the peace of the land, though realizing full well that his protection was precarious at best.

It was deep into the rainy season, just before the new crops ripened. People were running short of food and needed to supplement their meager supplies by gathering a wide variety of foodstuffs from the natural environment. There were leaves, berries and nuts from various trees, and there were fruits, vegetables and wild grain. But perhaps the most desired was wild rice — *lob* — and its finer variety — *bilit* — which grew in the marshlands near the villages and which women collected through a painstaking operation of swinging wide-open gourds over the top of the hay-like crop to harvest the seeds.

Aluel had been gone for most of the day collecting wild rice, leaving Bol under the care of women in the village. Missing his mother and presumably hungry for her milk, Bol cried so much that even Malengdit's attention was drawn. A junior stepmother sang to him, rattling the gourd in the vain hope of putting him to sleep, but all to no avail. Malengdit himself took the unusual step of holding the child and rocking him on his shoulders to soothe him, but that too did not help. Eventually, Bol exhausted himself and fell into a deep sleep from which he woke up only after his mother's return.

It was perhaps that episode which moved Malengdit to suggest that it was high time Bol was weaned and sent to his maternal grandparents. Bol was then only a year and a half old, and although Malengdit argued that he was too old to be nursing, it was unusually early for a Dinka child to be weaned. Two or three years were closer to the norm. But Malengdit also felt the need to compensate for the tragic loss of Achwil and the affliction of Madit by trying for another child sooner than normal.

"My dear wife," he addressed Aluel tenderly, "these are hard times and it is children born that ensure the survival of a people."

What he meant was not only that Aluel should stop nursing and Bol should be sent to his maternal grandparents for weaning, but that they should resume sleeping together, tabooed by the Dinka moral code during the nursing period. Violation of the taboo was not only believed to cause illness and perhaps death to the nursing child, but also to endanger the lives of other nursing children in the village.

Embarrassed by the insinuation of sex, Aluel sat on the ground opposite Malengdit's bed, her legs folded under her, her eyes aimlessly focused on the ground. Her instinct was against it, not only because she needed more time with her baby, but also because she was afraid of the gossip such an early weaning would arouse in the village. It would seem as though she was too eager to resume relations with her husband, and so compromise the interests of the child. Responding with an understatement, she said in a low, resigned voice, "How can I push him away at this tender age? Even the spirits would disapprove of my conduct."

Malengdit was challenged by the reference to the spirits, but he interpreted Aluel's reaction to be a statement of modesty, not criticism or opposition. Though not really offended, he nonetheless felt it necessary to assert his moral authority. "Since when have you become the spokesman for our ancestral spirits?" he said with a mildly sarcastic smile on his face. "Don't forget that it was I who released the sacred cows of our ancestral spirits for your marriage. I ought to know what is in the interest of my clan spirits. It was for children that the sacred cows were released."

As Aluel reflected on Malengdit's words, a thought which she had retained on a number of occasions flashed through her mind. If she had not insisted on nursing her twin children for as long as she had, they would probably have gone to her parents for weaning and would have avoided the tragedy. That thought always added to her feeling of guilt. Now, as the thought crossed her mind, she instinctively decided to recede. It was not really the kind of topic that could be debated by a couple sitting far apart. Nor could they risk getting close and allowing their desires to be kindled.

"Let's leave the matter," Aluel concluded on a conciliatory note. "I will talk to my mother and see what she has to say about having the boy at his age."

When she went to see her mother, carrying Bol in a sling hanging on her back, Aluel realized that she was in effect delivering the child to her mother. She and Malengdit had already agreed on the two milch cows that were to be sent with Bol for his weaning, but for now, the delivery of the cows must await a formal agreement with the grandparents. There was really nothing to be discussed, for Aluel's parents were delighted to have the baby and at the prospect of their daughter bearing another child. There was also another reason for their readiness to go along with Aluel's suggestion. They had heard her lament on several occasions that if she had sent the twins to her parents for an earlier weaning, she would have avoided the tragedy that had befallen them. No one could tell what other hazards were in store for Bol. They felt they should go along with the mother's instinct. "Who knows, God willing, you might have another set of twins," her mother commented jokingly.

Although Bol clearly missed his mother, he received intense love and affection from his grandparents. His grandfather, Monychol, was, as his name suggested, very dark, even for a Dinka. Tall, lean, with a long thin face and protruding cheekbones, he looked older than his age, which was around sixty. When he was not naked, which he usually was in the normal course of life in his village, he wore a jallabiya which he evidently found uncomfortable and suffered only when he was having visitors or visiting others.

Monychol was not a chief, but he was a descendent of a chiefly lineage, second to Malengdit's clan in divine preeminence in the Mathiang tribe. He himself was known for his devotion to spiritual matters and was esteemed as a highly respectable nobleman. His wife, Nyankir, a name which meant "Girl of the Nile," because she had been born during a period of severe drought when smaller rivers had dried up and people had been forced to migrate to the river banks for water, was contrastingly brown by Dinka standards. It was rumored that her great grandmother was an Arab princess who had been captured by the Dinka and offered to a chief. But that was a long time ago, now only vaguely remembered. Nyankir was shorter and several years younger than her husband, but that did not show in her lean figure, drained more by toil than by want. Dressed in leather skirts tied around her waist and hanging low to the ankles in front and back and overlapping on the sides, she stood thin and erect, her naked figure from the waist up lean to the bone, her drawn-in face accentuating her high cheekbones, her breasts hanging flatly over her exposed ribs like a pair of folded leathers.

Monychol and Nyankir had suffered a horrifying loss of children to the spirit of death. First, they had a son who died shortly after he was weaned. Then they had a daughter who died in infancy. She was soon followed by yet another daughter whom they named Nyanngoth, "Girl in Whom There is Hope," who died when, at about the age of seven, they were beginning to believe that she would indeed survive. That was when prominent elders of the tribe, moved by compassion, got together and decided to do something about the couple's plight. They went to visit Monychol one morning with a pregnant brown cow, which bore the name Aluel. Monychol and his family were startled by the visit. They had no idea what it signified. But it was of course their duty to welcome the visitors. A lamb was slaughtered and lavish hospitality shown them. Then came the moment for solemn talk. The initiative came from the spokesman of the group.

"Monychol, son of our land, we are not here because someone asked us to render a favor; we are here to fulfil an obligation we feel we owe to every member of our society and especially one who has lived up to the ideals of his people. We feel that you are such a person. That is why we have shared with you the pains of your family tragedy. We have come with this brown cow, Aluel, which we would like to sacrifice to God and pray for you to beget a child which will survive and be a fruit of salvation to your family. We have brought a cow and not a bull because we are going to pray for a daughter and not a son. We would like to sacrifice the cow to the spirit, Abuk, and not to her son Deng, or to the Supreme Spirit, Nhialic--God. Most people would pray for a son; we want God to hear a different word: we are going to pray for a woman in whom shall be sown the seeds of future generations. We have brought Aluel pregnant to fill the eyes of the spirit of death. This is a word that does not call for a response from you; it is a gesture by your fellow tribesmen and we only hope you accept it in good grace, for without that grace, our blessing will not be worth anything."

Then another member of the group spoke. "Our words are not going to be long, Monychol. We are here to do something different from the way things are usually done. As our brother said, normally people pray for a son to continue the lineage. And in their prayers, they address themselves to God, the Spirit Deng, or any one of the male spirits. We decided to invoke the Mother-God and rely on her maternal compassion. That is why we thought of Abuk, the mother of Deng. If our prayers are answered and you have a daughter, and she survives, she will not only be a mother of generations to come, but may pave the way for a brother to follow."

"Monychol," yet another man spoke up, "no man can survive without breathing the air around him. Your people are the air around you. Just as you do not decide to breathe, but do so any way, you do not decide to accept or reject the word of your people, uttered on your behalf. So, there is really nothing to discuss. We have brought our cow Aluel, and we are going to pray for a heifer of a child to be called Aluel. All this talk is only a matter of information, just to let you know what we are doing. It does not call for a discussion. But of course your acceptance would be desirable and is called for."

Monychol had listened to all of them very attentively, his head bent down, clearly moved by what he had heard. "My fellow tribesmen," he managed to speak after considerable silence, "I do not know what to say; what I feel is better expressed in silence. Nor will I tell you that I wish you would pray for a son; you know what you want and why you want it that way. I will not contradict your word. All I can say is I hope that Abuk will listen to your prayers and that God and the ancestors will back her."

The sacrifice was conducted accordingly. Monychol and Nyankir were seated on a sleeping skin with a bladed leaf-like spear, a female symbol, lying across their laps. After lengthy prayers in which the elders repeated the themes of their talk with Monychol, several times they placed the spear on Nyankir's belly and ended by pointing it upward, pronouncing in unison the word *nguoth*, symbolizing the successful delivery and acceptance of their message.

Nyankir became pregnant shortly afterward and in due course bore her daughter Aluel, named after the sacrificial cow. Although her life was threatened by a childhood illness that made people fear that she too might die, Aluel survived and was followed by a son whom they chose to name Alier, "Cool Breeze," that connoted health and survival.

The prayers of the elders had been fully answered; Aluel had grown up to be the mother of their grandchildren. Although she had lost her first set of twins Ngor and Chan, and tragedy had struck the second set of twins, there was now Bol, a symbol of continuity with which they were exceedingly pleased.

It was as though the blessings they had received effectively balanced the curse of tragedy and vindicated them from any allegation of spiritual contamination as an explanation for the tragedy they had suffered. Indeed, those who knew the couple felt that their suffering had been totally unwarranted. Although it was most unusual among the Dinka for such misfortune to be unaccounted for in terms of moral wrongs, no one ever attributed their fate to any hidden violation of the moral code. The Dinka believed that God and the spirits could be capricious, sometimes even sadistic, and it was up to man to accept this as part of the supreme will of the forces above and below. And to the Dinka, somehow, ancestral spirits were ultimately always right even when the justification was sometimes obscure to humans.

Monychol had other children by a second wife, Alimo, whose name was a perversion of the Arabic Halima, suggesting that she was from a non-Dinka tribe, and had been adopted or of slave origin. But it was taboo among the Dinka to speak of such indignities. Even the fact that her elder two children, both daughters, one of whom was married, had come with her, was kept within the family. Her two younger children, both boys, were begotten by Monychol. The youngest, Marial, who was about four and was quite close to his father, was to become Bol's close companion. On the whole, it was clear that Alimo and her children occupied an inferior position in the family which could not be accounted for in terms of her order in marriage alone.

The two wives lived in homes that were several miles apart, separated by a large complex of adjacent farms owned and cultivated by individual families whose homes lined the periphery of this extensive farmland. Each of the homes had two huts, one for sleeping and one for cooking, and a cattle byre. Monychol, like all Dinkas, sent the bulk of his herds of cattle, sheep and goats with young men and women in the wet season to the distant camps in the highlands of the North, but he kept a small number in the village to provide the family with milk and for other needs, such as slaughtering for hospitality or in sacrifice to God and the ancestral spirits.

While Monychol moved to and fro between the homes of his two wives, and helped them both with their individual farms, he resided more regularly with Nyankir. Their oldest child and only girl, Aluel was very close to her parents. This helped endear Bol to his grandparents, even more than is usual.

The emotional fervor that had been associated with Bol's life together with his status as the son of the chief also added to the special attention he received, not only from his grandparents but also from a wide circle of maternal relatives. They pampered him, flattered him, and exalted him in every way. But he was not spoiled in the negative sense. On the contrary, as he grew up and became more aware of things, he relished the attention he was receiving from his elders, but also strove to earn it by proper conduct. Even at that early phase of his life, he began to reflect a level of comprehension, consciousness and articulation that was astounding. He would sit with his grandfather in the evening, listening to him as he chanted prayers in response to the sounds of animals or of nature in which were embodied the symbols of the ancestral spirits. His absorbed attention on those solemn occasions combined with his deferential manner, somewhat exaggerated by reputation, won him the nickname of Wen-Yaath, "Sacred Child."

One morning, Bol woke up complaining of a headache. As the day progressed, he became lethargic and grew visibly worse until, by the late afternoon, he shivered with chills. It was the middle of the rainy season and, as Bol lay outside in the sun to warm himself, clouds soon covered the sky, suddenly turning the day into darkness. Then it began to thunder. Suspecting a downpour, people hurriedly moved their possessions into the byres and the huts, and went indoors for shelter. A dusty wind preceded the rain and then came the downpour with thunder and lightning, combined with a chilling drop in temperature. Nyankir was busy kindling the fire to warm the hut when Monychol surprised her by lifting Bol from the sleeping skin on the ground near the fire and said, "Nyankir, please open the door for me."

"What are you doing?" Nyankir asked in dismay.

"I am going out with the child."

"Why?" she remarked in disbelief.

"What this child needs is not the heat of your fire, but the cold breeze from the spirit of Dengdit, thundering and pouring down."

"Oh Monychol, you are taking our child to certain death," Nyankir complained. "How can you add cold rain to his chills and expect him to live?"

"My dear Nyankir, how can you question my ancestral duty? I want to offer his fate to God and let the blessings of the holy water fall on his body: I am entrusting his fate to God. If God wants to take him, this hut will not protect him. And if God wants to save him, what better way can there be than blessing him with the sacred water from Deng, the son of Abuk, Deng, the firstborn of God? Do not argue with me anymore, open the door."

As though pushed by invisible hands, Nyankir pulled the tightly fixed doorcovers apart, opening just enough for Monychol to squeeze himself through with Bol, screaming in terror. As soon as he was outside, the rain, thunder and lightning at their worst, Nyankir could hear Monychol singing hymns and chanting prayers as Bol continued to cry to the full capacity of his lungs. As though the cries of the child were insignificant, Monychol went on praying and singing a hymn to Deng, The Spirit of The Rain:

Great Father Deng
Our Father Deng, son of Abuk,
You are the shade under which all people rest,
You are the shield behind which we find protection,
You are the thundering voice of our Father in the sky;
I offer you my child for blessing,
If I have done nothing wrong
Then save him and make him recover tonight;
If I have committed a grievous wrong,
Then strike me down and save the child.

Kill me to save my child,
If he and I both survive the night,
Let me see him wake up tomorrow with smiles on his face
Let him play and enjoy his nimble age;
You are the Father of All!
You are the power over all!
Bless us and praised be your name.

When he returned into the hut, Nyankir thanked God that the child was still crying, alive. Within a short time, Bol fell into a deep sleep from which he did not wake until the following morning. Monychol and Nyankir could hardly believe their eyes when they saw him smiling cheerfully and full of vitality.

The season of scarcity was receding as the new crops started to ripen. Bol and Marial were among the first in the village to sneak into the cornfields behind the homestead garden and break off a few ears that were ripe enough to eat. But soon elders gratified the children's craving by selecting for them riper ears of corn and roasting them over the open fire or inside the smoldering conical mound made from dried cow dung. There was something unique about the delicacy of that early yield.

As Bol and Marial walked to and fro between their two homes across the fields, they gratified their craving for sugarcane from the sorghum crop, first the early ripening variety cultivated near the homestead, *ngai*, and then the longer maturing varieties, the brown *rwath* or the white *amarak* which were grown in the larger and more distant fields. With wet clay glued to their bare feet, not infrequently pierced by long thorns buried in the mud, the boys made something of an adventure out of going through the fields of tall sorghum stalks, inspecting the color on the veins of the leaves. White indicated that the cane was sugarless, while a creamy color meant a promise of sweetness. The custom of the land, which they realized even at that early age, gave everyone a certain freedom to fell the sugary stalks of any field, so long as one did not exaggerate the gathering beyond limited consumption, or damage a good head of sorghum. Bol and Marial chewed until their jaws ached. As the season progressed, it soon became evident that they were not alone. As more people joined the chewing, the sharp, sometimes treacherous, slivers from the peels of the sugar cane and the remains of the chewed pulp became scattered around the villages and along the pathways through the fields.

While Bol and Marial, like all children below the age of puberty or, in the case of boys, still uninitiated, were permitted to gorge themselves with these fresh foods as soon as they ripened, adults were prohibited from partaking of them until a thanksgiving feast had been performed and offerings made to the ancestral spirits. When the big day came, food was lavishly prepared from the freshly harvested sorghum. Other food varieties made from new sorghum soon followed. There was *akop* which was prepared from dough made of whole grain flour, broken into tiny balls which were then steamed in a frying pan and served with ground sesame seeds, dairy products, or gravy from fish or meat. And there was *aror*, prepared from the same kind of dough, but with a pudding-like consistency. Although they could be prepared from sorghum flour throughout the year, there was something uniquely tasteful about these dishes prepared from newly harvested grains. They were considered very special when mixed with melted butter. Beer was brewed in plenty and shared by all, including the children. Animals were slaughtered for meat. Ritual offerings were made on the shrines and in the rivers. Everyone feasted and from then on was free to partake of the food prepared from the new harvest.

Bol's euphoria about the season climaxed when, toward the end of the harvest, cattle were brought back to the villages to feed on the stems of the harvested second crop, *angwol*, which was believed to be especially nutritious and milk-producing.

It was the season in which Dinka preoccupation with cattle and the convenience of the village merged to make the ambiance aesthetically exciting: the land spotted with animals of all sizes, shapes and colors; the air filled with bellows of varying pitches and volumes; young men and women displaying flirtatious figures adorned with articles of beautification; songs of love, catharsis, lamentation, or glorification accompanied every conceivable activity. Even a child could not miss the sensuous flavor of life.

It was during this period that Bol got to know his mother's younger brother, Alier, who had previously been away in the distant camps. Alier was a member of the Buffalo age-set, the last to be initiated and therefore aspiring to the position of the dominant regiment. Like his parents, Alier was very fond of Bol. Despite the age difference, Alier being in his late teens, it was as though Bol represented the younger brother he did not have. And yet, his fondness for Bol was unfettered by the usual rivalry between siblings and consolidated by the special bond which the Dinka recognize as existing between maternal uncles and their sister's sons: a bond sanctioned by the power to bless or curse which the maternal uncle is believed to wield over his nephew.

Alier had not been home for long when his father called him for a confidential talk one evening. Monychol told him of the incident of Bol's illness, his prayers for his grandchild's recovery and the miraculous way the boy had recovered from his acute illness. Becoming more solemn in his account, Monychol then revealed an aspect of the story which his son found painful. "I offered myself to redeem Bol from death," he intimated. "The lightning did not strike me dead that night, but my self-sacrifice for my grandson was heard. No one knows the ways of the spirits. Bol was saved because I surrendered myself to the spirit of death. I do not know when the spirit will claim my life. What I know is that I will not live to see my prayers for Bol's leadership answered; that will be a thing for you and your sister's son. But I have no doubt that Bol will live to be a leader of his people. However long it may take, it will be as I tell you, my son."

Alier was disturbed by his father's talk of death, but he could not say anything wise or meaningful to counter his self-condemnation. All he could think of saying was, "Father, you are still too young to think of death!"

His father could not let that pass. "What makes you think that age has anything to do with God's will? The spirit of death chooses from all ages; it can prevent a child from being conceived, destroy a child in the mother's womb, end the life of a child in infancy or kill a man or woman at the prime of life. The spirit of death almost took Bol and I offered to die instead. But do not worry my son; my words will not kill me if my day has not come."

Monychol often reinforced the uncle-nephew bond by counselling his son that Bol was his extended arm in the chiefly circles, that a single son needed the protection of the chief, and that his sister's son would need all the moral and spiritual support he could get from his maternal relatives to be effective as a leader in his paternal clan. He urged Alier to always have a "white" heart for Bol and to never hold any grievances against him, his mother, his father, or any members of his family which the ancestors might interpret as a curse. Instead, he should always pray for Bol's well-being, prosperity, and leadership as he grew up.

FIVE

TIME PASSED AS BOL enjoyed the weaning period
with his maternal relatives. Season after season came with its
distinctive features and pleasures. One ambition Bol had was
to be allowed to go to the cattle camp, far away from home.
Of course, depending on the season, cattle were brought to
camps closer to the villages, but going to far-off camps was
the romantic dream of every Dinka.

On several occasions, Alier expressed his wish to take Bol
with him to the camps, but Bol's parents argued that he was
still too young to go that far without the care of his mother
or grandmother. Bol was about five years of age when he was
at last allowed to go to the cattle camp. Monychol decided to
give himself the unusual treat of accompanying his grandson
on the journey. As the distance was long, Alier carried his
nephew. Bol sat on Alier's shoulders, his legs hanging around
his uncle's neck, with Alier holding both feet for balance, while
his nephew wrapped his arms around his head for added
security.

Being in a cattle camp was, for the Dinka, a superior order
of existence to village life. For one thing, it was believed to be
healthier. Few people were known to have caught illnesses or
died in the cattle camp. This might be because those who fell
seriously ill were taken home to the village where they
recovered or died. But it was also believed to have been due
to the diet of cattle campers, for whom dairy products and

grain-based foods, supplemented with occasional fish and meat, were the staple forms of food. The dignity of the cattle camp however went far beyond diet and became an embodiment of the cattle culture that made the Dinka the superior herders they believed themselves to be.

Bol was not old enough to fully comprehend the social and moral significance of the cattle camp, but he instinctively realized that there was a sense of elevation and an aura of superiority there.

The night of their coming, once the commotion caused by their arrival subsided, Bol became aware of the jubilation and sensual displays of the cattle camp, an establishment about a mile in diameter. As with all Dinka social organizations, the camp was divided along autonomous segments that were based on family units and individuals within those units. The cattle hearth, where a conically shaped mound of dried cow dung smoldered into ashes that were soothing to the body, was the male sitting place. At the edge of the cattle camp were fenced-in areas where the girls cooked, slept, and every morning churned their milk gourds to make butter as they chanted their favorite songs. These might be their own, those of other women, or men's. Young men would entertain the camp by singing to their personality oxen as they displayed them around the camp in the morning or at night. Personality oxen were bulls castrated from early calf-hood and raised for beautification and aesthetic display. The tips of their horns would be sliced at an angle to make the horns grow into a desired shape. And when the horns had fully grown, they would be pierced at the tip to carry tassels. Since these chosen animals combined the docility of the castrated bull, which was essential to their social function, with the aggressiveness and vitality normally associated with bulls, they symbolized the contradictions inherent in the status of young men. Though subjected to the authority of their elders, to whom they must show filial piety, as warriors they are expected to demonstrate the martial qualities of physical courage, valor, and vitality, often in exaggerated forms.

Bol had seen and heard many a man sing of a personality ox, with the man wearing a large ivory bangle on his upper left arm, beads around the waist and the neck, an ostrich feather stuck into the colorful piece of cloth neatly wound around a thick hairdo, a bundle of spears in his left hand and a ball-headed club held high in his right hand. As though in concert with the singer, the animal would bellow melodic tunes, jingle the bell hanging from its collar and from time to time toss the tassels tied to the tip of its horns, fully part of the pride and glory of the "Father," as the Dinka call the owner of a personality ox. At the end of the performance, the singer would receive a "release" gift or prize from an admiring girl and the most popular songs would soon become widely known and sung as symbols of the man's social identity and influence.

Although Bol regularly enjoyed this popular entertainment, he was especially moved with pride and excitement when his uncle Alier rose up one late evening and chanted a high-pitched song that announced he was about to go on a singing display around the cattle camp. His bull, Mijok, a handsome animal of pied color pattern, white with black spots on the front and hind quarters, bellowed in response to his owner's voice. Alier tied a bell on Mijok's neck and bushy tassels on the tip of his horns. Spears and club in hand, he began the performance in bright moonlight that showed off the decorations on his animal and himself. When he came around their side of the camp, Alier was singing a song which had a profound effect on Bol. Although he could only partially understand the words, he lay seemingly asleep but in fact mesmerized by the tune and the words, the gist of which somehow conveyed itself to him:

> Women of our clan, wail
> Wail, Oh daughters of doom!
> Each year comes
> And with it death on our doors;
> Each year comes
> And with it we must mourn.
> The evil eyes have cast a spell on our clan,
> Cursing us, they shout for all to hear:
> "Beware, beware of the clan of death!"

Oh people, do not mock our blood
We did not feed on our dead,
We are only victims of misfortune.
Oh victims of misfortune, gaze on God's eyes:
Elders came and prayed on our shrine,
They called on Abuk, the mother of Deng,
"Your son, Monychol, has been sad for too long
Grant him a child to be a mother of sons."
Abuk answered and my sister Aluel was born.
Then came the spirit of death and called:
"Aluel, your brothers and sisters want you,
Come with me that you may join them."
Our women saw the creeping hands of death and wailed
Aluel heard them cry and pleaded for calm:
"Do not cry for me, I am not about to die,
Our mother Abuk has not surrendered me,
I hear her voice calling on God:
Save this one child, she will be the soil,
The soil in which will grow the seeds of life
The crop of the clan of Malengdit, the Chief."
Our Chief spotted my sister Aluel and gave me Mijok
That's why I pride myself on the ox of the divine Chief.
My Mijok which my sister Aluel dislodged from the Byre
    of God
Your name will hoist the head of our clan
For you I sing to raise the name of my father Monychol
I sing to raise the name of our clan.

In their ox songs, it was customary for men to praise their
female relatives from whose marriages they acquired their
oxen, either directly or by being born to one of the cows of the
original bride wealth. Bol was moved by both the praise for
his mother and the tragedy of the family recollected in the
song. Thinking of the deaths in his maternal and paternal
families, and the misfortune which the Arabs had inflicted on
his own family, he could not help linking the fate of the two
sets of families. Alier's song soon became very popular in the
cattle camp and was repeated by many a man and woman.
Without an effort, Bol found himself memorizing the words

and he often sang the song to himself, always feeling as moved as he had felt the first time Alier had introduced him to the song.

The seasonal cycle took its course. The rains began to fall; it was time to head back home for cultivation, a labor in which all generations of both sexes cooperated. The first task to be accomplished was *chum*, sowing the seeds, for which timing was critical and which therefore had to be done under pressure. Work started very early in the morning, with Monychol and Alier digging the holes, using long sticks with sharpened tips, while Nyankir and Bol, and in the field of the other "house," Alimo and her children, dropped the seeds into the holes and covered them with their feet. As they worked, men and women filled the air with the sounds of their voices singing loudly, each on his or her own, all hearing one another but listening only to their own voices. What was more, those songs depended as much on the meaning of their words as on their tune. And yet, there was something authentic and cathartic about the manner in which individuality expressed itself in autonomous harmony and mutual accommodation with the communal spirit.

Nyankir and Alimo would break at appropriate times and return to prepare meals. And of course the children worked only according to their stamina. But the men continued from morning to evening, pausing only for food.

Once the crops had grown to a reasonable height, it was time for the first weeding in which Monychol and Alier worked side by side with the women, crawling on their knees and using hoes with short wooden handles. Because the hoe was rather dangerous, children did not take part in the weeding.

Weeding was laborious and time-consuming. In fact, it had to be done twice to ensure good growth for the crops. But Monychol and his family were able to procure additional hands by brewing large quantities of beer and slaughtering a bull for a working feast to which members of Alier's age-group and male neighbors were invited. However, the contribution of age-mates and neighbors was not a substitute for the labor of the family members. Every one had to work.

It was customary for families to exempt the newly initiated young men and some members of the older age-groups from working on the farm and allow them to spend the season in the summer camps. Monychol gave Alier permission to take time off work and go with his age-mates for the camping retreat. Realizing that his father was short of male hands in the family, Alier chose to join his age-mates after assisting with the weeding. Bol asked to be allowed to accompany his uncle and was given permission.

Although Bol and other children were included, the occasion was really for adults. Boys and girls helped take care of the cattle and render menial services to "the gentlemen," *adheng*. The custom known as *toc*, "lying down," was exactly what the word said. The young men gorged themselves with milk supplemented with meat, moved as little as possible, and otherwise fattened themselves. Far from making them obese, this could only improve their long, lean figures. During the period of the retreat, they composed songs about matters of vital concern, from restatements of family histories glorifying the high points in their ancestral legends, to love songs aimed at winning a girl's acceptance and imploring the relatives on both sides to grant approval and make the necessary arrangements for the proposed marriage. Relatives who had generously exempted the young men from farming or provided them with milch cows for their fattening retreat were acknowledged and praised in these songs, known as *waak*, "cleansing." When the retreat ended, the men returned home, went from village to village as a group performing a special dance for the occasion and presenting their cathartic songs. The songs were presented to those for whom they were intended and often prompted them to act in dramatic response to the request.

Alier had nothing dramatic to announce in his song, only more lamentation for the family tragedies and words of exultation for the heroic deeds of the ancestors, whose continued influence depended largely on the creative recollections of successive generations. In his song were these words:

Our clan has remained a line of single sons,
Our ancestor was a single son;

My father remained a single son;
And I have become a single son.
Oh clan of single sons, uphold the name,
Uphold the name that brightened the path
And showed the Dinka the way of God
And how to live together in this world.
My pied bull Mijok, raise your horns to the sky,
And I will raise my voice singing over you:
I will sing the names of our forefathers;
I will sing to be heard by the people of this land;
I will sing to be heard by our forefathers beneath
    and the Spirits above.

By identifying with his uncle, Bol for his part enjoyed the retreat and its highlights of song and dance, including both the tragedy and the pride in his song. It was as though he himself had become a little "gentleman," who, despite his age, shared in the aesthetic sensibilities and moral responsibilities of adulthood and of the families he represented.

It was one of the complexities of Dinka moral values that the mother of an *adheng*, a "gentleman," should not continue to have children. Once the eldest child of a woman was old enough to be initiated, if a boy, or to be married, if a girl, the mother must stop having children. This implied that she should then abstain from sexual relations. Bol was too young to think in those terms, but when his mother came to visit him after their return from the camping retreat, he looked at her enlarged belly and turned away with a shy smile when he saw that Uncle Alier had read his mind. To the adults who were knowledgeable on such matters, Aluel's pregnancy had long been overdue. She had been expected to conceive shortly after Bol's weaning, but those wishes had not been fulfilled. Bol himself did not have any timetable in mind. All he was concerned about was that his mother looked pregnant. As soon as they were alone, Bol engaged Aluel in a conversation.

"Mother, why is your stomach so big?"

His mother hushed him up. "You don't speak that way about an unborn baby. That may attract the evil eye to do harm to the child."

"Are you carrying a baby there?"

"Yes."

"Why do you want another baby?" Bol asked, revealing his ambivalence.

"Why not? Don't you want another brother or sister?"

"Is that where I was before I was born?" Bol tried to change the direction of his investigation.

"Yes, dear."

"But no one asked me to give my place to him."

Aluel was not prepared for that, but she had to give an answer. "No one asks anyone to give his or her place in a mother's tummy. It's God who decides who is to occupy that place. No one except God even knows whether it's going to be a boy or girl."

Bol wished to be positive about the prospects in a childlike manner. "Since I have a brother, can you tell God that I want a sister?"

"Well, we can pray for a sister, but God knows best what to give, when he gives. You see, having a baby in the mother's tummy is not a guarantee that a child will be born. And even when a child is born, you never know what God will choose to do, whether the child will live or not."

"I want to live, Mother," interjected Bol, obviously frightened by what his mother had said. Besides, the theme of death had been recurrent with his maternal relatives, especially in Alier's songs at the cattle camps. "I don't want to leave my grandpa and grandma. And I don't want to leave you and Daddy and Madit either."

"Well, God willing, you will live."

"What about the baby inside you? I also want her to live."

"Well, we also pray to God to let the baby be born and live."

"How will the baby be born, Mother? Is she going to make a hole in your tummy? Won't that hurt?"

"It will surely hurt," Aluel confirmed, pleased that the last part of the question was posed, which made it easier to avoid the first. "But God has his ways of doing things. Although it hurt when you came, you did not leave a wound on me."

Aluel had not been back at Dak-Jur for long when, one

evening, as Bol sat with his grandparents near a fire, a visitor broke the sorrowful news of Aluel's poor health. "People were waiting for the diviner to come when I left this morning," the newcomer reported. "But there was also serious fear that she might not survive another day."

Bol was too young to comprehend the full meaning of his mother's condition, but he understood from what was said, the solemnness of the atmosphere and the sorrow of his grandparents' faces that his mother was in serious danger. Neither Monychol nor Nyankir slept that night. Monychol did not even lie down for most of the night. Instead, he sat up "calling the word," his prayers addressed to God and the ancestral spirits. "God and you our ancestors," Monychol's prayers went on, "what have I done to deserve all this? Why have I lost my place in your heart? Am I not of the blood of this clan? Did my mother bring me into the clan from another man? One cannot see you to talk to you in the face, but you hear the words of your children in this world. Should my daughter die, then I will have to accept that I have no fathers to look to in the spiritual world. But if she survives, then I will know that my words have reached your ears and your hearts and I will honor your names as a pious son."

Monychol left before dawn for Dak-Jur. Nyankir also wanted to go, but he persuaded her that she should remain to look after Bol. Both agreed that the boy should not witness the agony of his mother's condition. The distance to Dak-Jur was not long even for the feeble legs of an elder. Monychol arrived before the cattle were released to graze for the day. Throughout the journey, he had prayed and talked to himself. As he approached the village, he observed the scene very keenly for any signs of the fate that might have befallen his daughter at night. A sensation of relief overtook his spirit when he heard no wails of death. However, that was not conclusive; they might have cried earlier in the morning. But no burial was underway and that surely was a good sign; digging the grave was not a small feat that could be conducted without obvious indicators.

Monychol was immediately spotted and escorted to the courthouse of Chief Malengdit. Someone was sent to alert the chief. Although Monychol was eager to hurry to Aluel's hut, a Dinka father-in-law was expected to observe and show certain norms of respect. It would have been indiscreet for him to enter huts without warning or preparation. Monychol inquired about Aluel immediately and was assured that she had at least survived the night. He was offered a bed to sit on, but he refused, preferring instead to use his *adet*, a hollowed piece of light wood which Dinka elders of his time carried and used as a container, a seat and a headrest. Malengdit's half-brother, Akol, came just as Monychol sat on his modest seat.

"Father, that cannot be," Akol protested, addressing Monychol with the appropriate Dinka term of deference for a brother's father-in-law. "As an elder, you know better than I do, that to sit on the ground and refuse the bed would be as though you were mourning a daughter who is still alive. Surely that is dangerous. Please sit on the bed."

"Son, truth must be acknowledged even if pronounced by a child," Monychol remarked as he rose to sit on the bed.

Chief Malengdit joined them shortly afterward. The guest was served with water, as was the practice, and the lengthy greeting that was customary in those days began.

"*Wa*—Father," Malengdit began the greeting.

"Yes," responded Monychol.

"Have you come?"

"Yes."

"In good health?"

"Yes."

"Have you passed the summer?"

"Yes."

"And the winter?"

"Yes."

"The people are there?"

"Yes."

"And your possessions are there?"

"Yes."

"So, all is well?"

"Yes."

Then Monychol responded in the like manner of greeting.

"*Wendi*—my son."

"Yes."

"Have you stayed?"

"Yes."

"In good health?"

"Yes."

And on, the greeting went, covering all the areas of concern. Akol then followed. And so did others.

When the formalities of the greetings were over, attention was then turned to the condition of Aluel. Malengdit explained that she had slept quite well for the first time, but she had sadly lost the child.

"She delivered yesterday after the diviner came and suggested the sacrifice of a bull," Malengdit explained. "As soon as the bull was invoked and slaughtered, she gave birth to a son, a very handsome baby. We were all overjoyed. At first, the baby seemed to be in good health, but then suddenly, late in the afternoon, he passed away in his sleep."

Monychol listened silently. When Malengdit's account was completed, all he said by way of comment was, "*Yen ka*. So, that's that."

"Yes," confirmed Malengdit as a matter of course.

Again, Monychol became silent. Then he remarked, "*Acien ke rac*—Nothing is bad." In a way, he felt relieved that at least Aluel was still alive and seemed to have survived the threat of death.

As soon as arrangements were made, Monychol was escorted to Aluel's hut. Crawling on his knees, he entered to find Aluel sitting on a sleeping skin. She was reduced to skin and bones, her condition worsened by the loss of her child. The skin on which she sat and she herself were smeared with ashes, evidence of a mother's mourning condition among the Dinka. As soon as Aluel saw her father, she broke down in tears.

"Father, nothing will kill me now," she cried. "I believe I have survived. But what pains me is that my child has been taken away to redeem my life. I wish it had been the other way round and that I had died to save my child."

Monychol now felt the need to present a positive front. "You have spoken the words of a child," he said with an affectionate affront. "Have you ever heard of a child giving birth to a mother? It's the mother who bears the child, not just one, but with God's blessing, many children. Some die and some live. If the mother dies, that's the end to having children. Let's be grateful that you are alive. And let's pray that you recover fully and compensate yourself and the family with another child."

Secretly, Monychol was pleased that his prayers for Aluel's survival had been answered. It was now a question of making sure that she fully recovered. Toward that end, he had to keep on praying. Asking for water in a fresh gourd and a sacred cucumber, he prayed for Aluel's recovery, cut the cucumber into halves and threw them up in the air. They both fell facing upwards, a sign that his prayers were heard and would be heeded. Expressing his gratitude to the Fathers above and below, he sprayed Aluel with the water in the gourd after having blessed it with his spit. Then he rejoined the men, but not for long, for he wanted to rush back home to reassure Aluel's mother. So, having graciously accepted to wait for breakfast, he ate and left.

When Monychol returned, Nyankir decided to come to Dak-Jur not only to visit Aluel, but also to nurse her and in particular to "bathe" her, a customary treatment of regular hot baths which the Dinka consider essential to recovery from the ailments of delivery.

Since Malengdit had told Monychol that he thought it was time for Bol to return home, his grandparents decided that he might as well go with Nyankir. And so, the weaning period, which had been most formative for Bol, came to an end.

For Bol, the loss of the special attention, indeed devotion, which he had enjoyed with his grandparents was compensated by his return to the love and affection which had always surrounded his life among his paternal relatives. There was also the element of continuity in his grandmother's presence at Dak-Jur. Besides, he would be reunited with his brother, Madit.

SIX

SADLY, THE FAVORABLE ATTENTION that Bol enjoyed went hand in hand with the plight of his lame brother, Madit. To be sure, Malengdit left no stone unturned in his efforts to have Madit's hip treated by traditional bonesetters. But all that was to no avail. Eventually, everyone gave up hope of ever seeing Madit without the painful limp, which made him a cripple, an especially sad state given the conventional vanity of the Dinka.

It certainly wasn't easy to grow up as a limping child in Dinkaland. Almost every game the children played involved some physical fitness and peers would never hesitate to point out how unfit Madit was. It pained Aluel deeply to see how much her son was suffering from the afflictions of that accursed night. But Madit seemed to develop a strength of will to match his tragedy. Whatever the other boys did, he wanted to try even when he knew full well that he would be ridiculed by his peers.

Since he was a twin, Madit was supposed to be a manifestation of divine will. He and the spirit of his missing brother, Achwil, owned certain sacred cows that had been consecrated for the purpose and which his father could not dispose of. From this ritual status and the number of cattle in his possession, even at that young age, he certainly had a social position which merited recognition. But that was only among the adults; the children could not think of him other than as a *ngol*, a derogatory description of lameness.

One evening, while the moon was full and bright, the children went to the edge of the village to play. Madit was then about ten years old. He had only been gone for a little while when he returned looking unusually sad. "What is the matter, my dear bird?" Aluel asked, using the Dinka metaphor for a twin.

"Nothing," responded Madit, visibly holding back the tears from his eyes.

"How can you tell me that there is nothing when you are only pretending not to cry?" argued his mother, "Have you not heard that a child who does not cry with his eyes cries with his belly and that can cause serious stomach problems?"

The way she said it brought back to her own mind and to Madit's that cursed night when she took the children out because of diarrhea. As her mind flashed back, she almost broke down in tears, but quickly remembered that her task was to encourage the poor boy. "Come on, tell your mother the truth. Did one of those good-for-nothing bullies of the village offend you?"

"Mother, we were playing the game of *alalepoke*," Madit confessed, sobbing as he did so. "And as I ran from the row of boys towards where the girls stood, they all laughed. Then Adol shouted so loud that everyone could hear: 'Just see how he runs, would he not be more at home among the hyenas?' I could not face the girls after that, so I came back home. Oh Mother, why did the Arabs do this to me? Why did they not take me with Achwil? I would now be a normal person, even as a captive of the Arabs. I wish I were dead!" He then broke into a loud wail.

Aluel was infuriated. She got up and went to where the children were playing, breaking a branch of a tree as she went. "Where is this dog of a boy called Adol?"

Adol was the son of Akol, Malengdit's younger half-brother from the second wife. He was older than Madit, but shorter and tougher-looking. Everyone realized what was about to happen and no one volunteered to help. But Aluel spotted Adol even as she asked about him, and grabbing him with her left hand, she applied the branch, beating him on the buttocks. When he freed himself and ran off, Aluel ran after him, beating him on the shoulders or wherever the whipping branch could reach. Adol yelled as he escaped to his mother's hut, and Aluel returned to her home still fuming with anger. She had not been back for long when Nyandeng, Adol's mother, came dragging her son behind her. Addressing Aluel sarcastically, she shouted, "Noble wife of the chief, it is merciless to leave a person half dead. Here he is; I beg you to finish him off. Here, have him; kill him."

Aluel, who was still in a rage, realized that Nyandeng was challenging her to a fight. The two women were about the same age. Akol had married Nyandeng soon after Malengdit had married Aluel. Nyandeng's son was older than Madit not only because Aluel had lost her first set of twins, but also because Adol had been conceived out of wedlock, the main reason Akol had been urged to marry Nyandeng.

Nyandeng was an attractive woman, a little shorter and heavier than Aluel, but lively and dramatic in her mannerisms. The way she staged her protest was part of her personality. As she talked to Aluel, she was already tucking her leather skirts between her thighs, the way women did when they were about to fight.

Aluel responded the same way, shouting angrily. "And so, you bullwoman have come to teach me a lesson! I am ready for you. If you think that fat belly of yours, which carried a child before marriage to produce this animal of a son, is going to deter me, you are mistaken. None of us was born in this family; but everyone knows that my son was begotten here. I did not bitch around to beget a dog who could call his cousin a hyena."

Nyandeng attacked first and the two women became entangled, arm on arm and leg on leg, as they wrestled. People gathered, and as they pulled them apart, shouted at them to stop. "Aluel, how can you do such a thing when you are the seat of this family?" cried an elderly kinswoman in a shaking voice. "Do you think leadership is a simple thing? How can you behave like a junior wife? You are the chief among the women of this tribe; behave like one."

Nyandeng also got her share of the blame: "Is Aluel not

your mother?" shouted the old woman at her. "It is not only age that determines respect. How can you raise your hands against a woman who is your senior? Don't you realize that she is the senior wife in this clan? You have committed a grievous mistake."

But Aluel and Nyandeng ignored these pleas and continued to trade insults. "Let go of me," screamed Nyandeng. "I want her to know how a mother feels about women who punish other people's children for their own mistakes. Was it my child who made you go out with your children that night? Why make him suffer for a tragedy you yourself brought upon?"

Aluel countered, "Mother," using the Dinka slang for "woman," "I know how you feel about children, sleeping the way you did to trap a man over a child. I am not like the elders you fooled, I will not allow your tricks to have their way in this family."

Suddenly, Malengdit was heard approaching. "You women have gone far enough with your foul mouths. I do not want to hear another word from either one of you. Go back to your huts."

Silence prevailed as the two women were pushed back to their respective compounds.

"And all of you, go back to your places," Malengdit commanded.

Order gradually returned to Dak-Jur. Nonetheless, a serious feud began. The two wives would not speak to one another. And Akol felt that the insult against his wife having conceived out of wedlock was an insult against him. He refused to eat any food from Aluel's house, and since she was the senior wife who controlled the services of the junior wives, he preferred to abstain from all food from Malengdit's wives. The conflict even extended to the brothers.

Malengdit first noticed early the next morning that Akol did not take tea with him as was his usual custom. He chose to ignore it and see what he would do at mealtimes. When Akol refused to eat at breakfast and began to excuse himself as soon as food was being brought from Malengdit's house, he decided to open up the matter for discussion. He chose a time when their uncle Mijangdit was also present.

"Uncle," said Malengdit, "I have a small word to tell you and the elders present here. You might have heard that the women quarreled because of the children. In the ways of women, they got carried away and said things they should not have said because they touch on the integrity of the family. These things should have been dismissed as trifles, for which women are known. Unfortunately, my brother took them seriously. I have noticed that he has been refraining from taking food from my wives. This is far too serious for us to overlook, for it threatens kinship ties. To think that this can happen because of strangers that we brought into our family to serve our ancestral goals is terrible. I thought I should bring it to your attention."

Faces all turned to Akol for response. He sat burying his head in the palms of his hands. When he realized that he was called upon to speak, he cleared his throat, removed his hands from his cheeks and spoke. "My brother is right that wives should not be allowed to drag kinship ties into the jealousies for which women are known. But this is more than the usual squabbles of women. My brother's wife was questioning my marriage and the legitimacy of my son when she said that my wife had tricked me and forced the clan into marrying her to me. This goes beyond the quarrels of women; it is an insult to my integrity and my moral character. That is why I am abstaining from her food. I do not want to involve all my brother's family, but then Aluel is the leader of the family's women. How can I distinguish between what is hers and what belongs to the others?"

"Perhaps I should respond to what Akol has just said," Malengdit interjected.

"No!" protested Mijangdit. "We do not want to turn this into a court case. You do not need to speak again at this point. After all, Akol has not directed anything against you and what he has said against your wife can be answered by others."

Turning to Akol as he removed tobacco from his mouth and spat the remaining pieces, Mijangdit said, "Have you never heard that it is women who break kinship ties? Yes, they are indeed strangers who have left their own families to join the clans of their husbands. Now, that is a lot to expect of a person. On the whole, they do a wonderful job in serving the interests of their marital clans. But we have to remember that they are strangers after all. When all that is combined with their jealousies, you must expect real dangers to the solidarity of the clan. How can an elder like you succumb to such divisive ways and honor them to the point of boycotting food from your own brother? That is wrong. Did Aluel bring this food from her father and mother? And even if she had brought it from her own family, would you disregard the fact that she is here because your senior brother, who is like your father, paid your cattle, among them sacred cows of your clan, to acquire her? Is she not yours by divine right? Or do you want to make her the head of your family so that her actions determine your relations? It is for you to control and direct her and not for her to determine your conduct."

Mijangdit spat again and continued. "Equally important, by taking the line you have taken, you are siding with your wife against your brother's wife. Are you saying that your wife was right in supporting her child who had called the twin son of your elder brother a member of the hyena family? Your wife should have been the first to punish her own child for such heartless language. We forgive her because she did not hear the insult herself. And yet, when she saw her child beaten by her sister-in-law, she should have investigated the cause before becoming defensive. She should not have defended her child blindly. She was wrong and you are wrong in appearing to side with her. As your uncle, the ancestral representative in this world, I ask you to repent and share your brother's food with him."

Akol remained silent, his head bent down, but it was quite obvious that the words of his uncle had penetrated and were taking effect.

A woman came in with a tray of tea as Mijangdit concluded his words. A young boy stood up to receive the tea from her and help serve it to the assembled elders. Taking advantage of Akol's silence and the availability of tea, Mijangdit said, "Pour your uncle a cup of tea and let me see him break this unbecoming abstention."

That was when Malengdit intervened and said, "Uncle Mijangdit, I do not want to contradict your words in any way, but I feel responsible for the foolish words my wife uttered. I would like to appease my brother with two cows and beg his forgiveness. I also suggest that if he is willing to forgive and forget, we ask him to break his abstinence in a ritual feast tomorrow so that we can make offerings to our ancestors and beseech them to join us in the reconciliation."

"Spoken like a chief," said one of the elderly relatives at the meeting. "What else can Akol say? I suggest we do not embarrass him by asking him to respond. His brother has concluded the case very wisely."

Akol nevertheless decided to speak. "I think I should be allowed the opportunity of acknowledging wisdom. You, our elders, and you, my brother, have helped open my eyes. I would say that I owe my brother more than he is offering because I might have fallen captive to the ways of women. I offer him four cows for appeasement and reconciliation, but I will gladly accept his two as a token of mutual support and solidarity."

"You both are truly the sons of my brother," concluded Mijangdit. "With this attitude, we have no need to worry about the future of this family and of the tribe we lead."

The payments of appeasement and reconciliation were carried out accordingly and the rituals of food-sharing performed with festivity. The spirit of harmony and solidarity appeared to have been restored to the family.

It had been days since the events that brought about the family crisis. It was mid morning. The cattle had already been released to graze but the sheep and goats were still tethered in the cattle byres. Malengdit and a crowd sat under the court tree. Madit, who had been sitting in his father's court, got up to walk to the cattle byre and release the sheep and goats to graze. Malengdit, moved by his son's limp, could not control his emotions. Not realizing and perhaps not even thinking that his son was still within earshot, he lamented as though thinking out loud to himself: "What a tragedy my son has fallen into. Sometimes I wish he had never been born at all or had died when he fell."

Madit continued to walk toward the cattle byre as though he had heard nothing. But internally, his world was in turmoil. Once he was inside the byre, all by himself, except for the goats and the sheep, he broke down and cried.

Ajak, Nyandeng's youngest sister and therefore Adol's aunt, saw Madit walking to the byre and decided to follow him, giving as a pretext that she had forgotten to milk some of the goats. Whether it was because she was suffering from some guilt connected with her nephew's attitude toward Madit or her sister's defense of her son, or just because of some natural sentiment, she had taken a fancy to Madit.

Ajak was strikingly beautiful: medium height, brown within the range of Dinka skin colors, with a set of separated teeth, the Dinka ideal of how teeth should be. Although she was about Madit's age, she had matured beyond her years, a condition that added to her attractiveness. As soon as Madit realized someone had entered the byre, and even before he knew who it was, he quickly adjusted himself to look normal, but his puffy eyelids betrayed his state.

"Is anything the matter?" inquired Ajak, unable to conceal her sadness at the sight of Madit.

"No, nothing at all," responded Madit, determined not to reveal the truth. "I suppose my eyes were irritated by the smoke in the byre."

Although there must have been more to it than that, Madit's explanation sounded plausible. In any case, it provided a face-saving device for them both.

"I thought I would come to see whether there were goats not milked," Ajak attempted to explain her presence.

It was unusual for a girl to be uncertain whether all the goats and sheep had been milked. Madit understood her reasoning and was pleased about her visit to the byre. He decided not to respond to the girl's explanation. Feeling exposed, Ajak tested the teats of several goats in the hope of extracting some milk to reinforce her argument. But she did not spend much time doing this. She preferred to talk to Madit.

"I am sorry I've not found a chance to talk to you in private since the unfortunate incident with Akol."

Madit acknowledged her with a gesture of concealed appreciation.

"I want you to know how ashamed I was of both my nephew and my sister. I only hope that you do not lump me with them in their conduct."

"Why should I when you did not do anything offensive to me?"

"Perhaps it is not sufficient not to do something offensive," responded Ajak with a wisdom more adult than her years.

"I don't understand what you are saying," replied Madit childishly.

"I mean that I should perhaps have spoken out against them at the time."

"What good would that have done?" asked Madit with a soundness of reasoning that appeared to match Ajak's maturity.

"At least it would have told you more convincingly that I was not with them but with you."

Madit remained silent. Ajak too became silent. Then, as though to break the impasse, she said, "I suppose I should leave you to your work."

"I want you to know that your words have fallen on my heart," replied Madit. "I will remember them."

Ajak stepped out of the byre leaving Madit to ponder their encounter. They were too young to think of love, but there was something in the tenderness of Ajak's attitude and her beauty which made his heart throb with infatuation. As he reflected on Ajak and how he felt, he thought that perhaps he should turn his tragedy into an artistic beauty. He decided to venture the composition of a song which, being uninitiated into manhood, could only be taken as a tune of childhood play. His tragedy was the theme of the song:

I am a lad afflicted with tragedy
When I hear the drums beat,
I wonder whether to sleep or go;
Then I go and wonder whether to watch or dance.
With a hip which barking dogs call that of a hyena
Should I hide myself from the girls

Sit and watch the lucky ones play
Or should I ride on a sturdy heart
And compete for the attention of the girls?
I will not despair
I will struggle like a wounded lion
And like a buffalo with a broken horn.

Despite his struggle to achieve aesthetic self-esteem as a basis for winning social recognition and respect, Madit's problems persisted.

When he was about twelve, he attended a children's dance, with boys and girls. For his age, he was tall, but his height only made his limp more noticeable. In Dinka dance, the men or the boys line up and begin to dance in front of the girls. After watching for a while, to scrutinize the dancers, the girls join in, each in front of the man of her choice. Several girls may choose to dance with one man while some men may remain without dance partners. Dinka girls are generally honest in their choice so that being popular or unpopular generally reflects sincere feelings.

As the boys began to dance, Madit joined in, chanting loudly as though to compensate for his physical defect:

Girl, I am a hidden treasure;
I will dance with the beauty that sees the treasure.
Girl, close your ears to the gossipers of the tribe
Follow me and relish the fruit.

His words were so far above his age that it was hard to believe that they came from him. And yet, as the girls fell in and chose their partners, it seemed as though no one would come to Madit. The moon was full and bright; the drums were loud. The children, young and innocent as they were, filled their hearts with romantic dreams. Madit was about to recognize the cruel realities of Dinka life when he saw Ajak approach him to dance. Dressed in a bright cloth wound around her waist, with rings hanging from her ears and beads on her neck and waist, she was truly beautiful. Madit had made up his mind that he liked Ajak, even fancied her. He had never dreamed that she would choose him in such a public dance! He was dancing with Ajak as these thoughts crossed his mind. And as they danced, they hardly talked, except for his one-sided chanting, which was a Dinka custom.

Somehow, although he hoped for romantic sentiments rather than sympathy, Madit found Ajak's friendship a source of support and strength that helped to counterbalance the self-doubts caused by his lameness.

SEVEN

THE CHILDHOOD ROMANCE BETWEEN Madit and Ajak continued to grow. In the various games that the village children played—those in which the boys and girls were paired—whether the game was a dance or the imitation of adult roles—they nearly always managed to select themselves as partners. In the marriage games, in which boys and girls acted out the social roles of husband and wife, they acted as a couple. To be sure, these games were quite innocent. Some might describe their friendship as Platonic love; others would find a sensuous factor in their association, at least enough to bother both Nyandeng and Aluel for their different reasons.

"Why are you clinging to that boy like *anuet-thok-yol* (the plant whose seeds stick to the tail of the goats and sheep)?" Nyandeng asked Ajak reproachfully late one evening, as villagers were retiring for the evening. "Is this whole village without other boys to play with?"

"What is wrong with Madit, may I ask?" Ajak was now determined not to miss another opportunity to have it out with her sister.

"You with your roving eyes!" Nyandeng retorted. "Don't you realize that this is the way it begins? If you start choosing a *ngol* for a friend at this early age, who knows where you will end up when you are a grown-up? You must train your eyes to make a good choice from an early age."

"Nyandeng, how can you say such a mean thing?" Ajak

asked, outraged. "Is it not enough that you backed the beastly behavior of your son toward Madit? I am ashamed of you. And let me tell you right now that if this is the way you intend to guide me, I would rather look to strangers for guidance."

"How dare you speak to me that way, you fool?" said Nyandeng, now beside herself with anger. "I am not going to permit you to develop this promiscuous attitude toward a cripple. I did not bring you here to stray away and be a loss to our family. If you don't stop this outrageous behavior, I am going to send you back home where you belong."

Ajak spent a sleepless night. She had been challenged. Naturally, she wanted to stay where she could continue to play with Madit or at least be near him. But she was not going to allow her sister to blackmail her. And she knew that under no circumstances would she pull away from Madit to please her sister. Ajak made up her mind, but decided not to share her thoughts with her sister. Instead, she spoke to Madit at the earliest opportunity. As though to relive their earlier setting, she chose the cattle byre just as the sheep and goats were about to be released for grazing.

"Nyandeng and I had a quarrel," she said. "She does not want us to continue to play together. She has threatened to send me home if I continue to see you. I don't want to leave, but I also know that if I stay I don't want to stop seeing you. So, instead of having Nyandeng expel me from her home, I have decided to leave and go back to my family."

Ajak stopped to see Madit's reaction. He remained silent for a while. Although Madit looked rather sad, his face focused on the ground, it was not really possible to tell how he truly felt.

"I also had a quarrel with Aluel," he eventually managed to say. "She, too, wanted me to stop playing with you."

Ajak was amazed. She had not revealed her sister's reasons for opposing their friendship, for she felt that it must be too obvious to require an explanation. As for Madit's mother, what reason on earth could she have given for opposing their friendship?

"Did she give you any reasons?" she reluctantly inquired.

"Yes," responded Madit without elaboration.

"Can you tell me what they are?"

"There is no need to," he said. "Besides I just don't care what she thinks."

"Will you please tell me all the same!" Ajak persisted.

"It was not really directed against you, I don't think; it was directed against your sister. She said that it was not wise to get too close to people like your sister."

"What did you say to her?" Ajak probed.

"I explained to her that you had nothing to do with your sister's ways and that you disapproved of her attitude. Besides, I told her, I was not a son to be directed by a mother."

"What did she say?"

"She smiled and said, 'My son, do as you will. Ajak is a nice girl. As long as you are happy in your friendship, that is what matters to me.'"

"Madit, I will leave as I have said," concluded Ajak. "But if our friendship means anything to you, then we shall meet again. At least I will remember you always."

Madit felt his heart beat faster, but otherwise he betrayed no visible emotion. He chose to speak with silence. And they parted without words.

Bol was rapidly catching up with his older brother. Despite Madit's plight, Bol looked up to him and even shared the agony of his physical affliction. Indeed, the more he himself enjoyed the limelight of admiration, the more he felt the pain of his brother's disability. It hurt him to hear any compliments which contrasted his appearance with his brother's condition. It was as though there was a link between the two realities, as though his brother's tragedy was the price for his being physically whole. That gave him a deep sense of guilt which he could not really explain, but which was all-consuming; the less he understood it, the more consuming it was.

One day when Madit and Bol were cleaning the cattle byre—crawling on their knees in the slush of cow dung and urine and lifting their spirits with songs as they worked—they heard a piercing cry that came from the direction of their mother's hut. It was the unmistakable cry of a woman wailing over death. They recognized their mother's voice and, without exchanging words, knew instinctively that their maternal grandfather had died. Although they knew he had been ill and was said to have improved significantly, that cry could only mean that he had lost his battle for life. Without asking, they came from the cattle byre covered with cow dung, urine and sweat, crying at the peak of their voices. The whole village was in turmoil as people poured in the direction of Aluel's hut, some constraining her from physically hurting herself, for she was throwing herself on the ground as she wailed:

Oh my father!
Oh my father!
My father, Monychol!
My father, Monychol!
My father is dead!
My father is dead!
Oh my poor mother!
My poor mother!
My mother is left alone!
My mother is left alone!
Oh what misery!
What misery!

As the boys saw their mother screaming in agony, they felt a profound sense of helplessness and despair; it was as though the world as they knew it had been shattered. Gradually, however, their mother's wail began to subside and with it their own cries.

By now, she had already ripped off all the beads and other objects of beautification which she had been wearing. She had smeared her body with ashes and dust as mourning women did, and she projected a desolation and loneliness amidst the crowd that gathered around her. It was as though she herself was the medium of death, a symbol and a reminder of the age old cruelty from the spiritual world of God and the deities to which humanity was condemned from the Byre of Creation.

As people came and went, trying to console Aluel with words, the boys sat there sharing their mother's grief and hating the words they heard said to her. "What can you do?" one elderly woman asked Aluel rhetorically. "When God has

chosen to torture a person, the only thing to do is succumb
to His will. Can you fight God? And will your sorrow bring
your father back? Not at all! There is no denying that you are
indeed a tragic woman, having suffered numerous deaths
among your brothers and sisters and then fallen victim to the
inhumanity of Arab invaders. And now, your father who had
remained a consolation to you suddenly succumbs to the spirit
of death. It is heartbreaking. But that is your fate. You cannot
change it; you must accept it."

Then turning to the children, the woman went on to say,
"If God saves this one child of yours, Bol, at least he will be
some consolation for your loss." Bol could not believe that any
human being could be so insensitive to the feelings of others,
in this case his brother Madit. As though that was not enough,
the woman was even more explicit. "As for this other son
whom the Arabs have destroyed, I am not even mentioning
him. It is as though he too is dead. His affliction is part of the
abomination with which you must live. But this one Bol is
enough; even one child can be a source of salvation for a clan."

Bol noticed Madit walk away, his eyes brimming with tears
that were about to fall. He got up and followed his brother,
forgetting for the moment that they were there because they
had lost their grandfather, a man he himself had come to see
as his true Great Father. In some mysterious way, he recalled
the night his grandfather had taken him into the rain and
prayed for his recovery. He was too ill and too young then to
realize the full significance of what was happening and the
words of prayer which his grandfather had said. But he had
subsequently heard it said that his grandfather had not only
prayed for his recovery, but had sacrificed himself to redeem
his grandson. Alier had even intimated to him that his father
did not expect to live long because he had offered himself
to save Bol. Since his prayers had been answered, the old
man expected the side of the bargain concerning himself to
be fulfilled.

A sense of guilt flashed through his mind and heart, but
he also realized that there was nothing he could do about his
poor grandfather. Instead, he thought of Madit. For now the
priority was to offer whatever support he could to him.

As time passed, the sense of solidarity between the two brothers continued to grow even as the gap between their social standings also continued to widen.

One day Madit and Bol had just returned from a swim in the river when Malengdit called Bol. Madit continued toward the cattle byre while Bol went to his father, who was sitting with his usual crowd under the tree. Pulling Bol toward him with an affectionate smile on his face, Malengdit broke the news: "Son, I have just been thinking that it is time you went to school. You are still a child, but you are also old enough to be away from your parents. After all, that's what young boys do when they go to the cattle camp."

Bol did not know enough about going to school to react positively or negatively to his father's suggestion. But others under the tree reacted.

"Chief, how can you say such a thing?" one elder ventured. "Is Bol a child whose future you can risk in that way? Is a child sent to the missionaries not a child lost? And how can you send an only son to the missionaries when he is the hope of your people as their future leader?"

What the man of course meant was that Madit, who would normally be expected to succeed his father as Chief was physically unqualified for the role; that left Bol the only qualified son of the first wife.

Malengdit laughed at the response. But one of his uncles did not think it was funny.

"Son of my brother, do not laugh," he commented. "Whom do you expect to shoulder the responsibilities of leadership when you are gone or too old to lead? Your older son is only a reminder of our unending feud with the Arabs. Leadership requires knowledge of the spiritual words of our ancestors, not these profane new words with which the missionaries fill the heads of our children. Don't let the idea of going to school get into this boy's head. He is needed by his people."

Bol was angry with the dismissal of Madit, but he said nothing. In fact, he was also intrigued by the discussion between his father and the other elders, which continued.

"Uncle and all you people sitting here," Malengdit spoke,

"can't you really see what is going on around you? Almost all the important Dinka chiefs I know have sent their children to school. And why do you think they have done that? Do you think that it is because they expect their children to learn from the missionaries more about God and the words of our ancestors than we, their fathers, can teach them? Of course not. They have sent their children to missionary schools to learn to write and read, to know more about European medicine, and to prepare themselves for the new world in which the government of the English has incorporated our people. These are things about which we, their elders, including the chiefs, know nothing. We are like people who are blind, deaf and dumb. How can we be effective as leaders in a world we do not understand? Future leadership lies with these small boys whom you see being sent to school. That is why I want my Bol to be there. As for my other son, whom the Arabs have destroyed, nothing can be done about him; let him suffer his fate among his people."

Judging from the silence that followed, Malengdit had made an effective case. In fact, one elder chose to speak in his support.

"You people of our land," he said, "can't you understand that a leader, even when not educated, can see more and is wiser than the ordinary people? Chief Malengdit is looking far into that distant future which we cannot see. That is why he is there in the lead. And that is how he can guide us to the path of right and make us avoid the pitfalls on the way. Chief, you have persuaded me. And even though my son is not going to be a leader, because of the words I have heard you say, I will send him to school to prepare him for the new world which you have described so well."

Aluel also opposed sending her son to school for much the same reasons as the others had voiced, but was overruled by Malengdit.

"Look here, woman, I paid the sacred cows of my ancestors so that you should come and bear a leader for my people," he said to Aluel. "Bol is not your child; you were only a vessel by which God delivered him to me and my people. He is my son, the son of the ancestral cows, the son of the tribe. Do not cross my word."

The first school Bol went to was Nyamlel, one of the centers of missionary education in Western Bahr el Ghazal. Nyamlel was a vibrant institution where Catholicism was nourished by traditional Dinka devotion. The Christian message was particularly brought to life by the collective singing so characteristic of the Dinka. The priests and the nuns, who were Italian, wore heavy clerical garbs and decorated the school church with paintings of Christ, Mary, the saints and angels. Outside, the compound was landscaped with tropical trees and flowers of bright colors. Bol saw Nyamlel as a symbol of the heaven which the missionaries promised the converts. Traditional Dinka life and religion were condemned as primitive, depraved, and immoral, even as Dinka concepts of morality and well-being were invoked to reinforce the Christian message. Nor was Islam spared condemnation, for far from being recognized as one of the religions of the Book, it was presented as a source of evil and spiritual contamination, not very different from the primitive beliefs of the African pagans. Salvation lay only with Christ and his Church. And the message came loud and clear in the songs, which Bol and his fellow converts were taught to sing in prayers or in their public displays:

Nyamlel is our home,
Nyamlel is our summer camp.
The bishop is the one keeping our land in order:
Father, Master, the land is threatened by pagans;
The land is threatened by Mohammedans.
Oh what will the Christians do?
I turn this way and it is the evil spirit
And Mohammedans are facing east;
They are facing where the sun rises.
What misfortune, what misfortune?
We are tangled with bad spirits,
Some have evil eyes,
Some inflict evil spells,
Some are evil men who disturb the innocent,
The land is confused;

The land has its head in a knot.
Maria, our Mother is feared by the evil spirits
Cries arose in the middle of the day
Mother! Mother! Help!
Help us in the war with evil spirits
It's *wei*—health! It's *wei*!
Wei is what we want.

For Bol and the other Dinka boys in the missionary school, *wei* meant the full physical, moral and spiritual well-being of man in this world. The success of Christian missionary work among the Dinka, as reflected by Malengdit's argument for sending Bol to school, lay in the close connection between spreading the word of God and providing the people with such worldly goods as modern medicine and education. But their success was mixed, for the Dinka accepted the new message where they saw advantage and dismissed it where it conflicted with their basic values and world view. Of course, there were also generational differences in this response. Sometimes, the children accepted the message as it was given to them by the missionaries while their elders dismissed it as part of the fantasy world of fairy tales, which was naturally exciting to the children, but meaningless to the adult mind.

When Bol sought his father's permission to become a Christian, Malengdit wondered why his son would want to join a religion where he, the son of a chief, could marry only one wife.

"Because, unless one is reborn by being baptized as a Christian, one will not enter the home of God—heaven," Bol explained to his father. "Instead, one will be condemned to burn in the home of fire—hell."

Malengdit wondered what these homes meant after one was dead. Bol explained that on the day of the "big court," all the dead would rise again and people would be judged according to how they had behaved in this world. "Those who have led an evil life will be put into the house of fire," he said, "while those who have lived a virtuous life will be put in the home of God."

"What lies the missionaries teach you," Malengdit

remarked. "Once a person is dead and is consumed by termites, how can he rise again and be judged?"

Bol dismissed his father's question as a sign of his ignorance about the word of God. That was indeed the ignorance which their school songs had addressed in verses imploring their teachers to enlighten them:

> Learning is good, learning is good.
> Open our minds, masters, open our minds;
> Our minds like rocks, our minds like rocks,
> Our minds like the earth, our minds like the earth
> We shall enlighten them with rays of light.
> Our mothers all cry, "Our children have gone astray
> The land has remained without a child."
> Mother, I do not blame you,
> There is nothing you know, nothing you know,
> The word of the world is creeping on
> It comes crossing the land beyond
> In Khartoum, a child is born and goes,
> Am I to appease you only with a white cow
> What about the white clothes and my pen?

Fear of hell and yearning for heaven, though dismissed by the uneducated elders as childish fantasy, had become a reality to the young converts:

> Mary, our white mother
> Help us to go to God's home above.
> Oh! Oh! The home of fire!
> That's the place for misery.

"If we assume that the missionaries are right and we Dinka wrong," commented Chief Malengdit, "and that those who are baptized will go to the home of God while those who are not burn in the house of fire, are you going to be happy alone in God's home while the rest of the family burn in the home of fire?"

To Bol, that was again the wisdom of ignorance, for he had been taught by the missionaries that on the day of the big court, people would face God as individuals and not as groups or relatives. No one would be held responsible for the sins of others nor would it be possible for anyone to save another from God's punishment.

Malengdit smiled with the spiritual superiority of an elder and said, "Go ahead my son; get baptized as a Christian. At least you will save my cattle from the multiple marriages of the Dinka."

Bol was accordingly baptized and acquired the Christian name of Elias.

From his first days at Nyamlel, Bol's introduction to education was a dramatic turning point whose advantages, though not fully realized at the beginning, became increasingly obvious. Returning home after having been taught to read and write, he reinforced his popularity with a display of his modern skills. As his literacy advanced, his father began to make use of him in writing his official and private letters and keeping the books for taxes, all of which enhanced his social standing considerably.

Nevertheless, Bol still kept Madit's company. During his vacation time, he would strip himself naked and revert to the traditional lifestyle. Bol continued to be particularly fond of the cattle camp which he and Madit frequented. One visit left an indelible mark on Bol. Accompanied by several cattle campers, they started late one afternoon toward the camp, and as darkness fell, they saw reaching into the sky a beacon from the camp fires, that fused the evening's glow with smoke and dust. The sight seemed to dramatize the flair associated with the superior culture of the cattle camp. As they approached the camp, stretching over a mile in diameter, they were greeted by the roar of barking dogs, and then by the abusive cries and jeers from the youngsters already there. "They are bringing disease to the camp," they shouted, one after another. Such was the snobbery of the cattle campers. But when they were recognized in their own part of the camp, they were given an affectionate welcome.

Life in the cattle camp was very colorful, with men and women self-consciously working on attracting each other's attention by the way they walked, talked, joked, sang, danced, and flirted. In all of this, cattle offered them the symbols of identity, self-expression and social standing. For the children, and especially the boys, this was all part of the art and skill of aggressive self-assertiveness, often expressed in fighting as a sport. These skills were developed in boys as a means of training them for the important role of warriors which they would assume after being initiated into a military regiment.

The importance of the age-group as an agency for exacting moral and social sanctions against members was dramatically brought home to Madit and Bol on their second day at the camp. It was early in the morning and the cattle were still tied to their pegs. A crowd quickly formed outside the camp and soon began to boom with war songs as they moved toward a particular section of the camp. They were members of the dominant warrior age-group, the Crocodiles, who happened to be in the camp. Some of them ran about in the war-like ballet called *gor*, parrying and thrusting their spears. As they approached their destination, feelings seemed to rise high, and the tempo peaked. Suddenly, two of the men ran toward a handsome looking pied bull with long diverging horns. First, they pointed their spears at the bull in what seemed like a symbolic display of warring skills. Then one darted his spear at the nape of the bull's neck. The other aimed at the heart and threw his spear into the animal. Within moments, it was as though spears were all over the bull as it struggled in vain to free itself from the rope tying it to the peg. Even after it fell, warriors descended upon it with spears, skewering and dismembering it in a most distasteful and disgusting manner. Before long, it was as though the bull had been the victim of attack by carnivorous beasts, shredding it into pieces.

Everyone who cared soon got a slice of the animal, but the objective of the operation was not meat; it was to punish a member of the age-group who was said to have disgraced it by stealing. While herding, he had caught someone else's lamb, slaughtered it, skinned it, and roasted some of the meat for his own consumption. He had then brought the rest of the meat back to the camp, claiming to have hunted and killed an antelope. He had made sure that none of the meat he brought back to the camp betrayed the true identity of the animal.

However he had been unknowingly spotted by two boys who had later returned to the scene and found the head and skin of the lamb to show in support of their allegation. Once the man learned that he had been caught and that evidence against him was available, he could not face his peers and the rest of the camp. He therefore disappeared at night, leaving no evidence of where he had gone. But that did not affect the conventional way by which the age-group punished its members.

The same punitive measures were taken against offenses such as rape or any moral misconduct which would severely compromise the integrity of the individual and the age-group. Nor was the punishment limited to male age-mates; the same action could be taken by a female age-group against a member. Indeed, Madit and Bol knew of a famous incident in which a girl had been accused of having stolen a gourd of butter. The personality ox of her brother had been similarly speared to death and skewered by members of her age-group with the assistance of the corresponding male age-group. The animal had been a handsome ox decorated with tassels on its horns and a bell hanging from a collar on its neck. It had been a painful operation to watch. But even worse had been its effect on the girl's life.

As though the manner in which the brother's personality ox had been butchered had not been enough, a man had come to the cattle camp the next day, attired in bangles, beads, a feather in his cloth-bound hairdo, a bundle of decorative spears in his left hand, and a ball headed club in his right hand. He had been engaged to the disgraced girl. Singing and chanting, he walked over to a personality ox that he had paid as part of his advanced bride wealth, and releasing the bull from the peg as he sang, he symbolically repudiated the marriage and claimed the return of the cattle he had paid. "Why was I never warned? How could I have been expected to marry a thief? Let withdrawing my ox be a signal to our people that I wash my hands of this girl. May I die, I will not dishonor the name of my family by paying our ancestral cows for a girl with a tainted name." He had kept chanting these words as he had unleashed the bull.

It became evident to Madit and Bol that theft was among the worst moral wrongs one could commit in Dinka society.

For Madit and Bol, moreover, these dramatic incidents demonstrated the vital role of the age-group system. When they had been in the camp for two days, the senior boys called for an all-boys dance at night. Barely had the dance begun when the oldest boy, burly and clearly the biggest bully in the crowd, called for attention. The drums stopped beating and silence prevailed. It was obvious that he was in full control.

"As you know, we have new arrivals among us," he announced. "I am of course talking of Madit and his baby brother, Bol."

Noticing that Bol looked offended by the description, the speaker qualified himself. "I am not insulting you, Bol; I just mean to say that you are of course our younger brother and cannot be challenged to prove yourself a member of our age-group. As for your brother, if he wants to join us, which he is old enough to do, he will have to fight his way. We know that he is a *ngol* but we assume that his testicles are intact and that he remains a man at heart and in body. Our system is that the man who wants to join the age-group must choose one of us to fight. If he wins the fight or is at least not forced to surrender, then he has qualified for membership. Defeat means that he must go down to a junior set."

All the members of the senior age-group then formed a horseshoe around Madit, who was urged to make his pick. He could not accept the humiliation of declining the offer; that would be sheer cowardice. Nor did he feel inadequate for the challenge. His only problem was how to select. Naturally, it would seem foolish to choose the toughest-looking boy, but it would also be unmanly to look for the weakest. As he sized up the crowd, his eyes fell on a one-eyed boy who seemed otherwise quite fit and strong. As though he matched his broken hip with the missing eye, Madit chose that boy for the contest.

Wrestling was the first part of the fight. They soon got entangled. The crowd cheered without bias. Madit was not prepared for that. Besides, his opponent proved to be truly a fighter who, he learned later, had lost his eye in a fight. Madit was quickly thrown. But as they wrestled on the ground for dominance, he was able to overturn his opponent. They were then put to their feet for another go. Again, he was thrown and as they struggled on the ground, they reversed their positions several times.

Then followed the second part when the fighters were given slim branches of trees to beat one another freely. Madit fared well in this. He was not only good at enduring the physical pain, he was also skillful at aiming his hits. The chanting of the crowds now seemed to favor him. "Thrash him Bull-Man," they cried. "Show him that manhood is not in the hip! That's it, man! Make him bow to a tough *ngol*." Suddenly, and to everyone's surprise, his opponent threw down his whipping branch and caught Madit's right hand to constrain his thrashing. "Stop them!" chanted the crowd. That opened the door for the last part in which the fighters were free to use their hands to strike at one another. It was a form of boxing, except that the fighters were free to clench their hands into fists or leave them open to slap the opponent on the face or anywhere on the body. Madit's hip impeded his movements considerably, while his opponent displayed nimble moves that turned the fight into an entertaining game. What had been an objective crowd that cheered the fighters for merit now seemed partial, chanting enthusiastically for Madit's opponent.

Madit's movements, far from matching his opponent's, only received scornful laughter. "He jumps more like a monkey than a human being," shouted one.

"That's a lie," responded another. His ups and downs resemble those of a hyena more than a monkey's."

On hearing the comparison with the hyena, Madit turned away and ran from the scene crying. Torn between following his brother and fighting those who had provoked him, Bol shouted a stream of insults at the crowd: "Damn your mothers, you sons of dogs. He is better than anyone of you beasts. You will pay for this, you heartless dogs." He spoke as he ran to follow his brother.

Madit was heading for the wilderness, not for the camp. But word of his flight soon reached the elders in the camp and a group went searching for him in the woods, shouting the names of the brothers alternately. Bol responded and they were rescued and taken back to the camp.

Whether because of anger or humiliation, Madit suddenly felt very ill indeed. It was decided to send both brothers back home where word of the episode had already been spread. When Madit was well again, Malengdit had hard words for him. "How could you accept defeat and run away in tears? Are you the first ever to be lame in this tribe? Have you never heard of the man called Kur Allor who had a wooden leg, but was one of the bravest warriors this tribe has ever known? And have you not heard of Maluk Ker-Kou whose one leg was crippled and bent above the ground so that he supported his good leg with a stick? He was also a brave man, a singer, very popular with girls. From where did you inherit this cowardly attitude?"

Madit walked away from his father, struggling to contain himself. But as soon as he felt secure in the privacy of a shady tree behind the village, he again burst into tears. Crying had become his response to the endless episodes of his chronic affliction. And the more he was seen crying, the more he demeaned himself in the chauvinistic world of the Dinka.

Some of his adversaries seemed to be particularly adept at spotting his vulnerable moments and rubbing salt into his emotional wounds. The day he isolated himself to cry over his father's reproach, someone sneaked behind the tree and startled him with an unexpected voice. "Son of my uncle," said Adol with a deceptive tone of affinity, "is it true that you were thrown down several times and that you retreated and ran away from the fight crying?"

Without waiting for a response from Madit, whose head remained bent in sorrow, Adol proceeded to say, "I thought people with defects compensated themselves in other ways. In what ways do you compensate yourself for *ngol*?"

As though all his power had been conserved for this moment of reckoning, Madit got up in a rage, pushed Adol off his feet, throwing him to the ground, and sat on him, his knees bent over Adol's arms to constrain him, his hands pressing on his throat. Adol, unable to make a sound through his tightly pressed throat, struggled in vain to free himself.

As though resolved to kill Adol, Madit continued to tighten his hold on his neck until his eyes began to bulge and his resistance diminished. Suddenly Madit heard Bol shouting at him to stop. Madit then felt his brother trying to pull him away from Adol.

As though his younger brother had a magical spell on him, Madit immediately stopped and got up, leaving Adol lying down, a heap of lifeless body.

"He is dead," cried Bol. "You killed him. What shall we do?"

"He deserved it," was all Madit said.

Bol had a spontaneous trust in his brother's judgment, even though he could not see what could possibly justify Adol's murder. After all, he realized fully that Adol was a bully who was capable of any provocation. He also knew of the incident which nearly divided the family and which Adol had provoked. He did not even want to investigate the cause of the fight. His main concern was what would follow. And what should he do? Should he run to inform the elders or should they try to invent a cover up story to protect his brother?

As he pondered and Madit still breathed heavily with rage, Adol began to move and sigh. "He is alive," cried Bol with excitement. Falling on their barely conscious cousin, he began to shake him vigorously. "Adol, Adol, wake up; come on, wake up!"

Adol slowly opened his eyes and began to look around as though recollecting the sequence of events. Madit stood, still looking away and seemingly indifferent to Adol's return to life. Adol now seemed almost fully revived and aware of what had just occurred. Perhaps recalling how his insulting attitude toward Madit had nearly caused a family feud, he decided that as long as he was not seriously hurt, the least said about this last incident the better. He got up, went to Madit and placing his right hand on his shoulder, said, "Son of my uncle, forgive me. I was wrong and I promise you that it will never occur again."

Madit looked at him with a forgiving smile on his face. They then shook hands and laughed together hilariously. Bol too joined them in the laughter.

To everybody's astonishment and satisfaction, Adol and Madit now became close friends, although Madit continued to suffer from social prejudice. Not all of it was ill-intentioned. Indeed, much was a spontaneous reflection of Dinka attitudes toward physical disability. Whether you were blind, crippled, mentally deranged, or afflicted with any abnormality, society mockingly made you well aware of the fact, even though you were also cared for.

The more Madit was mocked, the more his younger brother hated the Arabs for having caused him such indignity. He still felt guilty for being perfect, compared to his brother. The more he felt guilty, the more he personalized his hatred for the Arabs and turned it into an obsession.

It was the lean season before the new harvest when the Arab traders went to Dinkaland on their bulls, carrying grain to barter for cattle, sheep, and goats. Relative peace had been restored between the tribes so that the trade was conducted without violence. But scornful attitudes still prevailed between the Dinka and the Arabs. Madit, Bol, and Adol accompanied their mothers to barter a calf for grain. As they stood amidst the crowd, trying to push their way, the Arab trader shouted at the people to step back. Signaling Madit out, he pointed his finger at him saying, "You *a'araj*, get back!" Although the trader had merely used the Arabic word for "lame," Madit was outraged and both his brother Bol and his cousin Adol were even more so. Without any warning, they fell on the Arab, hitting him and kicking him as he cried for help. Within minutes, the Dinka shouted *thuk aci dhuong*, "the market has broken down," which was a way of saying that anyone could help himself to anything.

When it was all over, the Arabs had lost most of their grain and the animals they had brought. But they were not hurt. Their only resort was to apply to Chief Malengdit for help. Malengdit eventually traced their animals and had them returned. He also collected additional cattle from the tribe to compensate the Arabs for their grain.

Bol's resentment toward the Arabs had now gone beyond anger over the loss of his brother, Achwil, and the indignity they had inflicted upon Madit. Education had opened his eyes to the inequities which the central government had imposed on the Dinka in favor of the Arabs. Although slavery was outlawed, the Arabs occupied a superior position from which they still looked down on the Dinka as an inferior race that deserved to be called *abid*, slaves, free as they were. As a result, Bol became politically conscious and began to play the role of a political counsel to his people.

But the more Bol became aware of his assets in modern terms, the more he consciously subordinated himself to his lame and illiterate brother. Yet, Madit was a disabled person to be pitied and supported, not to be copied as a role model. Bol realized this, but did not want to accept it, which created tensions and conflicts within him.

Bol's identification with Madit was perhaps all the greater because he did not have a younger brother. When Aluel became pregnant again and carried the child to the full term, the baby, this time a girl, was stillborn. The shock was aggravated by the fact that Aluel had lost her mother only a short time before. After that tragedy, she was unable to have another child. Diviners were called to diagnose the cause of her barrenness. They all theorized on it and recommended the dedication or sacrifice of animals, but to no avail. It was even said that the Arab spell that had caused the difficulty in Bol's delivery was responsible for her barrenness and ways of eradicating the curse were prescribed, but nothing helped. In the end, Malengdit and Aluel resigned themselves to their fate and focused their love and affection on Bol as though to compensate themselves for the loss of Achwil and the lameness of Madit.

Bol had heard that his mother had composed a song about her misfortunes, but he did not really know what the song contained until one day when, watching a woman's dance, someone moved into the circle and introduced Aluel's song:

Each year comes and I bury another child!
Each year comes and I mourn another child!
The ancient curse of the owl has fallen on me:
The curse when the owl sat on Aluel's hut
And cried, "Aluel, daughter of Black Man,

When it dawns you will bury another child."
I have become a black dog in the family of the chief,
The witches of the land look at me and laugh:
"There goes the black dog with no colors!"
Oh people, I did not eat my children.
Those whose mothers cook for the spirit of death,
They are the ones who never die,
Ours has always been a clan of mortals;
Since life began in the Byre of Creation
Our eyes have rained with the tears of mourning death.
Oh child of doom, surrender to the will of God!
I must leave; I must go!
To be in the wilderness with animals.
Do not blame me, Oh people of our tribe,
A woman keeps her home because of the children she has
    borne.
Brother Alier, Oh brother Alier,
What misfortune I have brought upon you?
Great Malek, Oh Chief Malengdit,
Your sacred cows have fallen into the graves,
The grave of the children of doom;
Oh, the ancient curse of the owl!

As the women clapped, ululated and jumped about
dancing to the tune, Bol withdrew into the privacy of an empty
cattle byre and wept, lamenting the tragic burden that his
mother was obviously bearing in society. He was glad at least
that nothing was said in the song about Madit's misfortune
or the notorious reference to himself as the only hope for the
survival of the clan.

PART THREE
GROWTH

EIGHT

ALTHOUGH MADIT WAS A little younger than his cousin, Adol, they were both in their teens and therefore qualified for initiation as members of the same age-group. Adol's father Akol was chosen as the spiritual father of the age-group. Somehow, Madit saw in his initiation the prospect for liberating himself from the social stigma of being a *ngol* to that of an *adheng*, or gentleman, who, despite his physical disability and perhaps even because of it, would be respected. So, although he was barely old enough for the painful operation of initiation, he managed to talk his father into allowing him to lead the age-group in the operation. After all, he was the oldest son of the chief and therefore the one rightly entitled to be the leader of his group. This meant that he should be the first to lie down and receive the initiation marks.

Chief Malengdit felt torn. On the one hand, he wanted his son to lead the group, which was his right and duty as the oldest son of the chief. On the other hand, he realized that his son was an invalid who had been so traumatized by his condition that crying like a child persisted as his way of responding to crises well into his teens. Besides, he was still too young for initiation; could he endure the ordeal? And what a scandal it would be if he should cry at the ceremony. Chief Malengdit decided to go ahead with the ritual. "Even if he should die at the ceremony, it is proper that my son should lead the group" was the logic he eventually adopted.

Madit's age-group was named Ater, the Feud, to signify the tragic raids by the Arabs which had led to the loss of the chief's twin son Achwil and to Madit's disability. Madit displayed a surprising degree of courage. He pleaded to be allowed to take time off from the bloody operation to chant verses of valor and honor to his family and supporters. And so, after one half of his forehead had received the painful initiation marks, he was permitted to rise with blood streaming from his face, chanting verses which he himself had composed and memorized for the occasion:

> The eldest son of the chief does not fear the knife!
> Even if my veins should pour blood like a broken dam
> I will not accept the shame of remaining a boy;
> I want to be a gentleman after the girls.
> Even if I should die, I will not disgrace my family
> I will not disgrace the leaders of the tribe from the Byre
>   of Creation.
> I will receive the knife with unflinching eyes;
> If I should flinch, slaughter me,
> May I die for disgracing a family of lasting pride.

His body smeared with blood, he went back to lie down and receive the rest of his initiation marks. Suddenly, the voice of a woman was heard chanting loudly. It was Ajak. Unknown to Madit or indeed to any member of his family, not even to his mother Nyandeng, Ajak had traveled from her village to witness this unique event. In a silvery voice that echoed her beauty, she chanted with a freedom that was only possible in songs among the Dinka:

> There goes the eldest son of the chief to lie down for
>   a second time,
> My man is the leader of our tribe, valorous and un-
>   flinching.
> How proudly we watch him lie among his people.
> I sing to my freedom to befriend the man of my heart

He is no longer a boy to be pushed aside
He is a man;
And I am no longer a girl to be hushed away
I am a woman in pursuit of her man;
May I die, he is the man of my heart
The man whose courage has brought pride and joy to
   my heart.

It was unbelievable—a miracle of the divine leadership
which Madit's ancestry represented. It was not unknown for
a girl to display pleasure at her boyfriend's initiation. But
Ajak's was certainly excessive. What did all that mean in real
terms? Had Madit proposed marriage to her? And had she
accepted? That must be what her declaration meant. But how
had the family responded? No one knew.

And so, the initiation ceremony went exceedingly well;
his father slaughtered bulls to celebrate it and Ajak played
the role of the favorite girl—the girlfriend. But then no one
really knew what all that meant. Would Madit marry her?
And would she accept to marry him? It was the last question
that really preoccupied people most as they watched the
rituals and celebrations of initiation.

The recovery period was perhaps the most festive for the
initiated: well fed with nutritious food, endowed with a
freedom that knew no bounds, and intoxicated with the
euphoria of their elevation from "boys" to gentlemen. Singing
their initiation songs of courage and self-esteem, carrying a
bundle of sorghum stalks as their initiation spears and
displaying long whips, the only weapons allowed them at
this stage, they gorged themselves with food, danced their
slow-moving initiation dance, and otherwise brought havoc
on any home which they honored with their performance.
It was a status which one would leave reluctantly because
it led to the even more esteemed status of a full-fledged
gentleman.

The graduation ceremony into this senior status was
marked by all night singing and dancing that ended in a
playful chase by the older age-group, beating the newly
initiated into the river and forcing them to swim across,

emerging on the other side as *adheng*, gentlemen, who must now be shown all the respect due to a young warrior. It is then that relatives and admirers "released" them with gifts of spears, personality bulls, or any objects signifying the aesthetics of adulthood.

Ajak released Madit with friendship, a special gift which signified an advanced stage of courtship that was most likely to result in engagement and marriage. Madit was very proud of the gift and soon acknowledged it in a song dedicated to Ajak:

> Brown beauty
> Brown beauty that has dazzled the tribe,
> I receive your friendship as a precious gift
> A gift as precious as the tusk of the mighty elephant
> And as the gold with which the Europeans crown their
>   queens and kings.
> I ask you to turn your friendship into tassels
> To be tossed with pride by my pied bull,
> The bull of the first born of Malengdit.
> I ask you to turn your friendship into a bell collar,
> From which the pied bull will jingle the brass bells of
>   the Jur-Col tribe,
> And announce the glory of our friendship
> The friendship of the son and daughter of noblemen.
> Ajak, I will never leave you:
> Even if you should be taken to the moon
> I will fly and catch up with you;
> And even if you should be taken to the sun
> I will fly and burn together with you
> Ajak, let us honor the bonds we created in childhood
> Let us be a man and a woman forever united.

The song was Madit's declaration of intent to marry Ajak, and provided it was accepted, a public announcement of their engagement. But for the same reason, it was an invitation for competitors to rise to the contest. And who but the same one-eyed boy with whom he had fought in the cattle camp would emerge to contest for the girl? Madit had come to know

him as Lith, the Hawk, a name befitting his reputation as
a brave warrior. Lith was the first born of a wealthy nobleman
who was prepared to "buy" any beauty for his one-eyed son.
But that his son would choose to compete with the chief's
son was something he had not anticipated, far less prepared
for. Lith's father tried to talk his son out of the competition,
but to no avail. Instead, Lith chose to challenge his rival by
attempting to win the girl through courtship.

The arrangements for Dinka marriages occurred on two
levels: the legal and social arrangements were conducted by
the elders while winning the girl's consent was the function
of courtship to be carried out by the groom and his age-mates,
friends, and young relatives.

Bol was a youth in his early teens when toward the end
of his vacation his brother Madit invited him to join him and
his friends in a courtship expedition to Ajak. As Bol was not
initiated, he could not strictly speaking be regarded as a
gentleman entitled to befriend or court girls according to the
Dinka code of conduct. Since he was educated, which somewhat advanced his status, he was accepted as an older youth.
Bol too was intrigued by the opportunity to experience a tribal
courtship, as he had become distant from the Dinka culture.

Madit and his party had an early dinner and walked for
several hours, reaching Ajak's village close to bedtime. Ajak
had been alerted by a prior message and according to Dinka
practice had in turn invited several of her girlfriends to keep
company with the visitors. This was generally expected in
courtship situations, especially when the bride was known
to be receptive to the marriage.

When they got to Ajak's house, the group, composed of
the two brothers and four others, stood a distance away while
one of them went closer to the place where a group of young
women sat chattering in front of a nearby hut. It was clear that
they were expecting them. After coughing to draw attention to
the group, Bol said, "There is a man standing here," a manner
typical of courtship announcement. A young girl verified this
fact, and two long mats were spread out on the ground to seat
the guests. Ajak came and greeted the visitors, and in accordance with custom, pretended not to know why they had come.

"You cannot face this battle front alone," Madit commented teasingly. "I hope you have prepared your forces."

"I had an idea that you might come, but I don't know what to expect," Ajak replied.

"A surprise attack must also be met," Bol ventured to say. "You have no choice."

"Every guest has a purpose," argued one of Madit's friends, "and in the ways of our people, a guest cannot be asked to state his purpose standing or sitting outside the village. He should first be welcomed and accommodated."

He was hinting at being accommodated inside a hut, which was thought to facilitate a courtship.

"Words are words whether they are said under the open sky or in the darkness of the hut." Ajak put on a show of resistance to the implied suggestion to move the guests inside the hut.

"Ajak, we are your guests," intervened another friend of Madit. "You cannot be the one to hold us at bay. Instead, you should be the one to present our case to your friends in the village so that your guests are not rebuffed."

"The sooner you go, the better the chances that they will not have already gone to bed," Bol interjected, eliciting laughter.

"With such persistence, what can I say but see what I can do?" Ajak conceded. "But do not be surprised if all you have is a single, overwhelmed girl."

"If you have the confidence to fight alone, we shall accept your challenge," commented one of the men.

Ajak had been gone for what seemed like so long a time that the group began to fear that something might have gone amiss in the plans. Now the village was quiet and presumably all were asleep. Then to their relief, they saw two figures approaching. Could it be that Ajak had secured the company of only one additional girl? Disappointment went silently through their minds and hearts.

Ajak's report was different. The girls had obliged and an empty hut on the outskirts of the village had been prepared. The two of them had come to escort the group.

The girls carried the mats and led the way toward a hut that seemed abandoned and dilapidated. But that was part

of the night adventures of courtship. As they approached the
hut, they could hear the other four girls giggling. Suddenly,
silence fell upon the girls as they heard the guests approach.
Ajak and her friends were the first to enter with the mats
to prepare the seating arrangements. A small fire was burning
which made the hut glow with a dim romantic light. An air
of solemnity seemed to greet the group as they entered. Then
everyone sat down for the night-long courtship conversation
that began with self-introductions. These included the names
of the individual, the father, the clan and the section or sub-
tribe. As the night progressed, the conversation was extended
horizontally, as couples lay down together on the mats, and
touching and flirting within certain bounds of propriety. At
this point their conversation assumed verbal wittiness, much
of which was poetic and humorous, the object being to
cultivate bonds between the bride-to-be and the bridegroom.
Yet nothing direct could be said. Everything had to be kept
on a flirtatious level.

"Can you have a herd of sheep in the same cattle byre
with lions and not expect a mauling to occur?" one of the
men said, with a certain bravado.

"And do you expect the lions to get away without retaliation from the owners of the herd?" retorted one of the girls.

"Yet how could the lions get into the cattle byre in the
first place," another of the men commented.

His comment provoked one of them to respond: "Our
Dinka tales are full of humans who get received, accommodated and shown generosity, only to turn into devouring
lions who must then be hunted like wild beasts."

"This conversation seems to be getting out of hand," Bol
announced. "Why don't we think of stories of the lion and
the fox instead."

One of the girls saw the sense of his remark and
exclaimed, "That's correct! Why think of the helpless sheep
who must fall victims to the lion? What about animals, who,
though physically weak, can redeem themselves with the
words in their heads?"

"That is my point," Bol resumed. "You see, in all those
stories, the fox tricks the lion and lands him in such ridiculous

situations that the animal, which was supposed to be the aggressor in the first place, ends up in pitiful failure and even humiliation. It is often difficult to tell whether one admires the fox or pities the lion."

"But if the lion had not been outwitted, what would be the fate of the fox?" argued a female voice. "At least the fox does not threaten to eat the lion, but merely to protect himself. Now it must be obvious where sympathies should go."

"Except that a feature of those stories is that the cleverness of the fox keeps turning against him," Bol continued with his front. "After all, is it not an accepted moral of the stories of the fox that trickery always returns to its master?"

"Ajak," cried one of the girls, "what has your man brought with him? I thought you said he was a younger brother coming to witness the affairs of conversation. He sounds more like the teacher than the pupil."

"Why are you asking me?" retorted Ajak. "He is here, why not ask him?"

"Tell me young man," the girl turned to Bol, "are you the *boy* you are said to be or some spirit in a child's body?"

"It's me talking to you," responded Bol. "I don't know about the spirit, the *boy* or the *child* as you call them."

Everyone laughed. It was clear that Bol was winning the battle of wits. One of the girls decided to pick up the challenge. "Applying your own argument, I must warn you that you are being very clever. Beware of its returning to you."

To this Bol responded with relish, "Ah, but you see it only turns against you after you succeed or appear to have succeeded in achieving your end through cleverness. Have I achieved that end? Do I even seem to have succeeded?"

They all laughed again, fully realizing what that end meant.

"Don't worry," a girl's voice rose above the laughter. "I don't know what you look like, but hearing the way you talk, you will have no trouble achieving that end."

No comparison with Madit was intended, but it flashed in everyone's mind, including perhaps Madit's. Madit made it easier by choosing to speak, somehow complementing Bol's words: "I have always wondered why women guard so jealously what God had obviously intended to be shared."

"But not every food is available for consumption all the time," Ajak decided to display her own view of things. "There are times when women must not drink cows' milk but only goats' milk. There are seasons for eating fish, fruits and vegetables, and seasons when other kinds of food are made available by nature. There is a time to hunt and a time to slaughter domestic animals. God has given man and woman a code of conduct that regulates these things. And God knows best."

"But it is God who has given eyes to these things to pursue one another," Madit stood his ground.

"He has not given them legs to travel on their own," Ajak persisted. "They must be guided by those who carry them. And to attain the purpose for which they were meant, they must be wisely managed. Just as a fisherman uses bait to attract the fish to the hook without giving too much meat to fill their desires prematurely, men and women must learn to sustain each other's desires until they can fulfil what God had intended for them since the Byre of Creation."

Ajak had the last word on the issue and Madit was pleased with the implication of what she was saying.

The conversation had gone on non-stop for the entire night and although some dozed off and rejoined it, no one had slept for any length of time when the cock began to crow. They all realized that they would have to end their courtship session and remove all traces of their night adventure from the hut, and that the girls would have to quietly return to their regular huts before the village woke up.

As they were breaking up, the girl who had complimented Bol for his comments announced, "Let me have a close look at the younger brother who was so eloquent last night so that I can put the words together with the face!"

They all laughed.

"No conflict at all," she declared. "You are as fine looking a lad as you are well spoken."

"With such sweet words, what more can I say?" Bol remarked in closing.

They parted realizing that they were all likely to spend a drowsy day, most of it perhaps in bed, because of *luar*, the tiredness resulting from a sleepless night in a courtship conversation.

As the two contenders, Madit and Lith, competed in courtship, Ajak showed considerable courtesy to both men, even though her preference was clearly for Madit. Lith at first tried to discredit his opponent by drawing attention to his disability, but he could not go far with that, especially as he himself was one-eyed, not much better off than *ngol* in Dinka aesthetics. Lith then looked for other points of weakness and found a particularly vulnerable spot. Word eventually reached Madit through Ajak. And it happened in a dramatically unexpected way.

Madit had called on Ajak several times and, contrary to her earlier responsiveness, she began to avoid him with the excuse of "a heavy body," which was the polite way of saying she was confined by her menstrual cycle. When the excuse became transparent by apparent overuse, Madit pressed for an explanation. Ajak agreed to see him under a clear sky with a bright full moon.

Both were radiant with the ornaments of their courtship. Ajak wore many wristlets, and beads on her waist, and silver metal coils on her arms and legs. Madit had a large ivory bangle on his left arm, his thick hairdo folded under a blue scarf with an ostrich feather stuck into it. But despite the decorations, the mood was ominous.

As they sat on a mat discreetly apart, it was impossible to imagine that the two had been sweethearts from childhood. Madit realized that something had seriously changed. "Tell me the truth," he demanded, "have I offended you in any way?"

"Not at all," Ajak answered, avoiding his eyes.

"Then, why are you behaving this way?"

Ajak was silent.

"I have to know tonight," Madit persisted. "There is no way I can continue in the darkness that has cast such a shadow on my life. Is it Lith?"

Ajak was silent. This clearly said something. It had to be Lith.

"Are you in love with him?" probed Madit.

"No!"

"Then why are you acting this way toward me? Have you ceased to love me?"

There was no answer, and Madit was left wondering what could possibly have caused the change.

As though Ajak read his mind, she broke the silence, "What happened the night you and Lith fought?"

"You mean when we were children?"

"Yes"

"Do you mean what happened at the fight?"

"No, I mean after the fight, late that night."

"I don't know what you are talking about," Madit responded defensively. "What does that have to do with us now?"

Realizing that she was making him acutely uncomfortable —perhaps too close to the truth—Ajak stopped probing. But Madit's curiosity was aroused, even though he appeared to dread the subject.

"Are you not going to explain yourself?" he pressed.

"I don't think so."

"Why not?"

"Because I don't see any need for it."

Madit recalled the conversation they had had in their childhood when their positions had been reversed and Ajak had pressed to know what Madit's mother had said against their friendship. He almost mentioned it now but changed his mind. Instead, he said, "But why was it significant in the first place?"

"I suppose I have changed my mind," responded Ajak.

"You mean you have made up your mind?"

"Do you really think it would help if I were more outspoken than I am now?" Ajak was becoming impatient.

"I would like to know the truth."

"Are you epileptic?"

Ajak dropped the bombshell she had been trying desperately to safeguard.

"Is it true," she continued, "that you had an epileptic fit the night of the fight and that was why you had to be taken home?"

It was Madit's turn to be silent. It was not because he had nothing to say; rather he was boiling with anger. He wanted to strike her and walk away. The longer he dithered, the more he felt enraged. In front of her eyes, Madit began to be transformed. He sucked on his lips; he fiddled with his fingers; and then, in a manner that was frightening, he opened his eyes wide and rolled them about in a glare without focus. Suddenly, his muscles began to tighten, making cracking sounds as he straightened and stiffened his limbs. As though wrestling with himself, he fell groaning to the ground, saliva and foam flowing from his mouth, his body still struggling aimlessly.

Ajak could no longer contain herself. In a shrieking voice, she cried out loud, and within minutes, a crowd had formed around writhing Madit. But as soon as they realized what had occurred, the elders shoved away the women and children, and held the struggling Madit to prevent him from hurting himself. It took several men to subdue him. When it was all over, Madit fell into a slumber and it was decided to let him sleep where he was rather than carry him into the compound. Some kept a watch on him as he slept.

When he woke in the middle of the night, he slowly recollected what had happened and then grabbed his spears to leave. People tried to persuade him to stay for the night, but he refused. It was suggested that he be accompanied by two persons or at least by one man, but his sense of pride had been too shattered and he refused this help too. But the elders knew it was unlikely that he would suffer another seizure soon, they did not press him, and let him leave alone.

Madit did not return home. Where he disappeared to, or even whether he was alive or dead, would haunt the family for years to come.

NINE

IN BUSSERE INTERMEDIATE SCHOOL, far from home, Bol had just returned from a game of football when he received a letter from a fellow Mathiang Dinka at Nyamlel mission school. "Dear Bol," it read, "it is with sadness that I bring the painful news of the disappearance of your beloved brother, Madit."

Bol, now about fourteen years old, interpreted disappearance to mean death. He felt the warm blood of shock pervading his body right to his head. Tears were already beginning to form. He wanted to stop the letter and cry. But his eyes had already caught the next sentence.

"No one knows where he has gone. All that is known is that he must have felt too ashamed of his condition to continue living in Dinkaland. Whether he has gone to live somewhere else or has killed himself no one knows. Let us hope that he is alive and will be found."

Bol felt a little relieved at the hope that his brother might still be alive. But where was he and how could he be found? His first instinct was to go home immediately and help in the search. He decided that he would seek the headmaster's permission. As it was already evening, he had to wait till the following morning to see him. That evening, Bol kept to himself. He neither had the appetite for dinner nor the desire for company. Instead, he went to bed and reflected on the plight of his older brother. The years he had known him kept running through his mind. His reflections turned to the night of the Arab raid: the capture of his mother and twin brothers; Madit's ill-fated escape from their captors; his mother's rescue; and the permanent loss of his brother, Achwil. Now Madit, too, was gone. Where could they be?

Early the next morning Bol sought out the headmaster, Father Archangelo. He knocked at the door and, without raising his head, the headmaster said, "Come in."

Bol stood for some time in front of him before he was acknowledged. Bearded with a stocky build, Father Archangelo looked younger than his late forties. Contrary to the general practice among the Catholic clergy, he dressed in regular trousers and a shirt, not in priestly garb.

"Oh, Elias, I am sorry I got absorbed in the papers," Father Archangelo apologized. "What is the matter? You look distressed. Did anyone misbehave toward you?"

Bol was popular in school and was clearly the head-master's pet. Father Archangelo's reaction was therefore more than the normal sympathy for a student in need.

"Father, I want to go home," said Bol abruptly.

"Home?" Father Archangelo repeated in surprise. He thought Elias was happy in school. They certainly were very happy to have him. "What is the matter, Elias? Has anyone done anything offensive to you?"

"No, Father," responded Elias, "I want to go home to help find my lost brother."

Father Archangelo was relieved. This promised to be a far less serious problem than he had feared. Elias proceeded to explain to him the news he had just received from home about Madit's disappearance, and went on to provide the background to his brother's plight. In doing so, Elias got carried away with his anti-Arab sentiments. "I hate them for what they did to my brothers," he said, almost breaking down in tears.

Father Archangelo was moved—was he even pleased to have further evidence of animosity between the Arab Muslim community of the North and the Africans of the South? Yet he felt it necessary to preach the Christian doctrine of love to the young convert.

"I am sorry to hear this, Elias. As Christians, we must always forgive even those who harm us. I know it is hard, but we must try. In any case, hate can only bring pain and suffering to you."

Father Archangelo felt good about preaching love for people he in fact despised.

The civil war between the Arab Muslim North and the African animist South, which had broken out just before independence, had ebbed and then intensified; it was now in full swing. The Christian missionaries, who had worked in close cooperation with the British administrators to introduce Christianity in the South, were blamed for the separatist policies that had segregated the two parts of the country, encouraging Islam and Arab culture in the North, while preserving the South in its primitive conditions or letting it evolve along indigenous lines, with Christian education as a "civilizing" factor. In the post-colonial era, the central governments tried to erase the Christian influence in the South by substituting Islam and Arab culture, but each successive government failed dismally in achieving these objectives. As a result, political instability had become the pattern.

Only two years after independence, General Abd el-Rahim Abdoun decided that civilian rule had failed to solve the problem of the South. He seized power and intensified the war in the hope of imposing a military solution on the Southerners. Within a few years, he moved from strict regulation and curtailment of missionary activities in the South to a total expulsion of all foreign missionaries. He also imposed Islamization and Arabization as ideological tools for national unification. Indeed, Father Archangelo and his Catholic colleagues in the missionary schools ironically survived the expulsions because they were educators, not missionaries, even though they still crusaded for the cause of Christianity in the South.

Despite its toughness, General Abdoun's dictatorship failed in its efforts to impose a military solution on the South. And yet the more the war escalated, the more repressive the regime became, not only in the South, but throughout the country. Eventually, the situation became intolerable and

Abdoun's regime was overthrown by a popular uprising backed by young revolutionary officers in the army. After a transitional period of one year, during which the government convened a round table conference and tried unsuccessfully to find a peaceful resolution to the conflict, elections were held and parliamentary democracy was restored. The sectarian government that came into power through the elections resumed the policies of Islamization and Arabization. The South resisted violently. Mutual animosity intensified with the collapse of efforts to find a peaceful solution to the war, the return of repression against the Christian Church in the South, and the determination of Southerners to use all forms of resistance, violent and non-violent alike.

But Father Archangelo's mind was not on the country's history but on the young man standing in front of him.

He advised Elias not to go back home. "There is nothing you can do that your elders are unable to do," he argued. "Remember that education in the long run will be the best contribution you can make to your family and people. Remember that you are now the representative of your lost brothers. God willing, your education may even prove to be their salvation. You will have access to a wider world than your elders at home, and who knows whether that access might not lead you to where your brothers are?"

Elias, seeing the headmaster's logic, was beginning to realize that his education could not only be useful to his people, but also help find his lost brothers.

"Now, come on, put on a better face," Father Archangelo said cheerfully. "The main thing is that we pray for their safety wherever they may be."

He offered to say a mass for Elias's brothers that evening.

When the time came, Elias, who had been baptized after years of Christian instruction, went to church full of spiritual consolation and gratitude. On entering, he dipped his right fingers into the holy water next to the door, knelt down as he made the sign of the cross, and got up and walked to the front row, where he knelt down again, his eyes fixed on the painting of Christ behind the altar.

Even before the mass started, Elias began to pray: "God, I know I have sinned many times before, but I promise you that I will try to be good in the future and will remain forever loyal to you, if you promise me that my brother, Madit, will be safe wherever he may chance to be." He focussed on Madit because Achwil had been gone far too long; indeed, he had never known him.

Father Archangelo appeared in a surplice followed by two boys dressed in white robes. Elias was deeply moved that his brothers received such spiritual attention. Father Archangelo said the mass in Latin; the congregation's participation was in Latin and Dinka. The prayers, the chanting, and the singing combined to give the occasion for Bol a deep mystical almost ecstatic significance.

After having confessed his sins and received Holy Communion, Elias sat with his eyes shut in deep meditation, fully assimilated in the Holy Spirit and the aura of God's presence. Then he felt an astonishing vibration, followed by a ring and a sound of music in his head, and finally, a heavenly voice spoke to him, saying, "Your prayers have been heard. You have nothing to fear; your brothers are alive and well. Maintain your faith in the power of God and all will be well."

"Thank you, my Lord," whispered Elias. "Thank you, thank you. I will not let you down."

The mass ended, and as the congregation got up to leave the church, Elias noticed a commotion at the door. "Are you not ashamed of yourselves, coming to harass the faithful in their church," Elias heard a voice scream. "You will pay for this in Hell! I assure you, you will."

"Take him away," said the commanding voice of a tall officer in military uniform whom Elias soon realized was the man in charge. He carried a piece of paper from which he was reading out the names of students who had been reported as ring leaders of a demonstration against the government for its anti-Christian policies in the South. Moreover, they had distributed leaflets, which may have been printed at the school's print shop, thus implicating school authorities.

As Elias emerged, he noticed someone whisper to the commanding officer, who immediately turned his eyes on him. "Take that one," he said to the soldiers. The sight of the soldiers, whom Southerners saw as an occupational Arab army from the North, almost drove Elias into a rage, but he remembered that he had just promised God that he would abide by His will; charity, even toward His enemies, was part of that promise. He obediently and silently surrendered himself to the officer.

At the security quarters, the boys were interrogated about their anti-government activities and the extent of missionary involvement. For some reason the officer, whose name the boys now came to know as Captain Ali Ahmed El-Jak, chose to interrogate Elias alone.

"Did you take part in distributing the leaflets?" he asked.

"Yes," answered Elias honestly and without any change in his voice or tone.

"Why?"

"Because the government policies interfered with my freedom of religion."

"You mean the missionary religion?" retorted the officer with deliberate sarcasm.

"I am a Christian," responded Elias, maintaining poise and calm.

"You are not even old enough to understand what the word means."

"All the same, I am a Christian."

"Why don't you want to be a Muslim?" asked the officer.

Elias chose to be silent.

"Tell me, why don't you want to be a Muslim?"

The officer persisted.

Harassed, Elias began to lose his patience, but he remembered his promise to God in good time.

"I suppose missionaries have poisoned your mind against Islam!"

Elias could no longer resist the pressure. "I don't know anything about Islam, but I know something about the Arabs who are Muslims. I hate them! I hate them!" He began to shout hysterically, crying as he did.

Captain Ali was taken by surprise. There was something about this young man that instinctively impressed him. In fact, his questions had been directed more toward establishing personal contact than anything else. That was why he separated him from the rest. He felt sad that he had antagonized Elias. But the youth's courage and honesty increased Ali's admiration of the boy. Placing his right arm around him, he said, "Son, I understand how you feel."

"No, you don't," Elias shouted back. "You think I hate the Arabs because I am here. You do not know what they have done to my family."

Suddenly Captain Ali understood. The boy's family must have suffered at one point or another. Was it during the civil war or did it go farther back?

"Tell me about it, son," Ali spoke with a compassion that instinctively disarmed Elias, sowing the seeds of trust in the man.

Elias slowly began to tell Ali the story of the Arab raid that led to the loss of one brother and the disability of another, who, he had just learnt, had also disappeared, the very reason they had been in church praying. Ali was moved by his account. He really had nothing to say that could soothe the boy, except the wishful assertion that his brother would probably be found. "And as for Achwil, you must trust that he is alive and will one day be reunited with your family."

Elias was pleased with Ali's optimism. It was just what he needed. Nor was Ali bluffing. Somehow, he had suddenly come to identify with Elias's problem. "But you must remember that your first obligation to yourself and your people is to take your education seriously," continued Captain Ali. "With a good education, your opportunities in life will increase, and so will the chances of your tracing your brothers."

Elias felt encouraged. He even felt a sense of gratitude to Ali, whom he now regarded more as a benevolent person than a typical Arab officer.

Ali wanted to let Elias go free, but he could not discriminate between him and the other students. So, he ordered that all be warned and let go.

Remembering Ali's advice, Elias worked hard for his final exams. Ali too did not stop with that casual word of advice. He resolved to keep in touch with the lad and to offer him continued encouragement and support. He realized that the worst thing he could do for Elias was to be seen in close contact with the head of the security forces in the area. He therefore maintained a close but discreet watch on the boy, from time to time sending his servant with small presents (sometimes pocket money) or inviting Elias to his house, where he offered him counsel.

Despite these precautions, rumors of a connection between Elias and the security officer spread in the school. One day, Elias received word that Father Archangelo wanted to see him.

"My son," Father Archangelo began, "some developments seem to have taken place since our discussion of your family tragedy."

The reference was too discreet for Elias to comprehend. His silence communicated the point.

"As I recall, the problem at the time was to urge you not to become bitter against the Arabs and to try to forgive them, despite the terrible things they have done to your family. Now I see that your forgiveness has gone much further than anticipated. I hear that you are in contact with Captain Ali. Is that true?"

Elias detected an underlying tone of criticism behind the headmaster's words, but he could not misrepresent the facts.

"Yes," he said without elaboration.

"I see," Father Archangelo said. "And why, may I ask?"

"Captain Ali has been very kind to me since the incident at the church," explained Elias. "My feelings about the Arabs have not changed, but Captain Ali seems to be different. He is kind, understanding, and generous."

"Oh no, my boy!" remarked the priest. "No! No! You must realize the subtle ways of the devil. One of the best means available to the devil is temptation and deceit. This means that you will be made to see things that tempt and deceive you to abandon the word of God and follow the path of evil. Even if you forget your own family tragedy and stop blaming the Arabs as a whole, can't you see that it is Captain Ali who is repressing the Church here? Can't you see that he is the tool of oppression? Was it not by his command that Christian youth were arrested and some tortured for defending the cause of Christianity? Is it not obvious that he is an instrument of the devil? My son, beware! Don't fall a victim of deception and material temptation."

Tears suddenly streamed from Elias's eyes and down his cheeks. Although he could not quite understand what he had done wrong, he felt overwhelmed by the words of the headmaster whose spiritual superiority and power over him he accepted without the slightest doubt. And as he thought of the magnitude of the wrong which must have compelled the Father to speak to him in this way, he broke down and sobbed loudly.

Father Archangelo got up and put his arms around him. "Do not cry, my son," he said with feeling. "God is merciful. He will forgive you and protect you. But you must pray and have faith in His love and grace." Then, making the sign of the cross, he blessed Elias, said a brief prayer in Latin, and counseled, "Now, with God's peace, go back to your studies and prepare for the exams."

As Elias left the headmaster's office, he was overcome by confusion. He appreciated the words of Father Archangelo and the blessing he had just received, but he could not quite make himself believe that Captain Ali was an agent of the devil. Or was he? He reasoned that by age, knowledge and God's grace, Father Archangelo obviously knew better. But he had come to like Ali and thought him a good man.

Elias thought more about this troubling problem and avoided seeing Ali or communicating with him. He concentrated on his studies and when the results were in, they confirmed his good feelings about his work. Elias was third in a class of thirty and was admitted to Rumbek Secondary School.

Ali had not realized that Elias had decided to avoid him because he himself had wanted to leave the boy alone to concentrate on his studies. When the exams were over and he sent for Elias with the intention of congratulating him, he received a negative response. After this was repeated several times, he became suspicious. He decided that he must see Elias and thought of a way to ensure his appearance. In a brief note, which his servant took to Elias, he wrote, "I have an important message for your father, which I would like to discuss with you before sending. It's most urgent. So, let's meet soonest possible."

Elias responded as predicted. He could not ignore an issue involving the head of the security forces and his family. What could the message be? Did it concern him or was it about his lost brothers perhaps? He went to see Ali immediately.

"Elias, my boy, where have you been?" Captain Ali could not wait to show his emotions as soon as Elias came into the house. "I really began to worry about you."

Although Elias had come with apprehensions and was intent to be on guard against this clever devil, the sincerity with which Captain Ali spoke reversed his frame of mind. Yet, his response betrayed what Ali had feared, for Elias could not give a straight answer.

"I was busy with the exams," he began clumsily.

"What about after the exams, which is when I first sent for you?"

Elias was silent. He now felt an urge to tell Ali the truth. But how could he say it? What could he possibly say that would not be offensive? And how could he come to someone's house to tell him that he had tried to avoid him because he saw him as an agent of the devil?

"What is the message you said you wanted to send to my father?" Elias tried to change the subject.

"We shall soon get to that," replied Ali. "But first, I would like to know what the problem is. It seems that you are hiding something. What is it, Elias?"

Somehow, the question was too direct for him to avoid. But he could not possibly tell the truth as he knew it.

"There is nothing," he again tried to be evasive.

"Come on, Elias, tell me," Ali insisted, now feeling a paternalistic urge to identify the problem and see if he could help. "Has anyone in school done something offensive?"

"No, not at all."

"Well, since you seem to be directing your unhappiness toward me, let me redirect my question: Have I offended you in any way?"

Even in his confused state of mind, it seemed impossible to Elias that this man, obviously so compassionate toward him and so deeply concerned for his welfare, could be an agent of the devil in disguise. Tormented by these inner tensions and contradictions, he could no longer contain himself; he broke down and cried.

"I don't know what's right and wrong any more," he said, tears streaming down his cheeks. "On the one hand, I am warned that you are the tool of oppression against our people, an enemy of the Christians and an agent of the devil. On the other hand, when I am with you, I see a kind and compassionate person, whom I cannot believe could be the evil man I have been warned about. Oh, Uncle Ali, what shall I do? Whom should I believe?"

It was the first time he called Captain Ali "Uncle" and he did so deliberately. As he continued to cry, Ali held his arms around him and tried to comfort him. "That's all right, Elias," he said. "You will eventually know the truth. Never mind what people say. Just direct your heart to God and he will reveal the truth to you himself."

By now, Ali had made up his mind not to react with anger against the accusations which had been leveled against him. He was not even going to ask for the identities of the people who had been talking to Elias. Nor was he going to try to defend himself against them. His best response would be to demonstrate compassion, love and support for Elias. Everything else would take care of itself from the positive common ground of a basic human bond. With those thoughts in mind, he took out a handkerchief from his pocket and, handing it to Elias said, "Have this; wipe your tears and stop crying. I am so pleased you have told me the truth. That's what I began to suspect, but now that you have admitted it yourself, there is no problem anymore. We shall clear the dust. In fact, God has already cleared the dust by making you talk this way."

If there was any doubt about the moral image of Captain Ali, the words he said completely put Elias's mind to rest. They could indeed have been said by a Dinka reflecting the values of traditional religion. Somehow, he felt a bond with

Ali that was far closer than he had ever felt toward Father Archangelo. For the first time, Ali did not appear as an Arab to him, whether in his color or in his behavior.

TEN

IT WAS AS THOUGH Captain Ali was reading Elias's mind, for he told him a story that could not have been more timely or appropriate. "Elias, let me tell you something you may find difficult to believe, but I think it is relevant to the present situation," he began with considerable solemness in his tone. "You see, I myself am of Dinka origin. My grandfather was a Dinka by the name Ajak, which was later changed by the Arabs to El-Jak, the name we use now. My grandfather was captured when he was still a small boy by an Arab slaver who treated him like his own son. As a result, he adopted Islam and became Arabized and fully integrated into the Arab Muslim community of the North. He married the daughter of a well-to-do Arab merchant and his children became racially and culturally assimilated into Arab society. In due course, the Negroid element became history to our family. I suppose to you, I am just an Arab. I accept that and I am proud of it.

"But let me tell you also that my having come to the South has rekindled in me a strong sense of awareness about my African origins. It has made me keenly aware that, although my grandfather was lucky enough to have been raised by a benevolent Arab, the plight of other black slaves was different. So, even in the North, most of the former slaves are Islamized and Arabized, but their lot still leaves much to be desired. And since coming to the South, I have opened my eyes much wider to the indignities that our people of slave origin in the North still suffer. This has made me more sensitive to the conditions of our brothers here in the South. I am a soldier with specific duties to perform and orders to obey, but I have a deep sense of solidarity with our people in the South which sometimes transcends my duties. I often try to harmonize between these two sets of obligations.

"So, you see, Elias, although I perfectly understand the emotions that drive people to think of me the way you have just described, I also have a clear sense of myself. My conscience is clear and I trust that the truth of our collective selves will sooner or later be revealed by God, even when man tries to cover it with fabrications and lies."

Again, Elias felt that Ali really sounded like a Dinka in his religious and moral convictions. Perhaps he had inherited from his grandfather something that was more Dinka than Arab or Muslim. He felt happy that he had revealed the truth to him and that they were reconciled again.

"Now, let me tell you about the message I wanted to write to your father," Ali resumed. "You must by now know full well that I have developed a keen interest in your future. I have felt for some time that your prospects would be considerably enhanced by pursuing your education in the North where you will learn Arabic and become attuned to the national culture." It also crossed Ali's mind that the experience might help Elias moderate his anti-Arab sentiment. But he chose not to mention this, although what he had just learned from Elias highlighted that consideration even more. "What do you say to my proposal?"

By now Elias was in a positive mood. Although he had no idea what studying in the North would be like, he accepted Ali's reasoning at face value. "If you think that the experience would be valuable, that I will be accepted, and that my performance there will live up to the challenge, what can I say except to thank you for the suggestion? The question is: how does one go about it?"

"Leave that to me," responded Ali. "Let me give you a private word of advice and I hope you take it in the spirit I am giving it to you. Knowing the mentality of the school authorities, which you were good enough to confirm to me today, I know that they will oppose your going to the North. They will argue that the people there are different from you in blood, religion, language and culture and that you will be miserable there. They will probably say things worse than that. In any case, whatever truth there is to such accusations, it should not stop you from acquiring a national advantage. So, I suggest that, rather than expose yourself to undue pressure, don't say anything to them. I will arrange it in my own way and if all goes well, you will hear the result while you are at home on leave."

They agreed and Elias returned to school feeling deeply elated about Ali's suggestion.

Ali wrote a security report asking the authorities to intervene on Elias's behalf to recommend his admission to Hantoub Secondary School in the North. "Elias is a remarkable boy," he wrote. "He is good natured, intelligent and, for his age, very astute. As a result of some unfortunate events in his past, he nurses a deep grievance against the Arabs, one that could destroy his future or make him dangerous, if not constructively contained. I believe that the best way of containing this destructive potential is to give him access to the best educational circles in the North. He should be made to see the other side and transcend his prejudices, which, I might add, are not unfounded."

Meanwhile, Elias returned to his village for a vacation. When he arrived, he was greeted with great excitement by his family—men, women and children alike, some breaking down in tears as though his presence reminded them of Madit's absence. But their tears were those of joy rather than sorrow. Yet, his father, who constrained his emotions the way a Dinka man should, reprimanded the women for crying. As Bol— who assumed his Dinka name at home—was well, crying over him was a bad omen; and if their crying was over Madit, that was even worse since it implied that he was dead.

Captain Ali's letter to the authorities was well received and Elias was admitted to Hantoub. He also wrote Chief Malengdit about his initiative. Elias read the letter to his father: "Although I do not know you, your son has brought us together. I am very fond of him and I strongly believe that he has a future in the leadership of this country. I feel sure that his prospects would be enhanced by his receiving part of his education in the North so that he is in touch with the country as a whole. I also think that it would be good for your leadership role to have your children educated in both the North and the South. I only hope you will share my point of view."

Malengdit was pleased with the arrangement. Despite his pride in the Dinka race, he realized that the Arabs had the upper hand in the country and it would clearly be an advantage for his son to learn their ways and be close to them. Malengdit celebrated his son's return home and his acceptance with a feast in which a bull was slaughtered, beer brewed in plenty, and large quantities of food prepared. Drums were even taken out to honor the occasion and there was singing and dancing.

But Bol soon learned that despite the festive atmosphere of his return, even as the disappearance of Madit had united the family in sorrow, it had also rekindled the tension and animosity between the families of his father and his uncle, Akol. Some time before Bol returned, new tension between the two families broke out. On hearing the news of Madit's disappearance and the circumstances under which it had occurred, Aluel was reported to have reacted insultingly toward the family of Nyandeng, the sister of Ajak.

"Was that not what I warned my son about?" she was said to have said in distress. "I told my Madit to keep away from that heartless breed. Now that she led him astray and then threw him down like a log on the open plains of their village, what can there be in that senseless relationship which she so lustfully pursued?" And as she cried, more words of lamentation poured: "Oh what a misfortune! That my son should die in the wilderness like a hyena! The death of my Madit will go after the witches who brought it upon him, however long it may take."

Aluel's complaints and curses reached Nyandeng's ears. She too had her biting response according to the rumors: "It is just as well that God has settled the matter for my sister. I told her to keep away from the afflictions of that breed and she would not heed my advice. Now that God has dictated his will, why are people throwing their words around in search of others to blame? Was it my sister who took the twins out at night to be seized by the Arabs or was it my sister who gave Madit the disease called epilepsy?"

Unlike the women's fight over the children, this ugly exchange of insults was hushed up and dismissed by their husbands as "rumors" or "the usual ways of women" in which men must not involve themselves.

It was perhaps Ajak's own conduct, as Elias understood from his father, that restored family unity and harmony after the last episode. On learning of Madit's disappearance, Ajak was reported to have stripped herself of all ornamentations, refused to eat for days, and even when she was persuaded to break her hunger strike, remained mournful and aloof from society. She also asked her family to return Lith's cattle as she had decided against marrying him, or, for that matter, any other man. She made it known that if Madit were ever to return, he was the man she was determined to marry. Meanwhile, she would remain single, however long it might take. When her family tried to persuade her otherwise, Ajak threatened to run away and go to Malengdit's home to await Madit's return, if her relatives failed to reach an understanding with his family.

Madit's disappearance had indeed become a tragedy for Ajak's family. Not knowing what else to do, they consulted Chief Malengdit.

"We have brought our problem to you not only because our daughter feels committed to your son, but also because, being the chief, you are the father of all people," they said. "The girl is threatening to run away and offer herself to your son, even though he is absent. She wants to wait here until he returns some day. If not, she is prepared to honor his name into old age and die as his wife. We have come to seek your advice. What should we do?"

Though moved by their mission, Malengdit felt unable to marry a girl to a son whose very survival was doubtful, a son whose whereabouts, if he were alive, were unknown, a son who might never again be seen in Dinkaland.

"Your words are good," the chief had said to Ajak's family.

"That is what living together in a land means. I could not understand it when I was told of what had happened. I have always thought very highly of Ajak. That she could disdain my son because of an illness which God had inflicted upon him without any moral wrong that could be revealed by a diviner was something that truly disturbed me. That is the kind of behavior which would anger the ancestors. And our ancestors never forget an insult.

"But Ajak has now lived up to the reputation she deserved. After all, she had overlooked Madit's disability and had demonstrated a noble compassion. If her ancestral spirits have redirected her back onto the path she almost missed, I am exceedingly pleased. But we must persuade Ajak to accept the truth. Madit is not with us and only God knows where he is."

And then, as though a thought just crossed his mind, Chief Malengdit went on: "But our people have the custom of *la ghot* for such situations. If Madit were known or presumed to have died, it would be for his living brother to 'enter the hut' of his widow and have children born to the name of the dead husband. Madit is not dead, we hope, but a prolonged absence is like death. Let's wait and see. Should Madit not come back, there is always that custom to follow. I shall talk with Bol when he comes back from school. The ways of the educated are different from our ways, but these are customs which our forefathers developed to help us in situations where they are needed. Bol is part of the situation confronting us, and I believe that, although he is still only a child, he will understand the need."

So when Bol listened to his father's account of these happenings, he was disbelieving. He was glad to hear of Ajak's concern for he liked her and had been genuinely distressed by her attitude toward Madit's epilepsy, which had seemed totally out of character with her personality. But the possibility of being asked to enter Madit's hut and have children with Ajak in place of his missing brother, presumed dead, was something he had never ever contemplated. In fact, he was totally caught off-guard.

"Son," his father began, "I know that you are educated and that, as a child of the missionaries, you may have your own words about life and what follows death. The missionaries even tell you that people will rise again from death and be judged by God; those who have lived a virtuous life will go to the home of God and those who have been evil will go to the home of fire. But those are not the words of our ancestors. According to our beliefs, when people die and are buried, their bodies are consumed by termites, even though the dead move on in some form to continue their life in an unknown world of the dead. Those who leave children behind become the ancestors who, though far removed from the living, watch over their descendants and protect them from evil. Those descendants who violate the word of God and the ancestors are punished by them and those who follow their word receive the ancestral reward. For us, what the missionaries call the home of God and the home of fire are here in this world. And people are blessed with the one or afflicted by the other depending on what they do or fail to do. Our ancestors working with God and the clan spirits are the judges.

"Every dead person is an ancestor or ought to be given the opportunity to be an ancestor. That is why our people have the custom of *la ghot* so that a man who dies leaving behind a wife of child-bearing age might continue to have children begotten in his name to stand his head upright in this world. And that is why any man who dies before marrying, even if a child, must have a wife married to his name and have children to stand his head upright. This is an ancestral duty which, if not fulfilled, can be a cause of illness and perhaps death.

"So, son, whether Madit is alive or dead, even if he were alive but away from us, we have the duty to let his name live among us through children born by a wife married to his name. In this case, Ajak is a girl he himself knew from childhood, courted and engaged. She is his wife. And she is also someone you know well. I think it is a duty that should give you a sense of fraternal fulfillment. I know you are still a boy, but you have also become a man. Besides, we are not talking of completing the marriage tomorrow and bringing Ajak home now. You have a few more years to grow. What we need now is a commitment. What do you say, son?"

Elias Bol was so dumbstruck that had he been a little younger he would have broken down and cried. But as his father said, he was becoming a man and it was as a man that he was being offered his brother's bride. How could he cry? Instead, he recalled the courtship visit to Ajak and how he had enjoyed his game of wits with the girls. It had been as though he was an age-mate of Madit and the other members of the courtship team. Was it God's will that he should assume this moral obligation?

But then the reasons against the proposal returned and, after an exaggerated silence in reflection, he responded to his father by admitting he was pulled in different directions.

"The moral obligation you have explained is not only a custom of our ancestors, but one which you want to apply to serve the interest of a brother for whom I feel boundless love and affection and whose disappearance still pains my heart deeply. And yet, Father, I cannot enter his hut and sleep with Ajak as Madit's representative. For one, there is the age difference between Madit and me and also between Ajak and me. But the real obstacle has to do with my own sense of moral obligation about assuming my brother's wife or even widow. This may be the missionary influence on me, but I think there is more to it than that. And it applies whether Madit is alive or dead. If he is alive, then I would be committing adultery with my brother's wife. If Madit were known to be dead, the situation might be different. I would also feel that his death would be on my bed with Ajak every time we were together, and it would be impossible to forget that we were together because of what had transpired between her and Madit. Ajak has acted commendably since Madit's disappearance, which has erased whatever wrong she committed earlier, but she and I would be reliving the tragedy continuously. Despite our intentions, I feel that we would be on opposing sides. And then, Father, I am a schoolboy, with my future still ahead of me. I cannot yet assume family responsibilities."

Malengdit listened to his son sympathetically, from time to time nodding his head in agreement. Elias Bol closely monitored his father's response to his stated feeling and was encouraged as he spoke. By the end, he was confident that he had persuaded his father to his point of view.

Malengdit coughed and looked around as though searching for inspiration. And then, after coughing again, almost artificially, as though to clear his throat, he said: "Son, you have spoken with powerful words. Let us think the situation over. But, as always, I fall back on the traditions of our forefathers and I can see that there is still another way out of our predicament. Perhaps Ajak is seeking this way because she is afraid of our ancestral curse for what she has done. And one is right to fear, for our ancestors are *bad*; they will never overlook such dishonor. But I will ask them to forgive Ajak, bless her and restore her maiden freedom to marry another man. I have no doubt in my mind that another son of a nobleman will release his cows for her. Let's leave the matter."

In due course, Malengdit sent for Ajak's relatives and conveyed to them the conclusion he and Bol had reached on the issue. "The girl is young, beautiful and from a noble family," he said. "I do not see any problem with her marital future. And I suppose I need not tell you that I am not interested in having my betrothal cows returned. Whoever marries her eventually, let my son's intentions to marry her be honored by those cows. Bring her to me next month and I will spray her with holy water, rub her with the sacred ashes of our cattle hearth, and release the robe of marriage from her neck. After that we can carry out the rituals of atonement between our clans to remove any bitterness from our hearts and restore our cordial relations. After all, marriage ties are not new to our families. Your daughter, Nyandeng, is established as a senior wife and mother of an initiated man in this family. Let's bless our relations and remain united and harmonious."

It had only been days since the meeting with Ajak's family when Malengdit saw a man approach his assembly under the court tree. After resting his spears against a nearby tree, the man came nearer, greeted the chief first, then proceeded to greet other notables and ended by raising and waving his hands in a collective greeting to the rest of the assembled crowd. Something deeply sorrowful was reflected on his face.

A few minutes later, the man revealed his story.

"Chief, I have just come from the family of Nyandeng's father. I was passing by and when they learned that I was coming this way, they requested me to stop and tell you that Ajak suddenly passed away."

The messenger stopped as though to watch Malengdit's reaction.

"Ajak dead?" Malengdit repeated the message with wide open eyes, as though challenging the bearer of this tragic news to retract what he had said.

"Yes, chief!" reaffirmed the messenger. As though struck dead by lightning, Malengdit sat back resting his head against the back of the canvas chair on which he sat and said not another word.

The messenger then explained the circumstances of her death. A few days after she had been informed of the results of the discussions with the chief, Ajak confided to her brother that she expected to die within a few days and that it was a destiny they should do nothing to prevent. She only wanted it to be known that she did not wish anyone to be blamed for her death; it was her own doing. If anyone even so much as raised a stick against another in pursuance of a feud over her death, her spirit would seek vengeance. Her death would be self-inflicted, to solve a problem she could not deal with otherwise.

Malengdit asked, "How did she kill herself?"

"It is said that she broke the taboo against drinking cows' milk while she was menstruating. In fact, she is said to have taken the milk of the sacred cows of the spirit Dengdit, mixed it with the juice of a poisonous plant that no one knows, and drunk it. Believing that she would hang herself, her brother had watched her closely and had also asked the women to do the same. But they looked for the wrong signals. One night, before going to bed, she went to her brother and informed him that the thing she had revealed to him would happen that night and that he should see to it that her wishes were fulfilled. Believing that she might leave the hut that night and go somewhere else to hang herself, her brother stayed awake watching the hut all night, but did not see his sister emerge. The following morning, Ajak lay motionless with a swollen body; she was dead."

When news of Ajak's death was conveyed to Nyandeng, she violently threw herself about, wailing with an uncontrollable flow of words that expressed both heart-piercing grief and hateful insinuations against her marital family, whom she took as the cause of her sister's tragedy. The family felt that it was time to show compassion and magnanimity, not recrimination and retaliation. Everyone felt a great grief for Ajak.

Things gradually resumed normalcy. In due course, even Nyandeng seemed to forget her behavior which in any case seemed to have been forgiven but not entirely forgotten.

Bol saw to it that he went out of his way to relate to Nyandeng in order to transcend any differences within the family, but deep within himself, he nursed resentment about what he saw as her heartlessness toward his family and especially toward Madit.

Nyandeng also reciprocated in kind. She displayed considerable warmth toward Bol, calling him by such flattering terms as chief, but everyone sensed that her inner feelings towards Aluel's son were adverse, not because of Madit and Ajak, but rather because of Bol's own image. The fact that her son, Adol, was an ordinary Dinka youth in the cattle camp, with no future in the modern world, while Bol appeared to shine brighter and brighter, caused in her a deep-rooted sense of jealousy and envy.

Bol's educational accomplishments were indeed exaggerated. It was even said that he had learned all that there was to be learned in the South, which was why he was being transferred to the North. Captain Ali's letter about his prospects for leadership was interpreted as virtual assurance that he would become a national leader.

Bol himself was embarrassed by all this, but there was nothing much he could do to counter it, except to deny the stories when confronted by them.

It was now close to the time of his departure for Hantoub. The more he thought of going to school in the North, the more he became anxious. Early one morning, before people began to assemble, Bol joined his father under the court tree, and as they sat next to one another on garden chairs, he seized the opportunity to voice his concerns.

"Father, I am somewhat apprehensive about going to the North. For one thing, it has given our people exaggerated expectations about my future. And for another thing, although I have come to admire Captain Ali and have even developed a liking for him, I still resent the Arabs and their attitude towards our people. I don't know how I will feel about being so close to the people who have brought such tragedy to our family. I do not even want to pretend that I do not hate the Arabs, but if I let them know how I feel about them, I cannot see how I can continue to live with them. I wonder whether I am doing the right thing."

Malengdit, who was informally dressed in a jibba, folded the garment between his thighs, as he often did when he was about to speak. Waving his finger at Bol as he spoke, he said, "You, son, let me tell you. The thing called feud, which you hear of, is not simple; it is a big thing which calls for a strong heart. It is true that according to the customs of our people, you should not partake of the food of anyone with whom you have a feud. But our people also have the saying: eat your enemies' food to acquire the strength to strike at him. The truth is somewhere there in between.

"Your brothers are gone. We know that Achwil is in Arabland, if he is alive. As for Madit, it is also to Arabland that people who leave Dinkaland go. If he is alive, he too is there. Go, my son, and acquire the knowledge of things and the strength that may one day lead to the path of your brothers. If our ancestors are watching over us, you will find them one day, however long it may take. And as for the words blown by the wind in this tribe, do not worry about them; they will pass with the wind. And why should you shy away from your people's expectations anyway? Are you not the son of their chief? And if God saves your life, will you not be their leader one day, whether here in the tribe or elsewhere in the country? Don't trouble your mind with nonsensical worries."

Malengdit's words soothed him a great deal. Elias felt that his move to the North was not merely a self-seeking exercise. It was now part of his obligation to his family and the tribe.

He now felt up to the challenge. However, this did not remove his anxieties about the strange environment which he was about to join. As he traveled by train, he wondered what the Northerners with whom he would live would be like. He realized how he felt about the Arabs, but then there were also people like Captain Ali who, though the symbol of oppression in the South, had proved himself kind and humane. He reminded himself that one should never overgeneralize.

As he traveled northward came the significant news that Jabir El Munir, who had seized military power several years before and had promised to solve the "Southern Problem," had just succeeded in negotiating a peace agreement with the Southern rebels, ending the civil war that had been raging since independence. The agreement granted the South regional autonomy and although it had not been uniformly accepted, it had almost miraculously restored peace and a measure of national unity to the country. Certainly, things were improving between the South and the North, the Dinka and the Arabs.

ELEVEN

THE TRAIN RIDE OF several days duration took Elias across a vast territory with widely ranging terrain and vegetation, a rich savannah zone of tall grass and forests of large trees with thick undergrowth, intermittently broken by villages on open plains of hard soil with only a sparse growth of acacia trees and short grass. As the train snaked its way through the villages, going from station to station, crossing forests and the extensive grasslands of the *toc* herds of Dinka cattle, sheep and goats spotted the grazing areas accompanied by their tall, naked or barely clothed herders. Occasionally, a man would be seen standing on one leg, holding a spear with the right hand to support himself, looking exaggeratedly tall in contrast to the flatness of the land. As the train rolled northward, sporadic highlands or hills began to break the monotony of the flatness. The vegetation too began to change, looking more arid and scrubby the further north the train went, until the green carpet of the irrigated Gezira land on the Blue Nile emerged and continued to Wad Medani, across the river from Hantoub.

The first school day, Elias was introduced to the headmaster, Mustafa Mukhtar, a heavily built man in his early fifties with a conscious, though hidden, sense of humor. As soon as Elias stepped into his office, accompanied by Abd el-Rahman Musa, the prefect Mustafa commented, as he shook hands with him, "You are more of an Arab in color than

I am." Abd el-Rahman and Elias laughed. And indeed although he would be described as blue by fellow Northerners, Mustafa was as black and negroid looking as any African could be. But in the Sudanese scheme of things he was an Arab.

Elias decided to respond in like manner on the race and color issue: "On my mother's side, somewhere in the generation of my great, great grandmother, there is some very strong Arab blood in our mainstream."

Mustafa Mukhtar saw the point and hastened to get out of the comparison. "Well, my boy," he said, "you have embarked on an exciting adventure. Colonialism kept the two parts of our country apart and saw to it that we were divided by race, religion and culture. We must work to break the barriers down. Your coming here is a small but significant step in that direction. It will not be easy for you, both in the classroom and among your colleagues outside, but you must work hard to let the dream of your mentor, Captain Ali, come true."

Elias did not like the reference to Ali as his mentor, but he chose to see things positively. "I will do my best," he said.

"Judging from your figure," resumed the headmaster, "the school has got itself a good catch for sports!"

Elias merely smiled as he saw his athletic potential take the front line in evaluation of his worth. "If you have any problems at all, feel free to come to me," said the headmaster as he ended the meeting.

Hantoub soon proved as challenging and formative as the headmaster had predicted. Academically, Elias was far behind in Arabic and had to receive remedial tutoring to reach the minimum standard for secondary school. His knowledge of Islamic studies was nil. But while he was not expected to participate in the class, he agreed to sit in on the study of Islam and the history of the Arabs, which were conducted in Arabic.

Although his poor record in Arabic and Islamic studies lowered his general standing in the class, his performance in other subjects continued to be good. His main problem was in cultural adjustment. In many ways, he felt very much out of context, unable to express himself well in Arabic, self-conscious in his mannerisms, and, all in all, a stranger in an alien environment. What was particularly perplexing was that he felt a sense of ethnic pride and even superiority as a Dinka, and yet recognized that the process of Arabization which he was undergoing was in essence a process of his own cultural self-enhancement. It was by no means an easy feat, but because of his intelligence, sensitivity and pride, he was able to adapt with relative ease. That, combined with his sports, made him popular.

His performance at sports might not have been so spectacular had it not been for the myth associating his race with physical abilities. And, in a way, the racial assumptions about his athletic skills were confirmed by the fact that he was quite prominent in virtually every game and sport. In addition to soccer, the most popular game, he played basketball, volleyball, and table tennis; he ran, high-jumped, long-jumped, threw the javelin, and swam. All in all, he filled any space for which a representative was needed. He knew that there was a certain amount of racism attached to his prominence in games and sports; it was not even disguised for often the crowd chanted: "Elias! Elias! Bol! Bol! *El-Abd*! *El-Abd*! Slave! Slave!" Elias Bol realized that the reference to slave had no insulting connotations for the Northern Sudanese. Far from it, for it was a term of endearment, even though it was rooted in racial prejudices. He decided to be understanding and not to condemn his audience of colleagues and friends for turning insult into praise.

Nevertheless, Elias was very lonely in Hantoub. Oftentimes, he would sneak away to walk alone along the Blue Nile, reminiscing about home or the friends he had left in the South. He would sing Dinka songs to himself and occasionally talk out loud, punctuating his words with laughter and wondering whether he was perhaps going insane from homesickness. And yet, Elias recognized, while he ached for his own people, his habits and culture had been transformed since coming north. He was clearly conscious of the Arabization process which he was undergoing, even though he was by no means an Arab. Far from it—the more he adopted Arab ways, the more his pride as a Dinka was reinforced. It was as though accepting Arab ways was a way of validating his inner pride, the roots of which went deep to his Dinka ancestry and cultural origin. But the issues involved were so complex that he himself was not clear on how he would rate his ethnicity against the sense of submission to Arab superiority.

One morning after breakfast, Elias found Motesim Mahmoud anxiously awaiting him. "A messenger just came looking for you," he reported. "He said the headmaster wants to see you." And with characteristic curiosity, he added, "What do you think he wants to see you about?"

"I haven't the faintest idea," replied Elias with nervous indifference as he hastened away.

As he entered the headmaster's office, he was greeted with "Oh! Elias, come in," and "I called you because I have just received some good news for you."

This was just what he needed to hear.

"As you may or may not know, we have a policy here that those who do not pay their school fees by the end of the second year, that is all their arrears, are not allowed to begin their third-year work, which is when the syllabus for the school certificate begins. I should hasten to add that we do make exceptions to this policy for poor students who receive assistance from their municipal or rural councils or from other reliable sources. Realizing your needs as a Southerner, I wrote to your friend, Captain Ali, whom I understand has now become a Major, enquiring as to how you would pay your fees. He has just responded by enclosing a check to cover not only your arrears, but also all the fees for the rest of your period in this school. You are truly lucky to have such a fine Muslim for your patron. How did you meet him by the way?"

Elias was confused. He had never been directly asked about school fees. How could the headmaster have concluded that he was too poor to pay? "May I ask what the school fees are?" he asked calmly, struggling to control his temper.

"You mean you do not know? How extraordinary!"

"No one ever told me."

"It's fifteen pounds a year," the headmaster continued. "I suppose in Dinka terms you would say it would be equivalent to a cow."

"Sir," interjected Elias quickly, "don't you think my father could have paid that cow?"

"Come now, boy, don't brag," the headmaster responded sincerely. "Be grateful, be grateful," repeating himself for emphasis. "If I were you, I would write to thank Major Ali. Besides, to honor his generosity, you should work hard to benefit from being in this school. And, by the way, have you not yet considered joining Islam, the religion of our Prophet Mohammed, on whom be the Grace of God? You see the example of a good Muslim in what Major Ali has done."

Elias was now boiling with anger, his mind in too much of a turmoil to think straight. He considered walking out of the office, but that would not do any good, only more harm. He thought of striking the headmaster, but who would understand his motive for such outrageous behavior? Instead, he remained outwardly calm, which only led the headmaster into believing that he was scoring points.

"Have you ever seen my daughters?" the headmaster said surprisingly. It was entirely abnormal for a Muslim to mention his womenfolk to a stranger in that way. Elias was intrigued. He had heard much about the beauty of the daughters. Born of an attractive Egyptian mother, who, although in her forties looked more like her daughters' sister than their mother, they were coppertone in skin color, long-necked, and slender, more like classic models from an ancient pharaonic painting than contemporary beauties.

"No, I have not had the pleasure," responded Elias. "But I have heard a great deal of praise for them."

"If you were a Muslim," continued the headmaster with a cynical smile on his face, "there would be no barrier between you and them. I would be pleased and honored to give you any one of your choice. You see, to us Muslims, what counts is religion, and to a certain extent language and culture. Thanks to Major Ali, you are now in a school where you are guaranteed the last two and you are being introduced to the first. All you need to do is say, 'There is no God but Allah and Mohammed is his Prophet.' You would instantly become a Muslim, as good as any and inferior to none."

Elias decided that there was no point in arguing, for to do so would certainly end in a quarrel. Instead, he smiled with the concealed condescension of an older and the wiser man.

Challenged by the response, Mustafa—the headmaster—came back with a different argument: "Do you realize that Islam is the religion of the majority in this country?"

"Yes, sir, I do."

"Why, then, don't you believe in democracy? Why disadvantage yourself by being in the minority? After all, if you entertain any thoughts of leadership in this nation, could you possibly realize such dreams by being a *nasrani* (Christian)? My boy, you are now old enough to be wise. I am talking to you this way because I want you to be a Muslim by conviction, not by intimidation. Islam is a religion of tolerance and persuasion, not of coercion."

Elias recognized an irony. He had been taught by the Christian missionaries that Islam was indeed a religion of force, which classified non-believers as enemies who must be brought to the faith by the sword. Did Mohammed not spread his religion by the sword? Christianity on the other hand, was a religion of love which required the believer to turn the other cheek to any violent assault. But Elias could not say any of this to the headmaster and kept his thoughts to himself.

"Think about it, son; should you be convinced about the merits of Islam, no one would be happier than I. I believe you are a fine lad with a good future. Help your Lord to help you realize it."

"Thank you, sir," Elias said, now feeling disarmed by the headmaster's naive chauvinism. He did not know whether to be angry or to feel sorry for the man and all that he represented.

Motesim was eager to hear what the headmaster had wanted Elias for. When he heard the report, his only response was, "He must really like you. He is certainly not known for such an open heart. And as for his offering you one of his daughters, I know many who would jump at the suggestion. Don't be a fool; save your soul and have one of his daughters. What will Christianity give you anyway?"

Elias knew Motesim well enough by now not to be

insulted by such slurs. He knew that they were well intentioned; at least he meant no harm.

But not everyone in Hantoub wanted Elias to convert to Islam. On the contrary, his leftist colleagues championed his anti-Islamic attitude, which they encouraged against their political rivals, the Muslim Brothers. There were two main political parties in the town: the leftist Democratic Front and the rightist Muslim Brotherhood. There were also many independents who did not care for either of these parties; Motesim was among them. But they tended to be generally dismissed as lacking principles, except perhaps, bookish learning, which was not respected among the peers.

Elias had been approached by the secretary-general of the Democratic Front during his first days in school. "If you do not support us," he had reasoned, "you will be supporting our rivals, the Muslim Brothers, in whose Islamic state you would be at best reduced to the status of *ahl al-dhimma*, a second class citizen, if not worse, *ahl al-harb*, with whom the Muslims are supposed to be at war. I cannot see how there can be any doubt about your choice."

Elias's leftist leaning was as much a quest for equality as it was anti-Islamic, ironically the result of his Christian indoctrination. The fact that he tended to argue in English in which he was more fluent than his adversaries, placed them at a considerable disadvantage, much to the delight of his leftist comrades.

"How can you call Mohammed the Seal of the Prophets when all he did was to refine the Judeo-Christian principles which he had picked up in the course of his trade between Christians and Jews?" Elias would argue. "And how do you explain the fact that this man, who symbolized your Islamic purity, made his astonishing profit in trading for his mentor, Khadija, whom he later married, despite the age difference between them? And how do you explain his double standards with respect to marriage, prescribing a limit of four wives for Muslims, while he himself married twelve?"

What particularly baffled Elias was the Muslims' claim that the Koran was literally the word of God, dictated by Him to Mohammed. "After all, parts are only revised versions of the

Old and the New Testaments."

The Muslims too had their points: "Was it not blasphemy to say that God could have a son? And if indeed Jesus was the Son of God, as Christians claimed, how could he be said to have been crucified? Even as the prophet that Muslims recognized him to be, God did not permit him, according to Islam, to be sacrificed. Instead, it was made to appear to his enemies as though they had crucified him, while he was in fact saved and lifted to heaven."

And so the debate went on endlessly, sometimes heatedly, sometimes humorously, and always with Elias as the star of the show, to the great pleasure of his comrades.

Elias spent his vacations at home as always. Promoted in social status, for secondary education in the Sudan was then considered a high achievement, he occupied one of the front seats near the driver. This was considered first class, for on the back of the lorry were the ordinary folk, sitting with folded legs on the luggage sacks, cartons and barrels of goods, a trying journey that rarely ended without some squabble.

One day Elias was immersed in conversation with the driver when they heard a frantic knock on the roof of the front seat. The driver stopped the lorry. The assistant driver, who was sitting on the roof, leaned downward and said to the driver, "The slaves are fighting!"

Elias, who was sitting on the opposite end of the front seat jumped out instinctively, offended by the assistant driver's slur. The passengers were mostly Dinka with a few Arab tribesmen.

"What's the matter with you people?" Elias spoke in a reprimanding voice that combined a sense of solidarity with embarrassment. "Can't you see how dangerous it is to fight in a moving vehicle? With the lorry so crowded, don't you realize that someone is certain to be pushed?"

The passengers were stunned. They had assumed that the man sitting in front with the Arabs was an Arab, and yet there he was, speaking their language perfectly.

The quarrel suddenly turned into laughter. "Where did you learn to speak Dinka so well?" asked one elder.

Elias was about to say, "I am a Dinka," but decided against

that. "In Dinkaland," he said instead.

"By all oaths, he speaks just like a Dinka," remarked the old man smiling.

Elias realized that his people associated being educated and especially being culturally at home in Arab circles with being an Arab. He attributed that to both ignorance and social subordination. Seeing no sense in discussing it with them, he jumped back into the lorry, but not before he gave the assistant driver a stern look. "Do you realize you could end up in jail with that careless use of words?" he said to him.

Humbled and intimidated by this confident but forgiving warning, he remarked apologetically, "We are all slaves of God; but I am sorry, I did not mean to be insulting."

Elias said no more and the journey resumed.

Back in Dak-Jur, Elias told his father of the generous act of Major Ali. He wanted to repay him, but his father felt differently.

"Son," he said, "it is more gratifying to give than to receive. But it is also humiliating to have one's gift returned. Don't pay him back in money. We shall think of an appropriate present for him when you come to go."

Elias's rise in social and cultural standing was quite apparent. His long white jallabiyas, which he now wore informally at home, became the symbol of his adaptation to Northern culture, which was generally accepted as a step up the national ladder of social mobility. He now played the role of interpreter in important cases and meetings involving Arabs. And he nearly always received considerable praise from the Arabs. "Your son is no longer a Dinka," said one Arab litigant to Malengdit with naive arrogance. "He has become an Arab."

Malengdit gracefully overlooked the unintended insult and replied instead, "Yes, he has become a son of the Sudan."

Elias was on vacation after his third year at Hantoub when he received shocking news from the school. He had just returned from his habitual walk along the river in the cool temperatures of the late afternoon when his father handed him an envelope containing a letter. It was from the headmaster. Elias nervously tore the envelope open and read:

"Dear Chief, I am writing to you about your son, Elias Bol. As you know, Elias is a wonderful boy, well mannered, socially adept and very popular with both his teachers and his colleagues. But I have to tell you that we are most concerned about his future. Although he has made significant progress in Arabic and Islamic studies, he still lags behind in both and he is not likely to bridge the gap between him and his colleagues in time for the School Certificate examination. The result, we fear, will be that he will not pass well enough to qualify for the university. On the other hand, if he were to take the examination in the South, the chances are that he would excel over the Southerners in these subjects and his grades would shine much more brilliantly. I am rather reluctantly suggesting that, for his own sake, it would be better to move him back to the South.

"I might add that I have brought this issue to the attention of Major Ali, Elias's mentor, and he agrees with us, even though he desperately wanted Elias to succeed in the North. Trusting that you would also see the wisdom of our decision, we have gone ahead and arranged for his transfer back to the South.

"I should emphasize that this measure pains us badly, for we are truly very fond of Elias. We all look forward to seeing him rise up the ladder of leadership in this country."

This came as a shock to Elias. It had never occurred to him that his school work could be that bad. Why had no one intimated to him that his performance was so unsatisfactory? And how could the headmaster, whom he had learned to appreciate and even trust, connive behind his back to discuss the matter with Major Ali and then write to his father without even so much as a hint to him directly? Elias felt betrayed. He could think of no one he could trust anymore in that Northern complex. He made up his mind neither to stay in the South, nor return to Hantoub. But what would he do? He had to answer that question by himself; no one could help him.

One day, in the late afternoon, as he walked alone along the river, a thought crossed his mind: he could join the army. After all, though educated, he was from a martial culture. He thought of the age-set system by which young men were initiated and trained as warriors. He was glad that he had been spared the ordeal of initiation, but would not the same pride and the same principles of organization come in good stead as a soldier? Would not the army provide a way out of his educational fiasco?

If so, he would need a school certificate and for this, it crossed his mind that now was the time for making use of Major Ali's paternalistic sympathies. He knew exactly what to say, but would it be more effective coming from him or from his father? Both, he decided.

"Dear Major Ali," went his letter, "you have been already so helpful to me that I do not even know how to thank you, let alone ask of you another favor." The letter then went on to summarize the facts of the situation. "I have concluded that in the circumstances, the army is my best alternative and indeed my first choice. I need your help to get into the army; I need you now more than I have ever done before. I know that I will have to pass the school certificate and I am determined to do so as a private student, not from the school. Please help me!"

His father's letter, of course also written by him, since his father could not write, was mainly a cover letter for various gifts in gratitude for the help Major Ali had already given. They included a five-gallon tin of honey, another of melted butter, and a variety of locally-produced food items and handicrafts, which Malengdit and his son knew were popular among urban Arabs. "I know my son is requesting of you more services," continued the letter. "I have nothing to add to his letter on that matter except that I believe he has become as much your son as he is mine."

A few days after the letters were sent off to Major Ali, hand-carried by someone who was going to Khartoum, Elias Bol received a surprise visit from his maternal uncle, Alier, whose coming was a special pleasure to Bol and his mother, Aluel. He was seated and given water to drink, and other forms of hospitality were ordered. Alier had visited Elias whenever he returned from school or whenever it was time for him to go back—mainly in order to give a maternal uncle's blessing—but what was the purpose of his visit this time? After conversing with the company of relations and visitors, Alier asked to have a private word with his nephew. They went and sat alone under a tree.

"Son of my sister, I have heard something which is disturbing me a great deal," Alier began. "That is why I decided to come and find out from you directly whether it is true or not."

Elias could not think of anything that would disturb his uncle so much, at least nothing he himself had done. Anxiety and curiosity were reflected on his intense face.

"I understand that you want to join the army. Is that true?"

Elias was relieved that Alier's concern was only about that. He answered in the affirmative.

"You, Bol, listen to my words very carefully," Alier spoke with the air and moral authority of an older person. "In the ways of our people, the Dinka, leadership is divided into two. There are those who conduct the affairs of war, who help the warriors plan for battle and perform certain rituals before people attack or confront an attack. And I am not speaking of those who actually fight; everyone, except the chiefs and the elderly, fights when people are confronted with war. But there is another kind of leadership, which is the most important for our people, and that is the leadership of peace, the leadership of divine word, the leadership which God gave our people from the day they came out of the Byre of Creation. Those are the leaders we call the Chiefs of the Flesh, and we call them that because their spiritual power is in their blood. Those are the leaders who, when things break up between people, when there is a quarrel or a fight among members of the community, when there is a war between factions of their people, or when their people are at war with others, intervene and mediate for peace. Those are the leaders whose words have the power to mend relations when they are spoiled.

"On both sides of your family, your father's and your mother's, your ancestors have always been leaders of peace, not of war. This does not mean that members of our clans do not go to war; we fight. In fact, we are known to be good warriors. But the chief of the clan cannot go to war. He is not even supposed to witness the sight of blood when animals are sacrificed, let alone when people are fighting and killing one another. His role is to remain at home and pray for peace or for the victory of the righteous and the defeat of the aggressor. He must not condone aggression; he must fight aggression with his spiritual powers. He will draw a line on the ground and place his sacred spears on that line and call upon God and the spirits to punish those who cross his line.

"Bol, son of my sister, Chief Malengdit has no other son to assume that leadership. You are the son. How can you decide to take up arms and fight? Who will fight with the power of the word? No, I have refused."

Elias was moved by his uncle's words and in particular by his sentiments about his leadership potential, but he was also convinced that they represented a voice from the past, for the kind of leadership Alier spoke of was fast fading. The leadership that had any chance of effectiveness in the modern world had to be that which was backed by the gun. Elias did not mince his words.

"Uncle, your words have touched my heart. But I have to tell you that our world is changing and that what was true for our society yesterday may no longer be valid for today. You see, although the chiefs still manage their people through their words of wisdom, the real power which is running our country today is that of the government and it ultimately rests on the police and the army. Even those politicians who seek power through elections cannot do anything when the people with the guns rise up and decide to take over. The man called Munir is ruling this country today not because he has any spiritual authority behind him, not because of his power of words, but simply because of the guns he and his soldiers are carrying. I think it is time we backed our power of the word with the power of the gun. That is why I am joining the army."

"I hear you," responded Alier, "but you see, Bol, my father used to tell me that you would one day be a leader of your people. And my father was a man who never said a word in vain. Words for my father were precious; he never threw them away in cheap talk. Whatever my father predicted, however long it might take, always came to be as he had seen it. He was very fond of you as you know. But that is not really the point. The fact is that he saw something about you and the future of our people. I am waiting for his word to be fulfilled. I don't think my father saw you leading, backed by the power of the gun. He was a man who believed in the power of the word, backed by the will of God."

Elias appreciated his uncle's reasoning, but he had no doubt in his mind that it reflected an archaic system of values that had little or no place in the world of the nation-state.

Despite his strong moral conviction, it was Alier who eventually concluded their talk on a compromising note. "Let us leave the matter," he said. "My father is watching over you, and if what he said has any value in the world of today, he will still find a way of making it come true. Join the army and acquire your power of the gun, but the power of the word will still accompany you wherever you go and one day you will see what I am telling you."

Colonel Ali, promoted to Lieutenant Colonel from Major and transferred to Headquarters in Khartoum, responded with the wish that Elias complete his secondary education in the regular way. He assured him of admission to the military college—if he passed the school certificate and if that was truly his preference. Elias decided to sit the examination within one year. Colonel Ali also offered him accommodations at his Omdurman home where he could study with relative quiet and be helped by private tutoring. Elias accepted and traveled north immediately.

Elias quickly adjusted to Ali's household. Khadija, his wife, treated him as a son and there was no question that to her four daughters, ranging in age between six and sixteen, he was an elder brother, especially as they had no brother of their own.

Nevertheless, Elias had reason to be cautious and to keep a certain distance from the female members of the family, partly to respect the sensibilities of the Muslim culture in which he lived and partly to avoid any temptations or even misunderstandings that might happen.

The need for this caution was brought home to him one day when the sixteen-year-old Nadia passed his room and spotted him in his underwear as he was getting dressed.

Instinctively, she stopped and looked at him. Their eyes met and as though she was helpless, she stood radiating a shy sensuous smile that conveyed an unmistakable desire. Elias smiled back, embarrassed. But that might not have been a problem had Khadija not chanced to notice the way Nadia was gazing through the open door into Elias's room. As though driven by the protective maternal instinct, she shouted loud enough for both to hear, "Nadia!"

The way she pronounced the name brought both to their senses. Elias was worried that in the extremely segregated social environment of the Muslim community, even this largely innocent flirtation, on Nadia's and not his side, would be misconstrued. He very much wanted to clear the air but did not dare raise the issue himself as he might be accused of a guilty conscience.

Several days later at morning tea time, Colonel Ali spoke to Elias in a solemn voice that initially filled him with fear. "Elias, I want to tell you something that you must not misunderstand in any way. Khadija and I were talking the other day about the girls. Nadia is now quite grown up; you can say that she is a young lady. And as you know, young people are full of curiosity and a zest for life. To prevent any possible adventures, Muslim culture imposes strict controls on the contacts between men and women, boys and girls. I need not tell you that both Khadija and I see you as our son and these girls as your sisters. I have no cause to doubt anything in your attitude toward them, but I thought as an elder I should emphasize the hazards of young women being in close contact with someone who is not, strictly speaking, a full brother. In Muslim culture even cousins would be separated because they can marry one another, let alone someone unrelated by blood. It is therefore our full faith in you that is making us place no restriction between you and the girls. I thought I should just say this for your own information."

For a moment, Elias was concerned that Ali might have had reason to doubt him, but he fully appreciated the reasons he gave and in any case he was very pleased that Ali had cleared the air following the incident with Nadia. He wanted to comment on the incident, but he had nothing to say that would not sound awkward and perhaps arouse suspicion. So all he said was, "Uncle Ali, I really appreciate your talking to me about this. And I would like to take this opportunity to tell you how grateful I am for the way you have accepted me into your family. There is no way I shall ever betray that trust—with God's help."

And so from that day on, Elias made sure that he kept a safe distance from the girls although without appearing distant in his relations with them as a member of the family.

And indeed, despite his failure to continue in Hantoub, Elias was now so well versed in Arabic and Islam that it would not have been easy to distinguish him as a Southerner without personal knowledge of his background. But that was a significant factor in his identity with Colonel Ali's household.

Once during the fast of Ramadan, the nine-year-old Haleema, the third daughter, asked Elias in absolute innocence why he was not fasting.

Elias explained that he was not a Muslim.

"Why?" Haleema wondered, evidently not seeing any difference between Elias and the people around her. Elias tried to explain, but he was not convincing. This prompted him to broach the matter with Colonel Ali.

Elias was particularly concerned to know if Colonel Ali felt let down by a lad whom he had assisted so much but who had not changed his religion to suit his benefactor. "I would be interested to know your views on our religious differences," he said casually.

"There was a time when I might have urged you to be a Muslim," said Colonel Ali. "I guess I told you that when we first met. But now, as far as I am concerned, I believe that we are all human beings in the eyes of God. What counts most is how good a person is, and on that score I have no doubts about you personally or your people in general. In the South, I got to know the people rather well. If being a Muslim is a matter of one's moral conduct toward fellow human beings, I don't think they need any religion other than what they have now. But if you speak to my brother, Mohammed, then I am sure you will hear a different story."

Sheikh Mohamed Ahmed El-Jak was considerably older than his brother Ali. He had been a livestock trader in the Western Sudan and rumors had it that he had trafficked in captives from tribal warfare, not to mention in captured herds. As far as he was concerned, at least from the stories Elias heard Ali and his family tell, the world was divided into the faithful, who were Muslims, and the rest, who were supporters of the devil and therefore the legitimate subjects of raids, slavery, robbery and domination. Even the tough hand of the government, both colonial and national, did not deter him.

Elias's year at Colonel Ali's home passed rapidly as he devoted himself to studies for the school certificate, and joined the family gatherings whenever the occasion warranted. One other thing Ali also succeeded in arranging was to have Elias take the special Southern Arabic as a private candidate.

When the examinations came, Elias felt quite prepared, even though he was not over-confident. All he wanted was to pass and qualify for the military college. He did better; he got Division Two, which was good enough to take him into the university. His choice was fixed on the army, and he was enthusiastically accepted by the military college.

That he was able to wear a uniform and receive a salary immediately made joining the military college the professional promotion Elias needed after his failure in Hantoub. He really enjoyed being a cadet and even looked forward keenly to being an officer. He was intelligent, cross-culturally astute, the very model of the new Sudan.

Elias did well at the military college, and the life of discipline and comradeship seemed to suit him. When the time came for his class to graduate, Lieutenant Colonel Ali was especially proud to see Elias march forward: erect, proud and confident to receive a prize as one of best officers in the graduating class. He also delivered the speech of the graduates in almost impeccable Arabic, punctuated from time to time with "Southern" Arabic, as though to underscore the transition he had made between cultures.

"While we are well trained and prepared to confront and repel any external aggression we would like to see peace and unity consolidated at the home front," he said. "*Dushman ben akhwan bad da mafi*! (No more fighting between brothers after this)." It was an amusing shift from a Koranic verse which translated to something like: "We created you as nations and tribes to become acquainted with one another."

TWELVE

THE YEARS THAT FOLLOWED were most formative for Elias. On returning to Khartoum to report for duty after a brief vacation back home, he was informed that he had been enrolled for a year's course at Munir's Academy, which had been newly established to provide comprehensive training to government officials, civilians and the military of all levels, in national administration. It was a year of hard work as students, young, mid-career and even accomplished leaders, discovered that what they had known about government and international politics was only fragmentary. The variety of the student body brought into the classroom an array of professional knowledge and perspectives. There were economists, historians, theologians, scientists, military officers, and diplomats. The teaching staff, which included regular members of the Academy and visiting lecturers, was equally varied.

Daunted by the realization of what there was to be learned and the richness of what others had to offer, everyone worked studiously to earn the diploma which the academy offered at the end of the course.

Strengthened by his brilliant performance at the military college and stimulated by the broad approach to knowledge and its application, Elias found his year at the Academy a most gratifying experience. He distinguished himself although some of his colleagues viewed his contribution with mixed feelings. They felt that he was both sharp witted and exhibitionist.

It was a full year for Elias and it certainly went by very fast. Apart from occasional weekend visits to Colonel Ali and other friends, his time was devoted to his classwork and reading relevant materials. Some of his friends at the Academy teased him by calling him *kabbab,* "Book-worm."

As the course was coming to an end, General Awad Mohamed Nimir, the head of the Academy, visited the class one morning, dressed in a dark civilian suit. The purpose of his visit was to discuss with the students their appraisal of the course and the Academy in general. As might be expected, everyone had glowing words of praise. But Elias felt uncomfortable about this. Weren't his classmates endearing themselves rather too transparently to a man who still had favors to hand out in the form of diplomas? Elias raised his hand to speak.

"Of course, I share what my colleagues have said about this wonderful institution. It is not only a source of tremendous knowledge, but it can make a major contribution in preparing citizens to play a constructive role in building this nation. But, I have two questions, and they are not really directed to the Academy, but to the government. First, why should such an excellent approach to knowledge be confined to one institution? It is true that students for the Academy come from a variety of professional backgrounds and government circles and they are expected to take back the lessons they learn here and apply them. But whatever the numbers admitted by the Academy, those who graduate from here will be a drop in the ocean. Their impact will remain minimal. What we are doing in this institution is training a select few who will become a superfluous elite that has no place in the real world out there, not because they have nothing to offer, but because what they know will seem out of place to those with whom they will work.

"And yet, the idea of seeing knowledge as an interrelated whole is a reflection of the real world, whether we are talking of the way the government actually functions or of life in general. The approach of the Academy is one which can apply to virtually all institutions of learning, from elementary schools to universities. Why do we have to wait until so much later in life and then restrict the approach to only one institution, called Munir's Academy. If anything at all, I believe the success of this academy highlights the failure of our educational system, both academic and professional. Perhaps this is a message which those responsible for the Academy should pass on to those in charge of the country.

"My second question may be more sensitive, but I voice it in a spirit of loyalty and dedication to this country. I wonder why the Academy was named after Munir. With due respect to the president of the republic, I believe that the name conveys the impression that the Academy is a place for political indoctrination. While political orientation may be an understandable part of the curriculum, political brain-washing certainly has no place in the Academy. If I were to think of a name, I would call it the Sudan Academy for National and Strategic Studies. Perhaps the administration of the institution might consider suggesting to the government that the name be changed to something which reflects its content, rather than a name which carries political or ideological overtones."

Elias argued his points effectively and it was obvious from the absorbed attention of the audience that he was receiving a favorable hearing, until the very end when he seemed to have entered some dangerous waters. The political system was, after all, a virtual dictatorship. Elias's criticism was directed at the country's leader, and therefore whatever merit there might be in what he said, his remarks could not be sympathetically received, far less publicly acknowledged.

General Nimir was plainly embarrassed. He may have agreed with Elias's point, but he could not let any degree of criticism of the government, especially criticism that went so close to the top, pass without scrutiny. Yet, to reprimand a young military officer for his astuteness was not an easy task. Looking confused and hesitant, he responded to Elias's statement by commending him on recognizing the wider contexts of lessons to be learned at the Academy, but went on to reprove him for criticisms of the government. "I really think it is illogical and unfair to criticize the government for having done the right thing in one place and not applied it everywhere immediately. The Academy is new. We are only beginning to see the fruits of our experiment. How can one say that we should have known that the idea would work so well and should have applied it everywhere? After all, that's what knowledge is about: you have to experience, learn from the experience and then find ways of applying the lessons learned. We have not even had enough time to know what we have learned, let alone apply the lessons elsewhere."

As if emboldened by the power of his reasoning, General Nimir became increasingly angry with Elias as he continued.

"As for your criticism of the name, may I point out that this is clearly a matter of high policy on which I see no room for a demonstration of egotistical wisdom? May I remind you that you have naively overlooked the wisdom of the whole national government? I find your views insubordinate."

But instead of being cowed by the general's remarks, Elias rose to rebutt him. He felt politically driven to state his views loudly and clearly. Raising his hand and half rising, he shouted, "Sir, sir, I beg your pardon. I must object to your treatment of my remarks. If this is the way the leadership is supposed to educate our youth, then I daresay that the rumors on the streets about the May Revolution being a dictatorship are not without foundation. I sincerely hope that what we have just seen displayed is a personal attitude that does not reflect the thinking of our national leadership, or else this country is in trouble. And frankly, I don't care what happens to me; where I come from, the youth are brought up to speak their minds as men."

Elias's anger surprised Nimir. He realized that his comments had been severe, but he never anticipated to receive that kind of reaction from a student. Strangely enough, however, Elias's anger had a pacifying effect on the general.

"If I may say one last word," he spoke with a contrasting calmness, "one of the lessons we hope to teach students in this institution is the value of the spoken word and knowing what to say and when to say it. Brother Elias, I am afraid that is all I need to tell you at this point. I wish you all the best back in your institutions. *Salaam aleikum."* And with those words,

General Nimir got up and left.

Elias was still fuming with anger and was in fact totally disorientated. He could say nothing to salvage the situation without humiliating himself. So he quietly withdrew to reflect. Those colleagues of his who were jealous of his conspicuousness, felt that he got what he deserved. One of his Southern colleagues told him later that, as the crowd left, he had heard someone say, "The slave has done it to himself." He told Elias that he had felt deeply angry not only at the man, but also at Elias for what seemed like blind faith in the Arabs. "Brother, I don't know what you see in these people that makes you trust them. I tell you, I almost cried when I heard that voice and recalled your ways with them."

Elias received the news with silence. He realized that his Southern colleague was speaking from the heart, and was sincere. But he was not impressed by simply reporting such things. He was indeed surprised that someone who had been so outraged would not care to know precisely who had made the statement and confront him directly. Elias felt that he himself would not have tolerated such a slur. His Southern colleague obviously wanted him to feel insulted and become politically antagonized against the Arabs.

Elias wondered whether he should go to General Nimir to try to explain himself and mend fences, but he felt his pride inhibited him. He had said what he believed and he still believed what he had said. But perhaps he should not have been so rude to the man. He could not help but worry about the possible implications. Time passed and nothing happened. Elias began to regain his equilibrium. It had perhaps been an episode that would be forgotten.

When the list of graduating students came out, Elias's name was not among them. He knew that the reason must be related to the episode with General Nimir. He immediately went to the general's office to ask for an appointment, but was informed that the general was in a meeting and had a full day. The secretary promised to call him back with a date. But Elias waited for days without a call and his own calls went unanswered. He concluded that something quite serious was amiss.

He decided to consult Ali, now a brigadier general, who immediately undertook to give General Nimir a call. Ali asked Elias to come to his office the following day. When he arrived, he greeted Elias and took the phone to dial. "Let me see what's up with these people."

"Is the general in?" he asked when the secretary answered, "this is Brigadier General Ali speaking."

Ali was well-regarded in military circles; his name was a password for cooperation.

"Hello!" came the deep voice of General Nimir. The usual courtesies of greetings were exchanged. And then Ali got to the point by simply asking why Elias's name was not on the list of graduates. It was apparent from his long silence and the way his face changed from smiles to a solemn look that the explanation given by General Nimir was both long-winded and unsatisfactory.

"So your opinion is that he should first wait until the president responds?" Ali posed a question that revealed the magnitude of the problem to Elias.

The response was clearly in the affirmative.

"Well, thank you General... Goodbye."

Ali turned to Elias with a melancholy face. "As you could probably tell, he didn't reveal much. He said there are some issues surrounding your graduation which are still being looked into by the President and that he was not at liberty to explain further. However, he expected that the President would give his opinion on the matter quite soon. So, he suggests that you just wait."

"What issues could possibly require a resolution by the president?" Elias asked.

"Well, you know this country," Ali tried to explain. "What you explained to me could be enough for someone to build an accusation with. Anyway, let me have a word with the Vice President, Field Marshal Khalid Abd el-Mageed. He is a very understanding man. You know him, don't you?"

"Oh yes!" responded Elias. "I first met him when he came to the college and gave a lecture on strategy. And I believe I told you that he has been teaching us 'Diplomacy and Military Intelligence' at the Academy. He is a sharp man."

Field Marshal Khalid Abd el-Mageed also held the portfolio of Minister of Defense in addition to being Vice President. He was widely known as a man of great courage and integrity. Khalid was a much younger man than his military rank and position in government reflected. He had been top of his class in military college and had studied in military academies abroad. He had gone through a series of accelerated promotions that rapidly took him to the top. He was a man who combined military discipline with a sense of camaraderie toward his officers and men. He was also a courteous person who seemed to believe that leaders owed their followers as much respect as they received. And in his case, the two clearly reinforced each other.

As is generally the case with teachers of bright students, Field Marshal Khalid felt a special sense of affection and support for Elias. He had always enjoyed his contributions in class. So, when Ali presented Elias's case and asked the field marshal to see the young officer, an appointment was immediately made.

The warm manner in which the field marshal greeted him relaxed Elias and made him realize that all could not be as hopeless as it had begun to seem. After a brief period of greeting, Khalid, who realized that Elias had come to see him with a serious problem, soon got to the point.

"I am delighted to see you, but I know you are here for a purpose. What is it?" The field marshal opened the subject.

Elias furnished the details as Khalid listened with deep absorption and without interruption. When Elias had finished, all Khalid said was, "You will appreciate that I cannot say anything until I have full information on the situation. As soon as I know what is going on, I will contact you. But one thing you can be sure of is that I will endeavor to see justice done, if indeed there has been injustice. On the other hand, if the facts reveal some other explanation that you may not know, I will tell you."

Elias waited for a week, but it seemed like a month as each day came and went with hopes fading by the hour. He wondered whether he should go back to Field Marshal Khalid. But he decided against it. After all, he had said he would call him. For Elias to take the initiative again would not only show too much anxiety but also indicate a lack of confidence. In any case if the field marshal had something positive to report he would certainly have heard from him.

Elias had virtually reconciled himself to his ill-fate when he received a call from General Nimir's secretary. The general wanted to see him. When he got to the office, he found the general in a friendly mood that seemed transparently contrived.

"Greetings, greetings!" he bellowed as he rose and extended his hand.

They shook hands and Elias sat across the desk from the general. "I apologize for not having been able to see you sooner," General Nimir began, " but it has been an extremely hectic period. I take it that you misread my not returning your call soon enough as some form of evasion."

"Well. . .," Elias began to comment.

"No, you don't have to explain," interrupted the general. "I perfectly understand. I would have concluded the same under similar circumstances. In any case, don't worry about it."

As though he had just resolved a critical dilemma, General Nimir smiled even more warmly and announced: "Now, Elias, I am going to be very frank with you and I hope you appreciate my situation. After our meeting in which you spoke about the Academy and how the government ought to apply the same idea to other educational institutions, as I had feared, your message was taken by responsible individuals and passed on to the President. In fairness to him, he called me to discuss the situation. His main concern was not that there was anything harmful or even wrong in what you had said, but rather to see in what way we could work with you to look more fully into your ideas and see whether we could even develop from them a government policy. That is why the President advised that we postpone your graduation to a later date.

"After you spoke with the Vice President, he apparently went and discussed the situation with the President and they agreed on a different approach. You will graduate and be assigned to the Vice President's Office, that is the Office of the Minister of Defense at the Armed Forces Headquarters. He would like you to be closely associated with the Department of Military Intelligence and hopes to work with you in formulating and developing the ideas you expressed here.

"And now, it is my greatest pleasure to inform you that you are not only graduating, but were among the best in your class. Congratulations."

Elias was overwhelmed. He had no words to express his profound gratitude for those who had turned the wheels of justice. He knew that Field Marshal Khalid must have been a prime mover even if General Nimir was not. He realized that the Sudan was a country of inbred egalitarianism and that no leader could really afford to disregard anyone, however junior, for his own day might come and with it reprisals. So, quite apart from acting in accordance with the dictates of his superiors, whom he was careful not to antagonize, General Nimir was also intent on becoming reconciled with Elias, especially as he was moving closer to the center of political power.

Although the names of those graduating had been published, the adjustment in Elias's situation happened in time for him to join his colleagues in the graduation ceremonies. The occasion was attended by President Munir who presented the prizes to the best students. As Elias received his prize, Munir commented teasingly, "You should have been awarded a prize for the improvement from a near-miss to a hit!"

As he had expected, Elias very much enjoyed his assignment with Khalid Abd el-Mageed. Through the Office of the Vice President, he acquired considerable insight into the way the system worked. And his sources were not merely the papers that passed his desk, but also the people who were eager to offer information as part of their sometimes subtle and sometimes blatant efforts to influence decisions at the vice presidential level.

Through his connections with Military Intelligence, Elias also acquired an understanding of the geopolitical situation of the country and of the potential sources of insecurity beyond the borders of its eight neighbors. The Ethiopian border continued to be a problem area and a source of massive refugee influx. Uganda and Zaire were also crisis areas and sources of refugees. The upheavals in Chad were spilling over the Sudanese borders and the balance of internal power oscillated from one group to another. And then there was Libya on the northwestern border, waiting to seize every opportunity to meddle. Indeed, several years back, a resistance movement had invaded the country from Libyan bases by smuggling large quantities of weapons and ammunition across the borders and transporting them to the capital city undetected. Having planted themselves in strategic positions throughout the Three Towns, they had waited for the zero hour and had staged a ferocious attack which, though eventually repelled, had been enormously costly in material and human terms. A subsequent reconciliation with the resistance had improved the security situation on that front, but the enmity between the Libyan leader and Jabir El-Munir remained acute.

With all these trouble spots surrounding its extensive and uncontrollable international borders, Sudan appeared to be an island with turbulent waters threatening to erode its every shore. The Egyptian front seemed relatively calm, with a program of close cooperation that some called collaboration and others gave a more involved title of integration. But even there, Sudan's support for the Camp David Accords between Egypt and Israel was provoking hardliners in the Arab world to distance themselves from a poor country in need of their material support, especially in the vital area of energy. Some of them even looked favorably on any internal weaknesses that might lead to the regime's downfall.

And indeed, internally, the country was in a precarious state. The peace accord that had granted autonomy to the South and ended a seventeen year civil war was beginning to crack as local leaders intrigued among themselves and fell easy prey to manipulation at the national level. And while the peace accord remained in a delicate balance, other regions in the North were beginning to assert their local identities and make demands for autonomy similar to that which the South had obtained by war. The Western provinces and Darfur in particular posed a formidable challenge to the centralization of power. Over and above that, intertribal warfare was on the increase. The Arab tribes of the West and the non-Arab tribes of that region and further South had frequent, violent clashes in which hundreds of people lost their lives, thousands of cattle and other forms of livestock were seized and misappropriated, and women and children were captured and subjected to various forms of indignity.

Time passed quickly as one incident after another brought news of the state of turmoil that the country was passing through to the headquarters. For Elias, tragic as these day-to-day events were, there was something positive about the way in which his vision was expanding to encompass the nation as a whole. It even began to make him sensible to the national dimensions of problems he had previously assumed to be peculiar to the South. He was increasingly realizing that what the South had suffered also affected the West, the East and perhaps areas of the North as well. The nation was painfully coming of age and discovering itself. Elias felt he was learning a great deal about the country he had chosen to defend, if need be with his own life.

His hatred of the Arabs was mellowing. What he hated now were not the Arabs as a race, but their prejudices and injustices against non-Arabs, notably Southerners and Westerners. Even here, he was conscious of exceptions, for he had discovered individual Northerners who were excellent human beings by any standard. How would he classify people like Ali and Field Marshal Khalid if he were to continue his blanket hatred of the Arabs, their prejudices or injustices? He even began to notice a pattern whereby those with merit reflected virtue while those with deep rooted insecurities and personal inadequacies tended to thrive on group prejudice and injustices which they believed were in their interests to pursue. Elias preferred to identify himself with the virtuous individuals whom he saw as having leadership opportunities and responsibilities for shaping the destiny of the nation.

Elias was reflecting on these issues when a file was brought to his desk bearing the tragic news of yet another outbreak of intertribal fighting between the Rizeigat of southern Darfur and the Dinka of northern Bahr El Ghazal. The reports from Darfur merely said that lives had been lost on both sides and cattle seized, but that security authorities had restored order and established full control over the situation. The reports from Bahr El Ghazal were more detailed. They said that the fighting had resulted from an escalation of minor incidents involving individual Dinkas and Arabs. An Arab had insulted Dinkas as *"abeed,"* slaves, and had been beaten to death. As a result, the Arabs had ambushed some Dinka youths and, after torturing them, killed them. They had then amputated their arms and used them for beating their drums. When the Dinka counterattacked, they had been met by the security forces mixed with Arab *marahleen,* armed tribal militiamen, who had opened fire on them and killed many people. As the Dinka ran, the security forces permitted the Arab tribesmen to seize their herds.

Elias was asked to prepare a file for the minister, including any comments he deemed appropriate. It was naturally a difficult assignment, since it concerned a conflict between his own people and the Arabs. But Elias also felt that this was an opportunity to display his widening national vision and to assure people like Field Marshal Khalid that their investment in him was in the service of the nation as a whole. Elias was determined to be cool-headed and objective in his analysis of the information available to him, both from the specific reports at hand and from other sources.

"What comes through in the different ways the incidents are reported by Bahr El Ghazal and Darfur regions," he wrote in a memorandum on the situation, "is that these divisive intertribal conflicts impose an enormous strain on our security forces in those areas. The Army is supposed to be national and our job is to defend the country from foreign threats. We are supposed to defend every inch of our national territory and every Sudanese life against foreign aggression. But soldiers are subject to human weaknesses. And they are not always above local problems; quite the contrary, they are often recruited from those very local communities with mutual animosities which their profession calls upon them to transcend. When a nation is divided into tribes, races, or religions which engage in internal wars, the military certainly gets confronted with a dilemma. On the one hand, they must be above the differences and fight to restore peace and order evenhandedly. On the other hand, they share the natural sentiments and loyalties of the communities to which they unavoidably belong. Many succeed in living up to the challenge of maintaining the integrity of the army; but I suspect that almost as many fall short of this ideal.

"The greatest challenge that will continue to face the leaders of this nation for some time to come is, I believe, how to rise above these dividing lines and work for the interest of the Sudanese people as a whole, without bias or prejudice on the grounds of tribe, race, or religion. The testing ground for that kind of leadership is now the army, since it is one of the institutions that takes pride in being national in philosophy, composition and manner of operation.

"Put in other words, it seems to me that while the army is national, the challenge of internal divisiveness on the basis of tribe, race, or religion seems to be taken so much for granted that it is not explicitly or consciously addressed in military college and on-the-job training. For a country as large and diverse as the Sudan with numerous warlike tribes where martial values are inculcated from an early age, I believe this dimension ought to be given special attention in preparing our army to meet all internal threats to our national security, unity and nation-building."

Two days after he had submitted his report, Elias was summoned by the minister. He felt his heart suddenly quicken: Was he in trouble again because of the views he had expressed? And yet, he was sure that he had expressed what he believed. Had this, too, been discussed in military college and had he been criticized for his views?

As soon as he entered the minister's office, the warm manner in which the field marshal greeted him made him relax immediately.

"Come on, sit down," Khalid said as he gestured Elias to one of the chairs in front of his large executive desk.

"I read your report. You certainly made a daring comment on our response to this chronic problem of intertribal warfare.

On the whole, I agree with your analysis. How one deals with the problem in devising curriculum for the military college or for the field training of officers and men is quite another matter. But I called you because reading your report gave me an idea which I thought I should test on you to see how amenable you would be to it.

"You see, you are a young man and judging from your performance to date, you have good leadership prospects in this country. I say this not to flatter you, but in fact to challenge you. It occurred to me that you should perhaps serve in situations that will expose you to the problems you so well describe, help broaden your understanding of them and develop a method of approaching them that is both creative and concretely based. I suggest that you undertake an assignment in Darfur which will combine your military duties with research and intelligence responsibilities. I would like you to observe firsthand how our security forces are dealing with local conflicts and how these problems intersect with the broader issues facing the nation. How would you like that?"

"Very much, sir," responded Elias with surprise and happiness. "It sounds most exciting."

"Wonderful," commented the minister. "My idea is that you carry on your other duties normally, but share with me your observations and analyses of this particular aspect in periodic reports addressed to me personally. I realize that your regular duties might be too demanding to allow time for this other assignment. But that should not worry you. Whatever time you are able to put into it will be adequate. Remember, this is a personal assignment, one that is entirely novel. Needless to say, you will have to discharge it very discreetly."

"That's very thoughtful of you, sir," responded Elias. "I really do appreciate the confidence you have placed in me."

"You deserve it," replied the minister. "Oh, by the way, when you come to go, I suggest that you travel to the West by land. That way you give yourself time to relax and reflect and also observe the physical environment of the country in which you will operate."

"Certainly, sir," agreed Elias.

Elias prudently decided to keep the information to

himself. If the minister wanted to say something to some-
body, that would be his own business. In due course, the list
of transfers came out and as he had expected, Elias was
transferred to El Fasher.

PART FOUR
SERVICE

THIRTEEN

WITHIN DAYS OF RECEIVING his assignment, Elias boarded the train and headed for Nyala, where he would proceed to El Fasher by military transport. Assisted with his luggage by friends and colleagues, he made his way through the crowds at the railway station toward the first-class car. Once inside, they began to look for his name on the lists posted on all the doors. He had a reservation in a compartment which he was to share with three other passengers.

Among the passengers in his cabin was a man who seemed to be in his late thirties, quite dark in color and dressed in a safari suit. It was obvious to Elias from the outset that the man was eager to talk to him. They had barely sat down when the man began to speak in an accented Arabic that indicated it was not his mother tongue. Elias gathered he must be from one of the non-Arab tribes of the West.

"Where are you going?" his compartment mate inquired.

"El Fasher."

"Are you visiting relatives or posted there?"

"I am going there on a new posting."

"A new posting?" he repeated. "Where were you before?"

"At the headquarters, where I was assigned after leaving the military college. Well, not quite, I first went to Munir's Academy."

"I take it you are from the South?" he asked, with qualified certainty in his voice.

Elias confirmed he was.

"To tell you the truth, you could have been from the West."

"Are you yourself from the West?"

"I am indeed. By the way, my name is Osman Jar-Ennabi. I am a trader."

"My name is Elias Bol Malek. Where do you come from in Darfur?"

"El Fasher. I trade between El Fasher, El Obeid, and Omdurman."

"What do you trade in?" Elias asked.

"Name it and I sell it; I may even buy it, too!" Osman responded and chuckled.

Something in the way he laughed made what he said about his trade sound somewhat sinister, even suspect. All three of the others in the cabin seemed to share the same thought: might Osman be engaged in an illegal trade, perhaps in elephant tusks or in some forbidden item? But Osman seemed to read what was on their minds and, speaking as if in an afterthought, said, "Seriously, I trade in gum arabic, livestock, groundnuts and hides. As you can see, that is quite a collection of items. But my biggest volume is in livestock and gum arabic, although the encroachment of the desert is affecting the production of gum."

The other two had engaged in a side conversation which left Elias and Osman on their own for a time. When they rejoined the conversation, the other two introduced themselves. One was the headmaster of an intermediate school in Dilling and the other was an engineer with Chevron in Muglad, both in southern Kordofan. With such a wide occupational range, they all had something to contribute as the evening progressed.

As though he had sized up the group and decided that he could afford to relax with them, Osman pulled out a bottle of Johnny Walker Black Label and suggested that it was time for a drink before the *farasheen*, the waiters, called them to the dining car for dinner. Raising the bottle as if to show his companions what he was about to offer them, he remarked, "Can you believe that the gentleman whose picture you see on this bottle was born in the 1880s and is still going strong because he drinks this stuff?"

"*Bi-llahi el-azim*? By God Almighty?" queried the headmaster naively.

"Got you!" Osman teased, much to the amusement of the others, who understood the joke from the whiskey advertisement. "I will have the first sip, not because I am selfish, which I am, but to prove that it is not poison, which it is."

His companions laughed. He took his sip and relished the taste with an "eeeh," then went on to say, "No wonder our Lord forbade it; it's too good." And then looking into his bag, he remarked, "I think I have two glasses," and looked for a response.

"I will have some, thank you," said the engineer.

He gave him a glass, poured another one and offered it to the headmaster. "*Lazim ya'ani*? Is it a must?" he said in a manner of politeness.

"Come on, *ya ustadh*—teacher—don't be vague or you might get a Haig instead of a Johnny Walker." Osman was recalling a big sign advertising Haig whiskey in the center of Khartoum. It read: "Don't be vague; ask for Haig."

The engineer got the joke and laughed. After explaining his joke to the headmaster, Osman went on to say, "*Ustadh*, we have a long way to go; I assure you this will make it shorter. Besides, we need educators in hell."

They all laughed as the headmaster surrendered with: "If you insist!"

"I sure do," Osman gave the expected response and poured a drink.

It was now Elias's turn. "Last, but by no means least, brother officer," declared Osman as he poured a drink. "It is the age not the job that relegates you to waiting," he said as he handed Elias the drink.

"Thank you, I don't drink," said Elias, "but not because our Lord forbade it."

"Propriety, I suppose," commented Osman with subtle indignation.

Elias understood Osman's sensitivity and responded

accordingly. "I have had my share in childhood, for at home we drink *merisa* freely. Then the older I got, the less I became inclined to drink. But I assure you, I have no qualms about people enjoying themselves."

Osman sipped the drink and breathing out rather heavily, looked as though he was deliberately getting himself into a state of rapid self-liberation. But it was not an obnoxious condition, merely more of the extroverted character he had already displayed.

"Well, officer, I do not know whether I would qualify for what you might call moderation," Osman said in his newly induced mood, "but I find myself sick and tired of these so-called holy men who come to the West and preach against alcohol while they commit worse crimes against humanity. It's as though they believe they can deceive the Almighty into thinking that they are innocent, even virtuous, because they do not drink. I tell you, they are among the things that drive me to drink."

"Well, as I said, far from prohibiting *merisa*, for us God and the ancestors expect to be honored with beer on special occasions and, in any case, always receive a share of libation on any festive occasions of beer drinking," Elias explained, as though to encourage Osman to feel at home with him. "You must first pour some drops on the ground before you proceed to drink."

"Now, *that* is the religion in which I would find devotion," remarked Osman. "What do you call the religion of your people?"

"It does not have a special name," explained Elias. "It is part of a way of life and it touches virtually all aspects of living. It is like asking a people what they call their culture. A culture is the people and so are their religious beliefs and practices."

"It sounds good to me," said Osman, "as long as someone who believes himself to be God's spokesman does not come to tell me what that culture is supposed to be, instead of what it is and has been for ages. Often, while posing as the mouthpiece for God, they bleed the poor innocent people to death with exploitation." Turning to the group as a whole, he went on, "In the name of God, can anyone of you honest men here tell me what the big shots whose families lead the religious sects do for a living? Let's go even further back: can you tell me what their fathers and grandfathers did for a living? I'll tell you: they made the poor ignorant masses toil the land for them in the superstitious belief that they would be blessed and guaranteed heaven after death. That is, if they did not extort contributions which the poor could ill afford, but which all combined made their masters millionaires before our language knew that figure in counting. As you know, we still do not have the word, even in Arabic, only an adopted version of the English word."

Osman's companions seemed to enjoy his wit, even though they realized that he was becoming increasingly intoxicated.

Facing the headmaster and addressing him as "sheikh," a title that carries pedagogic and spiritual connotations, Osman said, "You, our sheikh, answer this question for me. You are a man of learning and learning brings wisdom, which is disguised by God. Who should go to hell, the man who drinks and maybe gets drunk without hurting anyone or those who take advantage of the ignorant masses and make them slave for their gain?"

"I understand what you mean," the headmaster responded in a polite evasion.

"I should have known that you would be too polite to give me an honest to God answer," Osman said with a sense of humor that all, including the headmaster, appreciated with laughter.

Then turning to Elias, he said, "Brother officer," and stopping in mid sentence, he queried, "what did you say your name was again?"

"Elias."

"Yes, of course, Elias," he said. "You are a better Muslim than I am, even though you are a Southerner. Let me get your opinion on this."

"But I am not a Muslim," Elias intimated. "I am a Christian."

"By God?" Osman remarked. "What is a Christian doing with a Muslim name?"

"Well, Elias is also a Christian name!" Elias explained.

"I knew from the moment I saw you that you were a clever fellow! Imagine keeping your Christian faith with a name that makes the Muslim majority believe that you are a Muslim! That's really clever."

"It was never intended that way," Elias explained as he and others laughed.

"Never mind whether it was intended," Osman interjected. "It's the result that counts. And that is certainly clever."

By now, Osman seemed to have forgotten his original question. Instead, as though he had exhausted the topic, he suggested that it was time for them to eat something. "I always eat when I drink," he said. "They say that alcohol likes meat and when it finds no meat in the stomach, it starts eating the stomach itself. And that is when drinking really leads to hell."

They agreed to eat, but rather than go to the dining car, they decided to order their food in the compartment. Again it was Osman who got up to negotiate with the *farasheen* and returned victorious. "Certainly, money cannot buy everything, but it can do a great deal."

The waiter was very cooperative. He brought their food and cleared the compartment after they had eaten. It was then that the headmaster and the engineer adjusted their sleepers and went to bed. Before long, it was clear from their snores that they were fast asleep.

Elias was also thinking of going to sleep when Osman opened another topic with him. "Brother. . ." he began and realized that he had again forgotten his name.

"Elias!" Elias came to his aid.

"Brother Elias, I know that you are loyal to the regime. You have to be; after all, you are an officer in the army. So you must be loyal, correct?"

Elias did not respond in words, only with a gesture of smiling polite accommodation. But Osman could not be so easily dismissed.

"Am I not correct?" he repeated. But this time he did not wait for an answer. He went on: "Well, let me tell you the truth: I don't care what happens to me; I believe in telling the truth. And if the truth should kill me, my children will be there to carry my name with pride."

As though he had now in some way established his credentials, he continued, "You see, this Munir—people are not fair to him. Those who praise him and those who condemn him are both right and wrong. Like all of us, he has virtues and weaknesses. Can you question the remarkable virtue he has shown in granting autonomy to the South? May I be obliged to divorce my wife, I swear that the settlement with the South will remain his greatest achievement.

"The mistake he made was to think that the South was the only part of the country in which autonomy was needed. And what reason did he give? He said that the South was racially and culturally different from the North. My God, the man believed that all the rest of the country, the West, the East and the North, were Arab. How ignorant can one be of this country? You do not need to have studied history or geography to know that the North is not all Arab. I mean, here in the West, say in Darfur, how many Arab tribes are there?"

Counting with his fingers, he enumerated the tribes: "The cattle tribes, the Baggara, include the Habaniya, the Taisha, the Rizeigat and the Ben Halba. And their brothers who own camels are the Mahriya, with their branches, the Eregat and the Jallab. But what about the people after which the region is named, the Fur, my own people? We are not Arabs. And talk about numbers. Our people are really numerous. And how many branches are there among the Fur?"

And again using both hands, he counted on his fingers: "There are the Dajo, the Birgit, the Masalit, the Tamaa, and the Zaghawi. And we too have our Fertit tribes who are also non-Arab. Don't think that the Fertit exist only in your Southern province of Bahr El Ghazal. I take it you are from Bahr El Ghazal, aren't you?"

"Yes, I am," responded Elias.

"I don't know why I thought so. I suppose because you are a Dinka. Am I right?"

"Yes, you are," agreed Elias. "I am a Dinka. How did you know?"

"Didn't I tell you I had kidneys," he remarked, pointing

to his head. They laughed. "Who but the Dinka would be as tall as you are?" Osman observed.

"Well, there are the Nuer and the Shilluk, other Nilotic peoples," Elias explained.

"Of course. Actually, in Darfur we also have very tall people. But I have strayed away from my original point. Where were we?"

"You were talking about the tribes of Darfur, Arabs and non-Arabs," Elias recalled. "You were enumerating the Fur tribes and the Fertit as the non-Arab peoples of the region."

"Yes, thank you," acknowledged Osman. "I must confirm that forgetfulness is one of the evils of alcohol. Anyway, going back to the people of Darfur, for God's sake, even those tribes that are described as Arab are not full-blooded Arabs; they are a mixture of Arab and non-Arab blood.

"You see, I travel a great deal in this country. I have seen the people of the East, those tribes called the Beja, like the Hadendewa. Those people are no different from the Ethiopians. And they speak their own languages. As for Arabic, they speak it as a foreign language and very poorly too. Coming to the hinterland, the Danagala also have their own languages. And of course the Nubians of the extreme North remain to this day very proud of their non-Arab race and language.

"So, how can one say that the country is racially and culturally divided into the Africans of the South and the Arabs of the North? That is sheer nonsense."

Osman had stopped drinking. In fact, he had become quite sober and politically charged. Elias was interested in what he had to say, even when he had been a little tipsy. Now that he was becoming more coherent, the power of his words was growing stronger and stronger as was the logic of his argument.

"You see, the rulers in Khartoum are really ignorant of the country they are running," he went on. "They reproduce themselves and believe that they are the people of this country, while they remain isolated in their air-conditioned shelters over there in the Three Towns. They even forget that Darfur was an independent state until 1916 when the British had already subdued the rest of the country, or the North at least. Of course, we adopted Islam and elements of Arab culture, but we adapted them to our local conditions. We never claimed to be Arabs. What makes them think that we are going to be better people by claiming to be Arabs?

"What I really want to say is that the conditions that warranted granting regional autonomy to the South apply to the West and to the East as well. They include the unfair distribution of power and national resources between the center and the regions. And for many of us in the West, they also include the way our values have been misrepresented to the world as Arab.

"You remember we here in the West, in Darfur and in Kordofan, pressured the regime to extend the autonomy of the South to other areas of the North and especially the West. I assure you our people were prepared to take up arms and struggle the way the South had struggled. But Munir is no fool. He responded by giving regional autonomy to the rest of the North. For that, he also deserves to be praised."

Elias was becoming impressed by Osman's perceptiveness. He could not be the simple trader he introduced himself as. Who was he really? And what was his political stance on the critical issues facing the country?

Osman read Elias's mind and decided to press on. "Let me tell you where Munir fell short. He still seems to believe that the North is different from the South and that the West is part of the North. So, what does he do? He gives the North a system of autonomy far weaker than that of the South. And what is more, he himself retains the power to appoint governors of the northern regions. He even tried to impose his will on the people of Darfur. But again, our people asserted themselves and were prepared to fight and die for their rights. Once more, Munir was clever; he compromised in time. Actually, he conceded on two significant issues. First, he accepted the demand of Darfur to be a separate region instead of being lumped together with Kordofan, where we would have been subjected to the will of the Arab majority and their mentors in Khartoum. And when he wanted to appoint a man from Kordofan to be our governor, we stood firm until he conceded to our demand for one of our own people to be leader. That is how he appointed Hamid El-Dergawi, our present governor. His name, which I believe is that of his grandfather, means the shield; he is our shield against the powers in Khartoum."

Although it was now the early hours of the morning, Elias was engrossed by the conversation. He felt he could not have wished for a better introduction to the region. Osman too felt pleased with the opportunity of orienting an officer, for that matter a Southerner, who was about to commence duty in his region.

"Let me tell you, Brother. . ."

"Elias."

"Brother Elias, although our people have scored some victories against the authorities in Khartoum, our struggle is far from over. In fact, it has just begun. I can tell you in all honesty that the biggest obstacle facing our people in the South and the West is lack of unity. We are divided by the clever politicians in Khartoum. And they are using Islam and Arab culture to create barriers between peoples. Here is where I blame our leaders. Their vision has not gone beyond the walls which our enemies have so skillfully built to divide us.

"Brother, let me be absolutely candid with you. Many of us Westerners see you people from the South as slaves and even as heathens. But look at me, is there any difference between your color and mine? And if people were to judge from our features, do you really think that they could segregate you and me into two different racial groups? I mean this country is really confused, and the people responsible are right there in Khartoum, splendidly isolated from the real Sudan and yet playing with our lives in racial, cultural and religious terms that they know nothing about, and that certainly do not reflect reality. And our leaders in the South and the West allow them to get away with this insult to the dignity and integrity of our people."

Elias no longer saw Osman as a humorous drunk, but as a leader with a sound national vision.

"What do you think we should do to correct this error, or perhaps you would want to call it something more serious —

gross misunderstanding of the country?" Elias asked seriously.

Osman understood and decided to respond in kind.

"Brother. . ."

"Elias!"

"I am awfully sorry I keep forgetting the name. I probably cannot make up my mind whether you are Christian or Muslim. Anyway, I wish to be honest with you. You see, there is something about you that makes me trust you. I may be totally wrong and by the time we reach El Fasher, I may discover that I have made the biggest mistake of my life. But let me tell you the truth as I see it.

"Unless we, the disadvantaged groups in the country, who are considered to be minorities but are in fact the majority, unite and change the system to allow us our national rights as true sons and daughters of the land, we will remain slaves to the Arabs or those who call themselves Arabs. Our people have known what suffering and insults to human pride and dignity are. When we have united and freed ourselves from bondage, we will be able to create a Sudan in which tribe, race, and religion will not impose on any citizen a second-class status. Can you believe being told that the Sudan is one, that Khartoum is our capital, all of us Sudanese, and then when our people run away from the poverty they suffer and move to Khartoum in search of opportunities for employment, they get rounded up, crowded into football stadiums like cattle and then loaded onto trucks to be transported back to their rural areas as though they were undesirable aliens? And what reason does the government give for this outrageous *kesha*, as they call this raid on innocent citizens? The security of the people of the city. I tell you, this nation is a time bomb whose explosion is not far off."

"I could not agree with you more," Elias commented in a tired voice.

They both fell silent as though they had exhausted the subject. Certainly, the issues were crystal clear to them both. In any case, they felt too exhausted to probe any deeper. And so, at three o'clock in the morning, as they pulled out of Kosti, they agreed that they should try to catch some sleep before the next station, where they were almost certain to be wakened by the commotion.

The journey to Nyala took several days across a vast territory of considerable variation, with the desolate zone of the North gradually giving way to the savannah regions of the southwest. It was the beginning of the rainy season and, although it had not yet affected the desert areas surrounding Khartoum, here the vegetation was turning greener. The train passed Kosti and went on to Um Rwaba and then turned more to the south through the spectacular Nuba Mountains to Abu Zabad, Babanusa and on to Nyala. It was a long journey, lined with a string of stations, crowded with noisy vendors trying to make a sale before the next train load of passengers with means. Local items of all kinds, from foods to artifacts, were thrust through the windows, accompanied by promotional verses of varied forms, vernacular and Arabic, spoken and chanted. Invariably, people dressed in clean white jallabiyas and turbans, with prayer beads in hand, blind or pretending blindness, went from car to car, chanting Koranic verses about the virtues of charity to the needy and God's reward to the charitable.

These "noble" beggars walked through the train accompanied by children with containers into which donors were asked to place their donations. Here and there, individuals threw coins and occasionally notes into the bowls, but it was obvious that most of the passengers had heard the call before and chose to be quietly oblivious.

But there was another class of beggars who had to be paid or explicitly dismissed. These were men and women who were unmistakably blind, crippled, or otherwise ragged and needy, who would personally or through an agent extend a hand or a bowl asking for alms. Some would give and anything was good enough; but many would respond with "*Allah yadiik wa yadiina*: May God give to you and to us." That line was enough to make the beggars move on.

It was not the first time Elias had taken this train, but somehow, before, he had never really focused on what was going on all around him. He continued to reflect on what Osman had said. For the first time, he began to wonder how astonishing it was that the South had the reputation of being

the poorest part of the country and yet he could not recall ever
seeing such signs of want and misery in the South as he was
witnessing here in the North. He realized, however, that the
South was less "modernized" or "developed" than the North.
How did one explain this anomaly of the richer part of the
country having people who were clearly more destitute than
any people he had ever seen in the South?

As the train proceeded further west, and the headmaster
and the engineer departed, Elias and Osman had become firm
friends. They liked each other.

"Brother Elias, I am by no means the ruler of Darfur, but
I do have some influence in the region. I want you to know
that I am delighted you are beginning your field experience
here."

Elias found El Fasher to be a town with strikingly different
features from the towns he had seen in both the South and
the North. In some respects, it was similar to most Northern
towns: the architecture of the buildings was by and large non-
descript but functional, flavored by the cultural environment
and the poverty, with roughly thatched huts and tin and
carton shanty dwellings. Camels, horses and donkeys roamed
all over the place, animal-driven wagons competing for the
streets with cars and pedestrians. But perhaps what struck
Elias most were the racial and cultural characteristics of the
town. And particularly striking was the non-Arab element in
what he had assumed to be a Northern, therefore Arab,
environment. This was reflected in a variety of ways: from the
racial features to the manner of dress, which was less Arab
or Muslim, to the language, varying from a strongly accented
Arabic to local languages. El Fasher was certainly not what a
Southerner would consider a typical Arab town. Wau and
Deim Zubeir in Bahr El Ghazal could have looked equally
"Northern." Much of what Osman had said in the train was
being revealed to Elias in his first hours in El Fasher.

But El Fasher also had something quite distinctive as a
symbol of its exotic history. The palace of Sultan Ali Dinar, the
last ruler of Darfur, which was now a museum, was a reminder that this part of the country had been an independent
state which had defied British colonial rule until 1916 when

it eventually succumbed. Nor was that just history, for in the minds of the Furians and of the central government leaders, it represented something of a looming threat. If any region could aspire to separation, why not the one that had been an independent state, with a civilization whose relics were visible and treasured?

Elias had been in Fasher for just over a month when he received an invitation from Osman for "a private and informal dinner to introduce you to some friends."

Dressed in informal clothing, Elias chose to be driven by a military driver, since he did not know the place, on the understanding that he would drive back himself.

When Elias gave the driver the address and asked whether he knew how to get there, he quickly responded, "Of course, who would not know Osman Jar-Ennabi's house and be a resident of Fasher?"

What struck Elias as soon as he entered the gate was the ostentatiousness of the house, a palatial building on a spacious plot of land, enclosed by a high wall. Within was a beautifully decorated garden with a centrally located patio on which half a dozen chairs were arranged in a circle. Elias was the first to arrive. Osman embraced him with all the warmth of an old acquaintance.

"As I said in my note, it's a very informal gathering with a few friends," he explained. "You must feel at home with them. They are brothers."

They had barely sat down when the gate opened with a "*Salaam aleikum!*"

Osman rose to greet a man who must have been in his mid forties, rather short and somewhat rounded. "Brother Elias, meet my older brother, Gasim."

"So the Speaker of the Regional Assembly is your brother!" responded Elias.

"I have heard a great deal from my brother about you," said Gasim.

"Oh!" remarked Elias in a light-spirited manner.

"All favorable, I assure you," Gasim hastened to add. "Osman must have intended this as a surprise," Elias commented. "But in fairness to him, he indicated that he had *some* influence."

"Now, officer, don't assume that my brother has that much influence on me. He has to work harder than others to win my support!"

Two other guests came who were introduced as members of the Regional Assembly. Then came one who, judging from his abaya and turban, was obviously a traditional notable. "Meet one of our great Fur sultans, Sheikh Ibrahim El-Dergawi, whose cousin, Hamid El-Dergawi, is our governor."

"It's an honor to meet you," said Elias, shaking hands.

"The honor is ours," said the sultan. "We rarely meet our brothers from the South."

A few minutes later, there was a knock at the open gate and a tall, lean man dressed in a jallabiya and imma entered with a new round of *salaam aleikums*.

Osman rose and rushed to the door, knowing that it must be Sayed Hamid El-Dergawi, the governor himself.

A servant brought the refreshments: cold drinks, a bottle of Johnny Walker, and a bowl of ice cubes.

"My first duty, dear brothers, is to perform a ritual that Brother Elias taught me on our train journey," Osman announced. "The ancestors get served modest portions before we indulge ourselves." As he spoke, he poured drops on the ground. They all laughed, which indicated that he must already have talked to them about the custom.

"Now, next to the ancestors are two people: our sultan and our governor. I understand that they have decided on a separation of powers: one represents the ancestors, whom we have already honored; the other represents us worldly mortals, and should therefore be the first to partake of this sinfully pleasurable liquid."

Osman's words were greeted with roaring laughter.

"Your Excellency, the Black Johnny Walker of Scotland, born in the 1880s and still going strong," he said as he handed a glass of whiskey to Hamid El-Dergawi.

The others were then served according to their choices. As might be expected from the manner of introduction, the sultan refrained from alcohol. The reason he gave was not religion or social manners, but health, even though Elias thought that the argument was somewhat contrived. But everyone else asked for a drink.

Remembering Elias's reaction to alcohol during their journey, Osman served him a soft drink. But the governor challenged Elias on this matter in a characteristic fashion: "Unless your religion prohibits it or you are dangerously allergic to it, I dare you to share the blessing of the ancestors with your brothers." Elias found himself in a predicament. While he didn't drink and contrary to the myth about Southerners, was a teetotaler, he wished not to show too puritanical a nature and therefore express a social solidarity with his Western hosts. So he accepted the offer. "Now, I see how you got the landslide victory in the election for governor," Elias remarked as he succumbed to the pressure and nursed a symbolic drink.

Judging from the laughter that greeted this statement, the overall chemistry of the group could not have been better.

Osman wisely decided that people should interact on the human level without too much politics. Even when his brother Gasim injected a serious note, the intimacy and openness of the gathering did not suffer.

"Brothers," Gasim called for attention, "I don't mean to spoil this social occasion with speechmaking. But we are all busy people and it is not every day that we find the opportunity to get together and talk informally about serious matters. As you might expect, Osman has told me a great deal about our Brother Elias. It is just wonderful that the two of them met on the train. From what I gather, this contact seems to promise opportunities for friendship and a fruitful exchange of views between us and our Southern brother, Elias Bol. To that, let us raise our glasses and welcome Elias among his brothers and sisters in Darfur."

"Welcome to our brother," they said as they raised their glasses and drank to their friendship. The governor began the applause which was soon followed by everyone else, once they had put down their glasses.

"I suppose I should say something," Elias interjected.

"By all means!" remarked Osman as all eyes turned on Elias.

"I thank you for your friendship," Elias began. "I have really come to believe that this assignment is going to be a critical one for me. Brother Osman has given me a significant orientation on the train coming out. I am really here to learn and anything you can teach me would certainly be most appreciated and perhaps made use of in the interest of our country."

Elias received a burst of spontaneous applause that was as sincere as it was loud.

"Gentlemen, I really did not mean this to be a formal occasion for speechmaking," Osman intervened. "I merely wanted to introduce you to one another. Now, I believe dinner is about to be served."

"Not before the governor has spoken," interjected Hamid El-Dergawi. "The few words that have already been said are beautiful and meaningful. From what I have heard and witnessed this evening, we have a real brother amongst us. I am delighted Osman has taken this initiative. As my contribution, I would like to share with you two anecdotes.

"The first I was told by a Southern friend. He said that he arrived from abroad after several years' absence and got a taxi at the airport to go to his hotel. He said the driver was from Darfur, judging from his looks and accent.

"'How are things in Khartoum?' our Southern friend asked the driver in a lighthearted conversation.

"'Not so good,' he said. 'I think it is time for the likes of you and me to take over the reigns of power in this country.'"

"Let me tell you another story which a Southern friend told me recently. He was leaving the offices of the Socialist Union when a crowd of people from Darfur approached him.

"'We have been looking for you over the last few days and could not find you,' they said. 'We need your help; we are looking for jobs.'

"The Southern friend told them to go to the office of the governor of Darfur; perhaps he could help. It took some time before he realized that they thought he was the governor.

"These two incidents ought to tell us that we are really one people and our time is coming; perhaps, it is already here and we do not know it."

Again loud applause greeted Hamid's words.

"And now, I must offer you dinner before I am accused of political exploitation," remarked Osman with determination.

The rest of the evening was spent in more light spirited conversation, but it did not continue for long. They left almost immediately after they had eaten.

Elias said nothing to his colleagues in military head-quarters about the evening he had spent with the notables of Darfur, but El Fasher was a small place and he felt sure that at least the commander must have heard about it. On the other hand, unless the matter came up naturally, there was no reason to raise it with any of them. That would be simply like performing an intelligence function in a personal matter. In fact, it would be like reporting on his hosts, and therefore the betrayal of a personal relationship.

Elias's duties consisted mostly of patrols in the region and in particular in the Libyan and Chadian border areas, where the security situation remained tense and tenuous. Nothing dramatic happened, but everyone realized that a show of force on both the internal and external fronts was essential to preserving peace and security in the area. The regional authorities were equally interested in the peace, security and stability of the region.

Several months after the dinner at Osman's house, Elias received a note from the governor inviting him to join the friends who had been at Osman's dinner, with a few additional people, for a picnic in the governor's village some sixty miles south of El Fasher. Elias was happy because he wanted to have a closer look at a Fur village, free of the ostentatiousness of the military. As the journey would take several hours, it was necessary to have an early start on Friday morning.

Elias wore a safari suit while his companions were dressed in informal jallabiyas, the weekend form of dress in the Northern Sudan. The group drove in two jeeps over a rugged dirt road that meandered among bushy scrub that spotted the desert zone. Evidence of the surrounding desert and the drought that had afflicted the region of late was apparent in the desolation of the environment. Carcasses and skeletons of camels, horses, cattle, sheep and goats lay scattered along the road all the way.

Then, at mid morning, as the heat of the climbing sun was augmented by shimmering mirages, a village emerged majestically on the horizon, projecting trees and huts to the skyline and making them look more like castles and royal orchards than remnants of a dying environment. El-Dergawi proudly pointed in the direction of the village and announced, "There is my village, Dheleil Shader, so-called because of the cluster of trees you see there."

As they approached the village, what seemed at first like a cluster of shady trees became thorny acacia trees scattered around dwellings sparsely dotting a territory about a mile in radius with small family farms between them. As the jeeps rolled forward, a bull had already been slaughtered and placed across the path they were expected to follow. The governor's cousin, Sheikh Ibrahim El-Dergawi, the sultan, was standing on the opposite side of the sacrificial animal. The guests climbed out of the jeeps and led by the governor headed toward the dead bull. Governor El-Dergawi jumped over the carcass followed by his colleagues. Elias recalled occasions in the South when, after a prolonged absence from home, a similar ritual would be performed. Obviously, this was a pre-Islamic custom.

Having jumped over the bull, the guests were first greeted by Sheikh Ibrahim, after which they moved on to greet the crowd that was already forming rapidly. El-Dergawi's home was a large cluster of *tukuls,* circular huts, with a *kurnuk* or rectangular building which, like the huts, had mud walls and a thatched roof. A larger rectangular structure, *rakuba,* made of sorghum stalks and closed on three sides with the fourth side left wide open was furnished with canvas chairs all around the inside walls with large colorfully designed mats, *burush* thrown down in the center.

People continued to emerge from all over the village, while women greeted the honored guests with ululations. One by one, the crowd continued to build up until it seemed as though the whole village, men, women and children had assembled. Some of the men were dressed in immaculately white jallabiyas and jibbas with turbans neatly wound around their heads; others were less impressively dressed in the shorter version of the long garment, commonly known as *a'aragi* with trousers, *surwal*, showing below the garment and going down to the ankles, and shawls thrown across their shoulders. Yet others were dressed in more European looking safari suits. Women's dresses also varied a great deal, from the latest style in tobes modestly drawn across the face, leaving only a small opening for the eyes, to colorful cloths wound around the waist and leaving the top bare, except for adornment with decorative metals and beads. It was a juxtaposition of wealth and elegance and poverty and modesty. But whatever differences reflected themselves were more apparent than real and certainly only skin-deep, for most of the people in the village shared a common wealth which did not permit substantial differences in the houses in which they lived, the food they ate, and the culture they enjoyed.

What struck Elias most was that apart from the Arab Muslim accent of their clothing, these people looked very much like the people he had seen in different parts of the South. Even the flavor of the village was more reminiscent of the South than parts of the North he had known. In particular, he found the openness, with huts exposed instead of being enclosed, men and women mingling together instead of being dogmatically separated, and the apparent obliviousness to poverty to be characteristics which his people, the Dinka, seemed to share with their fellow Sudanese from Darfur.

Even the rapidly deteriorating environment was a common feature, though here there were differences in scale. Elias had heard his people talk about the way the rivers used to retain water for most of the dry season; now they dried up long before the normal cycle. They spoke of how big the trees used to be; now they were shrinking in size and dying long before their full life expectancy. They even realized that wildlife was retreating and that a wide variety of birds and animals like the giraffe and the antelope which had given occasional variation in diet seemed to have disappeared in recent years. Even the menace of the elephant, the hippo, or the carnivorous beasts of prey was fading, which was good news for the physical well-being of man, but tragic evidence of what was happening to the environment.

And indeed, no sooner had the guests sat down than the topic of the diminishing rains and the increasing drought came up. The leaders from El Fasher were trying to explain to the villagers the phenomenon of the encroaching desert. It was as though something they had observed over the years creeping in and slowly eating up their valuable soil was at last being exposed. Not that it helped them any; quite the contrary, it seemed to confirm that they were victims of forces beyond their control. Evidence of the drought and famine that had begun to bedevil the region was apparent in the animals, and especially the horses and the donkeys that stood in the blazing sun of the mid morning, quivering and shaking with the precious breath of life.

But whatever the threat of thirst and famine in the region, it was not going to be allowed to modify the quality or quantity of the village hospitality. As was the pattern, the guests were first served water and other cold drinks to quench their thirst of travellers. Lighthearted conversation began as village notables sat with the guests to keep their company.

But certain filial duties had to be performed too. Sheikh Ibrahim whispered to the governor that his mother had come to greet his guests. She was shown in immediately. Everyone rose as El-Haja Aisha was introduced. Dressed in a long frock and a black tobe covering her head without a veil on her face, Aisha was of medium height and straightfaced. She greeted everyone in a soft but firm and confident voice that seemed to describe the lady behind the man whom the people of Darfur regarded as their shield. Elias could not help reflect back to his village and recall the simple women, often only half-clothed, who were in effect great ladies behind great men, all of whom were now being pushed into a void of negated identity and even worse, non-entity. He felt encouraged that the experience was nationwide and at the same time deeply despondent for precisely the same reason.

Drums had begun to beat as the day developed into a festive holiday for the village. In addition to the bull that had been slaughtered, whose meat was to be for everybody, a lamb had also been slain, and all kinds of food preparations were underway.

Sheikh Ibrahim kept exiting and re-entering as he organized the hospitality and the entertainment. At one point, he stopped in front of his cousin to say, "We have your modern drinks, if you wish, and our women have brewed our native varieties to give you a choice. We have, in addition to whiskey from town, *kosheif*, *dooma*, *asaliya*, and of course the ordinary *merisa*. What is your wish?"

Governor El-Dergawi responded, "Bring them all and let our guests choose what their eyes dictate."

And so, the bottles of spirits came alongside pots and jars of the local drinks.

The festivities began with the crowd happily chattering. Whether by his choice or by social deference, the governor's voice rose above the rest: "I want to explain something to you all: Your Muslim fundamentalists tell you that those of you whose traditions permit drinking as an act of communal solidarity are engaging in sinful conduct. This brother from the South does not drink. But he has chosen to have some of your local brands not only to taste what you produce, but also to express social communion and solidarity with you. Tell me the truth according to your conscience, which of the two is a brother: the Muslim Brother who despises what you regularly drink as part of your diet or the brother from the South who is eager to live your life and identify himself with you?"

His was a rhetorical question, and the answer, shouted in unison, "Our brother from the South," was nonetheless pleasing.

Turning to Elias, Governor El-Dergawi said, "There, you have your answer about the so-called differences between the North and the South and the assumed cultural unity of the North along Arab Islamic lines. And remember, these are not politicians; they are speaking their minds and their hearts."

Elias smiled, obviously moved.

Everyone saw to it that there were no formalities, just relaxation and fun. And so, after several glasses or cups, depending on what they chose to drink, the group went to the dance site and participated in the fun. Girls in the prime of youth dangled their heads backward, shoving their breasts forward, with their young partners bending toward them as they vigorously stamped the ground, leapt, shook, and flirted.

Osman was at his best in exhibiting his already extroverted personality, throwing hundreds of pounds over the heads of the most obviously striking beauties in the dance. But no one showed any jealousy, for all understood that it was a game of aesthetic pleasure and innocent gratification. In the Islamic world, men and women could not so play together in a socially accepted manner. For Elias, here was yet another cultural similarity with the South. He realized he had been unbelievably privileged to be made part of the inner circles of Darfur.

With drinks was served *marara,* a local delicacy of raw liver and lungs washed in hot water and heavily spiced. It was a dish Elias's Dinka sense of taste found revolting, but he politely took a couple of bites and even made a polite comment. *Shiya,* a form of kebab, followed later. Elias liked that. With the drinking, nibbling, and dancing went a boisterous conversation with no protocol whatsoever. It was remarkable to see the governor joke and laugh with his people as a leader among peers, a case of true democracy in social action. Rather than detract from his dignity, the familiarity revealed his human touch of the governor and a shrewdness in reaching down to the lowest social strata of the community.

Then came the main meal served on platters laid out in enormous trays covered with the large colorful woven covers, *tabag,* for which Darfur was famed throughout the country. Tray after tray followed until the space in the center of the *rakuba* was filled. The crowd that was to be fed was equally impressive. Some sat with the governor and his guests in the *rakuba,* others were in the *kurnuk,* and yet others sat under the shade of the trees outside.

When it was time to eat, Sheikh Ibrahim El-Dergawi lifted the platters to see what was inside in order to determine the distribution. The selection was more to avoid duplication than to discriminate between people and the food they were to be served. When the dishes had been distributed accordingly, the governor rose and announced, *"Itfadalu, ya akhwana*—Brothers, be seated to the meal."

They all rose up and stepped outside the *rakuba* to wash their hands as one of the villagers held the *ibrig,* the container to pour water as they washed. Then they sat down on the mats in a large circle, with dishes placed at the center. As they ate, dishes came and went to make place for more dishes.

It was obvious that they were observing subtle but powerful rules of etiquette. Everyone tried to avoid crowding hands in the dish, took small bites and chewed in a way that combined respect for the food with modesty. People began to rise before they could make a dent in the large quantities before them.

"Bedri, bedri—too early, too early," the governor protested as one person after another rose up, claiming to be full.

"Zawidu ya akhwana—Brothers, have some more!" The governor continued to urge his guests, but to no avail.

"El hamdu lillah—Praised be God, for the food," they said in response as they rose and went to the *ibrig* holder outside to wash their hands again, this time even more vigorously with soap to remove any lingering smell of food.

Hillu, dessert, soon followed. It was comprised of cream caramel, jelly, and rice pudding.

Tea was next, served in small glasses decoratively narrowed in the center with gold trimming on the rim.

But no meal could be declared complete without *gahwa,* a cup of special Turkish coffee in a *jabana,* a beautifully crafted earthware jug with decorations of beads around it, served in small *demitasse, funjan,* and flavored with aromatic spices.

It was now late afternoon. The sun would soon disappear and the road being what it was, it was far safer to drive back to El Fasher in the light of day. So, with *" 'Am riin bi idhin-i-llahi*—May you continue to prosper by the will of God," they bade Sheikh Ibrahim and the rest of the village fare well and got into their jeeps to return to Fasher, continuing their merriment as they drove along.

Elias felt very grateful for the warm reception the leaders of Darfur had accorded him. As they had not known him before and as there were other officers, including senior ones

in the regional headquarters, there could be only one explanation: he was a Southerner and they identified with him as an
African or non-Arab. That had to have some significance in
his political outlook.

Where would all this lead, he wondered. Although he saw
the point and perhaps even sympathized with it, he made no
personal commitment to this new element of divisive
unification. But he saw it as part of his mission to understand it and to note it as a significant feature of the evolving
national scene.

FOURTEEN

PERHAPS BECAUSE OF THE racial politics that seemed to be in the making, Elias's colleagues—and especially the senior officers—were leery of his association with the leadership in Darfur. A few days after the weekend picnic at the governor's village, his commanding officer, General Abd el-Bagi Mahmoud, called him to his office.

"Brother Elias," he began with a deceptively cordial smile on his face, "I understand that you went with the governor to his village last weekend."

"Yes, sir."

"I have also heard that you met him and other notables at a dinner some months ago?"

Elias answered in the affirmative.

"I hate to pry into the private affairs of my officers, but don't you think that such association with the leadership of the region should have come to my attention from you directly?" The commander phrased the question rather courteously.

"I wondered about that, sir, but I thought that in addition to being a personal matter, it might not be polite to those leaders for me to report on their private affairs in that way." Elias attempted to answer the question as truthfully as he could.

"I see," remarked the commander. "I appreciate your concern for their privacy—or should I say your sense of loyalty toward them. But don't you think you owe us your loyalty too? And in fact, wouldn't you say that your first loyalty is due to the army rather than your friends?"

"Sir, I did not think it was a matter of competing loyalties," Elias tried to explain. "I thought it did not really matter to the army."

"But Brother Elias, you said that your first thought of letting us know and then decided against that because it would be unfair or impolite to those individuals. Was that not a case of competing loyalties and you chose to give them priority over the army?"

Elias felt angered by the way the commander had misconstrued his honest answers. "Sir, of course I thought about it — as I told you — but I concluded that these were totally separate aspects of my life and that accepting invitations from these people did not in any way compromise my duties. I still don't see any connection between the two."

Elias decided that it was his turn to be on the offensive. Didn't they say that the best defense was offense? And indeed he felt he had reason to be offended, for obviously the commander had been spying on him.

"How did you know anyway?" he asked. "Who told you?"

"Governor El-Dergawi."

"El-Dergawi?" Elias repeated to himself quietly. He wondered why he should have felt it necessary to report to the commander. For a moment, he felt a sense of betrayal, but quickly decided that there must be a good reason for the governor's conduct.

"Anyway, I thought I should share my views with you, Brother Elias," General Abd el-Bagi resumed after a moment of silence. "It's one of those delicate situations where views or feelings could easily differ. Ultimately, your own judgment has to be the crucial factor. But I want you to know that our responsibilities as a national army require sensitivity. We must try to be detached from those who may have some vested interests to serve through us. I am not saying that these people do, but you must agree that this is a region of considerable diversity. And although Governor El-Dergawi was elected, he belongs to a faction among factions which some day may come

into conflict with us. I hope you see what I am driving at. Just
bear that in mind."

"Thank you, sir." Elias spoke with a tone of sincerity,
pleased that the issue was ending on a note of some
conciliation. With that, the commander dismissed him.

Since arriving in Darfur, Elias had kept a diary of activities
and had already written several letters to Field Marshal Khalid,
sharing whatever information he thought useful to convey to
him. He had written, for instance, about his encounter with
Osman and about his meeting with the governor and other
prominent personalities in Darfur. Of course, he only reported
what he thought appropriate and was careful to exclude those
matters which he felt could be offensive to the minister. He
obviously could not report the views of the leaders of Darfur
about the racial situation in the country and the need for a
united stand between the South and the West. That was a
secret he shared only with the leaders of Darfur. Similarly,
Elias wrote to the minister about the weekend visit with the
governor and the reaction of his commanding officer. He knew
that the commander would probably report the matter to his
superiors in Khartoum and thought it wise to have his own
version on record as well. However, all he did was to report
the facts and not to ask for opinion or action by the minister.

A year rapidly slipped by as Elias combined his regular
duties with personal friendships not only among the leaders
of Darfur but increasingly among its ordinary people as well.
Osman Jar-Ennabi in particular had proved to be a loyal friend
and one with extensive contacts at all levels of society.
Whenever Elias needed some explanation or wanted to
cultivate a particular insight into the complex racial and tribal
composition of the region and its dynamics, he turned to
Osman. And Osman never failed him. Besides, he had come
to trust Elias so much that he even felt free to comment on
what he saw as the "racist" attitude of the security forces under
the command of General Abd el-Bagi Mahmoud. Again, Elias
reported some of the information he gathered from Osman,
but carefully censored it so as not to harm anyone.

One day, Elias received a circular note from General Abd
el-Bagi informing the officers that there would be a meeting

with the commander of the police force to brief them on the
security situation in the region. The meeting was held in a
conference room with the tables arranged to form a "T." The
attendees were the commissioned officers who, except for
Elias, were all Northerners from the so-called Arab tribes of
the river. They were chatting lightheartedly when General
Abd el-Bagi walked in with the commander of the police
forces, General Yahya Abd el-Aal, accompanied by a younger
officer who was carrying papers, presumably his secretary or
personal assistant. The officers stood at attention and saluted.
The generals saluted back and Abd el-Bagi gestured the group
to be seated.

General Abd el-Bagi briefly introduced General Yahya,
who quickly launched into an analysis of a developing
situation that posed a "serious threat not only to the security
of the region but to the country as a whole." He proceeded
to make a series of allegations, supported, he said, by
documentary evidence, that showed the Dinka of Bahr El
Ghazal were preparing for a revenge attack on the Rizeigat
once the Arabs moved in their seasonal migration to the river.
He said that evidence also suggested that some of the units
in the Southern command and police forces in Bahr El Ghazal
were implicated and might even be giving training to
individual Dinkas. The Dinka themselves were said to be
selling their cattle and acquiring arms. Some arms were even
said to be secretly passed on to them from official sources.

"If this weren't bad enough," General Yahya continued,
"we even have information that elements of the non-Arab
tribes in this region are in contact with the Dinka and
cooperating with them against the Arabs. More specifically,
certain individuals among the Fur are said to be passing on
information about the movement of the nomadic Arab tribes
of Darfur, and in particular the Rizeigat, including the routes
they are likely to take this coming year. It is even said that some
of the Fur are helping the Dinka to acquire firearms from
Libya. These Fur individuals are apparently trading guns for
cattle, and the whole operation is economically lucrative. But
it seems that the motive is more than financial reward. The
trade is in fact primarily motivated by racial politics here in

Darfur and on the national level. This is why it clearly goes beyond police competence and requires cooperation between us and the armed forces."

Elias was stunned by what he was hearing. If it was true, then the situation was very serious indeed. He couldn't help remembering the sentiments he had heard about the need for solidarity between Southerners and non-Arabs living in Darfur. But there was a radical difference, at least in degree, between anything he himself had ever heard and what the police chief was now alleging. Everything General Yahya said could easily apply to Elias's friends, especially Osman. And yet, never in all his conversations with Osman and the others had any evidence of military cooperation between the Dinka and the Fur against the Rizeigat even been hinted at, much less openly discussed. Was it that his friends did not yet trust him enough to put him in their confidence? Or was it that they had in fact exposed him to the situation and he had been too naive? Or was it possible that someone had fabricated a clever plot to implicate the Fur and the Dinka in a major conspiracy that would justify preemptive measures? Elias was more inclined to believe this latter idea, but was prepared to keep an open mind.

"And now comes what I believe to be the most difficult question as far as we in the police force are concerned," General Yahya continued. "What makes the problem so difficult to handle is not only that the people involved are operating in at least two regions, with collaborators probably spreading to other areas of the country and abroad, but also because those individuals who are involved here in Darfur extend into the highest levels of the regional leadership."

Now Elias fully understood that his friends, Osman, his brother Gasim, and perhaps the governor himself were all involved. Unbelievable, he thought. And yet, General Yahya sounded so persuasive. What should he believe?

"I will at this point stop short of mentioning names," General Yahya went on, "But I believe you can fully imagine the difficulties I am talking about. What do we do? That is the question on which I end my remarks and await your response."

General Abd el-Bagi was the first to respond, remarking that in his opinion the interest of the nation overrode all other considerations. "No individual is above the law," he averred. He then cautioned that the meeting was strictly confidential.

One of the officers chose to speak. "It seems to me that the two most critical aspects of the problem as presented to us by the general are the seriousness and the urgency of the situation. Failure to act decisively and quickly might result in far greater damage than need be."

Another went a step further. "General, you sound as though you know precisely who the individuals are, at least in this region. What is the difficulty with arresting them?"

People laughed.

"Should I answer that question?" General Yahya looked toward Abd el-Bagi.

"Well, I suspect that the answer is implicit in what you said earlier," observed General Abd el-Bagi, "but perhaps you should first listen to more comments and then come back with your reaction."

Yet another remarked, half jokingly, "I hope someone has kept the Rizeigat informed of the perils awaiting them." His comment was followed by a sardonic laugh.

Elias wondered whether he should speak or remain silent. But it was clear from the faces of all those in the room that he was expected to say something. He decided that silence might be construed as harboring something. And yet, he felt that if he spoke at all, he should say something meaningful. He decided to do so, even if what he said did not please his colleagues or the generals.

"Sir, the situation you have described is clearly most dangerous," Elias began. "The implications are certain to be very severe, whether preventive measures are taken or the situation develops to its logical conclusion. I listened to your words carefully and I heard you use such words as 'seem,' 'might,' 'said to,' and similar expressions. You will agree with me that these are tentative terms which do not indicate conclusive evidence. I do not mean to question the validity of your overall assessment of the situation, especially as the danger is so grave that it calls for the utmost precaution. But precisely because the allegations are so grave, and are bound to affect the lives of individuals very severely, it seems to me that the need for accurate information becomes particularly essential. For instance, there was an insinuation that the suspected individuals might be subject to arrest. Unless they are detained under some emergency measure, in itself subject to legal regulation, I don't see how any action can be taken against them on the basis of such circumstantial and tentative evidence without risking even worse consequences."

Silence followed these remarks. It was difficult to tell whether Elias had persuaded anyone or confirmed what they had already suspected, he being both a Dinka and a known friend of the people implicated in the alleged conspiracy. After a conspicuous silence, General Yahya responded.

"Brother Officer," he began with a deceptive courtesy, "I assure you we have no interest in imputing criminal liability to innocent people."

"I did not say that," interrupted Elias. "All I am saying is that acting on insufficient evidence to interfere with the lives of innocent people, especially ones as influential as the people you have in mind, could raise serious problems of injustice and endanger public security. That does not mean that I think you are interested in victimizing innocent people."

"Anyway, let me assure you that our intention in bringing the matter to this group is to think together and to come up with an approach that would best serve the national interest." General Yahya seemed to be in control of his nerves. "Now, let me respond to some of the questions raised. First the issue of arresting those suspected. What the brother here said is true. Any arrests made should be very well founded and we should take adequate precautions against any repercussions. Whether such arrests should be made, and if so, when, is a question worth serious consideration. On the lighthearted remark about the Rizeigat being informed, the answer is I do not know, but I would be surprised if they do not have their own intelligence network that is probably reasonably well informed. In fact, this is another reason why too much delay in acting could be very harmful indeed.

"Let me make one general comment. The reason we

brought this to the joint attention of the armed forces and the police is not only to discuss what should be done about the larger issues involved, but also to facilitate our own work for the security of the area. Knowing about what might be going on underground can be a significant way of ensuring that it does not surface. So, don't think that we are going to fold our hands and wait to see the time-bomb explode. Certainly not."

General Abd el-Bagi added, "I think Brother Yahya has really put his finger on a key issue. What we have heard today should open our eyes to what is going on in this region and within the borders of the Southern Region. That in itself is an important aspect of the exercise. As for the larger issues, as Brother Yahya called them, our task should be to report to the national security authorities in Khartoum and wait for their instructions or advice. Unless someone else has a contribution to make, I suggest that this be the main conclusion of our meeting."

The National Security Agency to which the report would go was the one headed by General Idris Abd el-Jabar, who was widely rumored to be a rival of Field Marshal Khalid, a situation which was known to be causing a strain between the institutions which they headed. Although the Defense Ministry was more concerned with external sources of insecurity and the National Security Agency with internal, there was no question about the overlap of their functions. Full cooperation should therefore have been natural.

Elias was personally torn on several fronts. He knew that the situation they had discussed concerned personal friends. There was therefore the question of whether he should say anything to them. He decided that he could not, for the information was strictly confidential. What about reporting to Field Marshal Khalid? He knew that a formal report would go to National Security, perhaps with copies to the Ministry of Defense, but he also felt he owed it to the Field Marshal to report to him personally and directly. He persuaded himself that there was no question of betraying secrets and that in any case his own reporting might help foster a balance that would somehow favor his friends.

And so he wrote a report that restated the facts as

furnished by General Yahya and offered an analysis which shed some light on the wider political, intertribal and inter-regional contexts in which they should be understood. In a discreet way, Elias was alluding to the hidden racial attitudes which he had been told existed and which he thought the reports wittingly or unwittingly substantiated. "My sense is that these people are making a lot of smoke from a small fire and, with all sirens at full blast, the fire engines are racing to the scene to extinguish the fire. That might be harmless in the case of a false alarm; but with a serious national security situation, overreaction might mean overkill and that is not conducive, in my book, to individual or national security."

Elias knew that his report and that of the security authorities went to Khartoum at about the same time. Everyone was now waiting for a reaction from the capital. Days turned into weeks and weeks were moving into months. Elias began to believe Khartoum had been wiser than the regional authorities and that the matter was being allowed to die a natural death.

Suddenly, one morning, General Abd el-Bagi called for an extraordinary meeting of the commissioned officers. Everyone intuitively felt that the meeting must have something to do with the security situation. They all hurried into the conference room in great expectation.

General Abd el-Bagi entered and, as though to tease them and heighten their anxiety and bring home the seriousness of the matter he was about to disclose, he sat silently for moments while all eyes were expectantly focused on him.

"Brothers, as you might expect, I have serious news for you," he said. "It really should not come as a surprise to you because I am sure you remember our last meeting with General Yahya Abd el-Aal. Well, Khartoum has reacted. We are ordered to be on alert as of today because some severe measures are going to be taken. A number of key personalities in this region and in Bahr El Ghazal as well as in Khartoum and elsewhere are going to be arrested in the next several days. We are to guard against any disturbances that might result from those arrests."

The general then proceeded to pass out assignments. Elias

did not get any assignment. He wondered whether he should ask and decided against it. When the meeting ended and the officers were leaving the room, General Abd el-Bagi called him back.

"Brother Elias, you noticed I did not give you an assignment." Then pulling out a sheet of paper from the file he was carrying, and handing it to Elias, he said, "Read this."

It read, "To General Abd el-Bagi Mahmoud, Commander, Darfur Region. You are hereby requested to arrange for the immediate travel of Officer Elias Bol Malek by air to Khartoum where his services are urgently needed at Headquarters. Regards. Chief of Staff."

Elias read the cable and said not a word.

"We will have the Hercules plane ready for you tomorrow morning at 7 o'clock. You may leave the office at any time today to go and pack your things. Good luck."

"Thank you, sir," Elias managed to say as they parted; he was too surprised to say anything else.

Elias chose to leave without saying goodbye to any of his Darfur friends. He thought that perhaps that would be the best way of conveying how he felt about the circumstances of his departure.

No one in Armed Forces Headquarters could explain to Elias the reason for his sudden recall. Brigadier General Ali himself knew nothing and Elias urged him not to do anything and leave it for him to find out himself. But even the chief of staff, who had signed the cable, had no explanation. "I followed the minister's instructions," was all he could say to both General Ali and Elias.

After meeting the chief of staff, Elias decided that as long as the order had come from Field Marshal Khalid, he should expect to get some explanation from him. Accordingly, he registered a request for an appointment with the minister and waited.

Elias had been waiting in Khartoum for four days when suddenly he heard General Idris Abd el-Jabar address the nation on the security situation.

"We have been observing a grave situation develop over the last two months, waiting to see whether the people involved would come to their senses and end their conspiracy," he said. "But, unfortunately, they seem to have misinterpreted our patience as weakness. They have continued to conspire within and between the regions and have even extended their networks across our frontiers.

"Dear compatriots, brothers and sisters, it is with heavy hearts that we feel obliged to take decisive and firm measures to end this insidious treachery before it consumes the nation. We have decided to arrest a number of people in Darfur and Bahr El Ghazal, some of them very prominent personalities and in due course to bring them to trial for high treason. Our philosophy and practice has been to keep the people of this nation fully informed on the security situation and any measures we take on their behalf. We shall continue to do so. And may Almighty God guide our steps."

Elias soon learned that among the people arrested were the Speaker of the Regional Assembly in Darfur, a wealthy businessman in El Fasher, the commissioner of Bahr El Ghazal province, a prominent Southern politician in Khartoum, and scores of other Westerners and Southerners. Elias had no doubt that those arrested in Darfur included Osman, the businessman, and his brother, the Speaker of the Regional Assembly.

It was as though daylight had suddenly given way to nightfall or light to darkness. Elias could not rationally explain what had happened. Suddenly, being in the Sudan in that day and age was like being in a nightmare; only he was not asleep; he was awake and living the nightmare.

Word eventually came that the Vice President and Minister of Defense, Field Marshal Khalid would see him. As he walked into the office and saluted, the minister rose and walked around his desk to give the young officer an embrace.

"When did you come?" he asked Elias.

"About four days ago."

"Four days ago?" he repeated with surprise. "I got the note requesting the appointment only yesterday. I had wanted to see you as soon as you came."

Gesturing Elias to sit down in one of the chairs before his desk, he said, "*Hasal kheir*—What has happened is well." It was a figure of speech, a way of saying "never mind." But Elias hoped that the minister meant more than the conversational idiom and that all was indeed well.

Obviously, the field marshal had asked for Elias's file, for even as they were exchanging conventional greetings, he opened it and was turning the pages.

"I guess I should not even ask you how it was because you probably want to know what is happening."

Elias smiled in agreement, looking at the minister intently.

Pulling out some reports from the file, the minister passed them on to Elias as he explained, "Read these, and then we will talk."

Elias read several letters from General Abd el-Bagi about his conduct. They reported his dinner and picnic with the governor and other notables, the overall friendship that had evolved between the Darfur leadership and the young officer from the South, and the underlying reasons for the relationship. Concluding that it was clearly racially motivated, the reports analyzed the implications for the security of the area and the integrity of the army in Darfur. General Abd el-Bagi went on to say that there was no way they could know what secret information the young officer might be passing on to his friends and what that might mean for the maintenance of peace and security in the region. Then there was the Southern dimension. "Given the fact that the problems of the area are often interregional between the Dinka and the Arabs, and the racial underpinnings of the officer's friendship with the leaders of the Fur tribes, we fear that the ultimate objective or outcome might be to undermine the interests of the Arabs in favor of their adversaries, the Dinka." The last report ended with the words, "It is of course for you at headquarters to decide, especially as we have reason to believe that the young man is a protégé of the vice president, to whom we know he sends periodic reports. But in our professional judgment, this young officer is at best an anomaly to our mission here and at worst a security risk. A sense of duty and loyalty to our country compels me to recommend his immediate transfer from the region. And may God be my witness."

Elias finished reading the letters and turned to the vice president, completely lost for words.

"You don't have to say anything," the field marshal broke the silence. "I know exactly what was going on and what the situation is. What I want you to know is that I consented to your coming back here because I realized the difficulties and even the dangers to which you were exposed. I have written my own comments on these letters and they are in the files. I hope you can guess what they contain. I obviously can't tell the future; we are always taking risks in whatever we do. But I believe that with these comments from me in your files, your professional career should not be affected by these ridiculous observations."

Then turning to a more positive view of his plans for Elias, he went on: "Now, let me tell you my thoughts on the situation. I am going to go beyond my official capacity and talk to you as a younger brother." He lowered his eyes with embarrassment as he became personal. "I believe I can say that I know you quite well now. I have certainly had great admiration and even affection for you from the first time I saw you in class. You are a young man with a future. I don't want you to fall victim to the crazy political paranoia that seems to be invading the regime. How else can one explain this ridiculous overreaction but as sheer madness?

"Anyway, what I have decided, and I hope it tallies with your own interests and ambitions, is to send you on a scholarship to the United States to study and continue research on the phenomenon of leadership in a country as racially and culturally diverse as ours. The army is obviously an important fact of life in the evolution of many developing countries, and the Sudan is no exception. My guess is that although we might go through a phase of swinging pendulums about the role of the military, it will continue to be critical. And if the army is to play its role constructively, it will have to improve the quality of its leadership. Obviously, we cannot educate everybody, nor can we prepare every officer for leadership. But we have to start somewhere. I am throwing in my lot with you."

Elias could not believe his ears. What seemed like a path

of doom was suddenly turning into a golden gate of opportunity. "I have no words to thank you adequately, sir," he said. "I only hope that I will prove myself worthy of your confidence."

"I have written to our cultural counsellor in Washington to find a university which will consider your military education, your diploma at the Academy and your experience in the service in determining your admission to a postgraduate course," the minister went on. "Let me have the necessary support documents to send to the cultural counsellor and we'll wait for his reply. Meanwhile, I suggest you take a vacation."

Elias reported these positive developments to General Ali, who responded with mixed feelings. He approved of the way Field Marshal Khalid had handled the situation. He was even delighted with the prospect of study in the United States. But he was saddened by the whole Darfur fiasco. "I just don't know what is happening to this country," he said with a sense of tragedy.

After a gloomy pause, Ali asked Elias how he was planning to spend his vacation.

"I hope to go home."

"Don't," Ali reacted unequivocally. "There is no need to risk what seems quite obvious. Don't you see that they have just started a witch hunt? How could you possibly escape trouble in an area which they probably regard as the spot of confrontation?"

"But should this scholarship abroad come through and I leave, I will not be able to see my family for a period of years," Elias argued.

"So what?" retorted Ali. "It's not worth it, son. Stay here where at least there are people who can make sure that this madness does not go beyond certain limits."

Elias conceded that he could spend much of his time in the library of the University of Khartoum, studying in anticipation of his course abroad.

One afternoon, a colleague came with a message that Governor El-Dergawi had been looking for him and would very much like to see him at the Darfur guest house in Khartoum North the following afternoon or evening. Elias was delighted by the prospect of seeing him again, a man for whom he had developed a profound respect and affection, and whom he considered a model popular leader: egalitarian, modest and considerate, but firm, dignified and charismatic.

Elias found the governor and Sultan Ibrahim Ahmed El-Dergawi sitting outside on a patio close to the bank of the Blue Nile. With them was a third man whom Elias did not know, but who also looked like a Fur. Elias figured that the governor and the sultan must have come to look into the recent arrests of their people.

On the table before them was a bottle of whiskey, a container of ice and several soda bottles, some already empty. Judging from the half empty glasses before them, all three had been drinking.

The first thing that struck Elias was that while he called an enthusiastic "*salaam aleikum*," he received a very cold response. He opened his arms to embrace the governor in greeting and was crushed to see him coldly extending his hand. Elias shook Governor El-Dergawi's hand and, having learned that humiliating lesson, extended his hand to Sultan Ibrahim.

When neither of them took the initiative to introduce him to the third person, he extended his hand to him, "Elias Bol is my name."

"Abdalla Jamuse," the man said as they shook hands.

"Of course!" Elias reacted, quickly connecting the name with the well-known representative from Darfur in the National Assembly. He had not met the man before, but Abdalla Jamuse was considered perhaps the most articulate and effective member of the Assembly from the West. He now realized why they had not been introduced to one another: of course, he should have known the Honorable Member.

But Elias still felt uneasy about the attitude of El-Dergawi and his cousin. He wondered why on earth they had asked to see him if all they could do was to appear so distant after the close friendship they had shared in Darfur. He certainly felt ambivalent about being with them. It was a choice between turning his back on them and walking away or staying and finding out as quickly as he could the reason for their behavior.

Since they had taken the initiative to see him, he had to find out their motive.

"What is the matter, is anything wrong?" he asked. And remembering the arrests he realized something was indeed seriously wrong. "I am sorry, I should have begun with expressions of sympathy," he said. "But what more can I say except that I am profoundly sorry about what happened."

Elias decided that they must be behaving that way out of grief.

It was Abdalla Jamuse, not either of the two he knew, who offered him a drink. "How about a glass of whiskey?"

"No, thanks," responded Elias.

Governor El-Dergawi was still thinking of Elias's words of sympathy.

"Who was it who said the word 'sorry' should never have been allowed to creep into the languages of civilized nations?" he said with obvious sarcasm.

Elias felt the sting of the comment, but did not fully understand the significance. "I am afraid that's all I can do."

"What the saying really means is that without the word 'sorry,' people might be more driven to do the right thing in the first place rather than count on apology and forgiveness." Hamid El-Dergawi persisted in his attack.

Something surely was wrong with the governor, Elias thought to himself. Was he all right or had the shock of the political onslaught taken him off balance? He chose not to react to the governor's impoliteness. In any case, it did not really have any relevance to himself, at least none that he could recognize. But Governor El-Dergawi must have decided that what they wanted to discuss with Elias was something that should not be obscured by courtesy. So without further ado, he decided to open the subject.

"Brother Elias, all of us who are sitting here are older than you," he began. "We have already witnessed much in the world that is enough to make a man cynical. But we are leaders of our people and we cannot afford to be cynical. We take people seriously and treat them according to what we think they are, be they relatives or strangers, friends or foes. Out of the experience of dealing with any people, one develops a reasonably sound way of judging people. Of course, one can be wrong in one's assessment of people. As they say, perfection is only with God. It is not unheard of to trust a person to the point of treating him like a brother, and he turns out to be a deadly enemy. The question I want to ask you is. . ." El-Dergawi stopped and reflected for a moment. "Well, I have several questions. First, has such a thing ever happened to you?"

"Nothing comes to mind immediately," replied Elias.

"I see," remarked El-Dergawi. "Then my second question: what would your reaction be if it happened to you?"

"Frankly, the question is so hypothetical that I have to say I don't know," Elias answered.

"You are a lucky man," interjected the sultan.

The others reacted with cynical laughter. Elias decided to be more assertive. "Tell me, I am completely at a loss," he remarked. "What's going on? I seem to be missing something quite important here."

"Is it perhaps deliberate?" Governor El-Dergawi posed the question.

"That's it, governor," said Elias as he stood up. "I am not going to sit here and listen to leaders talk like a bunch of kids. Goodbye."

As Elias walked away, he heard a voice which must have been Abdalla Jamuse's say, "Shame on you people, how can you?"

Jamuse was already running after Elias. "Come on, brother, you cannot leave this way," he pleaded with him. "You must understand that we are deeply upset about what happened. But there is no reason for you to be condemned before you have had the opportunity to state your case. Come on, let's talk this thing through."

"State my case?" Elias responded to Jamuse. "About what?"

"Well, that's what we should talk over," said Jamuse. "Please, please, come back. We have never met; this is my first request of you. In the name of God, I beg you to come back."

Reluctantly, Elias gave in. When they were together again, it was Abdalla Jamuse who spoke first. "Gentlemen, we are dealing with a very serious and delicate situation," he said. "We cannot and must not approach it emotionally. Instead of insinuations and what sound like insults, you should let Elias hear what you know and listen to what he has to say."

El-Dergawi had obviously worked himself into a fury from which it was not easy to disengage. "Look, Brother Jamuse," he said in response. "We are talking about the freedom and perhaps the lives of innocent people. I mean right now, we have not only several, but perhaps dozens of our brothers languishing behind bars. For what? What have they done to deserve that?"

"Well, talk about it to our brother here," Jamuse urged. "What do you really know about what he has done beyond what you have been told? I mean this is a unique opportunity. How often do you have situations where you know the man involved well enough to question him and get to the bottom of the truth? You should thank God that you know Brother Elias so well. And for God's sake let's still regard ourselves as brothers until we find absolutely convincing evidence to the contrary."

Gradually, the rage in Governor El-Dergawi began to subside and calmness came back to his speech. "Let me try to respond to our brother's call for a conciliatory discussion," he said. "Brother Elias, we have called you because frankly we could not persuade ourselves that the man we so much took into our hearts as a brother could do this to us. We have searched our minds and souls in an effort to find out what wrong we did to you to warrant such a punishment. What have they given you to betray innocent people who had taken you to be one of them?"

Elias's immediate response was anger, but on quick reflection, he decided to forgive them when he realized that they were under the misconception that he had been responsible for the arrest of their people.

"Are you gentlemen trying to tell me that you suspect me of having anything to do with the arrests that have taken place?" he managed to ask in a relatively calm manner.

When no response came, Elias urged, "Come on, tell me. Are you suspecting me of having betrayed your friendship?"

They remained silent, looking somewhat disconcerted as though not knowing what to say. Again, it was Abdalla Jamuse who broke the seeming impasse. "Why don't you tell Elias the whole story?"

"Well, you know the full story, why don't you tell him?" interjected Sultan Ibrahim to Jamuse.

"Let me give it a go then," conceded Jamuse. "As I understand the situation, Brother Elias, after your sudden departure from El Fasher, our brothers enquired about you and were told things that aroused their suspicions against you. Much of what they were told by General Abd el-Bagi of the Army was corroborated by General Yahya of the Police Forces. When the arrests were announced, General el-Bagi went back to our brothers and made it sound as though his statements about you had come true. Frankly, I can't tell you in specific terms just what he said that led people to that conclusion, but there was not the slightest doubt that you had not only endangered the security of the Rizeigat in favor of the Dinka, but had also betrayed the Fur to the central government, all because of your professional ambitions."

"My God!" said Elias. "Unbelievable! And you, whom I regarded as friends and brothers, went ahead and believed what you were told without so much as giving me the benefit of any doubt? I can now see that while you deceived me into thinking that you and I were together against them, you were all along allied as Northerners and I was the outsider. With them, yours is only a family quarrel while mine with all of you is the feud of strangers. Thank you for teaching me a lesson which I hope I will survive to benefit from."

"Come on, Brother Elias, don't also be unreasonable," Abdalla now tried to pacify the situation. "If we assume that we have been misled by circumstances to misjudge you, is that any reason to jump to the opposite extreme and misjudge us?"

"You see you are still saying 'if we assume' which means you still believe what you were told," replied Elias. "Can't you people see what you are doing? You are accusing me of treachery, one of the most dishonorable things according to my own code of ethics. I now know that I do not know the Fur well enough to understand your moral values, for if I had suspected anyone of doing what you think I have done to your people, I would not even talk to them, let alone ask them to my home and offer them a drink."

"Don't blame the brothers for that," Abdalla Jamuse interjected. "The meeting was my idea; so, if it was wrong, I am to blame. But I don't think it was a bad idea. In fact, I am sure it was the right thing to do."

"Yes, to the extent that it has taught me who is who and where I belong," Elias replied with bitterness.

"Are you telling us that there has been a misunderstanding?" asked Ibrahim El-Dergawi, now being swayed by Elias's reaction.

"I am not talking of a misunderstanding," returned Elias. "That's your own judgment, not mine. What I am talking about are the facts as I know them and these are what happened when I was in Darfur and your present attitude towards me. By God, you are among the most treacherous people I have ever known, making me believe that you were brothers while you were conspiring with my enemies behind my back. Now I understand perfectly why you kept General Abd el-Bagi informed of my meetings with you."

"What are you talking about?" said Governor El-Dergawi.

"I decided I would keep our social meetings our own affair and did not need to tell them about it," Elias explained. "When General Abd el-Bagi complained to me about not keeping them informed, in addition to telling him that I did not think it was any of his business, I asked him how he had heard about it any way. He said the governor had informed him. Now I know you were the commander's secret agent."

Governor El-Dergawi was in turn outraged, but he felt that he owed Elias an explanation. "For God's sake, the man told me point blank that he heard we had been to my village on the weekend. I merely confirmed it and added that we wanted to introduce his young Southern officer to life in Darfur. That was all. How dare you call me a secret agent for the commander?"

"Elias, there is no reason to be offensive," Abdalla Jamuse intervened. "The sultan is absolutely correct. Something is beginning to surface. Let us explore it without being emotional. Brothers, can't you see now that there is no limit to which these Arabs will go to create a *fitna* — a feud between kith and kin?"

Governor El-Dergawi now sat with his head buried between his hands. He was beginning to feel a combination of anger, embarrassment and shame at the way they had been manipulated.

"Frankly, I cannot think straight with anger, but I will try to respond to your plea to explore the situation calmly," Elias decided to be more conciliatory. "You see, until this Darfur business, I had never really known how evil human beings can be. I have seen people quarrel, fight, even kill one another. But I have never seen such a cold-blooded, cowardly way of destroying people as I learned in Darfur. If you want the facts, I will give them to you and you can use them as you will. At least I will tell you what I know; nothing but the truth, so help me God."

Now freed from his promise of secrecy by the way his superiors back in Darfur had violated all moral and professional codes of conduct, Elias decided to tell them details of the sequence of events, including his unexpected recall to Khartoum and all that he had come to know at Headquarters about the secret reports which his seniors were writing about his association with the Fur. "You have no idea how distraught I felt about the manner in which I was forced to leave. I decided to depart without contacting any one of you because I thought that would be the best way of bringing the message home. Now, all that has been turned around and used for precisely the opposite objective. By God, I cannot leave this matter. I will get to the roots of it even if it destroys my life, far less my career."

"Now Brother, you are falling into their trap," Abdalla Jamuse counselled. "Don't be foolish; that is exactly what they want you to do. We must play it cool. Rest assured that we will not betray your confidence. Let's turn this nasty lesson into something constructive."

"Abdalla is right," commented Ibrahim El-Dergawi. "I am particularly glad that he insisted on our talking to you. Frankly, I was against it because I did not see what good there was in discussion after what we had been led to believe. Now we know the circumstances leading to these outrageous requests. And that is really what counts. Our people are innocent and the truth is there. Even if they try to cloud it with smoke, all that smoke will be blown away and the truth will be uncovered, however long it might take. Listen to Hamid's advice, brother; let's play it cool. We have more to lose by getting upset."

"*Salaam aleikum*," a voice was heard at the gate as more people arrived. The fact that the governor was going through a painful political experience was reason enough in the socially orientated culture of the Sudan to invite visitors to express their personal sympathy. Given the lateness of the hour, they were probably members of his inner circle.

"*Aleikum salaam*," responded Governor El-Dergawi and his Fur companions. Elias remained silent.

"I ought to be going," said Elias.

"No, not yet," returned Jamuse. "Some of these brothers should meet you."

But Elias did not want to be subjected to undoing the harm that the security forces had done a second time; once was more than enough for the evening.

"I am sorry, but I really must go," he insisted.

One of the newcomers read the mood of Elias's farewell and commented, "I hope we are not interfering with your company?"

"No, no," replied the governor, "be seated."

As the governor invited the newcomers to sit, Abdalla Jamuse said to him and the sultan, "Let's see our brother off."

They followed Elias. When they reached the gate, Abdalla Jamuse stopped them with a few concluding remarks, "We now know what happened. I also realize that this has caused considerable harm to the trust and solidarity that has prevailed between you people. I did not know Brother Elias before, but I had heard a great deal about him. And what I have seen of him this evening has confirmed the excellent reputation that had preceded him. I really think it is for us to apologize to him, seek his forgiveness, and restore our brotherhood and solidarity."

Then turning to Hamid El-Dergawi, Jamuse said, "Governor, come, shake your brother's hand in apology."

"Brother Elias," Governor El-Dergawi spoke in full sincerity. "I am not merely responding to Brother Abdalla's call; I am following my conscience and heartfelt sentiments. Please forgive us for allowing ourselves to be misled. Now we know. And believe us, our sentiments towards you will not only go back to where they were, but have indeed grown deeper."

They embraced.

"Naturally, Hamid speaks for all of us," said Sultan Ibrahim. "Let this be a lesson for the future to us all."

He embraced Elias.

"Goodbye, brother," said Abdalla as he too embraced Elias. "We have even worse battles ahead. Let us not be distracted by small internal squabbles."

Elias headed for the mess to reflect on the evening's events and to decide how best he should handle the situation. But although he kept an open mind on the issue, he felt that his Fur friends were probably correct that the less noise he made the better. After all, did he not learn from his Dinka code that right will ultimately prevail and the truth will surface however long it might be covered?

FIFTEEN

WHETHER HE WAS INFLUENCED by the confrontation with his Fur friends or by the situation in general, Elias spent the night tossing about in a restless dream world. The dreams took him back to his early childhood in Dinkaland, through his educational institutions in the South and the North, and on to his military training and subsequent professional experiences in Khartoum and Darfur. When he woke up the next morning, a vision from one of his dreams remained vivid in his mind. His maternal grandfather Monychol had appeared. "Son of my daughter," Monychol had said, "I hear that you are about to go to foreign lands. They say it will probably be years before you return. I ask you to go home and visit your loved ones before you leave your country. You will break your peoples' hearts if you leave without visiting them. The sight of one's child is like food: offer it and you will have sustained your people; take it away from them and you will have starved them."

Elias went to General Ali the following day and explained his dream and his decision to go home. "I cannot disregard my ancestor's will; I must go whatever the risks."

"Well, what can I say?" Ali remarked. "Obviously, I cannot tell you to disregard the wishes of your ancestors. All I can say is take care and may God protect you."

As soon as Elias got home, he found that the political problems which he had first witnessed in Darfur were manifesting themselves in Dak-Jur and among his people, the Mathiang Dinka. His father was the first to indicate to him the state of insecurity that was prevailing.

"Son, we are pleased to see you, but you should not have come at this particular time," Malengdit told his son the moment they were alone. "The Arabs are going wild. I don't know what has possessed them to imagine things and then act upon their imagination to cause harm to others and even to themselves."

Malengdit then explained that as soon as the news was heard from Khartoum about the anti-Arab campaign in Darfur and Bahr El Ghazal, the commanding officer of the local security forces had come to him to explain the situation.

"So far our area is calm," the officer had said to the chief, "but we have to be on the look out and take preventive measures as soon as we detect anything so that we can protect our area from destructive elements."

"I thought there was nothing harmful in what he said," reported Malengdit to his son. "But he soon started arresting people here and there and interrogating others as though he suspected everyone. He is not even allowing the police to do their security work. He has taken everything into his own hands. I would not be surprised if he believes that I am myself a rebel chief."

"What's the name of the commanding officer?" asked Elias.

"A young man by the name of Ali Osman," said his father. "He looks barely old enough to be a soldier, let alone a commanding officer. Instead of working with the leaders, he has surrounded himself with informers to whom he throws scraps to obtain false information on innocent people. As a result of his recklessness, I am afraid many of our young people are being driven into rebellion. Several people have been tortured to death. Ali Osman himself admitted to having shot and killed a young man from the Akeu Dinka who had come into this area with his cattle looking for grazing. Now, as soon as people see a man arrested and taken by the army instead of to the police post, they expect him to be tortured, if not killed.

"They arrested your cousin Adol and tortured him until
I went and exploded in anger. And all that was because
informers claimed that Adol was the leader of the anti-Arab
campaign among the warriors. Now, as a result of the way they
treated him, Adol has taken to the bush and has indeed started
a local rebellion. We no longer have any control, let alone
influence, over what he is doing in the forest.

"They also arrested and tortured your uncle Alier simply
because he had a feast and young warriors went and shared
it. That was interpreted by the officer as a gathering to plan
an attack against the Rizeigat Arabs. When your young uncle
Marial saw the way the eldest son of his father had been
treated by the Arabs, he got angry and joined his age-mates
in the bush. I later succeeded in having Alier released, but the
harm had already been done. In fact, many young people are
now being driven into rebellion by the behavior of this young
officer and what they hear about the tension and conflict
between the Arabs and the Dinka."

Elias decided to make a courtesy call on the controversial
officer. Ali Osman, a young man in his early twenties, who
was light-colored and rather friendly, received Elias very
warmly and respectfully. Although Elias did not know him
because he was several years his junior, Ali knew of Elias
through his reputation as a promising Southern officer who
had been near the top of his class. He had not realized that
Elias was from Dak-Jur. Nor did he seem to know that Elias
had followed the rapidly deteriorating security situation in
Darfur and Bahr El Ghazal. Although Elias furnished Ali
Osman with information from Darfur and Khartoum, he
carefully avoided any details that might give him grounds for
suspicion or caution. All in all, their meeting was cordial, even
though Ali looked somewhat uneasy and apprehensive,
presumably because he realized that Elias might be unhappy
about what they were doing to his people.

It was Elias who introduced the issue of the security
situation. "I have heard a few things about the worsening
security situation," he began. "Of course, although some of
these were reported to me by my father who is the responsible
man in the area, much of it is in the form of gossip which one

cannot accept without verification. I thought I should hear your version of what is happening and to see whether I can be of any help to you in promoting the area's security."

"Brother Elias, thank you for your constructive and patriotic offer," responded Ali Osman with a naive sense of superiority, as though he were the senior officer. "What I see developing is a situation in which the leading families, which are also the most politically sophisticated, are seeking to combine government authority with the leadership of the growing rebellion. This could develop into a dangerous situation because the chiefs may not be as resolute against the rebel leaders as they otherwise could be. Now, I know that you are a son of the chief and the people I am talking about are probably related to you in some way or another. If there is a way you can help in that respect, I would be most grateful."

"Frankly, my personal opinion is that the security authorities should work closely with the legitimate community leaders because they too have a vested interest in peace and stability," commented Elias. "It may well be that there are members of their extended and even immediate families who find personal fulfillment in rebellion. But if they threaten the security of the area without any reasons which the chiefs could see as justification, I cannot see the chiefs collaborating. This means two things. First, one should cooperate with the chiefs. Second, one should do what one can to deny the rebels any moral cause which can win the sympathy of the community leaders and the public."

"I have no problem with that formulation," responded the officer. "In fact, I agree with you."

"Good," acknowledged Elias with satisfaction. "In that case, what I would like to do is discuss with my father and the other leaders of the tribe how we can move on both fronts: consolidating their cooperation with you and seeing to it that together you do not give the rebels a moral cause in the eyes of the people."

"Fine," responded Ali Osman, somewhat suspiciously, but not unconvinced. And then as though to change the subject, he said, "Let me give you an example of what I mean by the leaders cooperating with the rebels. You see, these so-called rebels are not really a force, but a bunch of criminals who roam about intimidating people and robbing them of food and money. Out of sheer fear, many young men join because they are confronted with the choice of being with them or against them and the consequences of being against them can be very severe indeed. It may not mean death, but it could mean the loss of all that one owns. And there are tribal leaders who are working to facilitate contact between the rebel leaders and young warriors. Right now, my men are looking for a man who has been offering the rebel leaders much logistical support. Two days ago for instance, they spent the night in his home and he slaughtered a bull for them. We cannot allow this kind of thing to continue unpunished or else we will lose credibility as security forces."

"I will go and talk to my father and the other leaders and will be in contact with you soon," remarked Elias as he rose to leave.

"Very well," responded Ali Osman. They shook hands and parted.

When Elias got back to Dak-Jur, he found his uncle Alier in his father's court. Alier had heard of his nephew's arrival and had hurried to see him. As Alier had something to tell his nephew, they went and stood a distance from the crowd.

"Son of my sister, I could not sleep when I heard that you had come," began Alier. "If people could send messages through dreams, I would have communicated my objection to your visit. The world is going crazy. You live with the Arabs, but you do not seem to understand them. They are not only cruel to us, they are also envious. When they see a black man get educated the way you are, they recognize that you are a fruit of redemption to your people and they don't like that. They will go out of their way to create trouble for you and as soon as they can, destroy you."

Elias could not help but remember what had happened to him in Darfur. If that experience were any guide, Alier was surprisingly correct.

"Things are bad, son of my sister," continued Alier. "People are accumulating guns and ammunition. The way I see the arms building up in this area, there will have to be war.

It is impossible to avoid it. We are all being pressured to take sides. And how can there be any doubts about the side one belongs to? We are Dinkas, and it is the Arabs who are trying to take us back to the days when they used to hunt us like animals and carry us away as slaves. Our young men are right to fight back and it is for us, their elders, to help them in any way we can."

Elias Bol was rather intrigued by his uncle's analysis of the political situation from the Dinka viewpoint. He recognized its oversimplifications, but on the whole, he was struck by Alier's level of consciousness and anger.

"They stopped in my place a few days ago, these young warriors whom they now call the people of the forest. I had a bull slaughtered for them and had quantities of food prepared to sustain them for some days."

Elias Bol could not believe his ears. "The rebels spent a night in your home and you slaughtered a bull for them?" he asked.

"Yes," Alier reaffirmed. "They included your cousin, Adol, and Marial, the son of my father."

"My God!" Elias exclaimed, shocked. "Uncle, you do not realize what trouble you are in." He then went on to explain to Alier that soldiers had been sent after him and were probably in his village at that very moment.

"You see, we Dinka deserve the treatment we get from the Arabs," Alier commented. "Just think that someone would run to inform on a person who has merely offered food to the sons of the land who are fighting for the dignity of their people! How can the Arab expect us to turn our backs on our sons?"

But Elias Bol was not interested in reasons. The main point was that his uncle was in trouble.

"Come, we must go immediately," he said.

"Where?"

"To the officer at the security quarters," responded Elias.

Alier's instinct was not to go, and he hesitated. But he also trusted his nephew's judgment. "There is no room for second thoughts," Elias spoke emphatically. "Right now, they are probably tracing you to this place and if they get to you before you approach them yourself, it will probably be too late to defend you. Let's go!"

Ali Osman was surprised to see Elias return so soon. He was even more surprised to see Alier, whom his men were seeking; what he did not know was the connection between the two.

"I have brought you the man you are looking for," Elias reported. "He is my maternal uncle."

"I see; I did not know that," Ali Osman replied.

"He came to report to me and I thought I should bring him to you directly."

"Did your nephew tell you that my people are looking for you right now?" Ali grew angry as he spoke to Alier. "What's your story anyway?"

Although Elias and Alier had not agreed on a story, Alier's presentation, interpreted by his nephew, was more persuasive than Elias could have expected.

"The rebels came to my home carrying arms and demanded that I offer them hospitality," he began. "Although there were relatives among them to whom I would in any case have felt morally obliged to offer food, it was really a choice between being generous to the whole group or dismissing them as rebels. The truth is that I had only spears and they carried guns.

"If I had denied them food, even those among them who are relatives would have seen me as an enemy. I showed them hospitality in the hope that the authorities would appreciate the precariousness of my position. I heard of my nephew's arrival just as they left, and I decided to come and report to him and his father immediately. Being himself an officer in the army, I thought he and you were the same. He suggested that we should come together to report to you personally. And here we are."

"Are you trying to be clever with me?" was Ali Osman's reaction.

"What does cleverness have to do with truth?" retorted Alier. "I have told you the truth as I know it. After all, did I not come here because you called for me? Did I not take the initiative myself to report?"

"Did you show them any resistance at all or did you decide

to cooperate with them from the beginning?"

"That's what I was trying to explain to you," responded Alier. "Those are no longer our people. They have found their own community in the forest. They no longer know their fathers or their brothers. How could I challenge them empty-handed and expect any sympathy from them?"

"You are truly a lucky man to have your nephew come at precisely this time," said Ali. "If he had not brought you and my people had found you at your home, you would have been brought back in chains."

"It's not luck, officer," remarked Elias. "It's just that God knows the truth and protects the righteous."

"Whatever, in deference to your nephew, who is my brother-in-arms, I am going to let you go," Ali announced. "But I have one condition: you should join us and cooperate with us by keeping us informed about the rebel activities in your area."

It was Elias who responded to Ali's proposition. "No," he objected, "that cannot be, for several reasons. My uncle is an elder who is highly regarded and respected in the community. You must realize that your informants, useful as they may be, have little or no social standing in the community. Indeed, they are despised and looked down upon. It would expose my uncle to almost certain physical danger, precisely because he would be too conspicuous to turn from a respected community leader into a secret security agent. What is more, my plan, as we discussed it, is to foster cooperation between the established leadership and the security forces. He will cooperate with you and the other leaders on that basis, but not as an informer."

"I can see your argument," conceded Ali Osman. "But in that case, you should move closer to us here or to Chief Malengdit's village so that your home is not used by rebels as a base for logistical support. You see, this is the second time you have been suspected of offering them support."

"I think your suggestion is a good one," responded Elias. "Even though it might entail some inconvenience, I don't think my uncle would object to coming closer to your protection. The countryside has become dangerous."

Alier accepted this suggestion. "I am myself becoming weary of these repeated incidents of suspicion and potential problems with the law," he added.

During the days and weeks that followed, Elias worked hard through his father and the security authorities to foster mutual understanding and cooperation. He suggested a public meeting with the people to discuss the overall security situation and what they saw to be the problem. Ali insisted that Elias should meet with the people alone without fear or inhibition, and he accepted. In the meeting that followed, there was an overwhelming condemnation of the Dinka informers as the source of mistrust, tension, and conflict between the security forces and the people. Several people argued that if the authorities could be persuaded to work only with the legitimate leaders and avoid rumormongers and self-appointed informers who were motivated by personal gain, the situation could be considerably improved.

A number of people had spoken when Akol, Chief Malengdit's half-brother, struggled for the floor with obvious impatience. He was recognized.

"You, Bol, let me tell you," he spoke angrily. "Don't push the people of your father into exposing themselves to the hyenas of this land who cannot distinguish between what is fresh and what is foul. How can you trust the Arabs? A few days from now you will go and our people will remain at the mercy of the security forces and their informers. They will get ambushed and tortured because of lies invented by those who want to live on the flesh and blood of innocent people. They will collect their reward and move on to fabricate more lies with impunity. Not even your father will be able to save the innocent. And somehow God and the ancestors too seem to have removed themselves from the affairs of this world. In the past, people like that would be struck dead by unseen powers. That's when spirits were watching over the affairs of men. But they have become confused by the kind of mixing between races and languages which has taken place. That is why a chief of one Dinka tribe never learned to speak Arabic. He said he asked God why he had denied him the knowledge of Arabic and God told him never to learn the language. 'Why?' he asked. God replied. 'The moment you learn Arabic, you will turn into an evil person.' What he meant was the sort of things happening here, where people learn a few words of Arabic and run to tell lies about others. Our Dinka language is not good for that; it is a language that fears God. Those who learn Arabic to feed themselves at the expense of the innocent do not know what God is.

"I am appealing this way because I have decided not to care. If they kill me, let them; I have begotten children whom I will leave behind. As for you Bol, if you really want to help your people, then do it from here. Let the people there hear the truth, and if they really care about all the people of the Sudan, they will do something.

"I doubt whether Munir really knows what is happening here. But Munir has always surprised us with his shifting behavior. At first, we could not understand where God found an Arab who could be brave enough to tell his people to stop killing the black man. Now, it seems that they are again forming a united front against the South. If Munir really cares about the good work he began in this country, then tell him and his people in Khartoum what is happening here and let us see what they will do. But for now, people of my father, close your mouths and keep them shut."

Akol's words were greeted with fervent applause. And as though his words had struck the crowd silent, not a hand was raised to request the floor.

At first, Elias tried to establish contact with the local rebel leaders to persuade them that much of the recent unrest had resulted from misconceptions and fabrications, and that he would restore full understanding and cooperation between the people and the security forces. Initially, Ali opposed the idea on the ground that it was a criminal offense to contact or communicate with rebels, but Elias convinced him that it was in the public interest and could not possibly be condemned by the central authorities. But despite intensive efforts, Elias failed to win the local rebel leaders back into the community, for, according to them, they could no longer trust the Arabs.

Elias found that he had no choice but to try to foster cooperation between the security forces and the established leaders even if that meant creating a rift between their followers and the rebels.

As they went to the meeting in which agreement for cooperation between the security forces and the community was to be finalized, Ali Osman complained to Elias about what his uncle, Akol, had said in the earlier public meeting. Elias was dismayed to learn that Ali, after having assured him of his commitment to freedom of expression, had infiltrated the meeting with his agents.

"I had to do it," Ali complained.

"I do not at all agree with you," responded Elias, "although I appreciate why you may have felt it necessary to do."

"And, frankly," Ali continued, "if it were not for my respect for you, that uncle of yours would be in serious trouble because of his irresponsible words to the public. You can see in his conduct precisely why it was necessary to cover the meeting. I am leaving him for your sake, but I hope you will ask him and other leading members of your family to stop playing a double game and be unequivocal in their cooperation with us. Otherwise we must assume that they are cooperating with the enemy and will treat them accordingly."

Realizing the uselessness of arguing with Ali, Elias appreciated the deference he showed him by taking no action against Akol.

At the public meeting, people of the tribe expressed the opinion that Elias's return had helped to save their perilous situation. Elias himself remained cautiously optimistic, even if the problems remained profoundly insoluable.

When Elias reported to his uncle and other elders what Ali had said about double-dealing and cooperating fully with the security authorities, Akol said, "Do the Arabs really expect us to work with them against our own children who are fighting the enslavement of their people? How could they even think of respecting us if they believed we could descend that low?"

The elders laughed in a way that indicated Akol had echoed the thoughts they all shared.

When Elias came to leave, Alier, after conducting his usual farewell blessings, was pulled aside by Elias who said, "Uncle, do you know that I would not have come had it not been because of my grandfather Monychol?"

Alier looked confused.

Elias explained. "He came to me in a dream and urged me to come and see my people before going to foreign lands. Many people, including senior government officials, advised me against coming because of the kind of problems I have found here. But because of Grandfather Monychol's words in the dream I refused to be persuaded."

"Son of my sister, that is what I mean when I call you a blessed son," Alier responded. "I told you that my father spoke to me about you being a sacred child with a mission in life. And that is the difference between ordinary people and divine leaders. My father and you saw something which your friends and I could not see. I told you that had I been able to see in the future and pass messages on through dreams, I would have advised you not to come the way your friends in Khartoum did. But my father knew the sacred mission for which he prayed over you and cursed himself to an early death to redeem you. Now you have saved the lives of many people who would have fallen by the hands of the army and their security hounds. I am glad you have told me the story of your dream. When I return home, I will sacrifice to my father to thank him for his word. The ancestors do indeed watch over us."

SIXTEEN

ELIAS CALLED ON GENERAL Ali the following Friday in order to brief him on what he had found in the South and to get news of what was going on at Headquarters. He arrived at about eleven o'clock to find that Ali's extended family had been visiting and were now leaving. It was then that Elias first met Ali's brother, Sheikh Mohamed Ahmed El-Jak, and his family. Mohamed was several years older than Ali, but his youthful exploits, when he had been a trader in the West, with adventures deep into the South — raiding for slaves and cattle — seemed to add weight to his age. Dressed in an ill-fitting jallabiya, with a shawl around his shoulders and a loosely wound imma on his head, he had a sardonic face. He rarely smiled and when he did, it seemed to be conceding to pressure and made those on whom he smiled feel uneasily grateful.

When Ali introduced Elias, Mohamed eyed the young officer closely and, as though he had never heard of him, asked with an air of superiority, "Which part of the South do you come from?"

"A village called Dak-Jur in the Northwest District of Bahr El Ghazal."

"That sounds like Dinkaland," Mohamed said in a tone that barely concealed familiarity with the territory.

"Yes, Dinkaland; I am Dinka from the Mathiang section," Elias explained.

General Ali interjected, "Mohamed speaks some Dinka as I recall."

"Really?" remarked Elias with some excitement.

Finding himself on the spot and for some reason desirous of playing down whatever knowledge of Dinka he might have had, Mohamed demurred, "Only a few words, and that was ages ago."

"When were you in Dinkaland?" Elias's curiosity was peaked.

But something about Elias bothered Mohamed. Appearing more distracted than impatient but obviously curt in his mannerism, he responded casually. "I wasn't really in Dinkaland," he said, deliberately looking away.

"But how did you get to know Dinka?" Elias was still intrigued.

Mohamed turned to Elias and gave him a stern glance that seemed to dissect the young man. As though he had definitely decided to dislike him, he said, "I passed through Dinkaland and picked up a few words here and there." In order to prevent Elias from raising another question, he turned to go, remarking as he walked away, "*Sheed heilak,*" a challenging imploration to work hard and prove one's self. And without waiting for a reaction from Elias, he shouted to his family as he strolled toward the car, "Come on, let's go!"

As though to compensate for his brother's rudeness, Ali attracted the attention of Mohamed's daughter, Fadheela, and introduced her to Elias.

"And here is my favorite niece," Ali said, holding Fadheela by the arm. "Come and meet my favorite and only son, the officer of whom I am so proud."

Ali was so solicitous that Fadheela seemed to forget her father's call. And her father seemed to prefer disappearing to having his voice heard again by Elias.

Fadheela had the rather unusual profession (at least in her father's eyes) of being a teacher at the Khartoum Institute of Fine Art. Her main interest was design, but she also sculpted and painted. She was of medium height, rich brown in color, with a set of slightly buck teeth, adding a touch of exotic imperfection, especially against the background of her black gums.

"So you are the young man about whom I have heard so much!" Fadheela, whose name meant 'Virtuous One,' commented as she extended her hand to Elias, with a sensuous smile and a twist of her slender figure.

Elias was too struck by the young lady to respond to her greeting appropriately. "How do you do?" he replied poorly.

The contrast between his glowing reputation and his apparent modesty intrigued Fadheela.

"I made up my mind even before meeting you that I would ask you to model for me," she said with disarming confidence. "And of course it would all be in the family; nothing suspicious."

Since Fadheela seemed to have thought of all possible implications and resolved them amicably, Elias decided not to worry about the social reaction. He was certainly taken offguard, but was instinctively captivated.

"Now that you have seen the object of your artistic design, are you sure you still want to proceed with the project?" he teased.

"Especially now that I have seen the object," she flirted. And fearing that Elias might dismiss her as frivolous, she added, "You may think I am joking, but I am dead serious."

"You realize that it would have to be in the evenings or weekends?" Elias was alluding to the fact that he would resume duties at the Ministry of Defense while waiting for admission to an American university.

"I don't mind," she responded. "I work in the evenings anyway."

General Ali, at first distracted, had caught the gist of their conversation. "Elias has some rather serious preoccupations these days," he interjected. "But, on the other hand, this might be perfect timing; the project may take his mind off some of these preoccupations. That would not be such a bad thing Elias, would it?"

"Not at all." Elias sounded enthusiastic.

"When do we begin?" was Fadheela's eager reply.

"As soon as you wish," conceded Elias without really thinking.

"How about the first day of next week?"

"That's fine with me."

Ali and Elias continued their conversation after the family had gone. Elias essentially briefed Ali on Dak-Jur and they agreed on a strategy of minimal reaction as the best way of countering the hysteria that was underway.

As Ali saw Elias off, their conversation returned to Fadheela's project. "I must admit to being intrigued by it," said Ali. "Fadheela is a very creative and original person. She could not have thought of a more worthwhile project."

Elias could not be sure whom Ali was complimenting.

"Who would be interested in that sculpture, Uncle Ali?" Elias remarked, more to elicit compliments than to disparage himself or Fadheela's artistic talent.

"I would hope you, certainly she, and if neither of you is interested, I would be."

It was now clear to Elias that Ali wanted him to proceed with the project, although he was not sure why.

Something about Fadheela struck Elias. What could it be? She was certainly enchanting as a woman. But she was a Muslim and he a Christian. What could there be between them other than her professional interest in art and his position as an all but adopted member of her uncle's family?

The first session went well, professionally speaking. Elias sat through it without betraying any ulterior motive. As for Fadheela, she could not have been more businesslike. In fact, she was surprisingly silent as she worked, only occasionally giving instructions such as: tilt your head slightly to the right; lower your head a bit; make your chin visible to the natural light; and so on and so forth. Her tobe fell off her head several times, exposing her long neck down to the shoulders, but she adjusted it matter-of-factly and neither of them interpreted her appearance as anything other than normal.

After the first day, she remarked to Elias, "You are a fine model; I believe we will work together very well. Remember it's all in the family." Something about her last sentence seemed to plant ideas in his head. But he took it as merely a flirtatious joke to be met with appropriate laughter, and not taken seriously.

They had had about five sessions and the figure was

beginning to emerge recognizably when Fadheela came into the studio one day looking distraught. Elias took his place; Fadheela sat on her stool and began to work quietly without a word and radiating currents of hostility which Elias could not understand, far less explain. So bothered by her mood was he that he could not relax. And it was as though her state of mind showed on his figure and interfered with the formation of the sculpture. Elias decided to do something about the chill in the atmosphere between them. "Fadheela, there ought to be more to what you say about this being in the family."

"What do you mean?" Fadheela asked, still cold, but sounding friendlier.

"I mean that since we started this project, it has all been too professional; we have never done anything else together."

A gentle smile came over Fadheela's face, reflecting more the warm extroverted personality Elias had initially taken her to be. "What do you suggest?" she asked.

"How about going to the movies?" responded Elias, as though anything other than working on the sculpture would do.

"Does that sound like a family activity?" she queried, smiling teasingly.

"If it is not, would you prefer the National Museum?"

"You know I wouldn't mind," Fadheela responded more seriously. "In fact, I would like it very much. But I am afraid."

"Of what?"

"You know!" She responded, again becoming reflective and dejected.

"I hope not of me!" Elias remarked, sounding rather serious.

She looked at him with a smile and said, "Perhaps I should be, but you are not what I am afraid of."

"Then what are you afraid of?" Elias pressed for an explanation.

"I don't know where to begin or what to say."

Fearing that he might have pressed her too much, Elias decided on a different approach. "Perhaps a change of atmosphere will help. How about going for dinner at the Officers' Club?"

"That might aggravate matters," she replied. "You know what kind of society we live in!"

Now Elias understood. Fadheela was afraid of gossip or social scandal. Obviously, it was not all in the family. And although he had been virtually adopted into Ali's family, Sheikh Mohamed's immediate family, to which Fadheela belonged, was quite another matter. On the other hand, he now felt an even greater need for a quiet talk with Fadheela. And he also felt sure that the Officers' Club was a respectable place for them to be.

"Most officers know my relationship with General Ali," he explained. "I am sure dinner at the Club with his niece would be viewed as normal or at least proper."

"I hate to think what my father might read into it if he knew," she said looking away as though thinking out loud. Turning to Elias once more, with an enchanting smile on her face, she added, "On the other hand, why not? Let's go."

The Club was a huge complex near the airport with a spacious garden, tastefully furnished with tables and chairs and decorative neon lighting. Inside the building were rooms of various sizes, elegantly furnished for various functional purposes. There were areas for lounging, rooms for formal meetings, and rooms for meals. The head waiter saw the couple and instinctively chose to lead them inside the building to a somewhat small, quiet and rather exclusive room. The trouble was that although it would guarantee them privacy, they would miss the ambiance of the greenery outside. They looked at one another and communicated in silence. Elias gestured with his hand, indicating that he would rather they sat outside. "Very well," responded the waiter with no sign of offense and led them to a table at the southern tip of the garden.

It was a pleasant evening. Couples or groups sat well apart enjoying the cool breeze off the desert. In the distance planes took off and landed and the sounds from their engines reached the spectators' ears indistinctly.

As Elias and Fadheela sat in their corner, it was quite obvious that they were more interested in conversing than in eating. They ordered a lemon drink, placed their orders for dinner, and started to talk.

"Would you now tell me what is on your mind?" Elias began as he leaned forward, his arms crossed and resting on the table, his face concentrated on Fadheela's face, his eyes radiating sensuously more than what his words said. Fadheela seemed to feel the message, but pretended not to. "Do you mind if I press for an answer?" Elias repeated his request.

"No, I don't," responded Fadheela, "but that doesn't make it any easier for me to talk." She fiddled with her knife and fork silently for a moment and then went on. "I might as well tell you. My father and I had a row before I came to the studio. He asked why I was doing a sculpture of you."

Fadheela paused as if to see the impact of her words on Elias. He could not resist the temptation. "What did you say?"

"My exact words were, 'Father, I am an artist.'"

Elias might have laughed and part of him wanted to. But the dominant part told him that laughing would be the wrong thing to do in the circumstances. Instead, he looked serious and deep in reflection.

"What's the matter?" Fadheela asked, somewhat surprised by Elias's response. "Have I said anything wrong?"

"No! No!" he reassured her.

"Then why are you looking offended?"

"'Offended' is not quite the right word," replied Elias without changing his posture or tone.

"Anyway, what is the matter?" Fadheela probed.

"I guess I had hoped that there was more to it than art."

Fadheela, who had raised her eyes to look at Elias, dropped them again and remained silent for a while. Elias chose not to disturb the silence and Fadheela seemed to appreciate it. After reflecting for a moment, she raised her eyes to Elias. He caught her look out of the corner of his eyes and reciprocated. She intensified her look and smiled.

The waiter came with their dinner. Their silence continued as the food was laid on the table, with an occasional word of appreciation to the waiter.

When they were once more alone, they seemed to be less interested in the food, even though they toyed with it and managed a bite now and then.

Fadheela remembered that Elias had been the last to speak

and that he had expressed some disappointment about her emphasis on the art side of their togetherness. She wanted to correct that, but decided to leave it ambiguous. That was probably a more meaningful response than being too explicit.

"I can understand my father's concern, our Muslim society being what it is," she chose to say instead. "But for God's sake, I am grown up and a professional at that."

Elias resorted to his Dinka upbringing on how to intercede constructively in a conflict in which one of the parties is closer to you: the best thing to do is to side with the party farthest removed from you; that way, you can better protect the interest of the person closest to you.

"If, as you say, one must try to understand your father's position in terms of the Islamic society in which we live, then you must realize that in Islam an unmarried woman is dependent on her father. You must also realize that there is no such thing as a professional woman in this Muslim society. So you can't blame the old man for not fully appreciating something neither his generation nor his religion can understand."

"Are you on his side or on mine?" Fadheela asked in a lighthearted manner that made Elias feel that his Dinka approach was working.

"Can you make a guess?" He threw the question back.

Fadheela understood. "What are you suggesting?" she asked, still speaking in a joking manner. "To succumb to the dictates of his generation and religion?"

"Begin first by appreciating his position!" Elias was now sounding even more serious. "Then with that frame of mind, you can begin to think of solutions that would avoid direct conflict and promote mutual understanding."

"You are sounding very wise, Elias," Fadheela replied, half-seriously and half-teasingly. "But could you tell me what that is supposed to mean in concrete terms?"

She had cornered him with a challenging question for which he could not in all honesty give a satisfactory answer.

"I hope it does not mean that you and I should not see one another," Elias responded. Then, "On a more serious note, I understand you have a brother."

"His name is Baraka. He is older than me. He is a *mawlana*, a sharia court judge."

"I wonder whether your father is acting alone or in accord with your brother Baraka?" Elias probed.

"You are indeed a genius," Fadheela decided to flatter Elias. "How did you guess?"

Elias decided to replay the joke Osman Jar-Ennabi had used during their train journey to El Fasher. Pointing his finger at his head, he said, "Kidneys!"

Fadheela caught on and decided to embellish the joke: "Brains, dummy!"

They both laughed. Perhaps for the first time they felt they stood on the same ground.

"Actually, I am not assuming anything," resumed Elias. "I am seriously wondering what Baraka's position is, being of a different generation."

"To tell you the truth, I really do not know either. I have not talked to him. All I know is what my father said."

"And what was that?" Elias seized the point. "In fact, tell me more about what happened between you and your father."

Fadheela remained silent. She looked down at the table, turned toward Elias and smiled, still without saying anything. It was quite clear that she was trying to conceal something, probably to avoid hurting Elias or fanning hostility between him and her family.

"Please tell me," he urged, "and don't worry about hurting me."

"What makes you think I am worried about hurting you?" she replied.

"I can tell; but please tell me anyway." Elias was pressing for the truth.

"Why do you want to know?" Fadheela tried to be evasive. "After all, it really doesn't matter much. Besides, I am sure you have other things to worry about."

"Right now, you have succeeded in making this my main worry," Elias was adamant. "Please tell me."

Fadheela looked torn. Of course, she now had to say more to Elias, but she worried that it would almost certainly result in more complications. She sighed, remained silent for a moment longer, and then looking somewhat reconciled to the risks involved, said, "Well, if you insist, I will tell you the whole truth, nothing else but the truth, as they say in courts of law. You see, just as I was about to leave for the studio, my mother asked me when I expected to be back. I said I did not know; it would depend on how the work on the sculpture was proceeding. My father heard me and, as if it were his first time to learn about the project, began to question me. When I gave him my arguments, he said, 'No one will understand how a young officer can innocently model for you. And what is more, this young man is a *nasrani*, a Christian. You know that your brother Baraka is a *qadi shar'i*, a Muslim judge, with leadership prospects in the country. How will it look to people if his own sister admires a *nasrani*, and for that matter, a *janubi*, a Southerner, to the point of making a sculpture of his head?'"

"And then?" Elias queried, when Fadheela paused.

"I said to him, 'Father, first, let me tell you that as an artist, I am interested in the object and not the man.'"

Elias lowered his head in disappointment, but secretly he hoped that Fadheela had not meant what she had said. Rather than embarrass her with a question, he asked her to continue.

"Then I went on to say, 'Besides, what makes you think I share your's and Baraka's political vision? Can't you see that as a woman, I would be relegated to an inferior status in an Islamic state? I am a professional woman, Father, and I aspire to being equal to the men of my profession. Besides, I am old enough to decide what I should do with my life. Why can't you understand that?'"

"What did he say?" Elias was now becoming intrigued.

"'Shut up, girl' was the way he reacted. I could tell that he barely stopped himself from striking me. 'This *janubi* has clearly poisoned your mind. I do not want you to see any more of him. That's final.'

"I got up and said as I was leaving the room, 'In that case, I am leaving and that too is final!' I stormed out and slammed the door behind me. Now you know why I was in a grumpy mood."

"What are you going to do now?"

"I am certainly not going back to that house," Fadheela

admitted. "I have my pride."

"But where will you stay?" Elias questioned, almost unavoidably.

"That's what I mean about being grown up," she began to explain. "I am sure my father cannot believe that I have alternatives to his house. Well, I do have a colleague who is also a friend. Her name is Awatif. She teaches at the Institute and she is single. I talked to her after the fight with my father and she offered me her apartment."

"Offered you her apartment?" remarked Elias, obviously surprised. "Are you going to share the apartment with her?"

"No, she left today to visit relatives in Port Sudan. But she gave me the keys and told me that I could use the apartment whenever I wanted."

"But, Fadheela, that could only confirm your father's suspicions!"

"I know," Fadheela agreed. "But he has to realize that I am an adult with my own views on these matters. I am also a professional woman and quite capable of being independent. Does he think that I am with them because I cannot manage on my own? I want to prove to him that I do not need his accommodation." Fadheela was getting carried away with anger.

"Come on, Fadheela, calm down," Elias intervened. "You must have patience with the old man."

"What do you mean by patience?" Fadheela replied.

"For now, it means going back home," responded Elias.

Fadheela reflected for a split second. Was it possible that Elias had misunderstood her intentions? Might he have thought that she was being suggestive? The more she thought, the more she felt insulted and suddenly became silent.

Elias noticed it and reacted. "What's the matter? Have I said anything offensive?"

"No, but I think it's getting late! And I have some preparation to make for tomorrow's class."

Elias understood that Fadheela had misread his intentions. "Don't be silly, Fadheela; of course I did not mean what I think you understood." Elias paused for a moment, then went on to say, "Let me answer your question about patience more fully. Haven't you heard it said that the father is the Second God?" Elias was repeating a sentiment he had heard expressed on numerous occasions in Dinkaland.

"Then let him behave like one," observed Fadheela, still looking offended.

"Do you think God always behaves like God?" Elias replied. "Haven't you come across seemingly capricious deeds for which He is held responsible? And yet we go out of our way to find justification in God's will. We even say to Him that He is always right. And why do we do that? Partly because we fear that He might do worse harm, if provoked, and partly because we feel grateful for His having created us and guarding over our lives."

"You are now beginning to sound like an imam," Fadheela responded.

"Not at all, this is sheer common sense," Elias argued. "You see, if you get yourself into a feud with your father, you end up not only hurting him very deeply, along with your mother, by the way, but you also hurt yourself. Your father will complain bitterly. You will be accused of disloyalty and ungratefulness. Even God will listen to his grievances. In many ways, some obvious and some subtle, you will feel the blame and suffer punishment. Eventually, you yourself will begin to regret, feel guilty, and even punish yourself. Like the prodigal child, you may choose to go back to your father and humbly beg for pardon or you may continue the inexorable path to self-destruction. Why undertake that dreadful journey?"

Elias felt as though he himself had embarked on a path he had not envisaged. He also felt that he was having an impact on Fadheela.

"You see, I am your father's satan who is supposedly leading you away from the path of God," he decided to establish his credibility. "From a purely selfish point of view, I have nothing to gain from a reconciliation between you and your father. But I believe I am giving you sound advice without ulterior motives. I think you should go back home and apologize to your father before things worsen between the two of you."

Silence fell between them. They were both gazing at the

table. Then Elias turned toward Fadheela and noticed tears forming behind her eyelids. Realizing that he was looking at her, she quickly grabbed the edge of her tobe and wiped her eyes.

"I don't know what to say to him," she remarked as she broke down, sobbing.

"Just go back and react to the situation as you find it. If he is asleep, that's fine, go to sleep and see what tomorrow brings. If he is awake, just say you are sorry for the way you behaved toward him and leave it at that. If he reacts, then listen to what he says and react accordingly but politely. Remember, the key idea is filial piety."

Again wiping her eyes with the tobe, Fadheela remarked, "I think you should take me home now, if you do not mind."

Elias caught the waiter's attention and asked for the bill. As soon as he paid, they rose to leave.

Once in Elias's car, Fadheela said, "My things are in Awatif's apartment. It will take me a minute to pick them up."

She directed Elias to Awatif's address. When they arrived, Fadheela got out of the car and walked the few steps into the building. Elias recalled that Awatif would not be there; indeed, the apartment was available for Fadheela to use for the night. He felt the urge to follow. What better chance could they have had to be together in full privacy? Was he really right to have persuaded Fadheela to return home that night? Should he follow her and perhaps persuade her to change her plans? But the voice of wisdom prevailed. He felt confident that he had given Fadheela good advice and that his second thoughts were from temptation. Once he had come to that conclusion, he drove Fadheela home without further complications.

He stopped a short distance away from Fadheela's house. But as she stepped out of the car, they agreed to meet the following evening at 6:30 at the studio.

Now that he was alone, Elias began to reconstruct what Fadheela had told him. He felt a sudden dislike for Mohamed which he realized had been latent in him from the very first moment he had met the man. Mohamed must have hated him too, judging from the look on his face when they had met. But Elias still felt confident about his advice to Fadheela. That she would risk breaking with her father for the sake of a sculpture added to the depth of his feelings for her.

Elias remembered that Fadheela had not responded when he had hoped there was more to it than art. He wondered whether there was indeed more to it than art. After all, they had never said anything about feelings. And why had Fadheela not remarked on his comment? Was it because she was too embarrassed to say the obvious or because her interest was indeed purely artistic? Elias could not find answers to the many questions that crossed his mind. Thoughts, doubts and hopes were overcome by exhaustion as he fell into a sound sleep.

Elias spent the next day eagerly waiting for 6:30 pm. When the time came, he had already been at the studio for ten minutes and was impatiently looking at his watch. Five minutes past the appointed time he began to feel anxious. At 6:45, he became worried. Why was Fadheela late? She was usually punctual. He tried to talk himself out of worrying. As they say in Arabic, *el ghaib bi sababu* — an absentee has a reason. By 7:00 pm, Elias was beside himself. Of course Fadheela had a reason, but what could it be? Had she had a fight with her father and been injured? Was she perhaps in the hospital? Or had her family prevailed upon her to forget him and the sculpture? But if so, why wouldn't she come to tell him? Or was she perhaps conveying a message through her absence.

By 7:15, Elias thought of giving up and leaving, but he kept giving Fadheela a few more minutes — until 8 o'clock. Then he walked away, but returned again to see if she had come. It was 8:30 when he finally decided that something quite serious must have happened.

As Elias drove back to the officers mess, it crossed his mind to drop in on General Ali. If something had happened to Fadheela, he would know. But he decided against that because it might muddy the clear waters. Ali would almost certainly ask questions and dig deeper than was advisable.

Elias hardly slept that night. A relationship that had begun so smoothly and resulted in a relaxed working association had suddenly become turbulent. Was he falling in love? Was he perhaps already in love?

Elias spent another restless day waiting for the evening. Again, he went to the studio well before 6:30 in the hope of finding Fadheela, but there was no Fadheela in sight. He nervously stood around, waiting. After half an hour, something propelled him to go toward the sculpture itself, as if it were Fadheela herself. Then he saw the envelope neatly placed on the table, right under the sculpture. He picked it up as though it were treasure or an explosive device. He knew it was from Fadheela. He opened it impatiently but carefully to avoid tearing the envelope.

"Dear Brother Elias," the letter began in standard Arabic form, "I must apologize to you for not having turned up yesterday as agreed. We had a family meeting which began at 5:00 pm and continued late into the night. I could not bring myself to tell the family that you were waiting for me, nor did I want to tell a lie. I thought omission would be a lesser evil and I trusted that somehow you would understand.

"I also discovered, in fact remembered, that the family had arranged to visit my father's brother, Abd el-Rahman, and his family in Kosti. His eldest son, Khalifa, is a medical doctor. He works in the Kosti Civil Hospital. I told them I had a small errand to do at the Institute before leaving and they agreed to pass that way for the purpose. My intention is of course to leave this note for you at the studio.

"Let me end by thanking you for a really wonderful evening. It might not have been a cheerful occasion, but I truly valued your counsel. I shall tell you more later; for now, let me just say that your wisdom seems to have worked.

"We will be back Friday night and I shall hope to see you at the studio earlier than usual—5:30—on Saturday afternoon."

It was signed, "Your sister, Fadheela."

The letter brought immediate relief to Elias, but it also raised new questions. What had the family met about? Did it have to do with Fadheela's disagreement with her father? And in what way had his advice worked? Obviously, the fact that the family had left together to visit Mohamed's brother meant that some reconciliation had been reached. But on what basis? Would Fadheela continue to work on the project or was she persuaded to abandon it? And what of their future?

Elias went over the letter one more time. Suddenly, the name of Khalifa jumped at him. Why did Fadheela specifically mention his name? Who was he and what was he to Fadheela? They were cousins, he reasoned. But he remembered that, unlike the Dinka, where the rules of exogamy prohibited marriage between blood relatives to a very distant degree, the Arabs favored cousin marriages as family obligations. Elias checked his vivid imagination and told himself he should be patient. Fadheela would clarify matters and hopefully remove all doubts on her return.

Since the family left on Thursday and would spend the Muslim day of rest, Friday, in Kosti, returning late in the evening, Elias calculated that it was going to be a short wait although it was bound to seem too long. Anyway, he could manage to distract himself by visiting friends. Or should he visit Uncle Ali? No, for the same reasons that he had decided against visiting the evening before.

When Elias turned up at the studio at 5.00 pm on the Saturday, he found Fadheela; she had arrived even earlier and was waiting.

"*Salaam aleikum*" he greeted, feeling as though a heavy cloud had moved away from the sun.

"*Wa aleikum salaam wa rahmat allah wa barkatu*," responded Fadheela with characteristic exuberance.

Although the first impressions brought relief, Elias still felt curious and anxious. "I have made up my mind that I am not going to model this evening," he declared with a trace of humor in his voice. "I would suggest a walk on the Nile, tea at the Officers' Club, going to the movies—no, not the movies— somewhere that we can talk."

Fadheela was relaxed and spirited, almost back to what she had been when they first met.

"Actually, a walk along the Nile sounds like an excellent idea," she said with a romantic look in her eyes. "Then we might stop somewhere for a cup of tea."

"Well, let's go before the sun disappears below the horizon." And indeed, as they strolled along the shady Nile Avenue, the setting could not have been more beautiful or romantic. The sun was spreading its golden rays over the Nile waters as they shimmered with the cool breeze of the season. The winds were soft enough to ruffle the leaves, synchronizing with the gentle waves across the river. They were walking toward the confluence of the White and the Blue Niles, their eyes inevitably drawn to the great red disk of the setting sun.

"Isn't it a sight to drown all worries?" Elias remarked.

Fadheela understood that there was a purpose behind the question. She also realized that she was expected to react. "Do you have any worries to drown?" she asked, smiling at Elias.

"Don't you?"

"I asked first," Fadheela argued.

"The last time we spoke, our main concern was you," Elias explained. "Don't I deserve a report?"

"You have the gist in my letter," Fadheela tried to answer. "Your advice seems to have worked miraculously."

"And what would that mean?" He pressed for more information.

"Well, after leaving you, I went inside and found my mother still up, apparently waiting for me. She immediately told me how upset my father had been. My brother, Baraka, had dropped in to find Father fuming with anger. According to Mother, Baraka had been wonderful in calming Father and pleading my case that I be allowed a certain degree of professional independence and discretion. But, apparently, even when Baraka had made such a strong argument on my behalf, Father continued to be enraged by what he regarded as my impudent way of talking back. As Mother was reporting to me, she began to sob and then broke down in tears. I was deeply moved by her compassion for both Father and me.

"And then she said something which suddenly made her sound as though it were you talking. 'Daughter, a father is like God,' she said. 'You should not hurt your father. Instead, you should be grateful to him.' The way I saw my mother cry and the way she repeated your words moved me to tears. After I had calmed down, it became my turn to console Mother.

"Then I asked, 'Is Daddy still awake?' When she assured me that he was, I immediately got up and walked to their room. I knocked on the door and Father responded. As soon as I entered, I walked straight to him, embraced him as I sobbed and apologized about the way I had talked to him. That did it. He said '*malesh*' and began to console me."

Concluding her dramatic account of what had transpired between her and her family, Fadheela said, "So, you see how well your wisdom worked."

Elias was moved that his advice had been so helpful. He also liked what he heard about the role of Baraka and the amicable way the conflict had been resolved.

"Are you going to continue with the project?" he queried.

"Father has apparently been persuaded that there is nothing improper in a work of art!"

"I see," Elias remarked, not sure how to take the explanation.

The sun had gone down and it was rapidly getting dark. It was time to go for a cup of tea somewhere. But where? Sitting outside on the large patio of the Grand Hotel along the Blue Nile would be perfect, but it would also be inviting gossip and might provoke new problems. They now realized that even the walk along the Nile might elicit talk. "Never mind," Fadheela remarked, "I have just made up with my father and that might hold at least for a while. Besides, it's the truth that counts. Let's go to the Grand Hotel."

They went and sat at a table strategically located in a corner. As soon as they were seated, Elias remarked, "You know, I have just realized that you have never really talked to me about your family. What sort of man is your father?"

"This is not a question to ask a daughter who has just reconciled with her father," protested Fadheela. "It's like asking a couple who have been separated and then reunited what they think of one another."

"Well, they probably could answer the question," Elias responded.

"And so can I," Fadheela replied. "To tell you the truth, everyone tells me that he loves me dearly. And he probably does. But it's difficult for him to show evidence of his love, not only for me, but for anyone, my poor mother included. I recall occasions when we were still small, when he would beat her until she would literally run away from the house and seek the protection of neighbors. And yet, he provides her with all her material needs. Nor is he always cruel to her. On the contrary, I believe he really loves her. It's just that, somehow, he seems incapable of showing tenderness."

"Is it true that he hates Southerners?"

Fadheela sat reflectively, using the coming of the waiter as an excuse for not answering immediately. They both ordered fresh lemon and tea. Once alone, Fadheela continued.

"'Hate' is certainly too strong a word," and she went on to explain. "I think it is probably the same problem aggravated by prejudice. I don't think he hates Southerners, but if I am to be honest with you, I believe he thinks that anyone who is not a Muslim and an Arab is somehow inferior. And being an Arab to him has something to do with being the right color. If you are too light, then you are a *halabi* or even a *khawaja*—a European and that means being religiously a Christian and racially something on the other side of the human spectrum. If you are too dark, that means you are a *zinji*, a Negro or a slave, and only a step removed from apes. *Janubiyin*, Southerners, fall into that category. But you see, Father does not even stop to think about these matters seriously. As soon as he sees a person, he fits him into a category and that determines his view of the person."

"I know what you mean," remarked Elias, recalling the time he had first met Sheikh Mohamed.

"Let me give you an example," Fadheela continued, almost interrupting Elias. At that point, the waiter returned with their orders. Fadheela decided to wait until he was gone. When Elias pressed her to continue, she hesitated, as though she had reconsidered the wisdom of saying so much about her family. "It's awful to talk this way about your own father," she commented.

"Come on, Fadheela," replied Elias. "I am no longer a stranger, even though I realize I am not a member of your family."

"Take my brother Baraka, for example," she resumed with a fresh determination to confide in Elias. "Without bias, he is really a wonderful person, very considerate, very civilized. Now, he is a little darker than me. I have heard my father call him ugly names because of his color. And yet, he is really proud and fond of Baraka. For my father, one has to be the right color, with the right religion, the right language, and the right family connection to be *wad ballad*, 'son of the land.' And that applies with even greater force to women."

"And yet he educated you and Baraka quite well," Elias observed. "You would think that only a progressive person would care so much about education, especially for women."

"Well, here credit should be given where it is due," Fadheela qualified.

"What do you mean?" Elias asked. "Someone other than your father deserves the credit for your education?"

"You see, Uncle Ali visited Father when we were children. My father was then in southern Darfur, trading cattle out of a small town whose name I now forget. When Uncle Ali came, Father made an *azuma*, a lunch party, to which he invited a number of government officials. I remember some of the visitors saying what a pity it was that such bright-looking children were being denied the benefit of education. Uncle Ali agreed and later insisted on taking us to the North to attend school.

"We were brought to Kosti to stay with Uncle Abd el-Rahman. First, we entered the *khalwa*, or Koranic school, where Baraka immediately distinguished himself. Actually, his interest in religious studies has never faltered. I also did quite well. Then we moved into the elementary school. The rest you know. Since we did well, we were promoted from school to school. Father, of course, paid our school fees and provided us with clothing and pocket money. He also visited us from time to time and we rejoined the family during our vacation times. But Uncle Abd el-Rahman was really the one who took care of us most of the time. And Uncle Ali also frequently sent us favors.

"So, although Father sustained our education with material support, it was not without considerable pressure from our uncles, especially Uncle Ali, and the home support of Uncle Abd el-Rahman.

"In fact, had it not been for Uncle Ali, we would probably not have gone on to higher education," Fadheela went on, as though propelled to tell everything. "Father wanted Baraka to help him in his cattle trade. But Baraka was so bright that the local sheikh, supported by Uncle Ali, pressured Father into allowing him to go to the sharia branch of the Faculty of Law at Khartoum University. At first Father argued that I should leave school because there was no marital future for a girl with a college education. But Uncle Ali insisted that I should be allowed to continue with my education and arranged for me to join the Institute of Fine Art."

And as though she felt she had been too hard on her father, Fadheela concluded, "I say all this to explain to you some of the odds we had to overcome, but although Father was initially reluctant and continued to have reservations, he certainly did not insist on stopping our education. He could have done so if he had really wished to, although he would have encountered opposition from our uncles."

"Tell me about your mother," said Elias shifting focus.

"She is a truly wonderful woman," Fadheela responded with obvious conviction. "And this is absolutely without bias. Someone who could cope with Father for that long has to be remarkable. She is very patient, loving, and giving. You know Baraka is not my real brother; he is a half-brother. His mother, Father's first wife, disappeared shortly after he was born. The story in the family is that she was captured by the Dinka in a raid. And yet, I have never seen my mother treat Baraka any differently from the way she treated me or my younger siblings. She really brought him up as her own son. In fact, although Baraka is Father's own blood and not my mother's, you could say that he has been far closer to my mother than to Father. But Baraka and Father have managed to contain their tensions; as I said, Father is very proud of Baraka. And I think Baraka, too, has been a very loyal son, especially after his remarkable success."

Fadheela looked at her watch and jumped up, almost involuntarily. "My God! It's nine o'clock. I told Mother that I would be home early. I must go!"

"No dinner?" Elias asked, already knowing the answer.

"No, thanks! I really must rush," insisted Fadheela, standing up. "It's far too soon to invite another row with the family."

Elias too got up and called the waiter. They paid and left.

As he reflected on the conversation with Fadheela, Elias had mixed feelings. It had been relaxed and pleasant, and she had certainly been very open with him. But it had also been a peculiar evening. He had not felt any clearer about their relationship. Equally, he had no real idea about Fadheela's feelings for him. And how about his own feelings for her? Even here, he was equivocal. Apart from brief romantic currents, the evening had been almost entirely devoted to intellectual discussion of Fadheela's family. And then, it occurred to him that he had not even asked about Khalifa, her cousin. From her own account, she must have grown up with him and presumably knew him quite well. "Oh well," Elias sighed to himself. "I guess that is a topic for next time."

When they next met, they decided to have an early dinner in the romantic garden of the Friendship Hotel on the Khartoum North bank of the Blue Nile.They had just sat down when Elias remarked, "You know, there are some very important questions which I forgot to ask you last time."

"Now, wait a minute," Fadheela replied swiftly. "This has been a one-sided flow of personal information. I have been telling you everything about me and my family, and I have not yet heard a thing about you."

"Well!" Elias sighed and waited silently for a moment. Then he went on, "First, I think you overstate your case when you say that you have told me everything about yourself and your family, and have heard nothing about me. I just told you that I had forgotten some questions last time; so, you could not have told me everything. And I know Uncle Ali has told you some things about me. But anyway, leaving that aside, what would you like to know?"

"Well, shall we say your family, yourself, your profession, your ambitions, everything," she said as she gave him a coquettish look.

"What is good about an impossible question is that you can answer it in any way you want," he responded, half jokingly. "Now, let me cut across all your questions and tell you something which I believe is relevant to our last conversation about your family. You see, I come from a family that combines self-sacrifice in the public interest with a sense of personal and collective pride in their racial and cultural identity and in being the leaders of their people.

"When you were talking about your father being something of a racist, I wanted to say that he was not exceptional."

"How do you mean?" Fadheela queried.

"It seems to me that racial consciousness and pride are inherent in our very existence as human beings," explained Elias. "I was born and raised among a people who consider their race and culture to be God's ideal of what human beings and their moral order ought to be. The only difference is that they did not dictate that view of themselves and of the world to others. They just regarded themselves as unique and superior, but they did not want to change others to be like them. Others were simply not Dinka and could never become Dinka."

"By God Almighty!" Fadheela remarked unbelievingly.

"But the Dinka realized that there were certain things the Europeans and the Arabs had which, if they learned from them, could improve their conditions," Elias went on. "In modern material terms, for example, the Arabs were seen as better off in clothing, horses, and market wealth. But the Dinka had the ideal wealth in the form of their special breed of cattle. Even more importantly, Arabs were Arabs and that made them inferior to the Dinka. Worse, they were considered to be morally depraved as shown by their trading in slaves, hunting human beings like animals and subjecting them to the indignity of slavery. When you ask the Dinka whether they had not themselves captured Arabs in war, they will admit that they had, but only in retaliation. They would also argue that the people they captured were always adopted and assimilated into their families as relatives. To them, slavery is totally alien and inherently Arab. That's the way they think God created the Arab. The Dinka was created differently."

"What a condemnation!" interjected Fadheela. "But considering how the Arabs have treated the non-Arabs in this country, the Dinka are right."

"The European, on the other hand, had the advantage of being far removed and less familiar to the Dinka," Elias explained. "He was viewed as a strange creature, who hardly qualified as a human—not to be judged by normal standards."

"That sounds like my father's view," Fadheela observed.

"But the European had one important thing working in his favor," Elias continued. "And that is he stopped the Arabs from enslaving the Dinka and other Southern people; he left a variety of peoples of different cultures alone to lead their own lives, ensuring peace and security. Then he brought education, medicine for people and their animals, and a market economy that had not existed before. These were some of the advantages that the Dinka felt could be acquired through education. And that was why they sent their children to school."

"Where did you learn all this?" asked Fadheela.

"In the school of life," Elias joked. "Didn't you know that there is such a school? Anyway, once we, the Dinka, went to school, that is, normal school, and came in contact with the wider world, we soon realized that the pride and prejudice that our people had maintained against the Arabs and the Europeans had been largely rooted in ignorance. Of course, they were not inferior as a people. Even more significantly, one began to know individuals who were far from the stereotypes of their groups. I mean, take, for instance, your Uncle Ali. Before I met him, I hated all Arabs. But over the years, he has really turned my view around. Field Marshal Khalid Abd el-Mageed is another person. And when you come to think of it, there are many individual cases who are exceptions to the stereotype of their people.

"You see, in a country like the Sudan, where you find so many different tribes or peoples, with each group viewing itself as superior, the only hope for our country to develop as a nation is for education to free as many people as possible from prejudices which their backgrounds have shaped in them from very early childhood."

Elias now spoke in a serious tone. "Unfortunately, not everyone who gets exposed to education overcomes these prejudices." As he spoke, he recalled the experiences he had had in Darfur and at home in Dak-Jur. Certainly, prejudice seemed to be the norm. But the exceptions were even more significant in shaping the future. "In fact, so deeply ingrained

are they that the overwhelming majority of people never
succeed in growing out of them. If they change at all, they
do so too slowly to have any positive impact on the society
as a whole.

"Only a small number of people succeeds in changing in
a way that can make a significant difference for the country.
What you were telling me about you and your father shows
that you are one of that number and that you are able to
transcend the social prejudices of your background."

"Flattering me will not help any," Fadheela interjected
humorously. "I am nobody. You had better confine yourself
to the big shots who can change the country in the direction
you want."

They laughed.

"I am not kidding," resumed Elias. "And with due
modesty, I too think of myself as being one of that number.
How else can one explain the fact that you and I are here
talking like this?"

When the waiter came to take their order, so engrossed
in their conversation were they that they did not acknowledge
his presence for some time. Eventually, they placed their
orders and quickly resumed their talk.

It was as though Fadheela had just discovered an aspect
of Elias that she had never known. And, in a way, that was
the case, for although they had been together on numerous
occasions, never before had they explored issues in such
depth. With that discovery quickly developed a new sense of
mutual understanding and respect for one another.

"You know, everything you say makes absolute sense to
me, except one thing," Fadheela commented.

"And that is?"

"That is, I never thought of you as a Southerner," she said.
"I heard from Uncle Ali that you were a Dinka, but I never took
you for a Southerner."

"Now, wait a minute," remarked Elias. "You are being
grossly inconsistent here."

"I realize there is nothing logical about what I am saying,"
conceded Fadheela. "Logically, you are a Dinka, Dinkas are
Southerners, so you must be a Southerner: simple. But I am

telling you that although I knew you were a Dinka and that Dinkas are Southerners, I did not think of you as a Southerner."

The waiter returned with their order sooner than they had anticipated. But, as usual, when they were engaged in conversation, food or drink appeared to be a justification and not a reason for getting together. And so, they slowly nursed their food while they continued to talk. Elias recalled that Fadheela had been the last to speak about not thinking of him as a Southerner.

"How do you explain that?" Elias asked.

"I have just confessed that it's not logical and you ask me to explain it?" replied Fadheela. "Well, let me try. You see, I have heard Uncle Ali and even my father speak highly of the Dinka; that they are proud, courageous and noble. I have also heard that there is Dinka blood somewhere in our ancestral background. But of Southerners in general, I have heard much disdain and condemnation: that they are lazy, primitive, wild, blood-thirsty and frankly animal-like. Now, can you see why I would think of you as a Dinka but not a Southerner?"

"Yes, I can," conceded Elias. "But it does not make you any less prejudiced against me as a Southerner."

"Now, wait a minute," Fadheela reacted with surprise. "How do I suddenly become prejudiced against you?"

"Because I am a Southerner."

"But I didn't think of you as a Southerner, so I couldn't be prejudiced against you."

"Are you prejudiced against Southerners?"

"If you made me swear on the Holy Koran, I would have to say: yes, to some extent."

"And you know that I am a Southerner?"

"Yes! But I have repeatedly told you that I don't think of you as a Southerner."

"You see what I am arguing is that when prejudice ceases to be a matter of personal or collective self-consciousness and becomes a matter of one group imposing its superiority over others, then you have racism, and that can no longer be tolerated by the people against whom it is exercised. Such racism can express itself in discrimination or, for that matter, in assimilation. The fact that you refuse to recognize my Southern identity is an attempt to negate that identity and to assimilate me into your Northerner identity and perception of the South. Now, my being a Dinka apparently does not threaten you because you were raised thinking that one could be Northern in one's identity and at the same time Dinka in one's background. You see, the kind of racism our country is confronted with today is not the type that discriminates as much as it is the type that wants to assimilate. The Dinka segregate by not requiring others to be Dinka; you, the Arabs of the North, assimilate by wanting others to be like you."

"That's terrible," remarked Fadheela, almost despite herself. "Why do we do that?"

"You should tell me, not me you," responded Elias. "Even worse, I think you do both," he decided to press on.

"How?"

"Because, while you work on assimilating, you discriminate against those who are not assimilated. In other words, you both have your cake and eat it, while you deprive others of either having their cake or eating it. And do you know what your men do to ensure this one-way assimilation?"

"What?" Fadheela asked.

"They marry girls from outside while preventing their girls from being married to outsiders," Elias explained. "Of course, the Dinka have that too, but in their case, it is social prejudice while yours is sanctioned by Islam, a powerful universal religion. And in the case of the Dinka, the prejudice against marrying outside the community is applied to both men and women, although it is stronger against women, while yours is applied only against women."

"But I don't understand something," remarked Fadheela.

"What?" queried Elias.

"I can understand what you say about Arab men wanting to keep their women, but I don't understand your saying that they like to marry from outside," Fadheela replied. "How do you explain the tendency in the North to favor cousin marriages?"

"Well, isn't that a perfect example of having your cake and eating it too?" responded Elias. "By encouraging men to marry their cousins, you ensure that the needs of the womenfolk are met, the internal front is catered for, and the group is consolidated. At the same time, you enlarge the circle by bringing in women from outside to come and bear offspring who will assume the identity of their fathers, and add their names to the male list. Now, if men were limited to marrying only one wife, there might be a conflict between keeping clanswomen and bringing in female outsiders. But since a man may marry several women, it is possible to keep the cousins and bring in the strangers. In other words, you have your cake and eat it at the same time."

"You make it sound so rational and logical," Fadheela observed. "And yet I understand that, genetically speaking, inbreeding of the type that occurs through cousin marriages is not healthy and leads to the weakening of the species. How do you relate the prejudices you have just explained to this scientific truism?"

"What makes you think that prejudice has anything to do with scientific truisms?" responded Elias. "If it did, it would no longer be prejudice."

"This sounds terribly complex," Fadheela said as she suppressed a yawn. "I believe I agree with you, but I am not sure I fully understand all the nuances and ramifications."

"Perhaps it is because it is getting rather late and you are tired," explained Elias indulgently.

"Oh my God," remarked Fadheela, having looked at her watch. "It's an hour past the time I said I would be home. But I would like to continue this conversation soon. I think it's fascinating."

"Next time, I want to ask you about the discussion you had in your family the evening before you went to your uncle for the weekend," said Elias. "And I also want to ask you some questions about your uncle's family and, in particular, your cousin, the young doctor."

"Well, well!" remarked Fadheela. "You certainly have a long agenda. Mine includes asking you what Uncle Ali meant when he said you had some serious preoccupations these days. I suspect that some of the things you have been saying must be relevant. It seems as though you have given them much thought."

Elias laughed. "You make pretty good guesses," he commented, as they said goodnight.

Elias and Fadheela continued to see a lot of one another and not always for the purposes of working on the sculpture. Their relationship grew closer and more intimate, and they began doing things together without worrying too much about what people would say. They frequented the movies, had dinners at the Officers' Club, went for tea at the Grand Hotel, visited the zoological gardens, and, at times, took advantage of the privacy offered by Awatif's apartment.

Meanwhile, at the Headquarters, Elias kept in close contact with the coordination officers of Darfur and Bahr El Ghazal regions to monitor the situation with respect to the detainees. But nothing dramatic took place. Although the security authorities responded to press questions from time to time with renewed threats to charge the detainees with treason and bring them to justice, it had become obvious that the state had no real case against them and intended only preventive detention and deterrence of potential political actors. The fact that even detention and imprisonment were not subject to the normal rule of law was a clear indication of the deteriorating situation of the country. Elias and all those concerned with the detainees consoled themselves with the rationalization that although the Government might not release them, they could also not do them any harm beyond detention without trial.

Word eventually came from the United States that Elias's admission to Columbia University in New York City could be arranged. Within a week of being notified, he obtained his passport, tickets, a U.S. visa and an exit visa. He would shortly be on his way to a new world—America.

He and Fadheela had been so distracted by their social activities that work on the sculpture suffered in consequence. But it was very close to completion.

They met for a working session late one afternoon at the studio. The *huboob* wind had been blowing that afternoon with blinding dust and most people had chosen to remain indoors. But since Elias and Fadheela could not communicate to cancel their appointment and in any case were eager to press on with their work, they had met as usual.

Fadheela sat on her working stool; Elias was half sitting at the edge of the table on which sat the sculpture. The *huboob* was subsiding and rain began to fall, pattering on the corrugated iron roof with sounds that were as intrusive as they were soothing.

"So you are about to take off to America?" Fadheela opened the conversation. "You know, when I first asked you to model for me, I really had no idea what I was getting myself into. Now I know what I have gotten myself into."

Elias let that pass and chose to counter with a question, "Fadheela, can I write to you from the United States?"

She did not respond in words. Instead, tears trickled down her cheeks. She reached for a handkerchief from her handbag and wiped her eyes. And as though answering Elias's question as an afterthought, she said, "If you want to."

Elias was visibly moved. "According to our Dinka ways, people do not cry over the living; that is a bad omen," he corrected Fadheela gently. Then, as though his own behavior would depend on her answer, he asked, "Fadheela, if I write, will you reply?"

"Yes," she said simply.

"That's a deal," Elias replied jubilantly. "Now, lets get back to creating Elias Bol Malek."

"I have one last request of you, Elias," Fadheela spoke solemnly. "When you return, will you remember the woman who gave herself to creating Elias Bol Malek, as you put it?"

"I will," responded Elias. "And may God approve."

PART FIVE
ACTION

SEVENTEEN

ALTHOUGH THE TIME ELIAS spent in the United States was filled with events, he continued to be preoccupied with the memory of his last days with Fadheela and the political developments back home. Not long after his arrival, he wrote to Fadheela:

"Although I have not been here for long, there is a great deal to distract me, and yet, I continue to be preoccupied with my last days in Khartoum and the wonderful time we spent together. I am not going to be presumptuous about what all those memories mean, but I want very much to relive them in my memory and to share them with you in my letters.

"America is a country where the issue of race is very much alive. I was shocked at the airport to see so many people who look like Northern Sudanese, with English as their language. These are Black Americans or Afro-Americans who until recently were called Negroes. In other words, our people in the North, who look down on the inhabitants of the South and the West as Negroes, are themselves considered to be Negroes in the United States. That shocks our Northern brothers and sisters when they come to the United States. For me, it has opened my eyes to the complexities of the race issue both locally and globally and I believe has made me a much wiser man in many respects.

"There is a great deal more to write, but I will wait until I hear from you before I say more."

273

When he did not hear from Fadheela, Elias wrote again, but again there was no reply.

He was saddened, but decided to forget; there was no alternative. Something must have happened. Fadheela had probably married, perhaps that cousin of hers. He began to rationalize how it was in any case a senseless relationship, she being an Arab and he a Southerner, she a Muslim and he a Christian. Sometimes he would laugh and speak to himself out loud, "To think that I could have been so foolish as to become so involved? What possible objective could it have served? Anyway, things are now clearer and that's the way it should be. Forget her, you fool."

And indeed, with time and the determination to be constructive with his studies, his preoccupation with Fadheela gradually receded. And yet, he could not forget her completely. He thought of writing to General Ali to ask about the political situation and to enquire about Fadheela in passing. But what he heard about political developments discouraged him from writing and, in any case, probing into the situation with Fadheela could be explosive, should Ali suspect something in Elias's enquiry. So, he decided that the prudent course of action was to do nothing.

Politically, almost as soon as he left, the country began to move from bad to worse on virtually every front. Elias frequented the Mission of the Sudan to the United Nations to read the papers and catch up on the news. But since the press was controlled by the government, it was not a reliable source of information. More dependable were the many individuals who passed through New York or were elsewhere in the United States and who were often eager to chat on the telephone and pass the word around. The democratic instincts of the Sudanese people seemed to have been aroused against the government and people relished transmitting information on the deteriorating situation of the regime.

Almost immediately after Elias's departure, news of sporadic acts of violence in retaliation to the massive arrests began to filter through from Bahr El Ghazal and Darfur.

To Elias's surprise and shock, he heard that his mentor, Field Marshal Khalid Abd el-Mageed, had been relieved of his duties. His rival, General Idris Abd el-Jabar, the chief of security, had taken his place as vice president, while still holding his security post. Another general had been promoted to the rank of field marshal and appointed as the minister of defense. Other problems were also coming to the forefront, as Elias heard from private sources.

"I tell you, brother, the South has long ceased to collaborate in the peace that was achieved some ten years ago," reported one recent arrival from the Sudan. "Anger at the way the area has been neglected is taking over from the jubilant celebration you used to see. The South is demanding social and economic development. Instead of responding positively, the government has adopted policies that have antagonized Southerners even more. Imagine trying to redefine the regional boundaries in order to take from the South valuable agricultural land and those areas in which commercial quantities of oil have been discovered! When that was successfully resisted, the government tried to move the crude oil from the South to be refined in the North. Is it any wonder that the South has totally lost confidence in the government? Even that big canal, which the government says will drain the swampy areas of the South and make land available for agricultural development, is now being seen as a way of salvaging water that is wasted through evaporation and making it available to the North and Egypt. This will be done at the risk of destroying the ecosystem of the South and endangering the life of the pastoral Nilotic people and their herds, not to mention the wild life in the area."

As days passed, anxiety continued to rise. Elias was following the situation through a Southerner who was at the mission.

Then one morning, when he was not thinking of the Sudan, Elias received a phone call from his Southern contact.

"Have you heard the latest?" asked the voice on the phone.

"No! What's new?"

"The government decided to move units from the South to the North, and when they disobeyed, the army moved in with force the day before yesterday," he reported. "Heavy fighting is reported to be continuing. And they say there are already considerable casualties on both sides."

With his knowledge of the military situation, Elias had little doubt that the incident was bound to have a ripple effect throughout the South. And sure enough, when it was over, not only had both sides suffered heavy casualties, but the remainder of the Southern units concerned had taken to the bush to start a guerrilla movement that would become the nucleus of armed struggle in the South.

A few days later, to the surprise of the country and indeed the world, Jabir El-Munir announced by presidential decree the division of the South into three regions and the reduction of each region's powers to the level of the country's other regional governments. That way, Munir had unilaterally abrogated the peace accord that had ended the civil war in the South.

One day, when he was least expecting it, Elias received a long letter in an impressive looking envelope with a British stamp on it. The name of the sender was printed on the envelope: Hamid El-Dergawi, the governor of Darfur. Elias eagerly opened the envelope:

"Dear Brother Elias," the letter began.

"I have just obtained your address from a brother here in London and hasten to write to you. First of all, let me tell you right away that I have fled the country. I could no longer stand it. My reasons for leaving are many. Some have to do with the neglect of Darfur by the central government, others have to do with what is happening to the country as a whole and especially to our brothers in the South.

"I have just returned from a visit to the brothers in Ethiopia. The rebel units have a new found legitimacy because of Munir's unilateral abrogation of the peace accord. With the assistance of Ethiopia and Munir's foes in Libya, they have organized themselves into a disciplined and well equipped army that will prove to be a formidable force for Munir's ailing regime to deal with. The movement is calling for the liberation of the whole country from any discrimination on account of race, religion or sex. This is an unexpected call that is bound to disconcert Northern politicians. And because of its formidable military power, the movement cannot be dismissed lightly.

"Nor is the news on the economic front helping the regime, for the gap between dreams and realities has begun to widen. Foreign loans have begun to mature and the cost of debt servicing has mounted beyond available revenue. When combined with the massive and lavish political mobilization of the country through the Socialist Union and the employment of large numbers of people in high-ranking but unproductive positions, not to mention ostentatious diplomatic presence in many international circles, the result is a financial burden far beyond our available means. Even the essential commodities have become scarce. The potential breadbasket has become a basket case. The nation is on the brink of collapse.

"As though entrusting the Sudan's fate to the powers above, Jabir El-Munir, in collaboration with the Muslim Brothers, has decided to set the country on the path of Islamic fundamentalism. With the infamous 'September Laws,' so-called because they were promulgated in the month of September, he has adopted Islamic law or sharia as the law of the land, ruthlessly enforced by ad hoc courts which are as simple in proceedings as they are simplistic in substance. Petty thieves, mostly from the poor regions of the South and Darfur, are subjected to amputations of hands for theft and to amputation of the foot on the opposite side for robbery. Pictures of Southern and Western youths, whose hands and feet have been amputated, are frequently appearing here in the European press, to the horror of the civilized world, including Muslim countries as conservative and religiously orientated as Saudi Arabia.

"My purpose in writing was to establish contact and let you know what's going on, in case you didn't know. I have been greatly saddened by the painful state of our nation. Anyway, let me hear from you and I will certainly write more."

Elias was gratified to have heard from El-Dergawi. They had not been in contact since the earlier misunderstanding. There was no question now that they had fully restored and even strengthened their friendship.

So Elias wrote back immediately, thanking him profusely for his letter and saying how he understood the circumstances leading to his leaving the country. "From where I am, the situation at home seems totally untenable. As a matter of fact, I have just learnt of the arrest, trial and public execution of Mohamed Ahmed Tahir, the Muslim leader and theologian who opposed sharia as undemocratic, discriminatory against non-Muslims and women, and out of tune with the modern values of contemporary society. How could Munir do this to a man who had supported him for bringing peace to the South and promoting equality between regions and in favor of women? The picture of this elderly man, smiling at the crowd of spectators with a rope around his neck as he was about to die, made the front page of major newspapers in this part of the world and is a devastating blow against Munir and his regime. I am sure the end is in sight."

Within months, the people of the Sudan had mobilized under the leadership of the professionals, doctors and lawyers, and, through repeated demonstrations, demanded an end to the regime. The army eventually sided with the people, and Munir, who had arrogantly left the country while the demonstrations were underway, was overthrown in a bloodless coup that virtually left the system intact, except for Munir himself and a few of his closest associates within the government, including, of course, his vice president and chief of national security.

An interim government was set up under the supreme authority of a transitional military council working with a transitional civilian cabinet to ease the country back to parliamentary government through elections to be held in twelve months.

But the liberation movement in the South, which claimed to be a national movement, dismissed the change as no more than a continuation of the Munir regime and a subversion of the true revolution which the people would bring about. As they saw it, the generals had stolen the show from the people and turned it into legitimizing window-dressing for the regime. As a result, the movement continued to appeal to the masses in both the North and the South to join hands with them in order to rid the country of its domination by a minority clique.

Elias watched these developments with keen interest, but continued to give his studies his overriding attention. When Munir was overthrown and the country began to move toward democracy, he was sitting for his final exams. He reflected a great deal about what his uncle Alier had argued when he had tried to persuade Elias against joining the army. "Son of my sister, leaders among our people, the Dinka, are men of words not of arms," he had said. "And from the time God created men, the power of the word has always been mightier than the power of the arm. A man defeated in a fight always wants to return to avenge his defeat. But a man persuaded by the strength of reasoning remains convinced and seeks no vengeance. Son of my sister, the spear and the force of the arm are for the warrior youth, but the pen, which you acquired in school and the word of mouth which you inherited from your ancestors, are the tools of a divine leadership which has descended to you from both your father's and your mother's lines. Do not throw them away for the gun."

Elias shared his uncle's advice with Hamid El-Dergawi in a letter. "Now I wonder whether my uncle had not been correct after all," he wrote. "Somehow, I feel that Munir's image as a dictator has tarnished the image of the army by association. I am seriously considering resigning my commission. But what would I do? I could join the rebel army. But that too is an army, even though the morale would be higher because of the justice of the cause. Well, the first thing is to complete my studies, then reassess the situation, and decide according to circumstance. But if you have any advice, I would be grateful."

Elias had been pondering these issues when the military attaché of the embassy in Washington telephoned to say that he had just received a letter from him marked "Urgent, Important and Confidential." What should he do with it? They agreed that it be sent by express mail. The attaché did not know who it was from, and because it was labeled "Confidential," he did not feel comfortable with Elias's suggestion that he open it and identify the sender. Elias eagerly awaited the arrival of the letter the following day. When it came, he nervously tore it open to find that it was written on behalf of his father by the clerk. He could not believe his eyes. He and his father had never corresponded before and he could not understand how the idea of a letter had occurred to his father.

"Dearest son," the letter began. "I am having this letter written in the hope that it finds you in peace and good health. And if you ask about us, we are all in good health, missing only your precious presence. I trust that you have been following the developments in the country. Much has happened since you left, but perhaps the most important has been the change of the system. Not everybody is satisfied with the change, and, as you undoubtedly know, some of our brothers in the South have chosen to reject it as inadequate and have decided to continue to fight against the system.

"Son, I know that you have chosen to be a fighter. That is why you joined the army. But I am writing to you because I believe that there are many ways of fighting. There is the gun and there is the word. The government has opened the front for words, but we must have people who can speak in this new system which they call democracy. Even more significantly, unless our own children come to represent us in this new assembly, the government will fill our slots with hand-picked individuals who will be mouthpieces of the Arabs posing as our representatives. The government will then claim that we are indeed represented. That is why your people, the elders at home and the educated youth, got together and decided to ask you to come back home and run for the forthcoming elections to the Assembly. If you come, we will be sure to have a representative in the Assembly. If you don't, I am afraid my people will not agree on any other person to represent them and we will lose our position to the puppets.

"Your people need you and I trust that you will heed the call of duty."

The following morning, although he had not received a response to his last letter, Elias placed an overseas call to Governor El-Dergawi to discuss his father's letter and seek his advice. The governor agreed with his father, even though he himself did not have much confidence in the new regime and the forthcoming elections. He advised Elias that, although the call of his people was noble and worthy of a positive response, he should leave the army in an honorable way, if he were to expect to exert influence within the system later on. He therefore suggested that Elias write a letter through the military attaché, explaining his people's call to him, his acceptance of the challenge to represent them, and the regretful but inevitable consequence of his having to resign from the army. Elias accepted this advice and the attaché promised to support his letter of resignation. Painfully he withdrew from his degree program at Columbia and made preparations to return to the Sudan.

Some days later Elias took an overnight flight to London where he met briefly with Hamid El-Dergawi and caught up with developments on both the internal and rebel fronts, and then connected with a Sudan Airways flight the same afternoon. He arrived in Khartoum during the early hours of Friday morning. Making up for almost thirty hours without sleep, he went to bed and slept until about noon. Having showered, he got dressed and headed for General Ali's house.

Elias had already heard that, toward the end of Munir's dictatorship, Ali had fallen out of favor and had been retired from the army. Despite his retirement, however, he followed political developments in the country quite closely. Elias found him lying on a bed on his veranda, listening to the radio.

While Elias approached his old mentor with warmth, he sensed a reserve in Ali's greeting to him. He wondered whether the former general disapproved of the activist political role he had chosen, but he felt that he had been too liberal to be so affected by that. What was the matter then? Had something gone wrong in the family?

Without betraying his concern, Elias asked Ali about the family.

"They are all well," he said in a cool, matter-of-fact manner. "At least they are alive," he added sarcastically.

Elias next asked about Fadheela with concealed eagerness.

"She is fine," said Ali, looking distinctively uncomfortable.

"What about her art work?" Elias probed rather innocently. "How is it progressing?"

"Well, more important things had to be taken care of before any professional interests."

"I don't understand! Like what?"

Ali now realized that Elias was ignorant of the developments which had followed his departure.

"Have you kept in touch with her news?" Ali asked prudently.

"Not at all; I tried, but couldn't." Elias did not want to mention that he had written but had received no response from Fadheela. "Has anything happened to her?" He was becoming quite anxious.

"You mean no one has told you what has become of her?" Ali asked in genuine astonishment.

"No one!"

"How strange!" pondered Ali. "I thought it was an act of faith in me that brought you to my house, despite what has happened."

"What has happened?" Elias was now anxious beyond control.

"Strictly speaking, you should not be here," Ali proceeded to explain. "And frankly, if anyone from my brother's family, or for that matter from our extended family, saw you here, I would have to struggle hard to prevent them from killing you."

"Please you are torturing me; tell me what has happened." Elias was beside himself.

"Fadheela had a serious disagreement with her father, and indeed with the rest of the family!" Ali decided to sidetrack the trend of investigation.

"What was the disagreement about?"

"Marriage!" Ali mentioned the word in a matter-of-fact way, but caught the look on Elias's face.

"Marriage?" repeated Elias. "Is Fadheela married?"

"No! That's the problem. Her father wanted her to marry her cousin, but she wouldn't."

Elias felt relieved, although he was careful not to reveal his feelings. He was silent for a while, not knowing how to react without saying too much.

"I suppose in this day and age, one cannot count on these

modern women following the traditions unquestioningly," Ali broke the silence.

Feeling encouraged by the comment, Elias probed for more information. "What actually happened?"

"Do you know Khalifa, the son of our brother, Abd el-Rahman, who is next to Mohamed in age?"

"I have not met Abd el-Rahman or his son Khalifa, but I have heard about them."

"Abd el-Rahman lives in Kosti and his son Khalifa is a doctor, working in Kosti Hospital."

"Well?" Elias queried, now remembering his original instincts about what might be between the young cousins.

"Fadheela objected on the grounds that she did not want to marry a cousin. She argued that it was not advisable for medical reasons. Besides, she considered Khalifa like a brother. Although the doctor himself was sympathetic to her point of view, the argument did not persuade the family. After all, cousin marriages are common in the North."

"That's where we Dinka differ from the Arabs," interjected Elias. "Fadheela's view is typically Dinka. But anyway, what then?"

"Then she said that she was in love with another man. That, of course, did it for Khalifa."

Elias was tempted to ask whether Fadheela had identified the man, but he questioned the wisdom of digging too deep too soon.

"But that was not all," Ali went on. "She then announced that she was pregnant."

"Pregnant?" repeated Elias with a sense of shock. "Fadheela pregnant?"

"Yes, Fadheela became pregnant shortly after you left."

Elias was overcome with emotion. "I must see Fadheela," he managed to say to Ali. "How do I do that?"

"Elias," Ali spoke in earnest, "I was a young man myself and I know the temptations of the flesh. I treated you like my son and Fadheela as my daughter. The first thing I want from you is the truth. Are you the father?"

Elias decided to be completely open. "Uncle Ali, it is with my whole heart that I now speak to you. I cannot answer your question, not because I do not want to, but because I do not know and I do not want to lie to you. But I can promise you one thing, if I were responsible, I would regard it as an honor to have Fadheela beget my child, and I would do all I could to be worthy of her and the baby. All I would want and ask for is to be accepted. Uncle Ali, you have not told me enough about Fadheela. Did she have an abortion or did she carry the child to term? And what has now become of her?"

Ali was visibly pleased with Elias's response, and particularly his concern for Fadheela. "The family wanted her, of course, to abort the child, but she adamantly refused. It was a dreadful confrontation. Her father went almost mad over the affair. He seriously wanted to kill her. I moved her to my house and we arranged to have her transferred to a school in Darfur to teach art, where no one would know her and where she could genuinely claim that the father of the child was on assignment abroad."

"I take it then that she has delivered?" enquired Elias.

"Yes, she had a son, a truly handsome boy. His father should be very proud of him. At first, Fadheela was totally repudiated by her own father, but I worked hard and eventually succeeded in bringing her back into the family. She has in fact come back to visit once or twice; that's when I saw the baby. But she prefers to stay with a woman friend called Awatif who teaches at the Institute where she herself used to teach.

"Anyway, my advice to you is to keep your distance from the family, at least for now. The answer you have given is a good one. I shall see to it that I facilitate matters between you and the family. And perhaps we can work things out."

By now Ali appeared almost as friendly as he had always been. He succeeded in persuading Elias to continue with his political campaign and to leave the matter of Fadheela for the time being. "Time is a good healer, remember. After you win the elections and are fully entrenched in Parliament, come back and we will talk. In the meantime, I will do my homework with the relatives, and especially with Fadheela's brother, Baraka, who is going to run on the ticket of the Nation of Islam and, if elected, is likely to be an important member of Parliament."

The elections came and went. Elias and Baraka both won and assumed important roles in their respective political parties. They maintained a degree of courtesy which testified to the propriety of their professional conduct, but also indicated that General Ali had worked hard to improve relations between Elias and the family. But as El-Jaylani, the Speaker, noticed, there was a coolness in their relations which could not be explained in purely political terms. But to those who knew of the feud over Fadheela, it was quite understandable. El-Jaylani did not know that, but when he spoke to the young men before Elias went home to his ailing father, his objective was to help clear the air and improve relations between them in the interest of their national responsibilities.

For Elias, the news of his father's serious condition dictated his going home immediately. Although Malengdit had been assured by the ancestors in a dream that he would survive the illness, Elias did not want to take any chances, which was why he chose to take his father to Khartoum for the best modern treatment available in the country.

EIGHTEEN

AS SOON AS ELIAS arrived back in Khartoum with his father, he had him admitted to a private room in the military hospital where the company of his wives, Elias's mother—Aluel—and one of his father's junior wives, was permitted. Although he himself did not stay with them in the hospital, Elias visited regularly and remained in close touch with the team of doctors who were taking care of his father.

One morning, as he went to visit, he happened to find Osman Awadallah, the head physician, leaving his father's room.

"I am glad you are here, Brother Elias," said Dr. Osman. "I want to talk to you about your father."

The way he spoke sent a chill through Elias. Something dreadful must be on the doctor's mind, he thought to himself.

"When would you want to see me?" he managed to ask.

"If you have time, how about now?"

"Well, that's what I'm here for," agreed Elias.

As soon as they were alone in Dr. Osman's office, the doctor got to the point. "Brother Elias, I have bad news for you," he began.

Elias gazed on the doctor's face without betraying any emotion. In a way, he had already suspected that much. He was ready to hear the specifics.

"Your father is suffering from terminal cancer," Dr. Osman said.

"No! It can't be, Doctor," Elias cried. "He told me he was feeling much better. I brought him here just to be sure!"

"Well, all I can do is tell you what I think I have found. It is for you to decide whether you believe me or not and what to do about the situation."

Elias detected a tone of offense in the doctor's words. "I am sorry, Doctor. I did not mean to question your finding. I suppose it's the shock of it."

Dr. Osman was reconciled. "I understand and I am sorry that I have to break such news; it's a sad duty. Anyway, I believe the cancer started in the liver and has now moved to his lungs; this means that it is quite advanced. The end could be within weeks or months. All we can do is alleviate the pain and give him comfort. We cannot do much to delay the end."

"But, Doctor, my father has never drunk alcohol or smoked tobacco in his life. How could his liver or lungs be susceptible to cancer?"

"Well, although you are reflecting a popular view, what you are saying has nothing to do with the cause of cancer. We do not really know the cause."

"Forgive me, Doctor, but I still don't really understand. You see, when I went home, I found my father very ill indeed. But then something happened and he seemed to miraculously recover. He even told me that he had been assured of life by ancestral spirits until certain events occurred. And indeed he began to feel much better after that."

Elias then proceeded to tell the story of his father's dream to Dr. Osman who listened with absorption. "I know this sounds ridiculously superstitious for an educated man like myself to repeat, let alone believe, but then the fact that his account was confirmed by his recovery made me see credibility in it. And now, when he is looking so much better, you tell me that my father is dying?"

"My dear Elias, the truth of the matter is that on the basis of clinical evidence, I believe your father has terminal cancer, and I have told you where I think it began and where it is now. In fact, his own account of the way he felt the disease develop confirms my finding. Now, having said that, let me hasten to add that we are not gods. And if God or your father's ancestral

spirits have communicated a message to him, it is not for me
to contradict their word. As you say, your father seemed much
improved after the dream in which his ancestral spirits
manifested themselves to him. All I can say in scientific terms
is that the power of faith and the will to live are considerable
in combating disease. I would not even rule out miraculous
recovery resulting from their impact. The fact is, however, that
your father still has the disease even if he looks improved.
Since I did not see him when he looked much worse, as you
say, I cannot make any comparison. Perhaps his faith and his
will to live not only caused his improvement, but are fighting
the progress of the disease. I must tell you, however, that in
my judgment he has the disease, the disease is spreading, and
the end is in sight. You should expect to have your father with
you for weeks and be grateful if he stays for months. My only
advice to you is to make his remaining days comfortable and
happy. How you do that I leave up to you. But we will give
him medication to combat the pain and give him comfort."

"Thank you, Doctor," said Elias as he got up to go, looking
depressed and reflective.

"I am sorry, Brother Elias," Dr. Osman spoke with deep
sympathy, "but death is an integral dimension of life. We must
learn to live with it." As he spoke, he extended a farewell hand
to Elias and said, "If you want your father released from the
hospital, which I would advise, just let me know."

"Thanks, Doctor."

"Goodbye, and make the best of a tragic situation," Dr.
Osman said as the two parted.

"God willing!" responded Elias as he stepped out of the
room.

Elias decided not to visit his father that day. His gloom was
too obvious to show his father or even his mother.

The thought crossed his mind that he should tell his father
the truth and persuade him to return home to put the affairs
of the family and tribe in order. But he decided that it would
be too cruel to satisfy the needs of the living with the comfort
of his father during the last days of his life.

Elias decided instead that lying under such circumstances
was quite justified. He went to his father and told him that

according to the doctors, all he needed was full rest. He would therefore be taken out of the hospital to rest at home in Khartoum.

Malengdit listened to his son with calm but inquisitive eyes. When Elias had finished, his father spoke in measured words.

"Son, I have heard your words. But I am an elder and elders have some insights into these matters. I saw something in the eyes of that doctor. And I know what is in my body. If the doctor says that what I need is to rest at home, then I want to go and rest at home in my village. I want to be near my people. My ancestors have assured me that certain things will happen before my death. But no one knows when that will be. We are now in the rainy season and the worst thing that can happen is for me to die away from home and not be buried according to the ways of our people. It is fitting that my life should end in the way God has ordained for our leaders since the Byre of Creation. So, when I leave the hospital, I want you to arrange for my return home as soon as possible. Those are my words."

Elias knew that his father was telling the truth and he did not think he should contradict his words of wisdom with false promises. And yet, there was no way he could admit the truth to his father. He felt tears coming to his eyes and quickly took out his handkerchief and wiped them.

"Father," he managed to say, "there is no need to think of the worst when the evidence of life is before us. We are still far from what you are guarding against."

"Son, what I say will not kill me," he said. "But I want to guard against any eventuality." Realizing that the subject was disturbing his son, the old man added, "Anyway, let us leave the matter now. We will have time to talk about it when I am out of here and back in your house."

Recalling his father's story of the promise which had been made to him by his ancestral spirits that he would live until his lost sons were found, Elias felt torn between respecting his people's religion and discrediting it as sheer superstition.

As he pondered the situation, Elias felt that in the circumstances the best thing for him to do was to resume his parliamentary duties as though there was nothing seriously wrong with his father.

That week, there was a debate on the relationship between the Association of the Revolutionary Minorities of the Sudan and the liberation movement in the South and its resort to violence. The central issue was whether ARMS, for which Elias was the spokesman, could be considered a legitimate participant in the democratic process or should be outlawed.

The case for the ruling parties was stated by Fadheela's brother Baraka. "Ladies and gentlemen, brothers and sisters, democracy speaks only one language and that is the language of words, the language of persuasion, the language of a civil and civilized society. Democracy does not speak the language of intimidation, the language of force, the language of the gun. This nation has twice overthrown dictators because of our love for democracy and our commitment to the defense of democracy. There is no room in this system for extremists who seek political influence through bigotry and racist agitation. We all know that the struggle has been perverted from a fight for democracy to a campaign against Arabism and Islam by those who call themselves the true sons and daughters of this land and dream of throwing out the so-called Arab immigrant minority. They sit here with us and enjoy the fruits of our struggle for democracy while, at the same time, they ruthlessly endeavor to destroy the foundations of that democracy. We have news for them. Democracy is not two-faced, one face enjoying the liberty of free speech and the other holding a gun to the head. Our question to our brothers in ARMS is which side are you on, the side of the word or the side of the gun?"

Baraka moved the Assembly to a roar of applause. "Yes, tell us Elias, tell us!" a voice was heard shouting. "We are tired of your hypocrisy, are you for war or for peace?" another shouted. Conflicting shouts came from all directions.

"Silence, silence!" El-Jaylani cried as he hit the table with his gavel. "Order is part of this democracy and it is my job to see that it is maintained. I now give the floor to Brother Elias."

Elias stood up slowly as though gauging the reaction around him. Then, adjusting his dark blue suit and straightening his tie, he cleared his throat, still tantalizing the audience by his preliminary silence.

"Thank you, Mr. Speaker," he began in low, measured tones. "For one who believes in democracy, I must compliment Brother Baraka on using his ammunition of words to a deadly end. For while his words may not kill the body, they are undoubtedly aimed at assassinating the character and the soul, and I am not sure which is worse. But in his verbal onslaught, he has deliberately sought to confuse the issues and mislead the representatives of the good people of the Sudan.

"Let us get the facts straight. No one can deny that for years the people of the Sudan have been subjected to the indignities, indeed the inhumanities, of racial and religious discrimination based on a clearly defined hierarchy. Since the Arabs and the Muslims came into this country, they established themselves as the superior race with a superior religion. But they were good enough to open their doors to anyone desirous of self-advancement by adopting Arab religion, language, culture and race, even when the claim to race was justified only by a few drops of blood and sometimes by no blood at all. The black African races, especially if not redeemed by conversion to Islam, were condemned to the lowest stratum of the hierarchy. The colonial powers came and added to the hierarchy the supreme status which they enjoyed as the ruling race. But at the same time they safeguarded and even reinforced the claims of the Arab Muslims to their God-given superiority.

"And now, Mr. Speaker, at a time when we pride ourselves on being an independent nation, whose very essence should be the full equality of citizens irrespective of race or religion, we find a persistent chauvinistic attitude which claims that some people are destined to be the rulers of men and that their religious beliefs reflect the immutable word of God. It is this simple reality which drove some of our brothers in the South to take up arms against Munir when he betrayed the understanding that had brought peace to our country.

"Yes, we have what some of us call a democracy. But have the old hierarchies really changed as a result of that democracy? Have we not merely fought to restore power to those who have always claimed superiority in accordance with God's ordinance? Have we not been tricked into believing that we had won our democracy by sweat and blood only to fall prey to the dictatorship of the misguided, who vote only for those they believe are chosen to be their lords?

"Well, Mr. Speaker, ladies and gentlemen, some of us are uncompromisingly opposed to slavery even when the slaves love their chains. We thought we had freed ourselves from the abominations of the nineteenth-century slave trade. But no, we are back into slavery, not only in more subtle forms, but, as current news glaringly tells us, even in its crude and classic forms.

"Who then is the racist, Mr. Speaker, the one fighting to end racism or the one inflicting racism on a people whom justice declares to have been born equal to any other members of the human race? Aren't the racists merely agitated by having their true identity and character exposed? But the truth can no longer be hidden. Jabir El-Munir was certainly guilty of major wrongs, but he provided our people, the rural majority of this nation, with sufficient power and resources to realize how much they had been denied and how much more there is to demand. We are at the threshold of a major political, economic, social and cultural revolution, a torrential current which, if the wielders of power are not wise enough to flow with it, will undoubtedly lead to a calamitous upheaval.

"Mr. Speaker, I believe in the power of the word; that much I learned at home and that is why I am here. But when words fail to achieve the desired results, other means must be pursued. Some changes cannot be brought about by words alone. Munir's downfall was not brought about by words. My own mother was captured by Arab slavers and had to be rescued. That was not done by pleading justice with words. It was done by force.

"This is what our brothers who are in the bush realize. They see no hope in working within this so-called democracy. Since talking is what those of us who are here have chosen, we will continue to inflate our democracy with ineffectual words. But by what moral justification can we tell our brothers in the bush to lay down their arms? What indicators can we point at to promise change by the power of words? What have we ourselves seen to persuade us that those who dominate our political life recognize a higher moral order, a code of humanity that must dictate a new deal, commensurate with the enlightenment, the sophistication, indeed the civilization of our nation? We will continue to speak, to invoke those principles, but we have no moral justification to discredit our brothers' use of the gun. If that is a crime, then let those who determine the principles of justice in this country do as they please with us."

As he sat down to deafening applause from the representatives of the regions most affected by his message, there was no doubt that Elias had carried the day.

Baraka frantically called for the right of reply and was recognized. Suffering from a half-defeat which even he could not help feeling, he chose to respond to one issue, the allegation of slavery and the contribution of the Arabs to the civilization of the country.

"Brother Elias has as always played with the facts to secure his special purpose. And he did this most superbly on the issue of slavery. The Arabs are sick and tired of always being branded as though we were the only race engaged in the trade. The Europeans whom the Africans praise as having saved them from the Arab raiders were not only involved in slavery, but were in fact the overlords of the trade. For God's sake, even the so-called Blacks who are now being pitied as the helpless victims of slavery not only sold their own people, but also captured slaves from the Arab tribes. Our Brother Elias spoke of his mother having been captured by the Arabs and later rescued by his people. I hate to involve personal sentiments in the affairs of state, but I have news for our brother Elias: I don't remember even seeing my mother and it is not because she died before I was old enough to know her—she was captured by the Dinka, and presumably made a slave.

"Elias also spoke of Arab immigration into the Sudan and their impact on this country. He spoke as though the only influence they brought was the subordination of the non-Arabs to the Arabs. Well, that is a negative way of stating a positive page in our history. Why don't we have the moral courage to call a spade a spade? Let us recognize the fact that throughout history, the world has been shaped by major waves of universalizing civilizations. The Arabs today may be viewed by some—perhaps by most—as relics of a by-gone civilization. And to some, even in this country, being called an Arab sometimes connotes the primitive Bedouin cherishing the company of his camel and an archaic set of values that can no longer sustain life in a modern global context. But let us not forget that the Arabs were the heralds of a flourishing civilization, sustained by the sophistications of science and technology at a time when Europe, the now accepted Lord of progress, was still immersed in the abyss of ignorance and barbarity. It was our forefathers who brought into this nation the ray of enlightenment and gave the peoples of the Sudan a superior vantage point that has elevated them above Black Africa to this very day.

"And so, Mr. Speaker, let us not be carried away by words. If you had a genuine choice, would you rather be grouped with a people and a continent whose image in the world is still one of material, moral and spiritual poverty, or with a universalizing civilization represented by the last of God's prophets? I will rely on your honesty in answering this question."

Baraka, too, received loud applause, mainly from the Arabs and the Muslim fundamentalists. Elias raised his hand to respond, but El-Jaylani, anticipating an escalating war of words, decided that there had been sufficient exchange between the two spokesmen and chose to give others a chance to speak on the agenda item. "We shall be debating the issue of religion next week and I have little doubt you will find reason to come back to some of these themes," he explained in denying Elias the floor. When the Assembly eventually voted on whether to outlaw ARMS, the motion was lost by a wide margin, which indicated the broad-based support which the concept of pluralism enjoyed even within the ruling parties.

Then came the debate on the question of sharia, the precise issue being whether the September Laws, the name given to a set of Islamic-based laws, should be retained, revised or abolished. The Muslim Brothers, who had re-organized and expanded their support under the name of the National Islamic Front wanted their retention. The ruling Nation of Islam Party, which was opposed by the National Islamic Front despite their common religious base, wanted the September Laws to be replaced by more appropriate Islamic laws. But, while no opinion polls were taken on the issue, it was quite apparent that a broad national consensus felt that the September Laws should be abolished altogether; not only because their application was divisive to the nation, but also because they were considered by experts to be a distortion of sharia. In particular, the brutal amputation of the hands and feet of petty thieves was regarded as unacceptable, not only on moral grounds, but also by the authoritative standards of Islamic jurisprudence. According to sharia, for such severe punishment to be justified, the state had to provide for the criminal's livelihood, which, considering the poverty prevailing in the Sudan, was far from being the case. It was indeed public knowledge that most of the offenders who suffered amputations were poor, unemployed migrants from the West and the South, many of whom were not even Muslim.

When Elias found out by sheer chance that the trial of one of the Dinka boys accused of theft was scheduled to take place two days before the debate, he decided to attend the court. Entering the court room discreetly, he sat among a crowd of the evidently mixed audience of Northerners, Southerners, Muslims, Christians, and animists. They radiated a diversity of sentiments ranging from excitement to anxiety and depression about the application of the tough Islamic laws.

It was one of those emergency courts, later re-named the "prompt justice courts," *mahakim al-adala al-najiza*, which Munir established by presidential decree to apply his September Laws or criminal justice. The court room was bare. Three court members sat on a raised platform. The chairman sat in the center. A light-skinned experienced judge in his late forties, he was well known for his fundamentalist beliefs. The other two were ad hoc lay magistrates, younger and evidently over-shadowed by the aura of the chairman.

On trial was a tall frail young man dressed in a worn pair of trousers and a shirt. He seemed to be in his late teens or early twenties. Standing behind him with a gun was a policeman with a bulging beer belly.

"What's your name?" the chairman asked with contempt.

"Akot," the young man replied simply, which was in part due to his poor Arabic, he having only recently entered town life.

"Don't you have a father?" the chairman continued.

"He is dead!"

"Did he die without a name?"

"His name was Aleu."

"Are you related to Nebel Aleu, the former vice president?"

"No, but we are both Dinkas!" explained the lad in his broken Arabic.

"That much I can tell," the chairman replied scornfully. "You don't have to say it with such pride as though the Dinka are the chosen people. Your grandfather's name?"

The boy, realizing that the trial was getting off to a bad start, decided to ignore the comment on the Dinka and gave his grandfather's name: "Marol."

"Well, what do you say? You are accused of stealing a window and a door and then selling them."

"Your honor, I saw them in what looked to me like a heap of rubbish. When I later heard someone needed materials for repairing an old house, I told him that I could get him a door and a window if he would pay me for them. He said he would, but had to see them first before discussing the price. To make them look better, I went and separated them from the rubbish and put them at a distance under the care of a watchman. The contractor apparently saw them at the watchman's place and when he was told that I had taken them there, he went and reported me to the police. I was arrested."

One of the young judges asked the accused, "What do you do?"

"I have no work, your honor."

"What do you mean you have no work? Aren't you doing something for a living?"

"Every now and then, I work on construction sites for a

daily wage, but they don't always need people. Besides, most of the foremen are Nuer and they prefer to recommend their own people to the contractors."

The chairman seemed uneasy at the trend of the questions. Cutting his colleague off almost rudely, he said, "We do not really care what you do or don't do. What is important is that you stole someone's property. And you know what sharia does with thieves?"

Almost by instinct, the young man spoke out in anger, "I am not a thief; I am not a thief."

Elias was outraged, but he nonetheless remained silent. He realized that the judge was totally ignorant of the Dinka moral code and did not have the slightest idea that theft among the Dinka was one of the worst offenses a man could be accused of.

"I told you that I thought the things were thrown away and that I took them because I found someone who was willing to pay for them." Akot was putting up a fight.

But the chairman continued his questioning. "You knew that they were worth some money. And you in fact took them to sell. Even if they were in a rubbish heap, you should have known, indeed you did know, that rubbish may have monetary value."

"Can't the Arab hear?" remarked Akot angrily in Dinka, which elicited a roar of laughter among the Dinka spectators. "Why do you keep calling me a thief when I have just explained to you that I am not a thief?"

"What did you say in Dinka?" asked the chairman suspiciously.

"I am a man like you and I have my dignity too. Why do you keep insulting me?"

"What did you say in Dinka?" persisted the chairman.

"A man should not be abused for nothing!" continued the young man. "Why can't you hear my words?"

"What did you say?"

"That's what I said: why can't you hear me?"

The chairman murmured to his colleagues in Arabic for a moment and then declared: "We have a long list of cases to hear. This is a straight-forward one; it should not engage our time unduly." Then turning to the accused, he said, "The court finds you guilty of theft and sentences you to amputation of the right hand." Then mumbling to himself in a voice that was nonetheless audible, he said, "Let the slave pay the price of combining theft with contempt of court. Next case. Bring the accused, Aluel Malek. Is this the Southern woman who trades in *merisa*?"

"Yes, your honor," responded the policeman. "She too is a Dinka."

Elias hurried to the Assembly the day the subject of the "September Laws" was being debated. Having passed a note to the Speaker, wanting to be given the floor at the earliest opportunity, he sat eagerly awaiting his turn. When it came, he was still fuming with anger.

"Ladies and gentlemen," he began, "Only two days ago I witnessed a scene so appalling, so disgraceful that if a majority of you had been there, we would now be acting with virtually no discussion. I have just attended the trial of a man accused of theft. He was found guilty and sentenced to amputation. But that is not the real issue, for those simple facts could be said to reflect a system of justice. The real crime is that the trial itself was a mockery, an unacceptable perversion of justice by any conceivable standards of humanity, let alone civilization. It was a trial from beginning to end fraught with racism, bigotry, and persecution."

Elias then proceeded to describe the trial in considerable detail, ending with the judge's aside about the "slave" before him.

"Honorable members of the Assembly," he said in concluding, "under Islamic jurisprudence, the application of these laws, and in particular the severe penalties against theft, is condoned only when the state has removed poverty and provided for the basic needs which could justify the poor into committing such offenses. No one can argue that we have succeeded in creating such conditions in the Sudan. If anything, we have deprived our people rather than provided them with the means to meet their basic needs. In that sense, this unscrupulous application of sharia is indeed anti-sharia.

"Ladies and gentlemen, we are the ultimate lawmakers in this country. If we do not promptly stop the courts from this dirty business, we shall have failed in our sacred duty, and I daresay the Supreme Being in whose name this outrageous abuse of power is being perpetrated will eventually make us account for our failure—that is if the people of the country allow us to continue to sanction this evil. I, for one, would have a hard time with my conscience if I were to continue pretending to be a lawmaker in an institution that would tolerate such practices in this day and age."

When he sat down, a deadly silence fell upon the Assembly, which made Baraka's request for the floor seem unusually loud.

"Mr. Speaker, sir," he said, "I have a very small word to say."

He was acknowledged and given the floor.

"Our brother Elias has spoken most eloquently and his words have undoubtedly achieved their desired objective. But I would like to remind this august Assembly that we are not here to legislate on the basis of emotion. All that Elias has said concerns a single alleged miscarriage of justice and is a purely procedural matter. Of course, we do not really know what happened, but even if we take what he said at face value, it does not in any way question the validity of applying sharia, only the manner in which that particular court applied it. There are established procedures for checking such abuses. We should not be carried away by emotionalism, or jump to conclusions about the entire system of justice and do anything that might undermine it. Sharia is the manifest wisdom of Almighty God. It cannot conceivably be repugnant to justice. It is only human error that may misrepresent it. This is a very tricky matter; we have to be extremely careful."

After he sat down to cheers from the fundamentalist front in the Assembly, Peter Maloda from Equatoria, a member of the Bari tribe, indicated a desire to speak.

Peter had a reputation for being anti-Arab. His political association with Elias, which became something of a friendship, had begun on a sour note that revealed Peter's deep rooted antipathy toward the Arabs. What he had learned about

Elias's educational background and association with General Ali at first had conditioned his view of him. Late one afternoon, Peter and a colleague dropped in on Elias, who had seated them and then stepped out of the living room to ask for refreshments to be served. He had barely left the room when he overheard Peter whisper, "I hate to see a brother in Arab clothes."

On rejoining his guests, Elias broke the ice by saying to Peter, "Brother, if we are fighting prejudice, should we ourselves become stereotypes of blind prejudice?" He spoke teasingly, with a smile on his face. To clarify the issue, he quickly added, "To hate clothing well adapted to the climate which you share with your political enemies and to which they have adjusted better than you is, in my book, blind prejudice."

His visitors laughed, both in surprise that he had overheard and in appreciation for the lighthearted way in which he reacted. "Brother Elias, truth must be admitted when said," Peter responded. "You are absolutely right and I thank you for teaching me that lesson."

From that day, the two drew closer and closer until they became known as the most complementary of the Southern politicians. And in a way, that was the truth, for, although the two were different in many respects, they maintained a solid political alliance. It was therefore to be expected that Peter would ask for the floor to counter Baraka's refutation of Elias's presentation.

"Mr. Speaker, sir," he said, "words more often than not reflect the level of cleverness, not the truth. We should not be deterred from emotions for emotionalism sometimes tells the truth better than cleverness. The last speaker has clearly succeeded in clouding the truth with cleverness and has distanced us from the will of God which our brother Elias reflected in his moving words. Who can tell where God is so that we can verify the truth with Him? Where does the poor man who is a victim of the worldly abuse of God's law go for justice? How do we separate the God Baraka is talking about from his self-designated agents on earth, ranging from Munir to the judges Elias saw in action? Does Baraka want us to live in the dream of godly perfection while the world crumbles in the name of that perfection?

"I have news for Brother Baraka. We see God differently. He speaks to us in different tongues and what we hear him say varies a great deal from society to society and from one person to another. How do we unify that message? That's the question. But while we seek an answer to that question, for God's sake, let's stop cutting off hands and legs as though we were the butchers of humanity."

The Assembly erupted into applause and anger, a good indication of the effectiveness of Peter's message and the extent to which the representatives were divided.

The debate continued until the late hours of the working day, but, in the end, the Assembly voted to establish a committee under the chairmanship of a respected senior member, Ahmed Wad Al-Sultan, from an aristocratic background in Darfur. The committee would investigate the situation and make recommendations on the extent to which crimes such as theft and dealing in alcoholic beverages were rooted in poverty and deprivation and therefore not subject to the harsh penalties of sharia. Both Elias Bol and Baraka Mohamed were appointed to the committee.

The committee met and heard from a large number of witnesses. Some of the evidence before it led to the discovery of an extensive underground network of "thieves" controlled by a man who was said to have amassed considerable wealth and power in the underworld of petty crime. His name was El-Tom Hassab El-Rasoul. It soon emerged that El-Tom controlled the market of stolen goods and that most stolen items went first to him. It was he who decided where they were to be marketed among extensive outlets that stretched far and wide across the country. It was also revealed that part of El-Tom's business was to "assist" victims of theft by tracking down their stolen goods, supposedly through his powers of divination and for a modest fee relative to the value of the stolen goods.

The police tracked down El-Tom and he was arrested. But it was quite obvious that El-Tom would not offer any informa-tion that would endanger his vast empire. He availed himself of the services of one of the best lawyers in Khartoum—who advised him to keep his mouth shut. The police were unable to get any additional information out of El-Tom about his criminal empire.

After extensive consultation with his lawyer, the committee decided that in the interest of the investigation and in order to better understand the social underpinnings of crime, especially in the Three Towns, El-Tom Hassab El-Rasoul was granted immunity from any criminal or civil prosecution. This was enough to induce El-Tom to cooperate.

The proceedings of the committee, which were broadcast and televised, provided popular entertainment for the urban population. The session in which El-Tom testified was particularly sensational. He was already in the committee room and was about to begin his testimony when Elias entered. Although he was sitting, El-Tom appeared to be a large, tall man. He was wearing a white jallabiya which seemed over-sized even for his voluminous body. On his head was a loosely wound imma that was tilted heavily to one side. In his hand was a set of prayer beads which he fiddled with as though to underscore that he was a devout Muslim, who could not possibly be a criminal offender, and certainly not a thief. And indeed, there was a look of innocence or perhaps calculated simplicity on his face. He was not naive looking, but he did not radiate the shrewdness of an experienced criminal either. In other words, El-Tom appeared to be a mystery, a perfect case for investigation.

"Please state your name in full," requested Ahmed Wad Al-Sultan, the chairman.

"El-Tom Hassab El-Rasoul."

"That includes only your name and your father's," remarked the chairman. "For the records, we usually need the grandfather's name as well."

"Actually, Hassab El-Rasoul is not my father's name."

This information seemed to surprise the committee.

"What do you mean?" asked Ahmed Wad Al-Sultan.

"Nor is El-Tom the name I was given at birth."

"I don't understand," continued Wad Al-Sultan.

"Well, you see, Mr. Chairman and distinguished members of the committee, my story is a long and complicated one. I came from the South as a young man looking for a job in the capital city. I could not find any employment that suited me. I was physically incapable of doing heavy manual labor and I did not consider myself suited for domestic service, physically or temperamentally." El-Tom's Arabic accent was almost perfect, a bit colloquial, otherwise without much accent.

"What job had you expected to do when you got here?" asked the chairman.

"I don't know and I don't think I had thought about it. For reasons that we need not get into here, I found myself in a desperate situation back home. Coming to town was my only salvation."

"What was the situation you found yourself in?" asked one of the committee members. "It might in fact be relevant, contrary to your own judgment."

"I would appreciate it if you would excuse me from answering that question."

"Well, let's go back to your name."

"When I reached the North, I really wanted to open a new page in my life. So, I gave myself the name El-Tom Hassab El-Rasoul."

"You said you could not find a suitable job, what did you do then?"

"I soon discovered that there were many young people from the South facing the same fate. Even those who were physically able to do any job could not find work. Many of them also got into trouble with the law for acts which they did not realize were offenses. So, we had to organize and do something to protect our people from the unscrupulous application of a law we did not feel belonged to us."

"Please tell the committee the whole truth," remarked the chairman. "You are under oath and you also know that you are free from any liability, criminal or civil."

"Somehow, they all seemed to look to me for guidance and assistance. I needed them and they seemed to need me. My daily bread came from their charity, even though they saw me as their leader. I had to rise to the challenge of the leadership they offered to me."

Silence prevailed in the committee room.

"I was very mindful of two sets of interests: those of my people, who were desperately in need and who found themselves victims of a society and a legal system to which they did not really belong, and those innocent victims of their acts of vengeance and crimes of necessity, who were not responsible for their plight. I therefore had to design a response that would cater for the needs of both."

"What a dilemma!" Elias thought to himself.

"I realized that the value of the stolen property was not so much in the object as it was in its sale value. I therefore decided to open a market for stolen goods. But I also wanted to give those whose goods were stolen a chance to retrieve them for a modest fee. In fact, as the really precious items were likely to be identified in the black market of stolen goods, I established a consultancy specialized in tracking down stolen goods, supposedly with the help of spiritual insights, which I was reputed to have. Of course, we traded on the superstition of our people, but there was no doubt that I had a genuine reputation for being able to divine the whereabouts of stolen goods."

"How did you do that?" Baraka asked.

El-Tom seemed to have anticipated the question. "By controlling the market for stolen goods and by offering guidance to the victims of the thefts, I was able to perfect my spiritual and scientific techniques of detection."

Everybody was absorbed in what El-Tom was saying. It was as though he was telling the whole truth, and nothing but the truth, to atone for his sins. But he did not display any sense of guilt or repentance for what he had done.

"How did you draw the attention of the victims of thefts to your services?" asked the chairman.

"Largely by word of mouth, occasionally directed to the individual victims, but ensuring that the word came naturally and not as part of a grand design."

"You said earlier that you were not able to get a suitable job," recalled the chairman. "You were obviously implying that you were unable to perform certain jobs. Could you elaborate on that? What was your problem?"

El-Tom did not respond immediately and he buried his head in the palms of his hands. Silence fell again upon the committee.

"I do not know where to begin; it's too painful a story to recall."

"We are sorry to push you, but it will help the committee to appreciate your position and that of others in a similar situation."

"I hope you can see that there is nothing wrong with my hands or my head." El-Tom's humor was met with laughter. "Those of you who saw me come in must have noticed where the problem is. It goes back a long way. I was not even old enough to remember how it happened. Our village was attacked by Arab raiders and in the raid my mother and my twin brother and I were seized and thrown on horses. I fell and broke my hip. The damage was too severe to be corrected. I have lived with this affliction all my life. It is the indignity I suffered in the tribe on account of it which forced me to migrate to the North. I changed my name in order to be anonymous and forget my past. But I named myself El-Tom to register the fact that I was a twin. My Dinka name was Madit, one of the names which the Dinka give to the second set of twins. My twin brother's name was Achwil. My father's name was Malengdit; he was the chief of the Mathiang Dinka tribe."

At that moment, Elias Bol could no longer contain himself. Jumping up from his seat, he shouted: "Praise be the Lord. I have found my brother at last! At last!" And as he shouted, he rushed over to El-Tom and embraced him. "I am Bol, your younger brother. Oh Madit, Oh Madit, my beloved brother. I have found you! I have found you!"

Pandemonium broke out. The scene was unbelievable. Everyone was flabbergasted. Members of the committee and the audience rose up, wondering what was happening and not knowing what to do. Had Elias suddenly gone mad? That seemed to be the most likely interpretation. And yet, it was also quite possible that they were brothers who had been separated by tragedy. Certain members of the committee now recalled how Elias had spoken of the way his mother had been seized and subsequently rescued. If El-Tom was his lost brother, then it was also quite understandable that their meeting under such circumstances would be emotional.

A number of people felt that it was better to protect the brothers from the live coverage of the cameras. They were led away from the room to a location of some privacy in the Assembly. The meeting was formally adjourned and the crowd dispersed in bewilderment.

NINETEEN

ALTHOUGH THE YEARS OF separation and change had transformed both brothers to the point that neither was able to recognize the other, Elias had been struck by El-Tom from the moment he had set eyes on him. He did not quite know why, but the man looked somewhat familiar. Of course, as Elias sat among the other committee members, El-Tom had no way of focusing on him. He therefore could not recognize anything special about him. Elias on the other hand kept wondering about El-Tom and the more the story unfolded, the more El-Tom looked familiar to him until, with the revelation of the tragedy and his family background, the prophesy of the ancestral will was fulfilled. For Elias, it was one of those unbelievable events that suddenly transformed the world into a kind of fairy land.

El-Tom, of course, had followed the fortunes of his family as closely as he was able. This had been easier for him to do since the election of Elias to Parliament, but even so, a combination of shame and fear had prevented him from ever communicating. And so, for him, too, the moment of recognition came as a shock—although less of a shock than for Elias.

Once Elias recovered from the shock of this miraculous reunion, the question was how to let their parents know. He was worried that the news and the emotional response it would evoke could be fatal to the old man in his frail condition. On the other hand, it could also give him a renewed zest for life, which could prolong his tragically numbered days.

With the discovery of Madit, Elias felt his faith in the spiritual traditions of his people reaffirmed and revitalized. But the recovery of his lost brother and the doctor's prognosis brought to mind the will of the ancestors that Malengdit would live until his lost children were found. Seen in that light, Madit's appearance was both a blessing and a curse. But Achwil was still missing and if the ancestors were right, their father would live until he too was found.

Elias and Madit—the old name was revived within the family—decided that their father should first be moved from the hospital and carefully prepared for the news in the home environment.

Elias wanted to celebrate his father's discharge from the hospital with a thanksgiving feast or *karama*, a Northern ritual of celebrating recovery from illness. Since their father had not recovered, the real idea was to offer him some encouragement in his grave condition. Many people, notables and ordinary folk, were invited to the feast, which was marked by the slaughtering of a bull and a lamb. With Madit's appearance, Elias felt that the idea had turned from false encouragement about the father's condition to a truly joyous celebration of the reunion of the family.

As the arrangements were underway and food was being prepared in large quantities, Elias decided to prepare his father for the news. Until then, he had given strict instructions that nothing should be leaked to him. Since the scene of their meeting had been covered by live television, the story had become widely known in the Three Towns. So, it was necessary to keep tight control over the possibility of someone mentioning it to the old man. When the moment was ripe, Elias had Madit come close to the house and stay with the neighbors until he was called. Elias sat with his father alone in the master bedroom.

"Father, I want you to be prepared for what I am going to tell you," he began. "I should not speak to you this way, being the child and you the father, but it is important that you remain calm as I tell you this. I want you to know, Father, that I have now become completely convinced about the spiritual powers of our ancestors. You said that they had promised you that our family would one day be re-united with our lost brothers. One major part of that reunion is about to be realized. Father, we have found your son, Madit, and he is doing very well."

"What did you say?" interrupted Malengdit, as though he had not been listening carefully all along. "Did I hear you say that you have found Madit?"

"Yes, Father."

"My Madit?"

"Yes!"

Malengdit laughed in what seemed like disbelief, but it was really the joy of concealed excitement. He suddenly put on a successful show of calm. "Where is he?" he asked with transparent composure.

"He is very near and will come in at any moment."

Malengdit uttered a chant of gratification: "My Great Pied Bull has thrown his bellows to the sky! I have nothing more to say until I set my eyes on Madit."

At that moment, Elias sent for Madit. He came accompanied by a crowd of Dinkas, while women shrieked with ululations.

As the crowd approached the gate of Elias's house and Malengdit became convinced that Madit must be within minutes of their reunion, he got up and chanted an ancestral hymn:

Lord, Master of all shades of color,
You are the Father of the human race;
We look to you on earth and in the sky,
Whatever ills befall us,
We rest in peace, trusting in your justice;
Your will manifests itself at selected times.
Blessed be your name on earth and above;
In your glory lies our destiny.

When the gate opened and the crowd entered, Malengdit cast an eye on his son and as though deliberately changing his vision, turned away and said, "Let him stop there. His path should be blessed before he enters his brother's house. Bring me a container of water."

A china bowl containing water was brought to him.

"Our ancestors do not know these modern things of yours," he protested. "Is there no fresh gourd in this house?"

But there was no gourd of any kind, let alone a fresh one.

"Let's do with what there is then," conceded Malengdit as he accepted the bowl. Spitting into it, he prayed:

"You, our ancestral spirits, and you, God, Father of all people, this is a word of praise for you. We praise you from the center of our hearts. If I were at home, this occasion would have called for the sacrifice of sacred bulls to your mighty names. But we are away from home; your expectations must be modified. I have always trusted that your promise to me would be fulfilled. I know that my son, Madit, has been gone for a long time. But what the ancestral spirits say will be, must be. I have never doubted that at all. And yet, when your will is fulfilled, as is now the case, we feel overjoyed with your benevolence. And that indeed is the obligation of a Father to a son. You have done nothing extraordinary. You have simply fulfilled your role as our fathers. But we acknowledge your blessing and are most grateful as your children. May this reunion be a point of strength for the children to serve you even more than they have done in the past. Although their hearts have been taken over by foreign words, what you have done today will strengthen their faith in their ancestral spirits. They will honor your names today more than they have done before." Then turning to the crowd, now absorbed in his prayers, he said, "Let Madit step forward."

Madit did so, and without touching him or even focusing his eyes on him, Malengdit sprayed some of the water from the bowl at Madit, as he touched his feet, hands, forehead and chest, an ancient ritual that resembled the Christian blessing. He then fell on his son's shoulders and embraced him.

"Son, is it truly you?" he said as he rested his chest on Madit's, his arms around him. "Have our ancestors truly brought us together again before I die? Blessed be the Lord. I can now die in peace."

The mother of the boys, Aluel, unable to deal with the

situation, looked away crying, as though she was in shock. She did not even want to face Madit. She did not seem to trust that reality. It was as though some evil spirit played tricks on them, making them believe that a son who must have died long ago was in fact still alive and before them. The figure that was in front of them did not seem to be that of their son, but some "ghost" that could be a source of spiritual contamination. How could Madit come back to life when he must have died so long ago?

When Aluel eventually recognized that her son had indeed arisen from the dead and that he was real, she had a new lease on her own life, her only wish being that her other son, Achwil, was also found. The fact that Madit had surfaced now made the possibility of Achwil being found far more realistic than she had ever dared to hope.

Aluel was not the only one whose expectations had been raised. Even Elias now believed that if the ancestral will had been fulfilled in finding Madit, there was no reason to believe that it would fail in tracing Achwil. Somehow, he had become a believer in Dinka prophesy and deep inside himself, he felt confident that the family would sooner or later be reunited with Achwil.

Madit's story after his disappearance was a long one and perhaps too painful to recall in the pleasant circumstances of the reunion; it must wait for more intimate sessions. Now, priority must go to public festivities and displays of sentiment over the coming together. People feasted and roared with laughter, especially over those matters pertaining to Madit's underground empire.

In due course, the crowd dwindled as the party gradually came to an end. When it was time for Madit himself to leave, he said to Bol, "Today was your day and a truly wonderful day it has been. With the will of God, may you continue to prosper. Tomorrow, I would like the family and our friends to come to my house to see my wife and children and join us in a modest feast."

That night, neither Malengdit nor Aluel slept. In their different areas, they murmured their prayers—calling the word, as the Dinka would put it. From time to time, Malengdit got up and walked around the enclosure, audibly addressing his ancestral spirits and singing a hymn. Much of what he said was not only in thanksgiving for Madit's return, but also for Achwil's well-being and future appearance. Although Achwil had disappeared in infancy, Madit's miraculous reappearance had convinced Malengdit that nothing was impossible, especially as it had been revealed to him in a dream by his ancestors.

When the time for the early afternoon festivity came, Madit sent his Mercedes with two vans to fetch his father and company. As they approached Madit's quarters in Omdurman, it was as though there was a wedding in the neighborhood, judging from the crowd and the ululations of the women. When their cars arrived, the cries of joy peaked. Malengdit was dressed in a white jallabiya with a neatly wound turban and his wives were comparably adorned in colorful tobes.

The gates opened to reveal unusually spacious quarters, with a large empty courtyard and two separate compartments, one for men and one for women. The crowds separated accordingly and Bol accompanied his father and the men into the male quarters, while the womenfolk entered the female quarters, where the ululations were deafening.

The sitting area in the male quarters was a large room, its walls lined with cushioned chairs, a table between each two, with floors carpeted with luxurious Oriental rugs. Beige silky drapes covered the windows, adding to the plushness of the surroundings. It was obvious that most of the furniture had been imported from abroad.

As though to satisfy his curiosity, Elias asked his brother, "Have you traveled abroad much?"

"Mostly to Egypt, Libya and the Gulf States," Madit replied. "And once to Europe. That was an adventure as I speak no European language."

Shortly after the crowd was seated, soft drinks were brought and served in shining silver pitchers on silver trays and in gold trimmed glasses. Madit's trips abroad were evidenced by his belongings.

"You certainly did not disappear for nothing!" remarked

Elias humorously. The remark was greeted with laughter. "That's more than I can say about my years in government."

Madit felt the need to respond. "Well, I hope you agree that these are merely different forms of struggling. At least that was the point I was trying to impress upon your committee."

"Absolutely," responded Elias. "And you did it very well. My reading is that you emerged a hero! And that is quite an accomplishment for someone who might have been branded a criminal and placed behind bars or had his limbs amputated for the same acts."

"And now to more pleasant topics," commented Madit. "Let me call my wife and the children to come and greet you. But before I do so, I hope you are not expecting to see a Dinka girl; after all, you know why I left."

Again there was laughter, although a painful note could be detected in the manner of laughing.

A white lady with an attractive gentle smile on her face walked in accompanied by five children, ranging from around four to fifteen years of age. Three were boys, the oldest, the youngest, and the middle one. Their names from the youngest were Samir, Munir, and Anis. The girls were Nadia and Dalia. They were all attractive children with a light brown skin that was typically Northern Sudanese. Their mother, Salama, was Egyptian. As they were soon to learn, she was a lady of noble qualities, intelligent, modest, deferential, and generous. She was more than a wife to her husband, for in addition to her responsibilities as the mother of five, she helped him run the business discreetly from home, since she was educated and knowledgeable in modern ways.

"*Ma sha'allah*," remarked Elias in a special tribute to God for his blessing. "A family to be truly proud of."

"*Shukran! Allah yabirik fik*. Thank you! And may God bless you!" Salama responded, as she discreetly turned away her half-veiled face to hide the blushes.

Neither Salama nor the children could speak Dinka, but that did not prevent everyone from demonstrating sentiments.

Malengdit called for water, spat into it, said a brief prayer and performed his rituals of blessing on Madit's wife and children.

"We are all children of God, whatever our skin color or place of birth," he said in his prayers, clearly thinking of Salama. "And when God has united two in marriage, they become members of each other's families and whatever differences of race, color, or religion there might be between them must then cease to be divisive. They become relatives and one people. So, you our ancestors and you spirits of our clan, this woman is yours together with her children. I thank you for having guided the steps of your son, Madit, toward this noble woman. She is an asset to your clan. She has extended your circle far and wide and that is what our people call a club thrown ahead to defend one in the unforeseeable future. In fact, that future is no longer unforseen; it has become visible and that is why we are here today."

Salama and the children did not understand Malengdit's words, but they realized the meaning. And even when they felt revolted by the thought of being sprayed with water containing spit, they endured the ritual with deference.

Food eventually came—lavish Sudanese and Egyptian dishes served elegantly on platters and plates of quality, all substantiating the luxury which the setting radiated. Had Madit not been a son, born and bred in his early years in a typical Dinka setting, his family might have been intimidated by all this material flair. But they were not; it was their son's and he was theirs, all united by the bond of common descent. They did not even reflect on all this—they took it naturally and in good grace.

During the party, General Ali, who had been among the invited guests, whispered to Elias that Fadheela had arrived in Khartoum, and that he was prepared to bring the two together as as soon as it was convenient. Fadheela chose the meeting place—the home of Awatif, her closest friend—and a date was set.

As Elias approached her home, he was both excited and awed. What should he say to Fadheela? The objective of the meeting, as he saw it, was straight-forward—to become convinced that he was the father of her boy. Once that was cleared, he saw no reason why he should not propose marriage. He wished that the situation would resolve itself that way for many reasons. First, he was sure of how he felt about Fadheela. Second, for the same reason, he felt bad about the suffering his conduct had inflicted upon her without the emotional support he could have offered her, had he been in the country. Last, but of course not least, he was ready to marry and assume family life. And what better timing could there be for announcing his plans, with his parents right there in Khartoum and his older brother, Madit, having surfaced?

Elias found the gate of the enclosure half opened and immediately understood that he was expected to walk in. But as he entered, he clapped his hands and shouted the conventional greeting "*Salaam aleikum!*"

She responded from the divan, a few yards beyond, "*Wa aleikum salaam wa rahmat-u-Allah. Itfadhal*—come in."

Alone—for Awatif had left to give them privacy—Elias became nervous. He did not know how he should behave. When he entered, Fadheela was seated in one of the chairs arranged around the room in a large rectangle with an opening facing the doorway. She got up to greet him. But, somehow, they both felt awkward and acted hesitantly, apparently uncertain as to the appropriate form of greeting. Fadheela's tobe fell off her head and shoulders so that she had to adjust it as she greeted Elias. His heart jumped. He wanted to embrace her passionately. But he checked himself, for she seemed to read through him. Perhaps that explained the cool manner in which she extended her hand in greeting. Elias now felt certain that it would be presumptuous to embrace her. After all, she had never responded to his letters; that certainly said something. It was as though they needed to renew their acquaintance all over again before they could behave with familiarity, let alone intimacy, toward each other. Almost instinctively, they sat some distance from one another, visibly constrained in their mannerism.

"How have you been?" said Elias, still feeling awkward.

Fadheela looked at him for a split second and turned away with a sarcastic smile. "Nothing bad, as you can see."

"You have changed somewhat, and I don't mean it in the way you will probably take it." Elias decided to strike a serious note, still feeling inept for the way he dispassionately alluded to Fadheela's situation.

"In that case, I guess you have to tell me in what way I have changed." She was still controlled, apparently more in command of her feelings and mannerism than Elias.

"For one thing, you are far less friendly than I recall."

"Really?" remarked Fadheela, still sarcastic. "How would you judge yourself?"

"I guess I must look the same way to you, judging from your question," Elias responded.

"I was simply asking."

"Well, the serious answer to your question then is that I have probably changed in response to your change."

Elias was being sincere, but he also sounded horribly equivocal.

"So, in other words, I am responsible?" Fadheela was beginning to take an offensive line.

"Not in any judgmental way," explained Elias. "Just right now you are in the driver's seat."

"In what way?" Fadheela probed.

"I have been the odd person out, away from the country. You have been here involved with the developments at home. Don't you agree that those developments are critical to our situation?"

"Strange!" she remarked in a whisper. Then raising her voice, she went on to say, "First you say that you have been away and do not know what has taken place in your absence. Then you say that what has taken place is critical to our situation. Does that not mean that you know what has happened? If so, why are you asking me?"

"I am sorry, I wanted to hear your account, rather than react to what others have said."

"What have others said?" Fadheela jumped in. "And who has said what?"

"Come on, Fadheela, tell me, how are you?" he spoke, moving to a closer chair, determined to be candid and to submit with humility.

"I have already told you that I am fine. If there is something you know that I have not told you, tell me."

"This is not going to lead us anywhere," announced Elias,

intent on getting to the point. "I understand that you have a child."

"Yes," Fadheela responded in a matter-of-fact manner, but clearly uneasy with the trend of the conversation.

Elias hesitated over the next question. He clearly wanted to know whether the child was his, but he could see that Fadheela was not comfortable with the subject, or at least the way he was pursuing it. The natural question to pose at that point was, "Whose child is it?" But Elias decided not to ask that question. Instead, he changed the tone of the conversation.

"Did you miss me?" he asked.

Fadheela seemed more responsive. "What do you think?"

"I know what I would like to think, but I would not want to be presumptuous."

"Don't give me the usual lies of men," she remarked lightly, but with an undercurrent of hostility. Elias was provoked, not so much by the insult, as by the implication that Fadheela seemed to know so much about men.

"What are they?"

"Fabrications aimed at deluding women into feeling appreciated and wanted."

"And how do you know that?"

"Because I am a woman and I live in a man's world." There was a plaintive tone in her voice.

Somehow, that triggered in Elias the courage to get to the point. "Fadheela, is it true that the child is mine?"

"Let me overlook the insult and ask you why you want to know."

"Of course, I want to know. If it is my child, don't you realize what a difference it would make?"

"For you, for me, or for the child?" she asked, fiercely.

"For all," he responded with unconsidered frankness.

"In what way?"

"Naturally, I would want to have my child!"

"I see," she remarked sarcastically. Then with a resolution on her face, she went on to say, "You may have him; he is yours. In fact, had I known that I was going to find you in Khartoum, I would have brought him with me. But Uncle

Ali's message did not tell me that he was calling me because of you."

There was a coldness in her voice and mannerism. It chilled Elias to the bone.

"Fadheela, if that is truly the case, then, of course, I want you and the baby."

"Mister, let me tell you something. I have had enough of this chain of insults. I fall for you, allow my feelings to lead me astray, get into trouble as a result, only to be left alone to fend for myself while you dart off to the promised land where you probably found all you wanted and forgot me. Now you come back, and not only are you questioning my fidelity, you dare tell me that if the child is yours, which you evidently doubt, then you want him and, of course, his mother along with him. I think the situation is clear. I have already suffered considerable indignity. The worst is over; I can weather the rest. Now, if you do not mind, I would like to leave."

"Now, wait a minute; is this what they mean when they say that the best defense is offense?" Elias remarked with equal agitation, which brought Fadheela to a standstill. "Which of us is entitled to be offended by the behavior of the other? I leave this country to study abroad, something which none of us questioned. From the day I left, and throughout my stay in America, all I did was my duty to my studies, worry about my country and think about you. I wrote letter after letter and got no response from you. Heartbroken and desperately anxious, I concluded that you must have fallen for another man, probably married that cousin doctor of yours. Then I come home to hear that you became pregnant and that I am suspected of being the father. How can a man who has been desperate for a response to what were devoted love letters and received nothing joyfully hear the news that he must indeed be the father? Why can't you see that I need clear evidence to persuade me that you still care or ever cared about me?"

On hearing this, Fadheela broke into tears. "Oh Elias, why did you not tell me from the beginning that you wrote? That was the whole point of my sad mood. I was crushed by not hearing from you. Of course, I looked changed because I persuaded myself to hate you so that I could forget you. Oh

Elias, believe me, if only I had received a single letter from you, if only I had even known your address, things would probably have developed very differently."

It was now Elias's turn to display emotions. "Fadheela, believe me, in the name of God Almighty, and I am telling you the absolute truth, it was agony leaving you when I did. And for all the time I spent in America, I suffered the pain of missing you. But I also sustained the memory of you. Fadheela, I love you very much and it has never crossed my mind to think that you could doubt that fact. I mentioned the child not to say that he would be the reason for my wanting you, but rather because he would be a confirmation of our love and a reinforcement for our being together. We cannot deny that our society sees the main objective of marriage as childbirth. If God has blessed our love with a child before marriage, is that not evidence that marriage is preordained for us?"

Fadheela was now totally disarmed. She bent her head down wordlessly, but she was clearly cherishing every word he uttered and seemed to want to hear more. Elias read her mind and went on. "Let us also not forget, Fadheela, that there is a great deal of prejudice among our people on both sides. I hate to say this, but it is a fact that if I asked to marry you under normal circumstances, it is most likely that both our families would oppose the idea. With a baby, we would be facing them with a situation they would be more likely to accept. What is important is what we want. How we get it is a secondary consideration."

As Elias spoke, Fadheela began to sense her original feelings for him coming back until she was certain that she cared for him very much, both intellectually and emotionally. And indeed, what could be better evidence of her sentiments toward him than the fact that she had borne him a child. Elias was correct; she had perhaps been romantic and he more realistic. As these thoughts ran in her mind, she felt her body yearning for him right there, but she quickly dismissed the thought as imprudent. Instead, she chose to tease Elias.

"You know, you have not even proposed marriage to me and yet you talk as though that is a foregone conclusion. What makes you think I would accept?"

But reading that the joke was missed or was not sitting well, she quickly added, "Elias, on a more serious note, I want you to know how happy I am. What I went through without you was hellfire. So often I cried in secret, longing for you to be there to share the burden with me. Somehow, I was counting on your strength, but I had no access to you. Of course, I am overjoyed as a woman to have borne you a son and I am happy that you want us both. How much I have longed for that! And how desperately I feared that it would probably never happen! So, you can see how happy I am. Perhaps you do not care to ask me, but if you do, my answer is 'Yes!'"

"I will talk immediately to Uncle Ali," said Elias, "I believe we can count on his support. It is also fortunate that my father is here. In Dinka society, it is not so unusual for a young couple in love to impose their marriage on their elders by having a child or even eloping. That is the least of my worries with my father."

As he spoke, he extended his hand to Fadheela and eyed her intensely, a wide smile on his face. She caught his hand and smiled back, but they both decided instinctively that they must stop there. Nothing would be gained by heating up their emotions; that would only end in frustration or in a worse scandal, should they be accidentally spotted.

"I guess I should be the first to leave," Elias concluded. "But one most important point: what do you call the boy?"

"I was wondering when you would ask. I call him El-Fahl to honor guess what? It's a personal secret."

"That's a manly name," commented Elias. "I approve."

TWENTY

ELIAS WONDERED WHETHER he should discuss the situation with Ali or with his family. There were good reasons for either: unless he was assured that Fadheela's family would not object, it would be hurtful to his father to give his approval and then have his son turned down. But, at the same time, what if Fadheela's family approved and his father refused? And, in any case, how would his father feel about his son discussing marriage with the girl's family before clearing it with his own family first? It was a gamble either way, but he chose to clear the matter with his family first.

They met in Madit's luxurious house in the privacy of his confidential sitting room. Both Malengdit and Madit had a hunch that Elias had something serious to discuss. If it was marriage, who on earth in the Khartoum setting did he have in mind?

Cold drinks and tea were served as the three prepared themselves for the talk. Aluel dropped in and was asked by Malengdit to leave them alone. "There have to be things for men to discuss without the presence of women—wives or mothers."

"Nothing is altogether bad," conceded Aluel, who had guessed the subject for discussion and was feeling happy about it. "Go ahead and discuss alone. If it is truly as important as it seems, it will eventually reach us anyway." She stepped out of the room.

"Father, and you, Brother Madit," Elias spoke. "I need not say how I feel about our being together at this moment. There are things in life which must, by their very nature, be considered by the family together. This could not have been possible only a while ago. Now, with you here, Father, and Madit having surfaced from his underworld" —they all laughed—"it seems as though it is God's will that this should be the moment for me to discuss with you a matter of great importance to me.

"My family has urged me to look for a wife, but, so far, it has not been possible for me to come up with a girl. Now, I believe I have found one suited to my interests. She is well-educated and courageous, but also considerate and beautiful. It may also interest you to know that she is the niece of Ali Ahmed El-Jak, who has been so good to me."

Elias then proceeded to give a detailed account of how he and Fadheela had met, the circumstances under which they had parted, the news he had found on his return about their child, and the ostracism Fadheela was subjected to. "I love her. I hope you will give me your blessing and move quickly to arrange the marriage, should her family approve."

Madit quickly responded, "Bol, my brother, let me tell you both that, although I left under desperate circumstances when I saw no alternative to self-exile, it was hell without my family. I have learned that there can never be a substitute for one's family. And it all begins with marriage and children. As you know, my wife is an Egyptian, but that fact is not relevant to me. What counts is that we are a family. I love her and she has borne me children, thank God. I don't know what Father will say, but as far as I am concerned, what counts is that you care about the girl, that she cares about you, and, as God has already shown, that she can bear children."

Madit was very clear-headed about the issue. "In any case," he concluded, "who am I to say anything different when I acquired a family without consulting you people?"

His humor elicited a smile from his father and a laugh from his brother.

The brothers now looked to their father for a comment. Malengdit remained silent for a moment, then cleared his throat and adjusted his jallabiya, tucking it between his thighs as he always did when he spoke. "Your words are good, my son," he began. "That is indeed the kind of topic a man should discuss with his elders."

Malengdit paused and turning to Elias posed a question, "Is El-Jak an Arab name?"

"Well," Elias responded, "in writing, and even in pronunciation, it is somewhat different from the Dinka name Ajak in that they call it El-Jak. But it is widely believed to be derived from the Dinka name. In this case, the great grandfather of the girl is said to have been a Dinka by the name of Ajak. The name was later Arabized into El-Jak."

"I see! I thought it sounded Dinka. From that generation of our fathers and grandfathers, many people were captured by the Arabs. Of course, it was such a long time ago that it is impossible to recall most of the names. It would not be unlikely to have had a man called Ajak among them. My concern in this respect is whether that Ajak is a relative. As you know, in our Dinka way, one must not marry a person related by blood, however distant. We make some exceptions after several generations for those descended through women—that is the daughters of the clan—but not for those descended from a common ancestor. In this case, it would not be easy to tell what the truth is, but there are ways of dealing with such a situation among our people. A ritual can be carried out to sever any ties of blood that there might be and any evil consequences that might result from a violation of the prohibition."

Malengdit again cleared his throat as though to announce that he was about to raise a new point. "As for the basic issue of your marrying this girl," he began and stopped, as he remembered a different point. "By the way, what is her name?"

"Fadheela is her name," responded Elias. "Fadheela, daughter of Mohamed Ahmed El-Jak. She is the sister of a colleague of mine in the Assembly. In fact, her brother is the spokesman of the ruling party."

"I see. As I was saying, on the specific issue of this girl— Fadheela—God has already made a decision for you by making her pregnant from a game of young people. If you did not like her or want her, that is the kind of problem that can cause a feud between families. But since you like her, that is a blessing from God and the ancestors. Of course, it is understandable that her relatives were offended, especially as you were away and they were left alone with a pregnant daughter, abandoned by the man who had made her pregnant. But since you have returned and are now asking to marry her, I don't see any problem with that.

"Another issue that would have concerned me would have been her family. A man does not marry the woman alone; he also marries her family and it is important to know what family your son marries into. In the case of your brother, Madit, we were not there to be consulted, but thank God, he seems to have done well on his own. In your case, as I understand you, the fact that she is from the family of Ali speaks well of her background. Besides, you say that her great-grandfather was a Dinka. That, too, should commend her background.

"My only other worry is that Ali has been like a father to you, which, in our Dinka ways, would make this girl like a sister to you. But I suppose your ways with the Arabs are different. I can carry out a ritual to sever that connection to permit your marriage. It does not even need to be mentioned to them."

So, all went well as far as the family of Elias was concerned. It was now a matter of talking to Fadheela's family. But before the formal talks with them, Elias wanted to clear the air with Ali. He therefore hurried to his house, entered the gate without knocking, and headed for the divan which Ali used as his sitting room. One glance at Ali and Elias understood that things were not well.

"*Salaam aleikum,*" Elias uttered the usual greeting with worry written on his face.

"*Aleikum a-salaam,*" responded Ali, making no effort to hide his gloom. "Take a seat," he gestured Elias to the chair close to him.

"Is all well, Uncle Ali?" Elias asked nervously. "It certainly doesn't seem so."

"We will have time to talk about that," Ali responded.

"First let me call someone to bring you something to drink. Would you like tea?"

"Not really, Uncle Ali. I don't want anything. I would rather talk. Besides, this is home. If I want something, I can get up and ask for it myself."

"That's right," remarked Ali, as though he had just been reminded of something he should have remembered.

"Well, in her enthusiasm, Fadheela told me about your talk," proceeded Ali. "And I, in my own enthusiasm, went on to discuss the matter with her father."

"What did he say?" probed Elias impatiently.

"He is absolutely adamant that he cannot allow such a thing."

"Why? Did he explain?" asked Elias.

"I don't think I would say he explained," Ali answered. "At least nothing he said sounded like an explanation to me. But when I pressed him, he mentioned something I had frankly not thought about. He reminded me that you are a Christian."

Elias was taken aback. Why did he not anticipate that issue? He had been aware that religion could be an obstacle. He had even voiced it to himself at times. But he must have subconsciously buried the issue. He had also become so assimilated into the family of Ali that religion had ceased to be an issue.

"To tell you the truth, I had forgotten that you were a Christian," explained Ali. "And with a name like Elias—which is also a Muslim name, perhaps written differently—you were like any Muslim I know. Of course, I know you do not pray, but then there are also many Muslims who don't."

Then becoming more serious in his demeanor, Ali commented, "You know that this question of religion is not important to me under normal circumstances, but frankly, this is one of those situations that are quite clear-cut. Sharia does not permit the marriage of a non-Muslim man to a Muslim girl, and whatever my personal view of religion, I cannot disregard this, nor would I be permitted by society to do so, even if I so desired."

Elias reflected quietly. This was clearly a dead end. Ali had been straightforward on the issue. And yet, how senseless it all seemed. He was not a practicing Christian in any way. Over the years, he had in fact become so assimilated into the Arab cultural ways that while he remained vocal in his opposition to Arab hegemony over the non-Arab communities, you could say that he had become culturally Arabized. In what way was he different from any other Northerner who was not a practicing Muslim?

As he immersed himself in these thoughts, Ali also appeared to be reflecting on his own. "Elias, I must say again that I feel toward you as though you were my son, and although Fadheela is my brother's daughter, I confess that I identify myself more with you than with my niece. It is as your father that I must now raise a very difficult question with you. What difference would it really make if you were to declare yourself a Muslim? You would bear the same name and your social status would remain exactly the same. The only difference I see is the positive one, which is that there would be no religious barrier between you and Fadheela. If I were you, I would become a Muslim."

Elias was amazed at how calm he felt as Ali spoke. Years earlier, a similar point of view had provoked him into thinking of walking out of a headmaster's office. The headmaster had, metaphorically speaking, offered him one of his daughters if he became a Muslim. Now he was hearing the same suggestion again and feeling no offense. Suddenly recognizing that he was thinking more about why he was reacting that way than about the issue itself, he remarked, "Uncle Ali, perhaps I should go now and reflect over what you have said."

"Very sensible," commented Ali. "It is certainly a big decision. You are right to think it over carefully."

As Elias drove back to his house, he was confused. On the one hand, religion was no longer an important issue for him. He remembered that he no longer knew what religion Madit followed, nor did he care. Most probably, since he had married a Muslim, he had become a Muslim. On the other hand, what would people think if he converted in order to marry? There was something almost shameful about that. But then, was love not a power that could make men do what they would not normally do? His analysis led him nowhere. He sighed and decided to consult his father and brother.

It was mid evening. They sat outside in the compound of Elias's house. Perhaps because of the manner in which he behaved or the subtle hints he made about wanting to have a family talk, casual visitors excused themselves earlier than usual, leaving the two brothers alone with their father. Elias began by explaining to them Fadheela's father's objection to the marriage on account of religion.

"I am not sure I understand what you are saying," queried Malengdit, who was oblivious to the subject.

"Well, Fadheela is a Muslim," Elias explained.

"And what are you?"

The question startled Elias. Didn't his father know all along that he was a Christian? Hadn't he gone to a missionary school? He questioned Malengdit on that line of thought.

His father responded, "But didn't you also go to a Muslim school in the North?"

Could his father believe he changed religion with schools, thought Elias? Or was the old man more pragmatic than Elias had previously considered? Madit, who had been listening carefully, now interjected. "Bol, I am perhaps the wrong person to speak on this matter. I suppose you know that my wife is a Muslim."

Elias answered with a nod of the head.

"What was interesting is that with us the issue of religion never really arose even though it applied to our situation. I think the reason was that they saw my acquired name, El-Tom Hassab El-Rasoul, and assumed I must be Muslim. I do not fast and I do not pray, nor do members of my wife's family. But I speak Arabic and I invoke the name of God and the Prophet Mohamed in my everyday language in the same way Muslims do. And as you saw in your committee, I even take the oath on the Koran and carry prayer beads. You may therefore say that in many ways I am a Muslim, although no one has ever bothered to make me undergo the formalities of conversion.

"What does all this mean in your situation? With your education, you are probably more of an Arab than I am. By that I mean that you know Arabic better than I do, you have studied Islam and read the Koran, and in your everyday language and way of life, you presumably conform to Muslim culture more than I do. Even your name is Muslim. So, why the fuss about religion? I suppose the only problem I see is that since the issue has been raised, it would require some ritual of conversion. The question, then, is whether that ritual would be worth it. Personally, I do not see any harm in going through with it."

"My word is like your word, my son," added Malengdit. "Whether you are called Muslim or Christian, you are still Dinka and protected by our ancestral spirits. And if you want the truth, that is what concerns me the most. If going through the rituals of Islam would give you what you want, why not?"

"But does it not make a man seem weak to change his religion because of a woman?" Elias posed the question to both.

"You call pursuing a woman weakness?" retorted his father. "That is determination my son; it has nothing to do with weakness. Let me tell you something. When the spirit of Dengdit descended on the man called Mohamed Ahmed, whom the Arabs called the Mahdi, prominent Dinka leaders went to see him and received his blessing. He had not yet succeeded in throwing out the Turks and the Egyptians from the country, but he was already acknowledged by all the tribes as the leading man of God in the land. Even my own grandfather went to see him. He blessed them, gave them Muslim names, and honored them with spears and other objects of his religious authority. These leaders returned with the word of the Mahdi behind their spiritual authority as Dinka Chiefs. Was that weakness? And did that in any way affect the respect and the power they wielded as the leaders of their people? Certainly not!"

Elias's perspective on the situation was being transformed by what he heard his father and brother say. He nevertheless realized that if he changed his religion, he might antagonize some of his Christian political allies. On the other hand, the group he represented, the Association of the Rural Minorities of the Sudan, cut across all regions and religions. Indeed, politically speaking, he might even become more broad-based if he, of unmistakenly Southern racial and cultural origin, could also be identified with Islam. It was still likely that the matter would pass unnoticed as his brother and father were insinuating. When all was said and done, what was really important was that he should marry, and where would he find a more suitable girl than Fadheela, for whom he cared a great deal? Besides, she had his son.

As Elias continued to reflect, he wondered if he had overlooked the Christian Southern perspective. Might he be blinded by self-interest? He decided to talk to Peter Maloda about the problem.

"You might have heard rumors, brother, about some aspects of my private life," Elias began.

Peter made an ambiguous gesture that indicated neither knowledge nor ignorance. "Well, I cannot say I have heard anything that should deny me the opportunity of hearing it from the horse's mouth!"

They both laughed.

"It's about prospective marriage!"

"That much I was beginning to guess," interjected Peter. "My ears are all yours."

"It's a long story, but the gist of it is that the girl is Muslim and do not ask me, 'And what are you?' as my father did." Again they laughed.

"It's a valid question, though!" Peter could not help commenting. "But it's one for which I know the answer. Continue."

"Your comment is very pertinent for neither the girl—her name is Fadheela Mohamed Ahmed El-Jak—nor myself practices religion. Culturally, she is quite liberal and I would say more modern than most Northerners in her mannerisms. But, as you know, Islam prohibits a Muslim woman from marrying a non-Muslim man. I have discussed the situation with some Northern friends and members of my family and their opinion is that since we are not practicing and would presumably continue that way, it would really not make any difference if I performed the ritual of becoming a Muslim, except in the positive sense of removing the obstacle to the marriage. I see their logic and I almost feel persuaded by their argument. But I am also afraid that it might be viewed as weakness and could have harmful political repercussions. That's why I am seeking your opinion."

Peter sat fully absorbed. When Elias had finished, Peter thanked him for the honor of consulting him.

"Let me say that you are the only political colleague I am consulting and, needless to say, it is in full confidence."

"All the more reason for my feeling specially honored. And in that spirit, I hope you will forgive me if I am frank with you."

"That's exactly why I am consulting you."

"First, let me ask you: did you say her name is Fadheela Mohamed El-Jak?"

"Yes, she is the sister of Baraka."

"I see! That's exactly what I was wondering about. Brother Elias, I must confess that for me the situation does not call for much thought. It's crystal clear. I cannot possibly recommend that you change your religion in order to marry this girl. You see, if you were convinced about Islam and you wanted to convert, I would have nothing to say; it would be a matter of conscience and, as a leader, your example would also be significant to your people. But in the circumstances, your conversion into Islam would not only have an element of hypocrisy—I must be frank, even at the risk of being brutal—it would also be pretentious, even dishonest. This is bad enough for any individual; for a leader, it is catastrophic.

"You see, to me, the issue of weakness is there, but what is worse is the connotation of surrender. I am sure you realize that our problem with the North is in part a struggle for cultural survival. And because our cultures have been so disadvantaged by the colonial policies of the Muslim and Christian worlds, this cultural survival is mostly thought of in negative terms such as non-Arab or non-Muslim, for it is the Arab and Muslim culture that now threatens us with extinction. Even when we call our culture 'African,' that, too, is diffused; it's our opposition to Arab-Muslim assimilation that gives our movement its vitality. If we, the leaders, begin to give into Muslim blackmail and surrender to assimilation, how can the struggle be sustained by our people?

"I speak of blackmail because I am convinced that this whole issue about Muslim women not marrying non-Muslim men is sheer Arab racism and chauvinism disguised in religious terms. In the South, you know that our Muslims give their daughters to non-Muslim Southerners. That's because they don't look down on them as inferior, whether racially or culturally. And that practice prevails throughout Black Africa. If it's a question of procedure, and they do not want their daughter to be married in a church, I can appreciate that. But there is also a civil form of marriage, which is religiously neutral. Why should that not be acceptable? My candid opinion is: No! No! No! You cannot do that."

As he spoke, Elias was persuaded by each line of argument. By the time Peter ended, it was obvious that Elias's mind had been changed.

The reference to civil marriage was a key point. Peter was a lawyer and ought to know, but even to Elias, a layman, it sounded reasonable.

"That was the kind of talk I had hoped for, brother," said Elias. "You have moved me a great deal with your words. I am convinced, especially about the alternative of civil marriage."

"You see, there are two legal issues here," Peter now elaborated. "One is who should determine whether sharia is binding on you as a mixed couple. The other is which alternative forms of marriage are open to you. In either case, the first principle to be established is that jurisdiction cannot be with sharia courts. It must be with the civil courts. I would suggest that the person you must first win to your side is Fadheela. If she is persuaded, I feel confident that you have a good case, although one cannot be sure of the law under the circumstances in our country these days. Anyway, loving the girl as I believe you do, it's certainly a cause very much worth the fight."

No sooner had he left Peter than Elias wondered whether he should in fact first talk to Ali. Ali was older, more experienced, wiser; on the other hand, Ali also argued in favor of conversion to Islam: could he be expected to change his opinion? Perhaps he should talk to Fadheela first. After all, they were really the two most directly concerned.

Elias went to Awatif's home where Fadheela was expecting him. He told her of the discussions he had had, ending with the suggestion that they seek a civil marriage. He was tense when he spoke, fearing that his words would prompt a negative reaction from Fadheela. Nor did it help him to read her face.

But Fadheela approved with surprising calm. "You know, I don't care much about this whole issue of religion. I am fully with you. What I don't know is what the law will say. But then you and your friend Peter seem to understand the situation well. So, why don't we proceed accordingly?"

"Do you think I should discuss the matter with Uncle Ali?"

"Well, the family will know sooner or later and he is as good a family member as any to deserve being told first. The real question is which of us should do it. And since you have better knowledge of the issues involved, I think it's appropriate that you talk to him."

Elias was eager to get the whole thing over with as soon as possible. So, he rushed over to Ali's house. It was late afternoon. Elias quickly introduced the subject of his visit. Ali watched him with an outwardly calm demeanor. Inwardly, he felt so close to Elias that he was worried the boy might have come to a disharmonious conclusion. On the other hand, he had persuaded himself that whatever Elias decided, his feelings for him would not be adversely affected.

"I hope you have reached a decision," he commented with detachment.

"Yes, I have decided that it would be wrong to convert. Besides, I have sought legal advice and convinced myself that there is an alternative way of getting married without involving religion."

Elias went on to give an account of the discussions he had had with his family, Peter, and Fadheela. The evidence and Elias's tone of conviction were overwhelming.

"Well, well!" said Ali with a sigh. "That sure is a dramatic turn of events. What can I say except that you are drawing quite sensational attention to your romance. Good luck, my boy. You deserve it."

"Aren't you going to tell me whether you support our approach or not, Uncle Ali?"

"Son, these matters of religion, especially in Islam, are very sensitive and tricky. A Muslim, whatever the degree of his persuasion about the faith, is in bondage to adhere to the dictates of Allah or at least not to question publicly. You know, I approve of your marriage to Fadheela. And that stands whatever form you adopt which is socially or at least legally sanctioned. So, you see, while you can surely count on my quiet moral support, do not expect me to be vocal about it at this stage. If and when you win your case, the decision of the judge, whom I assume will be a Muslim, will be my shield. My voice will then rise against those who persist in condemning the decision of the court in the name of Islam. Now, the right path for me is caution—silence is another way of putting it."

"I understand, Uncle Ali," Elias remarked, his head bent down, clearly appreciating the magnitude of the task he was undertaking.

When Elias met Peter the following morning, he was feeling somewhat dejected. Peter noticed it.

"What's the matter, Elias?"

"Nothing really—well, frankly, the way Ali reacted to our plan bothered me. I have always been able to predict his reaction to situations I presented and he has been consistently supportive. This time he was vague, almost politely adverse."

"Well, what do you expect? This question of religion goes right to the bone. Perhaps it is bringing out Ali's true colors. I would have been surprised if he, a Muslim, a Northerner and an Arab, had reacted otherwise. You see, we have to be realistic about our expectations from these people however much we may consider them friends or brothers."

"Now, be careful, Peter, I am about to marry one," Elias responded in a spirit of heavy humor.

"That's true brother, I apologize there," Peter conceded laughingly. "I guess this is a case of an exception to the rule."

"I must confess that in the case of Ali, I had ceased to label him as an Arab." Elias tried to explain, "You see, what I really couldn't tell was whether he was reflecting his personal opposition to the idea of going to court—that is seeking a civil marriage—or whether he was anticipating social and even legal difficulties in pursuing that path."

"Well, let's be practical," Peter said with a tone of confidence. "Let's at least be sure that the civil law will be on your side. I suggest that we visit our friend Molana Rasheed Dafalla, the deputy chief justice. As you may or may not know, he is a good man, relatively more liberated from conventional Northern thinking than most Northern judges. You know he has attended the London Institute of Advanced Legal Studies and has a graduate degree from Yale Law School in the United States."

"Strangely enough, those kinds of qualifications often do not seem to make much difference to our Muslim brothers, except to reinforce their conservative positions." Elias responded with some cynicism.

"Molana Rasheed Dafalla is surely not a Muslim Brother," replied Peter, correcting the coincidental use of words. "In any case, he is certainly an exception."

The telephone system in the Three Towns being what it was, they decided that they would do better to drive over to the Judiciary and drop in on the deputy chief justice. They found him in his office chatting with several of his colleagues. The warm manner in which he greeted the young members of Parliament from the South gave the hint to his colleagues that they should leave them alone.

Once alone, Peter went straight to the point, providing the background to the case in considerable detail, from time to time aided by Elias, who furnished relevant facts, sometimes in response to the justice's queries.

"I tried to assure Brother Elias that the civil law would be on his side," concluded Peter. "But with my preoccupation with politics, I am the first to concede that my law is rusting. And I thought I should let him hear it from an undisputable authority. Unless, of course, you think otherwise, in which case he should be well advised."

Although in his mid fifties, slim and of medium height, Rasheed Dafalla was quite gray, which, with his dignified mannerism and superior air of wisdom, gave him the fatherly look of an elder. He followed the story with intense interest and seriousness, never once even smiling. When Peter had finished, Elias took over to elaborate on some themes, and in particular the perspective of his family members, the reaction of Fadheela and the last exchange with Ali.

When it was his time to speak, Rasheed Dafalla remained silent for a moment, as though pondering what he should say. But eventually he said: "I will try to advise you, but you must realize that my position as someone who might subsequently be called upon to render a legal opinion is rather precarious. So, take this as personal advice that in no way prejudices what I might say if the case were ever to come before me.

"I believe we should distinguish between two sets of issues, the legal issues and the social consequences or repercussions of such issues. Opinions, I am sure, would be divided on the question of whether a Muslim woman is free to contravene Islamic law by marrying a Christian through the civil form of marriage. Personally, I believe that it is legally possible, but I would not want to prejudge without a close look at the arguments that would be presented by the parties.

"What I really want to draw your attention to are the social consequences of such a marriage and whether in your particular circumstances it is your best option. I perfectly understand, appreciate and even support the political considerations to which you are giving special attention. But also try to look at it from the social standpoint of the woman. She has already sacrificed a great deal for you by insisting on carrying and having your baby instead of aborting or otherwise trying to conceal the evidence. This is something for which she could have been literally killed by her family in accordance with traditional values. Although that was not her fate, thank God, she was virtually banished from her own society to a remote and totally different community. And in all of this, she did not have your company or support to give her solace. Now you are suggesting that she makes more sacrifices by making a major contravention of her religion and social norms. Islam is clear-cut on this. A Muslim woman cannot marry a non-Muslim. This has also become a social norm among Muslims. Instead of antagonizing only her family, she is now going to enrage the entire Muslim community. There may be a few who will go along with her actions. But, she is likely to be ostracized even more categorically than she was on the pregnancy issue. This is bound to be the case with the publicity that the court action will arouse, for even if the court were to permit the marriage quietly, her father will probably appeal to the highest judicial authority in the country. Don't you think this poor girl has suffered enough on your account? Don't you think it's your turn to sacrifice something on her behalf?

"Well, let's look at your own situation to assess the sacrifice you are called upon to make. As I understand it, on the personal level, while Christianity does not favor marriage outside of the faith, it does not categorically oppose it the way Islam does. That means that from the religious point of view you are relatively free to marry. The only obstacle for you is that you are proposing to marry someone whose religion does not permit such mixed marriage, nor, I might add, does it allow conversion from Islam. That would be heresy, punishable by death. Whether that would be enforced today or not is a different issue. The main point is that societal expectations are built around that concept of sharia. You are, thank God, free of that prospect.

"And as Ali and your family members have so cleverly argued, your conversion is not going to entail much change in your lifestyle or social position on the personal level.

"What is now left is the public significance of your conduct. I agree with what you have both said about the political dimension of the situation, especially considering that you, Elias, are a leader of your people. But let's also look at it this way: while the religious division among our people is obviously serious, you can say that since we have Southern Muslims and Northern Christians, religion may be used by politicians to serve their own ends, but is not really the pivotal issue between the South and the North. One can say that religion becomes only one factor in a complex situation in which racial and cultural sentiments are deep-rooted. There is even the question of whether the racial and cultural differences underlying the South-North tensions and conflicts are real, assumed or imagined! There is undoubtedly a great deal of myth in this simplistic categorization. But it has become established as a reality in people's minds. The myths of Arabism and Africanism are sometimes hidden behind religious differences, which are more difficult to bridge. The question, then, is, if one removes the religious issue, would the racial and cultural problems still play a pivotal role as barriers to intermarriage? I believe this case can help address that issue. I hope you understand what I am aiming at?"

Neither Elias nor Peter said a word. What Rasheed Dafalla said came as a surprise to them both. But they fully understood him; he sounded so objective in his analysis that they could hardly say anything about his reasoning. He had obviously shed more light on the complexities of the situation.

Peter broke the silence by bringing up his favorite comparison. "You see, in the South and in many parts of Black Africa, Islam is not a barrier to intermarriage. Christian men have married Muslim girls and Islam has not been invoked as an obstacle. That's because people feel that they are one and should not be divided by religion. That's why I believe that religion is used by our brothers in the North to cover up their racism."

"But that's exactly why I think that you would expose their underlying racial prejudices by removing the religious factor," the justice interjected. "Would it not be interesting and useful to your cause to see whether the family would still oppose the marriage if Elias converted to Islam?"

"Yes, but that would reinforce a one-way process of integration," replied Peter. "What we are after is a genuine two-way interaction and integration. What you are talking about, if followed, would eventually result in assimilating ourselves into the Muslim identity, which happens to be also racially and culturally Arab."

"Here again I must agree with you on the general principle," conceded Molana Rasheed. "But I still say that, in this particular case, Elias owes it to Fadheela—if he really wants to marry the girl—to make some concession or sacrifice on his part. For God's sake, the girl has done more than you can expect of any ordinary mortal. Why tax her devotion to the ultimate sacrifice without something significant to balance it on the part of Elias? Especially since it will not affect him on the personal level and might indeed serve a public interest by removing the religious factor and testing the other hidden factors."

"Well, Brother Elias, there you are," Peter remarked with a mixture of seriousness and lightheartedness. "The ball is in your court."

"It certainly is," agreed Elias.

As they drove back, Peter talked about the impact the Molana had made. "I can't say my position has changed, but I can at least say that I see his point of view, especially the argument of seeing the interest of Fadheela. I do not at all feel as convinced as I was before. Indeed, I find myself unable to give clear advice. So, good luck, dear friend, in a decision only you can make."

"You know, Peter," Elias said in a serious tone of voice, "I wonder whose side God is on."

Elias continued to be torn. Rationally persuaded by the Molana's argument to convert for Fadheela's sake, his gut reaction was against it. If he should do it for Fadheela, was Ali the right person to inform first or Fadheela herself? He decided that Fadheela should know first, since she was the person directly concerned.

As soon as they met, again in Awatif's house, he lost no time in letting her know his decision and his reasons. "I have come to agree with Molana Rasheed that you have suffered enough and it is not fair you should shoulder further acrimony on my behalf. Reason dictates that it is my turn to sacrifice for our togetherness."

When it was Fadheela's turn to speak, she began by disagreeing with him. "I will go even further and say that I don't even think you agree with yourself. What you have been telling me are not your own words, but the words of others and you don't even repeat them convincingly.

"Who are we trying to please: ourselves, God, or other people? I know you would not please yourself that way. As for me, be sure that, far from pleasing me, you will be giving me hell by sacrificing *your soul* for my sake. And as for God,

I daresay he knows only too well that we would be playing a game of deceit. To tell you the truth, even society will probably see through our deception. Do we stand a chance of winning the righteous to our side? Not a bit. And as for the hypocrites who would be pleased by our pretenses, knowing very well that we are merely acting, do they really deserve that much consideration? I certainly do not think so.

"Elias, my love, let us not be confused by others like the man with his son and his donkey, who could not please anyone. Let's first satisfy our conscience and get what we deserve. After all, our beliefs will continue to be what they are, whatever rituals we may adopt to please others.

"As for the argument that I have already sacrificed much and should not be called upon to sacrifice more, I will not say what I feel like saying. No one asked me to sacrifice. Besides, who defines what a sacrifice is anyway? By these criteria, I suspect that people continue to make sacrifices all their lives through the choices they make. Are we going to keep a record of our sacrifices and compare our respective contributions from time to time in order to maintain a healthy balance? How ridiculous!

"What I really care about is to get the sanction of the law of the land, especially in the interest of Fahl – our son. If the civil courts can legalize our union, who cares what anyone else thinks? Please never again entertain the thought of sacrificing your spiritual beliefs, political interests, pride and dignity for my sake. After all, if you lose your center of gravity and turn into a man easily swayed by the winds of floating opinions, how would I continue to find the weight and the anchor of stability in you, which I find now?"

By now, Elias was filled with emotions. He looked at Fadheela, eyes burning with passion, and said, "I was always sure I loved you. Now, I am overwhelmed by my love for you. I feel the happiest man alive."

"You see, you make me feel so happy by being happy. You were not as happy when you told me of your decision. Nor was I when I saw you struggling with it. Now, I see you obviously happy and I feel happy as well. Oh, Elias, I love you so much! I want you to be happy with me and Fahl and,

God willing, more little ones!"

"God willing!" he reaffirmed.

Their application for registration of a civil marriage found itself in front of Judge Mahmoud Ali Hassan, who had the reputation of being an expert in comparative private law, or conflict of laws. Mahmoud Hassan was said to have been a Muslim Brother in his student days. Those who knew him well believed that this had left him very knowledgeable on sharia and its place in comparative jurisprudence, but did not bias him in favor of sharia in the pluralistic legal system of the Sudan. If that were so, he did not seem to reflect it in his judgment on the case of Elias and Fadheela, for he rejected their application on the grounds that she was obliged to marry a Muslim in accordance with sharia.

Elias and Fadheela appealed and, ironically, Molana Rasheed Dafalla was asked by the chief justice to hear their appeal. At first, he excused himself on the grounds that he had already rendered personal advice to one of the applicants and therefore did not feel entirely neutral on the case. But the chief justice disagreed.

The Molana decided to play down any media involvement with the case, knowing how potentially explosive it could be. He heard the case in camera. Elias and Fadheela were accompanied by a very distinguished Coptic lawyer, Boutros Sammani. A group which called itself the Committee of Concerned Muslim Brothers lobbied the cause of Islam and offered Fadheela's family the services of an advocate by the name of Hussein Omer Abdeen, a well known Muslim Brother. General Ali took permission to sit as an observer.

In his plea, Boutros Sammani argued that in a country of multiple religions, where the constitution guaranteed freedom of conscience and religion, it was hard to see how one could be bound to the dictates of one's religion of birth without violating fundamental human rights. There was no doubt in his mind, he said, that the law had provided the civil marriage form to cater for those who did not want to follow the procedures set forth by their religious laws. "To deny anyone the right to that recourse was to negate both the letter and the spirit of the law," he reasoned. "How could Fadheela have any freedom of conscience or religion if she were bound to follow the Muslim code of law simply because she was born a Muslim? Besides, do all Muslims observe every aspect of God's law, such as fasting, praying, or paying zakat? I doubt it, to say the least. And where are the sanctions for religious failure? I believe they ultimately rest with God, as should the consequences of marrying outside the faith. The law of the land provides alternatives, and if these are resorted to by those of differing faiths, the ultimate judge must be God, for whom all these religions are, in any case, roads to the same destination."

"Your honor," Hussein Omer Abdeen then pleaded, "we are not talking of human choices or freedom of conscience; we are talking about obedience to God's law by a Muslim whose religious identity is not in question. There is no room for doubt in sharia about a Muslim woman marrying a non-Muslim man. To even discuss it is anathema. This is clearly not a debatable issue, your honor. Fadheela has already committed an offense which would be punishable with one hundred lashes, if we were properly observing sharia. Although that has not been applied, we cannot go to the extent of sanctioning by court order an illegal union between a Muslim woman and a non-Muslim man. By what law can we possibly do it? I have all respect for your legal expertise, your honor, but I would be curious as to whether you could possibly find an excuse for this ungodly situation."

Boutros Sammani responded by reminding his Muslim counterpart that the Sudan was not a nation of Muslims. "Even if we were an Islamic state, I would have serious questions to pose about fundamental liberties and human rights in this modern age of secularism. But I will not go that far in my humanitarian cause. I will simply ask the court— certainly not my learned colleague—whether there is no room left for those who choose to lead their own lives as their consciences dictate or reach their Lord through a path cleared for them by their own visions? If the answer is negative, then we have no system worthy of the word 'law' and, I daresay, my presence here would be entirely futile. I trust that is not the case."

The Molana ruled against Hussein's request to speak again on the grounds that the debate could continue endlessly. "No doubt you are both right. But it is my task to say which of you is more right and therefore merits my vote of support.

"The case is not entirely new to me as you presumably know. Nothing which has been said in this court has given me any new insights or changed my initial opinion. I believe one must distinguish between the legal and the social aspects of this case. Legally, I have no doubt that we cannot judge the couple by the criteria of only one of the two religions to which they adhere or at least nominally belong. To do so would be to discriminate between the two religions. I believe that is why the civil procedure of marriage was instituted. It offers an alternative to couples who may choose not to conform to their religious or tribal forms of marriage. To hold otherwise would be a contradiction in terms.

"But to give people the right to which the law entitles them is not to guarantee effective social acceptance of that right. Often, religion is a matter of social norm and etiquette and even when people meet legal requirements, unless their conduct is in conformity with the social climate, legal rights are merely words pronounced or documents written and signed. Of course, we have the police and ultimately the army to sanction the law, but who wants to live in a neighborhood overrun by policemen and soldiers enforcing the law, especially in such private family matters?

"What does this analysis mean in practical terms? It means, at least as I intend it, that legally, Elias and Fadheela are free to marry by the civil form of marriage. But socially, I believe they are at risk of harassment and annoyance. On the other hand, if they choose that path, they are entitled to all the protection the state can provide for its citizens. Some find that adequate; others find it an awesome way to live one's life. It's not for me to tell Elias and Fadheela which is best for them. They have evidently made their choice by coming here. I declare that they have the legal right to marry; how they sustain their marriage socially is their own affair. But I hasten to add that they will have the full protection of the law for the union which the law has ordained."

Upon his concluding remarks, Fadheela broke into a loud ululation—a joyous sound of victory. The justice's pronouncement also provoked an angry reaction from the Muslim fundamentalists who congregated outside the court room awaiting the outcome. *"Allahu akbar! Allahu akbar!* God is Great! God is Great!" they shouted, shooting their fists into the air, and spontaneously starting a demonstration against the court ruling.

"Let's die for God! Sharia, sharia, the Law of God! Let's be rid of secularists and infidels! Fadheela, Fadheela, the hostess of infidels! The sword, the sword! Off with the heads of Elias and Fadheela, the enemies of Islam."

The Molana anticipated such conduct and had warned the security authorities to be on guard. Measures were taken against the demonstrators and it was soon broken up.

But Mohamed Ahmed El-Jak would not be put down. Realizing that the court order on the issue of religion was final, he decided to use the only card left in his hand, as Elias was soon to discover. The stage was set for startling confessions.

TWENTY ONE

ELIAS DROPPED IN ON General Ali late in the afternoon at a time he had come to expect to find the general alone in his divan.

"How strange you should drop in at this precise moment," said Ali after he greeted Elias. "I have just been thinking of you."

"Uncle Ali, I need your thoughts and more," responded Elias. "I presume you know that despite the judgment in our favor, both Fadheela and I remain anxious about other people's reaction, as the judge intimated. And no one is more important to us than yourself. That's why we need to know your reaction to the judgment."

"By now you must know me well enough to know that what is in your interest certainly wins my approval. And so did the court judgment. But you are correct and so was the judge, for a legal right does not in itself guarantee social acceptance and therefore happiness.

"I went to see your prospective father-in-law," Ali continued, "and we had quite a row—more of a fight than a talk. He is determined to oppose the marriage by every means possible. He even told me that he has gone back and asked for an injunction to prevent you from marrying on the grounds that he has new evidence that would bar the marriage. That has been granted. He told me that as far as he is concerned, the marriage is not going to take place.

"I told him that he was being ridiculous, that he was not even Muslim enough to oppose your marriage on religious grounds and that he must have other reasons."

Elias looked discouraged. It was as though the fight was getting beyond him. "I guess I should have tried to forget about Fadheela," he said.

It was the way he said it which moved Ali the most. He gave Elias a look of paternal compassion, and then biting his lip, shook his head and said, "Elias, listen to me carefully. As I have indicated, my brother and I had a terrible fight about your case. I accused him of being a racist and he got very angry with me. In a desperate act of self-defense, he revealed to me something I have been reluctant to tell you, but I really think that it should be revealed. It's one of those no-win situations. Silence would have left sleeping dogs lying and that is essentially what I would have preferred. Mohamed and I had agreed to reflect further, but I know that deep, deep inside him, he wants the truth to come out and for more reasons than to vindicate himself of accusations of racism."

Elias looked at Ali, now completely absorbed. He could not imagine what could possibly make him so solemn. He was dying for Ali to get to the point.

"Elias, I have wondered since you and my brother Mohamed met why he behaved toward you the way he did. I thought it odd. I felt that he had a deep-rooted animosity toward you, but I could not really feel what it was. All I was sure about was that he was deeply sensitive toward you. Why? I could never tell."

By this time Elias was beside himself with impatience. But just then Ali went on to say, "Now I know. Mohamed believes that you are his son."

Elias was not sure he had heard correctly. "What did you say?"

"Mohamed believes that you are his son. He says that he had detected the family resemblance in you from the start, but as he could not explain it, he had dismissed the thought. And yet, every time he saw you, he felt uneasy about what he saw in you. Then, suddenly, the picture was clarified by the evidence your brother, El-Tom, gave to the committee."

Elias's mouth opened wide; his eyes glared without blinking. In shock he mumbled, "What did El-Tom say?"

"I am not sure. Mohamed watched the committee hearings on television. He claims that he was the Arab who seized your mother and brothers, that he and your mother lived together during the short period of her captivity and that before she was rescued by the Dinka, she told him that she was pregnant with his child. He believes that child is you, since you were born after the twins."

Elias's world seemed to shatter. He did not know what to think, what to say, or what to do. Worse, he did not know whether to be sad or happy. To be sad would be a rejection of a man who could well be his father. To be happy would imply a rejection of a man who had been a truly loving father, whether or not he was biologically his father. Nor could Ali help him. They just sat silently, avoiding each other's eyes and gazing aimlessly at objects, any objects, in their inwardly focused vision.

Elias had been absorbed in this way for some time when he came to the realization that he might as well be lying down on his bed reflecting in the privacy of his own room. It was certainly no use sitting there, in complete confusion. "He really could now be my uncle!" he thought to himself, as he got up to leave.

"I guess I better go."

" What are you going to do?"

"I don't know. First, I want to go home and get my thinking straight. I feel confused and disorientated."

"If you need to share your thoughts, come back," remarked Ali. "After all, irrespective of what you are to my brother, I consider you my son."

As Elias drove home, he felt as though he were in another world, crowded with tangled reflections and apprehensions he could not sort out. He was not at all aware of the other cars or people on the road and on one occasion he was able to avoid an accident only by instinct. When he arrived at his house, he entered as though sleep-walking and headed for his room. Aluel noticed him and followed. The mother's instinct in her signalled that something was the matter, perhaps because Bol did not greet her as he passed, perhaps because of the look on his face.

"Is anything the matter?" she asked as she opened his door to find him already lying down on his back.

"There's nothing the matter. I guess I am just tired and would like to rest for a while."

"Then I had better leave you to rest," she remarked as she left the room.

But, of course, Elias could not rest. He reviewed his life as the son of Malengdit and Aluel, his attachment to them both, his deep affection for his brothers, even Achwil, whom he never knew, and the happiness that recent developments, especially the discovery of his lost brother, Madit, had brought into the family. He felt grateful for the fulfillment of the ancestral will and now looked forward to the prospects of one day finding Achwil. But now, suddenly, he had just discovered that he was the son of someone else, an Arab, the very man who had caused his family so much suffering. "Well, that should really do it," he thought to himself. "How can I acknowledge as my father a man who had so cruelly victimized my own family?"

But which of the two was really his family? What if he were really Mohamed's son? He felt some consolation that he would still be his mother's son so that he would at least still be a relative, if only a stepson, as far as Malengdit was concerned. But how would he feel about his mother, not only for having had him with Mohamed, but for having lied to him and the world for all those years? Perhaps his mother had no choice in the circumstances of his conception. But if so, why did she hide the fact? He could not answer that question. Somehow, he felt betrayed by his mother for having misled him for all those years into accepting Malengdit as his father. Then it suddenly occurred to him that he had already condemned his mother on the word of Mohamed without verifying the story with her directly. After all, it was quite fortuitous that she happened to be in Khartoum at this time. He jumped up and called her.

Aluel entered, feeling both relieved that her son had decided to talk and apprehensive about what he wanted to say.

"Mother, I want to ask you a question and I want you to tell me the truth."

It was already obvious that something truly serious had happened, but Aluel did not have the faintest idea what it might be. She looked closely at her son.

"When you were captured by the Arabs, what happened?"

"What do you mean what happened? You know what happened only too well. Why are you asking me?"

"Mother, there is reason to believe that I have heard only part of the story. The most critical part, at least as far as I am concerned, has apparently remained a well guarded secret."

His words pierced with a sharpness that almost made her shriek in pain. But she cast those emotions aside. "Well, if there is something you know that I do not know, why don't you tell me?"

"Mother, did you become pregnant with me when you were with the Arabs?"

She had feared that Bol was up to something, but it never dawned on her that it would go that far. The impossible had happened. How could he have thought this way? And who had triggered in him such dreadful thoughts? As far as she knew, nothing of the kind had ever been talked about in the family. She had almost died in childbirth, but had refused to confess. Diviners had repeatedly speculated on why she had lost her next child and then never had another. Although no diviner had ever accused her, it was clear that they wondered whether she was hiding something. She herself wondered whether her tragic situation did not have to do with the secret she was concealing, but she had consistently refused to disgrace herself by revealing it. And now, all that had been in vain. How did Bol come to even speculate on the matter? Speechless and unable to think, she replied impulsively, "What son of a dog has been feeding you with these vile thoughts to poison your mind and destroy your life?"

Elias felt driven by forces he could no longer control. He felt hostility. "Mother, Mohamed, the Arab who captured you, has told me the whole truth. He claims that I am his son because before you were rescued, you told him that you were pregnant with his child. He heard the story of our family from the investigation of Madit, which he watched on television. Now that the truth has been revealed, what do you say?"

Aluel remained silent. She didn't need Bol to tell her about the Arab whom she had informed of her pregnancy with his child in order to protect herself and Achwil from further cruelty. Now, the worst thing conceivable had happened. Words could no longer help and there were indeed no more words to be said. In utter desperation, she screamed at the top of her voice, her hands raised above her head, which she shook vigorously as though she were seized by evil spirits. "Oh! Oh! I am destroyed," she cried. "The Arab has taken the last breath of my life. Oh my God, Oh spirits of our ancestors, what have I done to deserve all this?" She shrieked and jumped and swirled as though psychotic.

Within minutes a crowd had gathered, wondering what had happened. Since she was running the risk of hurting herself as she knocked herself about, occasionally falling down, she was caught and carried into her room. Nothing she was shouting made any sense to anyone, except to Elias Bol. At first, people thought someone had suddenly died, murdered by the Arabs. Then, when no evidence of that was apparent, they thought Aluel must have just received bad news from home, again involving the Arabs. Meanwhile, Elias who knew the truth, would not speak. Instead, he rushed out of the house, got into his car and drove off, giving no one any indication as to where he was going.

When he returned, it was late at night and most people had gone to sleep. Malengdit sat up with Aluel in the courtyard; with them was Madit. They were waiting for Elias. As he entered, his father, who was visibly suffering from pain but did not want to admit it, saw him and uttered the exclamation of relief and gratitude for divine benevolence: "*Thithiey.* Our ancestral spirits have brought him back." It was as though the sight of Elias Bol ameliorated his terminal condition.

Elias walked toward them and mumbled a controlled acknowledgement. Then he proceeded to his room to change, assuring them that he would be back. He got into his jallabiya and returned to join them. The two men were on chairs while

Aluel sat on a mat, her legs folded to one side, her arms resting on her thighs, her head bent low, clearly a different person from the woman Elias had known and trusted for all those years.

Malengdit was as composed as ever and Madit, too, was calm, betraying no emotions. When Elias had sat down, Malengdit spoke first, his voice weak, but soothingly smooth, his mannerism conciliatory, the wisdom of age and proximity to God and the ancestors showing in his handling of the situation.

" Son, this has been a very long day. I have spent most of the evening first calming your mother and then talking to her. After she had calmed down and we were able to discuss the situation reasonably, we began to worry where you had gone and what might become of you. Thank God, you are back, safe and sound."

Malengdit coughed painfully, as though to announce that the end was at hand. Then he stopped, as if to consider how best he should phrase what he was about to say next.

"Bol, my son, life is the creation of God, using the father and mother as mere tools of his work. God is the true Father and Mother of every human being. All the rest are only means to God's end. When God has chosen to bring a person into this world, the most important thing is that the person exists. He may exist through the father and mother whom God had used to bring him about, or he may exist through other individuals whom God might have chosen to take care of him. The two do not always come together. Among our people, the Dinka, it is said that a child belongs to the ancestral spirits, whose cows have been paid in marrying the mother. That is why our people say that a child belongs to the marriage cows before belonging to the biological father and mother. What that means is that if a child is begotten by a man to whom the woman is not married, that child goes to the man to whom she was married at the time of conception, whether or not he is the biological father. So, my son, you should have no doubt in your mind about that; you are my son. Now, if you should say that you have discovered your real father and wish to join him, I will, of course, not impose my Dinka legal rights of fatherhood on you. I will be pained by the loss of you, but I will let you pursue the choice of your heart."

Elias's calm now seemed to match Malengdit's. "Do I understand from what you are saying that what Mohamed said is indeed the truth and that I am his biological son?" he asked, contempt written on his face.

"Who knows what the truth is?" Malengdit responded, deliberately introducing the complexity of an elder's wisdom. "The whole truth is known only to God. That your mother was forced to be with Mohamed, we cannot deny. That she might have had his child or she thought or said she had his child is also natural. She is not denying it. But she says that she told the Arab that she was pregnant with his child in order to protect herself and your brother Achwil. Your mother was rescued soon after and was brought back to her ancestral family. What happened in her womb between the blood of the Arab and that of the Dinka is God's work. Which of us can speak for God? Let's not preoccupy ourselves with those questions. You are here and you have satisfied our hearts for all the years of your life. That's all that counts."

"Why did Mother keep all this from me for all these years?" Elias asked, a touch of bitterness in his tone.

"She kept it from me also. She did not confess, even when she was about to die in childbirth because, as she explained, she wanted to protect the image of the family from scandal. She also cared about the effect of that truth on her child among the Dinka. That child happens to be you. But frankly, this is where your mother has committed a grievous wrong. I now know why she was not able to have more children. Our ancestral spirits are tough. However long a wrong may be concealed, they will always pursue the wrongdoer to the bitter end. The way of our people is to confess a wrong and atone with the ancestral spirits. Even if a wrong should be covered and covered for a hundred years, God will in the end reveal the truth. Had she revealed the truth, the necessary rituals of atonement would have been carried out and she would have compensated our sacred cows of her marriage with more children."

The way Malengdit spoke made Aluel feel reprimanded

all over again. She had already gone through that with him and she felt betrayed by the lack of sympathy and the condemnation in his voice.

"Can't you people see that I have already suffered enough?" she said plaintively, as she started to sob. "I was a slave to a master who desired me and wanted to make me his wife. I had lost all hope of being rescued by my people, the people from whom we had been captured. I gave myself to my master, not only because I had no choice, but also in the hope that God and our ancestors would protect my son Achwil and me. When I begot Bol and saw him grow up as a Dinka, I felt myself rewarded for the degradation I had suffered at Arab hands. I had almost forgiven Mohamed because he gave me Bol, our Bol, who became a Dinka, as Dinka as any son of a nobleman can claim to be. Now, in my old age, after believing myself fulfilled through Bol, my self effacement is turned upon itself, and I am accused of immorality." Suddenly, Aluel cried out, louder and louder. "Why did God make me survive long enough to witness this?"

"Shut up, Aluel," shouted Malengdit. "Can't you see that you will wake people up? Haven't we already disgraced ourselves enough in front of the people? Have you not made your case already? Let me not hear a single sound from you any more."

Turning to Elias, Malengdit explained, "Son, your mother and I have already talked about most of these issues. You know that I am hurt by all this, but one cannot allow it to destroy our family."

Madit, who had been sitting silently, sought to make his presence felt. "Have none of you thought of my twin brother, Achwil? If this Mohamed claims to be the one who captured Mother and Achwil, then surely he ought to know what became of Achwil. Can't you see that amidst all this sorrow, there is a bright spot—the possible discovery of Achwil?"

There was a sudden silence, for the question had not occurred to anyone before.

After a pause, Malengdit spoke, "Well, Bol, has Ali told you anything about that?"

"No!"

"What do you think?"

"I think it's certainly something worth talking to Mohamed, I mean Ali, about."

"Actually you mean Mohamed, but through Ali," interjected Madit.

As soon as Madit had introduced the issue of Achwil, Elias began to see obvious physical resemblances between Baraka and Madit. Was the missing member of the family about to be found?

Elias did not sleep that night. Conscious thoughts, dreams and nightmares all mingled to make him restless. Early the following morning, he hurried to Ali's house to find him having tea alone in his divan.

"Strangely enough, I expected you to come this morning," remarked Ali. "I could not see you just leaving such a dramatic situation hanging in the air that way."

"Well, a number of pieces have fallen into place, Uncle Ali, but a few remain uncertain."

"Let me know what they are and I may help you fit them in," remarked Ali. "After all, since we talked, I have not been idle; I have also done my homework."

"One thing is—what became of my brother or, should I now say, my half-brother—that's my mother's son, Achwil—whom Mohamed captured with my mother and who was never returned?"

"That's simple," responded Ali, astonishingly calm. "Baraka is your brother, your half-brother or your mother's son, as you say. And now let me tell you another development which will surprise you. Fadheela came to see me yesterday, shortly after you had gone. I decided to take her with me to see her parents and try to come to some family resolution of this whole mess."

Elias seemed somewhat oblivious because he could not really see what difference anything Ali could say would make. But, distracted as he was, he continued to listen as Ali continued his account.

"All I wanted was to bring them all together to share the facts and to come to some understanding as to what should or should not be done for what reasons. Frankly, I expected

Mohamed to tell his daughter precisely what had happened, how the father of her child happened to be her half-brother. I mean, when you come to think of it, this may be the most bizarre story in the history of family annals. I don't even know why I wanted them to confront one another, but I thought it had to be done sooner or later.

"Anyway, after I had made my statement, Fadheela's mother suddenly surprised us all by breaking down and saying, as she sobbed, 'Mohamed, I will not allow my daughter to be tortured this way! I have endured enough of this insult; it is more than I can bear. You know the truth, why not admit it? You know Fadheela is not your daughter! How can you acknowledge your son and use that fact to punish my daughter, when you know they are not brother and sister? Elias is your son, but Fadheela is not your daughter, and I see no reason to oppose their marriage on the ground of blood relationship. And by God Almighty, I am prepared to testify in a court of law or wherever necessary, even if I should die for doing so.'

"The woman poured all this out nonstop. We were absolutely stunned, speechless. Mohamed became enraged. Right in front of me, he struck his wife a terrible blow on the face, shouting, 'Shut up you devil of a woman!' But his wife would not be cowed. She shouted back, 'Which of us is the devil, the one lying or the one telling the truth?' Meanwhile, Fadheela had herself broken into a loud cry and had moved in to defend her mother, hitting Mohamed with her bare hands as she shouted, 'He is killing my mother. Help! Help! He is killing her.' I tell you, it was a very ugly scene.

"I struggled to separate them as the neighbors poured in to try to help. We eventually succeeded in restoring some calm and I came back with Fadheela and her mother. Fadheela spent the night here; she left just before you came."

Elias was mesmerized by the story, even though he could not believe his ears. When Ali stopped, he asked, simply, "What is the story about Fadheela not being Mohamed's daughter?"

"You see, Fadheela's mother was married to one of Mohamed's best friends, a trading partner," began Ali. "He was killed in the same fight with the Dinka in which your mother was rescued. He left behind a young bride, Fadheela's mother. To offer her protection, Mohamed decided to marry the young widow according to the customs of our people.

"Islam requires that a remarried widow should observe an *idda* or period of abstinence from relations with her new husband for four months and ten days to ensure that there is no confusion in the paternity of a posthumous child. What happened in the case of Mohamed and Fadheela's mother was that the young woman had just become pregnant. They got married after observing the period of *idda*, but they wanted the baby to be accepted as Mohamed's. Since Islam does not recognize adoption as such, they felt that in the interest of the child, being perceived as Mohamed's biological child would remove that obstacle. So, when they moved from the South and came to the North, they presented Fadheela to the family and the community as their daughter together. It seems that only the parents knew the truth; society took Fadheela as unquestionably Mohamed's daughter. But, of course, in the end, her mother was moved by compassion for her daughter to reveal the family secret, which they had kept to themselves for all those years."

"How is Fadheela now?" asked Elias, still in disbelief.

"Deeply saddened. Perhaps shocked is a better word. But she is also relieved, in fact I should say overjoyed, that her father's scheme for opposing her marriage had been so strangely foiled."

Elias could think of nothing to say. He felt torn between the pleasure of vindication and the sadness wrought by the agonizing schism within Fadheela's family.

"I am sorry I have caused all this trouble, Uncle Ali," he eventually managed to say with a sincerity that was deeply moving to Ali.

"Don't worry, Elias. All Mohamed needs is time to calm down. I am sure he will get over it in the course of time. Meanwhile, Fadheela's mother will remain with us until we can sort out the mess and reconcile them. I am sure we will manage that. Don't allow this to interfere with your marriage plans or your feelings for one another. I will have to talk to